LAST BATTLE

Bill Bridges

TIME OF JUDGMENT

Act Two of the Time of Judgment

THE LAST BATTLE

To Jane, who patiently put up with my absence during the writing of **The Silver Crown** many years ago, and did so again with this one.

This is the Time of Judgment

Millennia ago, the Earth Mother Gaia birthed her protectors, the race of werewolves known as Garou. Half-flesh and half-spirit, the Garou were both cursed and blessed with a terrible rage, a seething righteous anger that allowed them to triumph over impossible odds, but plunged them into countless tribal battles with their own kind.

All the while, their enemy—the maddened spirit of corruption called the Wyrm—grew more and more powerful. The werewolves' spirit patrons warned that a time would come when the Wyrm's power would swallow Gaia whole, when the Garou would make their last stand. They called this time the Apocalypse.

Now, the prophecies have come true and the call to battle has been raised. The Last Battle is at hand.

A Matter of Perspective...

Each act of the **Time of Judgment** trilogy adopts the point of view of the supernatural creature whose story it tells. Astute readers will note nods and small references to the larger supernatural world, but most vampires, werewolves, and even mages find their attention drawn to their own problems in these terrible last days. Thus, the three acts of this trilogy are more akin to three facets of a larger happening than sequential sections of a single tale. Each builds upon the others, but tells its own story.

Prologue:
A Star of Blood

In the Last Days there shall appear
within the heavens a star of blood,
gyring as it falls toward Gaia's breast.

—The Prophecy of Speaks-in-Silence

The thunderwyrm writhed in pain below the earth. Her slow death throes shook the desert floor.

Zhyzhak screamed in frustration. She flung rocks across the sandy desert, smashing them into ancient stone outcroppings and exploding them to dust. The mica deposits sparkled in the full moon gleam like antiaircraft flak, flickering briefly before settling on the canyon floor.

Slatescrape-ikthya bit his lip in frustration, holding back an acerbic comment. Zhyzhak's screaming wasn't unusual—she was a klazomaniac, after all, gifted during her first Wyrm revelation with the screaming affliction. When she was angry or frustrated, she had to yell at the top of her lungs anytime she wanted to say something. It took enormous effort of will during these spells to speak in a normal voice or even a whisper. This wasn't a conscious oath or vow of piety; it was her only way of dealing with the awesome trauma the Wyrm had inflicted on her mind. They all had such glorious stigmata, psychoses worn like combat badges. Pain, hurt and affliction were borne as pridefully as battle scars by the Wyrm's chosen tribe, those who danced the Black Spiral Labyrinth.

Slatescrape himself had his own divine problems: the festering sores that bled pus and caused such infernal itching in his hindquarters, in addition to the constant insufferable runny nose and sweating. He rubbed his bottom violently as he watched Zhyzhak's midnight tantrum. She wore her usual black leather dominatrix outfit—at least two sizes too small for her frame—while he wore his worsted wool jacket and pants, squinting at her through spectacles fogged by watery eyes. An uninformed human might mistake him for a professor, perhaps one of the many nuclear scientists known to work in the region. Once, this wouldn't have been a completely mistaken assumption; He had been a scientist—a biologist, not a physicist—in his previous life when he counted himself among the Glass Walkers tribe. That was long ago, however, before Grammaw devoured him and excreted him inside an egg. He had hatched from its slimy womb, reborn in a warped but corruption-blessed body.

Grammaw. The thunderwyrm.

"If you're so damn smart," Zhyzhak screamed at Slatescrape, lifting a huge rock above her head, "why can't you fix her?!" She threw the rock over Slatescrape's shoulder. It shattered against the canyon wall, its dust coating the back of his jacket. He didn't flinch.

"I've told you before, you bitch," Slatescrape said, knowing she would interpret the vulgar appellation as a sign of respect, "her disease is spiritual, not biological. No one knows more about thunderwyrm anatomy than I, and there is no physical affliction. She wastes away because of some Umbral assault on her soul."

Zhyzhak leaped over a group of mangled rocks to stand inches from Slatescrape's face, breathing her rancid breath up his nose. "Yaargh! You're a shaman! Fix it!"

"For the thousandth time, I can't. This is White-Eye-ikthya's doing. He's laid some sort of curse, and I can't even detect it."

"Traitor!" Zhyzhak cried, screaming not at Slatescrape but out across the desert, to wherever White-Eye might be hiding. The ancient werewolf was legendary among the Black Spiral Dancer tribe for the vision he had been granted at the Trinity nuclear explosion, the blast that had stolen his sight, gifting him with great insight into the mysteries of the Wyrm and earning him the honorific suffix *–ikthya*. But White-Eye had disappeared recently. Soon after that, Grammaw took ill. Many in the caern whispered that White-Eye's true allegiance still lay with his old Garou tribe, the Uktena, and took his disappearance to be a defection back to his first tribe. Slatescrape doubted that. He suspected that whatever force had taken White-Eye had also wounded Grammaw.

"The point is not who did it," Slatescrape said, his nose wrinkling under the withering assault of Zhyzhak's breath, "but when are you going to quit yelling about it and go to Malfeas?"

Zhyzhak stood stock still, not breathing. Slatescrape knew she was conflicted, unsure whether to loose her rage and strike him down or actually do the long-contemplated deed, to travel to the spiritual heart of the Wyrm and seek relief for the thunderwyrm's suffering. Luckily for him, she chose the latter.

Zhyzhak whirled around and marched back to the cave in the canyon gully, toward the caern within. Slatescrape smiled, proud of himself and somewhat surprised that she actually had the balls to go through with it. Where she was going, there would be no return. Soon, the caern would be his. He followed behind her, crouching to enter the cave.

Zhyzhak shifted to her wolf form, a black-furred mongrel. As the cavern widened on all sides, she retained that form while following the winding path downwards. Finally, she reached a point where the cavern narrowed, with rows of symmetrical stalactites and stalagmites. Warm gases came from deep within, and nothing of the faint light from the cave entrance made its way here. Zhyzhak moved by sense of smell and sound alone, but Slatescrape's Wyrm-enhanced eyes could see dim shapes through a sickly green haze. Beyond the up-jutting and under-hanging rocks, the floor was slick and wet.

The large wolf paused and seemed to collect her thoughts. Then she lunged forward on all fours, charging past the rows of rocks and disappearing into the blackness. Slatescrape hoped she would fail to step over to the Other Side in time, but he knew that was unlikely. That had been the fate of Ghavaaldt, the previous caern leader, although many knew of Zhyzhak's role in that event. It was no accident that she was now leader.

He paused now himself and reached out with his senses, seeking the ephemeral fabric of the spirit world. He grasped it and pulled himself into its folds, struggling past the hot veil between worlds and emerging into an even darker, steamier cavern, the spiritual reflection of the material world.

He smiled. He always liked this next part. It felt like entering the womb again. He marched past the stalactites and stalagmites, running his hand against them as he went, thrilling to their bony, calcified texture. He wiggled to maintain his balance as he hit the slick spot and it undulated underneath him, pulling him in deeper, a magic carpet ride on Grammaw's tongue straight into her esophagus. It was a religious experience to walk boldly into her mouth and straight into her gut, to experience all the banes writhing within, to ride her innards from stomach to gizzard, through the intestinal labyrinth and then to the stomodaeal plexus—Grammaw's brain, the center of the Trinity Hive Caern.

He knew Grammaw's anatomy better than anyone, even Zhyzhak. He was sure he could find shortcuts through the intestines and beat her to the caern center, and so prepare his allies to seize the caern as soon as Zhyzhak was gone.

• • •

Zhyzhak already knew of Slatescrape's plotting and didn't care. If anything, she was glad that someone as Machiavellian as Slatescrape would assume leadership of her beloved caern. Somebody needed to keep the larvae in line. She had already warned her loyal soldiers that Slatescrape would attempt a bid for power the moment she left on her journey. What was power worth if you didn't have to fight to get it? She couldn't allow a true leader to assume command without the scars to show for it.

But such concerns were petty next to the greater need to cure Grammaw. Zhyzhak had realized that weeks ago. She pretended to procrastinate, delaying her necessary journey, so that she could secretly build weapons, for she would need more than her wits and spirit gifts where she was going. It had taken her weeks and the sacrifice of her most loyal soldier (whom the others believed had been killed by Wendigo warriors), but now she had her fetish, the one thing that would allow her to succeed where all others before her had failed.

She tumbled through the thunderwyrm's gut, barely avoiding the molten blood in the veins as she shot through the viscera at incredible speed. She flicked her tongue in her wolfish mouth, making sure that the small fetish was still there, tied to her back teeth. It was. It rubbed against her throat, almost causing her to gag now and then, but that was a small price to pay for the secrecy she needed. If any of the Wyrm's minions suspected what she had, they would try to seize it for themselves. She barked loudly as she imagined the looks on the faces of the Maeljin lords when they realized that they'd have to bow down to her, the Queen and Bride of the Wyrm itself.

As she was painfully squeezed through the gizzard, she shifted to the Crinos battle form. Her increased size would slow her, but she needed the extra power to withstand the grinding stones that tried to crush her into powder for her entry into the intestines. If she had been traveling through Grammaw in the material world, rather than its spiritual reflection, she would have been dead ten times over by now. Like poor Ghavaaldt.

She cautiously turned her thoughts to other matters, intentionally thinking about how she would flay White-Eye-ikthya alive. There were certain spirits and minions who could read minds, and she didn't want to risk them picking up her thoughts about her secret fetish. She contemplated the painful howls the old man would choke out as she slowly chewed his still-attached sinew like licorice.

As she entered the intestines, she purposefully reached out and grabbed a handful of slick, fecal-smeared flesh, pulling herself down a side-tunnel. She heard Slatescrape slide past behind her, hurrying to beat her to the caern center. Let him. Once he was past, she let go and let Grammaw's peristalsis take her wherever it

The Last Battle

wanted to. After an eternity of foul smells and the caress of hogling banes, she flopped greasily into the vast cavern of neural flesh that made up the caern center.

Her waiting soldiers, the elite caern guardians, immediately rushed to help her to her feet and surround her, growling at the other Garou gathered there. Zhyzhak kicked them away, rising on her own as she brushed off swaths of feces. She marched to the center and screamed at her broodlings.

"Listen up, scum! I'm going to Malfeas! I'll dance the Spiral, and no goddamn banes or bullshit excuses will stop me! Hear?! Anybody got something to say?!"

She looked around. Slatescrape, who had arrived while she still tumbled through Grammaw's labyrinthine intestines, stood at the periphery, trying to be as unassuming as possible. She could see a few other Garou, also at the edge of the congregation, trading knowing glances. Slatescrape's conspirators. She slapped Mange-Breath, her lead guardian, on the back, a powerful blow that almost caused him to lose his balance.

"Mange-Breath's in charge while I'm gone! Hear?! Anybody got a problem with that, take it up with me now!"

Slatescrape remained silent, as did his fellows. He would wait until she was gone before making his move. Good. Mange-Breath was a tough-ass warrior, but stupid. Slatescrape, if he was smart, which he was, would use his fellows to take him down, and then declare his leadership. His Wyrmish gifts would ensure that nobody else here would overcome him, but he'd have scars to remind him of it. His reign would be short-lived anyway; when she returned, she'd have them all killed.

Zhyzhak turned and walked over to a whitish lump rolling around on the floor. She kicked it and two eyes opened, looking up at her with fear. A mouth opened and closed, mewling sounds escaping from it. The thing slowly stood up on what passed for limbs: white doughy balloons barely capable of holding his obese weight.

"Palefish! Open the gate! Now!"

The albino metis croaked a reply and began the procedures for opening a moon bridge. He knew where she was going, so he didn't need to ask. A few minutes later, the portal appeared, its silvery light too bright for most of the Garou's eyes. Only the faint balefire in Grammaw's veins and the occasional electrical firing of the thunderwyrm's neurons usually lit the cavern.

Zhyzhak didn't look back as she stormed through the portal, ready to fight what challenges waited at her destination—one didn't enter the realm of the Green Dragon without a challenge. Even before the portal closed behind her, she could hear the howls of battle and the wet tearing sound of claws slicing flesh. As it should be….

• • •

The infernal hissing of a billion snakes made it hard to concentrate. Zhyzhak made her way by touch and smell through the tight, dirt-encrusted pit. The heat was nearly unbearable even for her, but her overcooked brain shrugged it off and kept her body stumbling forward. She could feel fangs sinking into her flesh with each step, their venom jetting through her bloodstream, but her superior Garou constitution nullified the poison. Every now and then she stopped to vomit up the inert toxins, and then stumbled on, suffering still more snake bites.

Finally, she felt a breeze and smelled the hot, tepid scent of a brackish marsh. She quickened her step and soon slipped from the tight tunnel into the welcoming embrace of a stagnant pool. Instantly, insects swarmed her, covering nearly every inch of her fur. It felt like a massage compared to the snakes. She moved sluggishly forward in the water, brushing aside wilting vines and snapping rotten logs with her stride.

Swamp gases engulfed her, killing the insects. In the split-second it took them to die, she heeded the warning and held her breath until the noxious fumes passed her by.

Zhyzhak felt something brush against her legs, something slimy and scaled, and she smiled. She opened her eyes, still stinging from the insect bites, and looked down. Through the murk, she could see the bulk of a dinosaur-huge tail disappearing to her left. She followed it, splashing through the mire with no care to what creatures she disturbed.

The tail led her to a clearing, a grassy knoll in the mists, upon which sat a huge, coiled bulk of green scales. Near the top of the small mountain of its body, she saw a single open, reptilian eye watching her.

Zhyzhak dropped to her knees in the water, her legs swallowed by mud. She closed her eyes and presented her throat to the creature. Its head slowly lifted, revealing a huge, hundred-fanged snout frilled with black feathers. Its head floated across the water toward Zhyzhak and hovered next to her face, sniffing her. It opened its mouth and two monstrous fangs slid from their sheaths, dripping acidic venom. The black poison splattered onto her fur and singed it, hurting more than anything she had ever experienced.

The burns formed shapes, pictograms spelling some blasphemous secret that even she could not read, but she knew she had been marked. She had passed the test. The Green Dragon favored her.

It slid back to its coiled mass and buried its head once more, appearing to sleep. Behind it, the faint flickering of light signaled the portal it had opened for her. She shifted to her prehistoric dire-wolf form and leaped over the dragon and through the portal before it could change its mind.

• • •

She landed with a skid on dusty flagstones. The stones cracked under her sudden bulk, sending loud echoes across the open, gray sky. She halted and listened. In the distance from all directions she heard various sounds: moans of terror and pain, screams of horror and delight, and the crack of whips or the clank of gears. But they didn't respond to her arrival.

She looked around the ruined courtyard. It looked like an ancient, long-abandoned medieval fortress. The walls stretched at least 18 feet high, and she could not see over the battlements. She knew that beyond each of the octagonal courtyard's walls, each of which bore a large iron door, a unique Malfean duchy could be found. None of them were her destination.

She shifted to her battle form—her head that of a wolf, her body a huge, hulking, furred humanoid—and dug her claws into the clefts in the masonry, climbing up one of the walls. When she could peer over it, she looked about in all directions, searching for one place in particular. The smoky haze of many fires, coupled with the black clouds blocking the sun (or whatever passed for the sun in this infernal realm), concealed much of the view. But she could see her destination: a huge, slender tower of green-veined black marble, jutting into the sky like a barbed arrow from a wound in the Earth. The Temple Obscura, home to the Black Spiral Labyrinth.

Zhyzhak moved slowly along the side of the wall, peering over the battlements to examine the stony maze on all sides. She saw the passage she wanted and the route needed to get there, and then dropped from the wall, heading for the west gate.

It was different from the last time she had been here. It was different every time. Once, the place looked new, as if it were still well maintained. Another time, it appeared somewhat Asian, as if she were in a different land. Now, she suspected she saw something of its true face.

She reached for the door-latch and tugged the metal ring, hauling it with all her strength. The door groaned and resisted, but slid open a crack, with a great grinding noise that echoed everywhere. They'd know she was here now; the curious would come to investigate. She dropped to all fours, still in her battle form, and ran through the maze, remembering the way from her reconnoitered climb.

When she reached the corridor that led to the temple, she found a parasitic crow waiting there for her. It cawed as she approached and shifted into human form. This surprised her; she had not expected to find one of the Corax changing breed here in Malfeas. They were servants of Helios, the Sun, and did not belong in these gray lands. This one must be a renegade, corrupted and pledged to one of the dreaded Dukes of Malfeas.

"What do you want, Crow Boy?!" she cried, refusing to stop as she ran past him.

He ran along behind her. "Hey, lady, no need to be hostile. I'm just curious about that shiny thing I see in your mouth."

Zhyzhak wheeled around without breaking her stride and snapped her fangs at the Corax's throat. He was quick but not quick enough. She tore out his jugular and slashed his knees with her rear claws. He gurgled some sort of surprised apology, but the light went out of his eyes and he collapsed.

She turned and kept moving. She didn't know how the little bastard had seen the fetish in her mouth—those crows had good eyes and a knack for seeing sparkling objects—but she didn't want to risk something truly threatening standing in her way, so speed was of the essence now. She bolted faster down the corridor, the temple a distant smudge at the end.

A giant pincer slammed down onto the flagstones in front of her, causing her to ram her shoulder into the wall to avoid the sudden attack. She looked up to see a giant mantis-like creature dressed in black and gold robes, a miter on its insectile head. It was royalty of some kind, perhaps a count or marquis from one of the nearby duchies. The clacking of its thorax made no sense to her (she had never learned the spirit speech), but she assumed that it, too, wanted her fetish. The bane she had forcibly bound into the thing must be calling out somehow, giving away her presence. She put on another burst of speed and tried to stay ready for its next strike.

When its other pincer came down, she dodged it easily and then leaped up the length of its arm in a single running stride, reaching its elbow before it could react. As it brought its mouth down to eat her—its clashing pincers large enough to sever her torso with one bite—she jumped again, landing on its head and knocking off its miter, the symbol of its rank. As it began to shake itself to throw her off, she drove a clawed hand straight into one multifaceted eye, shattering the orb like glass. It squealed at such volume and pitch that even Zhyzhak, well used to loud sounds, had to cover her ears.

Its convulsions were too manic; she lost her balance and fell, barely grabbing the top of the battlements in time to keep from falling into another duchy and losing her way. As she righted herself, the mantis lord's pincer came at her again. She barely dodged it, grunting as it scraped her thigh, and then wrapped her arms around it in a bear hug, twisting with all her weight and might. The lord couldn't adjust its footing in time, and the pincer snapped, the carapace cracking and leaking a thick, vile-smelling goo.

The mantis leaped backwards, stumbling over the battlements behind it, and fell into the neighboring duchy. A roar greeted its arrival, and the clash of metal signified a welter of swords and knives from the other side of the wall. Each duchy had countless legions, most of whom wandered aimlessly, desperate for any excuse for war. This mantis did not belong in that duchy and so was open game. Only Zhyzhak's markings from the Green Dragon allowed her to get this far without raising a cry from the neighboring duchies.

Zhyzhak quickly vaulted along the top of the battlement and then leaped back into the corridor. She put everything she had into running flat out. Now that the armies were alerted, she'd be mobbed within minutes—unless she reached the safety of the temple, which belonged to her tribe. The temple doors were near, hanging wide open. She barreled into the foyer and skidded to a stop across its slick marble floor just as a loud roar erupted behind her.

She turned to see the roiling armies of bane-spirits halt just outside the doors, unable to pass the wards that allowed access only to the Garou and their allies. She sneered at them and turned to face the foyer.

No guards ran to intercept her. A lone Garou sat on the floor by the stairs leading down. He wore his mis-shapen man-form, a shape from an earlier stage of human evolution, giving him the jutting brows and lean muscles of a cave man. He looked up as she marched toward him and gave a conspiratorial smirk, rising to greet her.

"So, another comes to try her soul on the forge of fear," he said.

"Shut up! I've danced the Spiral five times, you little turd!" Zhyzhak raised her hand, threatening to strike him.

His smile faded and his head hung low, like a child who has just been told a trip to Disneyland has been canceled. He sighed and sat back down. "It's downstairs. You know the way."

Zhyzhak grabbed his meaty ear and gave it a painful twist. He rose to his tiptoes to keep her from yanking it off entirely. "Who the fuck are you?!" she yelled.

"G-G-Galvarg" he cried, slipping from her grasp and nursing his hurt ear with both hands. "My duty is to lead any Gaian warriors to the Labyrinth."

"Gaians?! What the hell would *they* be doing *here*?"

Galvarg sighed. "They used to come here full of pride and glory, hoping to defeat the Wyrm or free our tribe from its allegiance." He cackled, remembering past victo-ries. "They always failed and joined us. To see them stumble from the Labyrinth, newborn madness in their eyes... oh, for the glories of yesterday."

Zhyzhak wrinkled her brow. "They don't come any more?"

"No. The word's out; nobody survives the Labyrinth whole and untainted. They don't even try anymore."

"Why don't you find something useful to do then, asshole?" Zhyzhak kicked the Garou, who doubled over, clutching his ribs.

"Gakh," he choked out, scuttling away from his attacker. "Can't. Bound. Duty...." He wheezed horribly and grimaced in pain, rolling around on the floor. In seconds, however, his shattered rib healed. He sat watching her warily, ready to bolt if she moved toward him.

Zhyzhak spat at him. The fool had been trapped into some sort of allegiance to Malfeas, and now wasted his time waiting for Garou who would never come. Idiot. She ignored him and headed for the stairs. Flickering green lights could be seen reflected on the walls from some source below. She walked down the steps, reaching into her mouth for the fetish she had tied there.

She paused as she came to the last step and looked at the strange patterns traced on the floor, pulsing green veins etched into black marble. There were no walls on any side, only mists deepening in the distance. The Labyrinth led in all directions. Only one path was the correct one, the one that would lead her to the Second Circle and from there to the Third and all the circles thereafter, to the fabled Ninth.

She took the fetish from her mouth and examined it, still coated in saliva and a remnant of the poison she had vomited in the Green Dragon's realm. She brushed the wet from its surface and examined it. The fetish appeared to be a simple Boy Scout's compass, a cheap one for beginners. However, on its back pictograms binding powerful banes were carved. She popped the latch—a magnifier—and peered through its glass at the mists. There, to her left, was a red glowing light on the horizon. She spun in a circle, seeing the mists rise and fall to disorient her, but the red glow remained, a fixed point in the changing landscape.

She threw back her head and roared with pleasure. The Eye of the Wyrm would guide her. In a place devoid of any consistency or stable space, the Eye of the Wyrm—Anthelios, the Red Star—remained unmoved. She would navigate by it, and so trace her path through chaos to its center, with no fear of getting lost.

Zhyzhak wrapped the compass's thong about her neck and carefully stepped onto the Labyrinth, in the direction of the Red Star. The mists immediately engulfed her and then receded, leaving complete darkness. She heard voices, distant yelling and screaming, and immediately recognized them as her own. She barked a scornful grunt, for she had experienced this before: the First Circle of Insight. Zhyzhak marched forward, peering through her lens, ignoring the apparitions and voices around her, concentrating on the Eye. She had already danced this circle, along with the four circles that came after; each was a requirement for attaining rank within her tribe. She could learn nothing more at this level. She sought the Inner Mysteries, the Sixth Circle and beyond. It would be a long dance to get there, but she could speed her progress by using her fetish to see the hidden path, the shortcuts through the Labyrinth.

Zhyzhak drew her barbed whip and snapped it. Its crack echoed through the darkness, loud, but unlike her previous echoes in the courtyard, these grew louder and threatened to shatter her eardrums. She ignored them and snapped her whip again at the mists, tearing a hole in them as one cuts through a hedge. The tendrils of fog screamed as they parted, torn by the devil whip's spirit powers, and she knew this was the right path—pain reveals all secrets.

Zhyzhak marched forward, snapping her whip and tearing away more mists that blocked her path, laughing loudly with each step. She traveled a route no other Garou before her had ever walked, following the lure of the Eye, invisible to all sight but hers thanks to her fetish. Ironic that the secret of its making had come from White-Eye-ikthya, old and blind, but who could nonetheless see the Red Star. He had not meant to give her the secret of its making. After she had wrested it from him, he fled. His fear of what she could become with it made him seek his old tribe in the hopes that their power could undo what he had done. Too late. With his lore, they somehow managed to wound Grammaw with their Gaian spells, but they could not stop Zhyzhak.

She was so exultant in her victorious march, cackling to herself as she swung her whip, that she did not notice the trail she left behind herself: a torn, trampled path of footprints and tattered mists that further unraveled as time advanced.

In the depths of the Umbra, in places far from Malfeas but still connected by bonds of taint and corruption, ancient bindings began to fray. Barriers and pathways stitched together by the twisted logic of the Black Spiral Labyrinth began to come apart. Creatures tied to the essence of the Labyrinth wept and moaned as they disintegrated. Others, freed from what little bondage to order the Labyrinth represented, leaped from their cages and ran far and wide, spreading chaos and destruction.

The old order began to crumble, and even the Weaver stumbled, sending shudders through the webs that bound all the worlds....

Part One:
Unholy Fires

Unholy fires fell to the ground,
burning us all, twisting us
and making us vomit blood.

—*The Prophecy of the Phoenix,* "The Seventh Sign"

Chapter One:
The Steps of the Ancestors

A lone howl echoed across the snowy pine forest until the nearby mountain peaks swallowed it. Complete silence descended. Not a single bird croak or snap of ice-laden branch could be heard.

King Albrecht cocked his head and listened for answering howls in the distance but heard nothing. He stood perfectly still, his tall, muscled frame a statue cloaked in thick furs, his hand gripping a sword hilt that jutted over his shoulder, its blade sheathed on his back. His white hair spilled over his shoulders from beneath a band of silver. He squinted at Lord Byeli with his single eye (of the other, only a mass of scar tissue remained hidden behind a rune-engraved patch). The large, white-bearded lord dressed in white furs stood in front of him, looking off at the mountains.

"She's talking about us, right?" Albrecht said, his frozen breath misting the air before him. "'They come.' Who's she warning?"

Byeli turned to meet Albrecht's eyes. "Yes, she speaks of us. She is on that peak there, I believe." He pointed to a mountaintop visible above the tree line. "She is one of the warders placed at the edge of the bawn."

"We're at the bawn?" Albrecht said, smiling. He let out a sigh of accomplishment as he punched a fist into a gloved hand. "Finally! I'm getting sick of all this snow and ice."

Byeli shook his head. "At the bawn, yes. Its edge. Those are the Ural Mountains ahead. But we still have a long journey before we arrive at the caern itself."

Albrecht's eyelids lowered and his smile became a grimace. "How freakin' big is this bawn? How do you defend something this huge?"

"There is no one here," Byeli said, tightening his hood against a chill breeze. "A few villagers to the south, and the occasional hunter or trapper, but no one else. We ran off Stalin's secret military projects long ago. The Urals are ours."

Albrecht looked at the distant mountains, brilliant white and dusty brown in the mid-day sun. "It really is something out of the old days, isn't it? Wild, forlorn and untrammeled."

"Not all the mountains. We can't defend the whole length. But here, in this place, it is pure. The oldest Garou caern from before humans built their first city."

Albrecht heard grunts and wistful intakes of breath among the warriors strung out on the path behind him. They were his elite Silver Fang guard, the best of the best. Some of them were homegrown—from his own sept in Vermont—but others had come to stand at his side from Silver Fang septs the world over. Now, they followed him across the tundra of Russia to see the ancestral caern of their tribe, the Caern of Kingship hallowed by Falcon himself.

They, like him, were dressed in thick, cold-weather furs with hoods, knit masks and dark goggles to dim the harsh snow glare. Two of them tended a sled filled with provisions, pulled by a pair of horses. Albrecht hadn't liked that part. The horses would get spooked if his crew had to take their battle forms. Apparently, though, modern vehicles weren't allowed. Not that the jeeps couldn't go where they needed to, but their hosts at the caern wouldn't allow such machines anywhere near their sacred home. In addition, there was some sort of ancient ritual crap about the "Steps of the Ancestors," a ceremonial journey by foot and sled in the same manner his kingly predecessors had traveled when returning to the Mother Caern. It was all legalistic bullshit as far as Albrecht was concerned, but anytime he brought it up, it seemed to scandalize Byeli's sept, especially coming from a king's mouth. So he finally shut up about it and went with the flow.

Albrecht turned to watch his guards as they scanned the horizon, the sky and the woods around them. They were seasoned troops, ever alert for any sign of approaching figures, whether human, wolf or other. Scattered among his own band of twelve Garou were five scouts from the Lord Byeli's Firebird sept, a pack called the Arrow's Fall. Ahead of their entourage, well out of sight and sound in the spirit world, Nightmane ran alone, scouting the path for signs of any enemies and making sure that the caern's spirit warders were properly appeased. She hailed also from Byeli's sept, based back in Zagorsk where Albrecht had first arrived in Russia by moon bridge.

"Let's get moving, then," Albrecht said. "It's time we got there already." He turned back toward the path and marched forward, nodding at Byeli as he passed him. The Silver Fang seneschal fell in behind Albrecht, following near enough to answer whatever questions the king asked of him. He was the king's advisor here for as long as Albrecht intended to stay in the Mother Country.

His stay had already proven to be longer than he originally intended. He had set up this parley with Queen Tamara Tvarivich months ago, but no meeting of two Silver Fang rulers ever went off without weeks of pre-arrival arrangements and logistics, trading ritual requests and concessions. He'd already made the first concession by agreeing to come to her, on her turf. She'd graciously accepted but had been pretty haughty about her own concessions, giving up precious little. The Queen needed Albrecht; he knew that. Her country was in ruins, only now recovering from an occult nightmare that had strangled all travel in and out of the region for years. The legendary hag Baba Yaga had ruled Russia with an iron fist, commanding legions of undead, and the crone had even managed to gain the allegiance of the dreaded Zmei dragons. But that was all past now; the Hag was dead, most of her legion destroyed or dispersed, and one of the Zmei had been slain by Tvarivich herself (with the aid of her massive armies, of course).

The clouds had finally parted, letting in the sun and with it, increased freedom for the Garou. This meant, however, freedom also for the Wyrm beasts who had not allied with the Hag, and they were many. The Hag had her own plans and chained all her servitors to her will, which often differed from the best interests of the corruptors. New things were already slithering across the Mother Country and the Garou here had lost precious warriors in their hard battles. They would need help from abroad, not just from fellow Silver Fangs but from the other tribes also. For Tvarivich, that meant an alliance with someone influential, someone who could advocate for her in the New World. That person had to be King Albrecht.

Albrecht couldn't help smiling as he marched forward, snow crunching loudly under his feet. He almost hoped that something was lurking ahead of them, some monster to fight, to give him a chance to prove his hotshot New World credentials to all the stuck-up traditionalists. There was nothing like blood on a klaive to convince the doubters that you meant business.

He glanced at Byeli and his closest guards, but they showed no signs of detecting anything unusual. He shrugged, stretching his shoulders, and accepted that the rest of the march might well be uneventful. At least he got a great view of the stark and majestic landscape.

In preparation for their meeting, Lord Byeli and Nightmane had come to the States to instruct Albrecht on Silver Fang traditions from the Mother Country. They had also come on a mission of their own, one they had kept secret. They had unleashed their sept's totem, the Firebird, upon Albrecht, and it demanded to know his role in banishing and defaming Lord Arkady.

That pissed Albrecht off. He'd put the whole Arkady affair in the past. Once he had claimed the Silver Crown for himself, it didn't matter what happened to that traitorous bastard. He'd only spared Arkady's life because Falcon advised him to (*advised*, but not demanded). Then the shifty creep had shown up again in Europe, apparently after making a new name for himself in Russia, claiming false credentials to new renown. But this time he'd damned himself by his own deeds for all to see. He had been spurned by the Garou Nation and disappeared. To everyone's surprise, not the least Albrecht's, he then redeemed himself by wounding the Wyrm creature Jo'cllath'mattric, allowing Albrecht's own war party to finally take the beast down.

So, redeemed but dead, Arkady once again haunted Albrecht's life, this time by causing a totem Incarna to doubt Albrecht's word. Albrecht had set the matter straight, though, and Firebird did more than accept it: He granted Albrecht a rare audience with the Silver Crown itself, one of the secret powers that the great fetish held. Albrecht had been tested by the Crown and passed, coming to realize certain truths about leadership and power—and when to give it up in the natural course of time.

The outcome of that event had been Albrecht's increased comfort with his role. He'd always had some lingering doubts about his fate, fearful that he'd go mad like his grandfather before him—like so many Silver Fang rulers. Nightmane imparted to him what she had called "The Secret of Rulership," a wild allegation that the Silver Fang tribe's penchant for madness was a curse from Luna in her split personality as the Betrayed Moon. Apparently, some ancient Silver Fang king had really pissed the old crone off when he pledged his tribe to Helios's servant, the Falcon totem.

If this so-called secret was true, and Silver Fang rulers had no more than seven years before they began to lose their grip on sanity, then Albrecht's own mind had to be compromised already. The funny thing was, he felt more sane and in control than ever before. Sure, he'd briefly wondered if that in itself was a sign of madness, but his experience with the Silver Crown showed otherwise—he had passed the test of power and proved that he could relinquish it if necessary. It was a tool, not a vital part of his identity.

"Do you see those tracks, my lord?" Byeli said, interrupting Albrecht's pondering. He pointed towards a set of animal prints that crossed their path.

The Last Battle

"Yeah. A hare. Big one at that," Albrecht said, squinting in the snow glare. "So?"

"It is no mere hare. Its tracks mark the boundary between the bawn and the outside world. It is the spirit we call Steadfast Friend. He aids the warders in keeping the territory."

"Yeah? And so once we cross over those tracks, this spirit'll know we're here?"

"Exactly. Of course, the Garou defenders already know, thanks to the lookout howl we heard. This is merely another line of defense."

Albrecht nodded and stepped over the tracks. He stopped and listened, glancing around, with an odd, unfocused look in his eyes. He called on a trick the spirits had taught him and peered into the Umbra, the spirit world reflection of the material world that lay just beyond the barrier called the Gauntlet. The Gauntlet was thin and weak in this pristine wilderness, allowing his vision easy access.

Surprisingly, the forest looked almost the same as it did in the material world. That was a positive sign; it meant there was a good accord between the two, that the spirits and their material counterparts—trees, animals and even the rocks—were thriving. Albrecht frowned as he looked closer. Things were indeed alive, but there were signs of ash in various places, as if fires had come through sometime in the near past and the forest had not reclaimed the burnt ground.

His eyes followed the tracks but saw no sign of movement or any sense that a spirit watched him, beyond the usual heebie-jeebies one got when looking into the Umbra. Things always watched you, but they weren't always animate or even sentient.

He blinked and looked back at Byeli, who waited patiently on the path behind him. "It's funny; I see signs of old fires in the Umbra, but not here in the physical world."

Byeli nodded. "Zmei fire. The dragons fought at the edges of the bawn, and destroyed much of the spirit landscape. There are a few dead trees and groves here as testament, but they are well off the path we travel."

Albrecht nodded and whistled. One of the Garou warriors from the train jogged forward. He was tall but somewhat thin and he carried a large silver knife in an ornate sheath at his side. "My lord?" he said as he bowed his head.

"Goldflame," Albrecht said, putting his hand on the warrior's shoulder, "I want you and Birchbark to scout the path ahead. Go about fifty paces in front. Don't get out of yelling distance—for a human throat, not a wolf's, although you two had best take to all fours."

"Yes, my lord!" Goldflame said, his form already shifting and reforming from human to white and yellow-furred wolf, his clothes disappearing but his knife remaining in its sheath, now wrapped about his back. He barked a command in the wolf tongue to the group behind him, and another warrior—a female—shifted into wolf form, this time a white-and-gray-maned one. She trotted forward, obviously happy to take her birth form, and she and Goldflame ran past Albrecht, kicking up snow as they sped down the path ahead.

Albrecht began walking again. The line of warriors followed behind him, the horses and sled in the middle, guarded from the front and behind.

"Hey, Byeli," Albrecht said.

"Yes, my lord?"

"That city your sept is in, Zagorsk. Do all the mon-asteries in Russia look like that one back there? With the Disney onion-top domes?"

"I don't understand…."

"You know, that brightly colored la-la stuff. Bright blue with gold stars, gold leaf, red and white designs and all."

"Ah. I think I know what you mean. Most people think Russians are bleak and boring. One look at the Trinity Monastery says otherwise. Yes, it is colorful. But no, not all monasteries are like that. Many are indeed bleak and gray."

"Just curious. I gotta admit, as soon as I saw it, I figured it was the sort of place Firebird would like. Lots of colors. Passionate monkdom."

"We do visit the monastery now and then, as do many tourists. Our own abode, I'm sure you'll agree, is much more humble and unremarked."

"If you can call catacombs humble. I did like the bit where you draw back the ceiling at night to reveal the moon and stars."

"Only during rituals. It stays closed most of the time. We perform most of our duties by candlelight."

"Pretty strange for a Firebird sept, you gotta admit. It's one of Helios's brood, after all."

"No, it is tradition. Realize that up here, many months are without sun. The candles signify our tend-ing the flame from which our totem can arise."

"But the Crescent Moon caern we're heading to-ward is all outdoors, right?"

"Not entirely. The ritual area is under the open sky, but the true spiritual center is… well, you shall see for yourself. I do not wish to spoil the wonderment."

Albrecht chuckled. "Okay. I can wait. I've waited a whole week so far, all of it on foot. I can wait a day or two more."

Albrecht had arrived with his hand-picked guard at the Firebird Sept, Lord Byeli's home—or at least, his adopted home, for he was native to the British Isles. He had been trapped in Russia by Baba Yaga's Shadow Curtain and made the Firebird Sept his new home.

The weird thing was that it had been Arkady's sept also. In fact, he'd been its leader once he returned to Russia, exiled from the States by Albrecht. The problem was, he hadn't told anybody about his exile, and had made himself out to be a hero. He'd gotten away with it for as long as he had because—damn him—he *was* a hero. When the chips were down, he came through with flying colors. He wasn't stupid or a coward, just self-obsessed to the point of arrogance, little realizing that allying with the Wyrm did not mean he could control the Wyrm.

Albrecht had met with the sept's new leader, Rustarivich, who was desperate to be seen as an ally of a powerful Silver Fang king. Tvarivich was consolidating Russia under her rule, with each sept leader capitulating to her demands. But Rustarivich wanted some degree of autonomy, and the only way to get that was with strong allies who could balance Tvarivich's power. Rustarivich was by no means disloyal to Tvarivich or unwilling to work with her; he just wanted to do so on his terms, which ironically meant conceding to some of Albrecht's own.

Those terms involved allowing his crew to open moon bridges to the Firebird Sept anytime they wanted, and some training for his seers in spirit secrets developed during the long night of the Shadow Curtain.

What's more, his Silver Fang packs could pledge to the Firebird if they chose to, giving those packs strange powers in a part of the world where that totem was largely unknown.

Then, with the gift of provisions, the horses and sled, and the counsel of Lord Byeli and Nightmane, Albrecht had set off for the Crescent Moon caern, to meet Tvarivich and make pacts between their respective septs. He had initially assumed they'd just hop a moon bridge from Zagorsk to the heart of the Urals, but the Crescent Moon was denying any moon bridges that didn't originate in septs already aligned with Tvarivich. In an emergency, he could force the issue, but this was all about diplomacy, not expedience. Once he and Tvarivich came to terms, he could have his moon bridge, not before then.

At first, he'd fumed and taken his rage out on a number of trees outside of Zagorsk, felling them with his grand klaive in single sweeps. That effort tired him enough to make him finally sit and think about the situation, and accept it. He still had the upper hand, and Tvarivich knew it. Her tactics were measures to keep her dignity and the illusion of supreme power, but Albrecht wasn't the one defending the most ancient caern from newly hatched Wyrm beasts. She needed him, and that knowledge was enough to make him smirk at the insulting demands and rude welcomes.

Albrecht's entourage walked the rest of the day and into the night, stopping only to let the horses rest and eat. Around midnight, they made camp in a clearing and took shifts sleeping while others did guard duty. Albrecht stayed awake for a while longer, pondering some of his diplomatic tactics. He wasn't that great at the subtle stuff, but his earnestness and reputation usually got him what he wanted... eventually. He knew he'd have to be firm and withstand a lot of false offers, and probably walk away (or threaten to) a number of times before Tvarivich finally realized that bluffing wasn't his style. In the end, they'd surely come to some sort of accord. He hoped she was as reasonable as Byeli and Nightmane made her out to be, behind her legendary icy mask of bitter anger. She'd certainly seemed so when they'd met last year at the Margrave's caern to tackle the Jo'cllath'mattric affair.

He heard some gruff commands from one of his guards—Black Hammer, it sounded like, the big guy from Montana who'd joined his sept a few summers ago— and then heard a soft barking reply. Nightmane entered the clearing, her black fur a shadow on the snow. He raised his arm and Black Hammer lowered his hammer— the fetish he carried that earned him his name. Nightmane padded over to Albrecht and sat down. He motioned to the cooling fire and the meat still hanging over it on a spit. She nodded thankfully, rose up and began to chew straight from the spit.

"So, what are the spirits saying? I bet they haven't seen anything like us for quite some time."

Nightmane shifted into human form. Her thick furs transformed into an old, hand-sewn bear pelt coat and hood. "They are curious," she said, sitting next to Albrecht again. "They can see the crown upon your brow, so they know you are important. Falcon himself often perches in the mountains surrounding the caern, so they are quick to bow to his allies. They recognize the crown as something bearing his power, although it also bears other powers even greater than he."

"Yeah, Luna and Helios both. I know. Well, as long as they know we're friendly and don't try anything funny, we'll get along okay."

The Last Battle

"They will not interfere. They will gather, however, in increasing numbers to watch what occurs here. Any major pact between Garou septs is a matter important to the spirits, especially those who might one day be called upon to teach secrets or to enter into fetish pacts."

Albrecht nodded. He was glad Nightmane was here; she was a good Theurge, a spirit seer, and seemed quite loyal to him even though they'd known each other only a few weeks. But he missed Mari, his packmate. He was used to turning to her for shamanic advice. She didn't give him any bullshit about it or try to put honey on top. He missed that sort of frankness. As a king, he got a lot of obeisance, both willing and grudging, but he usually had to force a frank statement out of his followers; they were too used to proper etiquette, the kind enforced by most Silver Fang kings. Albrecht was nothing like most kings.

He also missed Evan. The kid was a good diplomat. A little too trusting, sometimes, willing to give others the benefit of the doubt even when he knew they'd squander it, but that willingness made him a lot of allies and won him a lot of respect even among the Get of Fenris back home—and those Adirondack hunters were no softies. He could sure use the kid's advice here. Not that Evan was a kid anymore, but he was still younger than Albrecht or Mari.

He'd wanted them to come, but he also knew how tough that would be on them. This was a Silver Fang affair; they'd be fifth wheels with little to do and almost no renown to win for themselves. Besides, Evan had this big affair to take care of with his own tribe. He'd finally wedged his way into the trust of the big honchos, like Aurak Moondancer, and had been invited north to hang with them. That would be a great opportunity to win some honor and steer some folks to his way of thinking. If he could get the Wendigo to put aside some of their hatred of the "Wyrmcomer" tribes, as the European immigrant Garou were often called, they'd have a real coup when it came to uniting against an enemy.

Mari hadn't wanted to come in the first place. She wanted to support him, but she knew that a month or two among Silver Fangs would try her patience. She'd decided to stay in New York, but was only a moon bridge jump away at the Finger Lakes if it came to trouble.

Nightmane's form melted into that of a wolf. She curled up into a ball and buried her face in her fur, falling asleep within minutes. She'd earned the right after trekking ahead of their party for days on end without sleep.

Albrecht stood up and stretched, and went to relieve the guards. He felt wide awake; it would do no good to have a warrior who needed sleep wasting his time watching for enemies when Albrecht could handle that duty. He passed the night uneventfully, pacing back and forth around the edge of the clearing.

Upon first light, they struck camp and took to the old trail again. It was a hunter's trail, cleared generations ago and still maintained by the occasional trapper or Garou. They soon reached the mountains, where Byeli led them to a small path, surrounded by high walls on either side, wide enough for two Garou, but tight for the horses and sled. They re-hitched the pair single-file and began wending their way through the pass. Around noon, the trail grew too treacherous for the horses; they would have to leave them behind.

"I don't like leaving them here to get eaten," Albrecht said. "They've served us all right, and deserve better."

"Agreed," Byeli said. "Now is when we summon aid. With your permission…?"

"What, you're gonna call out to the locals?" Albrecht looked around, watching for any signs of hidden Garou.

"Exactly. They're expecting it. They will guard our sled while we continue on foot."

Albrecht nodded and Byeli threw back his head and let out a loud howl. A distant howl somewhere down the trail answered within moments. Byeli responded with another howl, and soon a pack of wolves could be seen at the far end of the trail, coming from around a bend. They were a mix of gray and white, magnificent specimens. As they approached, the lead wolf shifted into human form, a towering man with close-cropped hair and a bull neck, dressed in military snow fatigues.

"Greetings, King Albrecht," he said in English with a heavy Russian accent, bowing his head and shoulders. The wolves behind bent their knees and lowered their heads. "Welcome to the Sept of the Crescent Moon. We are much pleased that you have come so far, following in the steps of your ancestors."

"Thanks," Albrecht said, nodding but not bowing. He was the king here. "It was a good trip. I don't often get back to nature for so long at a stretch. I can't wait to see this caern you got; it's legendary all over."

The man responded with a faint smile. It looked genuine, but he seemed unused to smiling and unsure how to do it. He instead bowed again and swept his hand back toward the trail. "My name is Broken Talon. I would be honored to guide you, o king."

Albrecht nodded. "Lead the way. Is there someone who can watch over these horses?"

"Of course." Broken Talon motioned to two of the wolves. They both shifted forms and now appeared to be Russian youths, dressed in well-worn outdoor clothing. They stepped forward and took the horses' reins. "Please, follow me," Broken Talon said, and turned to walk back up the trail.

Albrecht followed, with Byeli and his warriors behind him. The trail grew more treacherous in places, requiring them to climb up steep, gravel-strewn clefts, but they could navigate these easily by shifting to four-legged forms. As dusk approached—earlier in the mountains, as the sun disappeared beyond the western peaks—the trail inclined downwards and they soon broke into a small field, the walls stretching far on either side, revealing a vast, forested valley. In the distance, the sound of roaring water signified more than one waterfall.

"My lord," Broken Talon said. "My lady Queen Tvarivich awaits you at the caern center, ahead and to our right through the woods. However, she has bid me lead you first to a unique feature of our caern, to our left." He motioned in that direction, waiting for Albrecht's consent.

Albrecht frowned, looking at Byeli. "I guess I've waited this long; a short detour won't matter." Byeli nodded but said nothing. "Lead on."

They followed Broken Talon through an ancient forest, old growth untouched for millennia. The ground rose as they ascended to a higher section of the valley. Finally, they broke from the tree coverage to see a wide, roaring river split the center of the valley, thundering downwards to their right over a steep cliff face, continuing on for at least two more waterfall drops in the distance, though they could barely see that far through the mist and deepening gloom.

A bridge led across the water at a slight bend, where the river narrowed. On the far side, Albrecht could see wolves moving through the forest, watching them. They followed Broken Talon out over the bridge.

"King Albrecht!" Byeli cried. "Look there!"

Albrecht followed Byeli's outstretched hand, pointing to a cliff across the river, a huge, flat surface. The sight took his breath away. He halted on the bridge, staring at it.

Its surface was carved with reliefs depicting Garou warriors, shamans and leaders, battling Wyrm beasts, appeasing spirits and sacrificing themselves for the Earth.

"The Wall of Heroes," Albrecht said. "I'd heard of it, but didn't imagine it'd be so… huge."

"It is truly ancient, my lord," Byeli said. "Its first carvings date from the time of Earth's last ice age. They are… hard to read, but stirring nonetheless, speaking to a part of our soul that understands."

"My lady has asked that you see the wall," Broken Talon said, "especially the most recent carvings upon it."

"Yeah, let's see it. I can make out some stuff from here, but not most of it." Albrecht followed Broken Talon across to the far side of the valley, past the forest and onto a small plain from which the entire wall could be seen. It was phenomenal. The ancient past stretched leftwards to primitive carvings in the far distance. The more recent past lay rightward, with the freshest carvings. He walked up to examine them and was shocked to see himself depicted on the wall.

Standing over a battlefield of fallen Wyrm creatures was his image, marked by a glowing Silver Crown and his well-known eye patch. They even got the details of his grand klaive right.

Beneath his image, something had been carved over, scratched with multiple claw marks. He peered at it, but couldn't clearly make it out. It looked like a Garou warrior of some sort, his image stricken from the surface.

"Lord Arkady," Broken Talon said. "His honor has been abolished."

Albrecht frowned. "Look, I hated that guy. I wouldn't mind seeing him get some comeuppance, but he did sacrifice himself against the Wyrm. It doesn't seem fair to completely wipe him from the record."

"His feats still stand, my lord," Broken Talon said, pointing out another image of Arkady, this one to his left, farther back in time. In this picture, he led a pack of Garou against a horde of undead soldiers, his aura glowing like that of the Firebird, his sept's patron totem.

"Well, I guess he deserves that at least. Who did this picture of me, anyway? It's pretty accurate."

"We have shamans and skalds who sculpt the shapes, but the spirits inform them, sending them dreams of what to depict. They dare not impose their own wills onto these images, lest they mar the record. If you stare intently at these scenes, they will awaken and engulf you, displaying their events as if you were a witness. Do you wish to see any of them now?"

Albrecht scanned the wall, but also looked up at the sky. It was completely dark now and the moon was rising. "Damn it, I do. But not yet. I came all this way to see Tvarivich. I'm damn well going to do that. Let's move on and get this over with."

Broken Talon nodded but seemed disappointed. He led them into the nearby woods, skirting the far side of the enclosed valley, and down a series of descending paths. After passing what sounded like another waterfall invisible through the thick tree cover, they came out into a field.

Standing before them was the largest tree Albrecht had ever seen. It made the giant oak that served as his own throne back home look small. The fir tree stretched so far into the sky that Albrecht had no way of estimating its height.

"It is even bigger in the Umbra," Broken Talon said, noting Albrecht's obvious awe.

They moved past the fir tree to a small lake created by the waterfall they could now see. From the lake, the river continued on, now to their left. Across the banks, standing stones encircled a clearing. Some people gathered there, watching Albrecht with curiosity. He scanned their ranks but saw no one that resembled Tvarivich.

Instead of taking them across the nearby ford in the river, Broken Talon led them back along the lake toward the cliff face. There, a slender path hugged the cliff, leading under and through the raging torrent of the waterfall.

"My lord," Broken Talon said, halting before the path. "My Queen awaits you in the crystal grotto. She asks that you come with only two warriors, for the grotto is small."

Normally, Albrecht would have been suspicious of such a request, but he didn't think Tvarivich would try anything here. He looked to his group and waved over a single warrior, Erik Honnunger, a Silver Fang from his own sept. He patted Byeli on the shoulder. "You've got me this far, I figure I can trust you further."

Byeli nodded, smiling at the compliment and gesture of respect. Broken Talon stepped back. "I cannot accompany you. Be careful as you pass the water; the spirits must first judge you. If they do not like you, they will not let you pass and the torrent will take you. This is, of course, unlikely." He bowed as he said this.

Albrecht snorted and shook his head. "It takes all kinds. Let's go." He started down the path, Erik behind him and Byeli following last. When he reached the falling water, he slowed and peered into it, trying to see signs of the spirits. He couldn't see anything but water. He walked through it, figuring if the spirits wanted to try something, let them; he'd rip their ephemeral guts out if they judged him wrong. He had no doubts that a bunch of water spirits couldn't begin to match him.

He emerged into a small cave and followed a dim light coming from within, some sort of phosphorescence. As soon as Erik and Byeli were through, he moved onward, noticing the crystals that studded the walls of the place. The light, from a source he still couldn't pinpoint, made them sparkle, giving off a rainbow of colors. He couldn't help but stare at one of them as it sent off a shimmer of multi-faceted light. He blinked, somewhat dazed, and opened his eyes in another world.

He started, reaching for his klaive, but then calmed. The place was larger, the walls wider and taller. He had somehow been shifted over the Gauntlet and into the Umbra. Erik and Byeli were with him, both also blinking their eyes.

"Welcome, King Albrecht," Queen Tamara Tvarivich said in her Russian-accented English. Her midnight black mane seemed even darker against her silver rune-embroidered white robes. She had a sly, playful smile on her face. "I wondered if you'd ever get here."

Chapter Two:
The Reluctant Third

Queen Tvarivich spread her arms, gesturing toward the brilliant, crystal-laden grotto around her. It was larger in the spirit world than it had been in the physical world, but it was still only about thirty yards across and wide, with an uneven floor. Shimmering light reflected from a pool somewhere behind her, throwing wavering shadows and light across the walls and ceiling. Sitting by the pool, two wolves watched Albrecht with curiosity, their pure white fur practically glowing in the light.

Albrecht bowed his head and shoulders, but didn't take his eyes from the queen. "Tamara," he said, addressing her by her first name. If she couldn't be bothered to bow, or even to bid her fellows incline their heads, then he could bloody well call her whatever he wanted to. "It's good to see you again. This time, in better circumstances." They had last met amid war at the caern of the Margrave Konietzko.

Tvarivich's nose wrinkled, a wolfish gesture that looked somewhat odd in her human form, but her smile never wavered. "It is also good to see you healthy and whole. *Spasibo, chto priekhala v takuiu dal*. Word of your march against the Dragon of the Tisza speaks well of you. Congratulations on your victory." She bowed her head, finally.

"Thanks. It was a tough one. Some of my crew didn't make it out alive, but their names are hallowed and will always be sung. Interestingly, we couldn't have done it without Lord Arkady's help. He softened the thing up for us. I owe him for that. I hope your people remember that."

Tvarivich's smile softened and seemed more genuine. "Yes, so I had heard. He walked the Silver Spiral, the legendary path through the Weaver's web to the heart of the Wyrm. Many of us had believed it to be a myth, and yet it led him to secret powers. He shall be remembered for his glorious deeds. But we shall also not forget his errors; they will instruct cubs on the dangers of arrogance. Nonetheless, I am glad that you asked. Come." She gestured to the pool and walked to its edge, the silver runes on her robe shimmering in the light. "I wish to show you something."

Albrecht joined her by the edge of the water. The two wolves stood and backed away, making room for them. As they did so, they lowered their heads to him. *That's more like it,* Albrecht thought.

"This is the Pool of Sorrows," Tvarivich said, dipping her hand into the water. The source of the light came from deep within the pool, unseen somewhere far down in its milky waters. "It holds the memories of our losses, our tears for our fallen comrades and our crushed hopes for our native land. But it also holds our triumphs, our victories, gained at great cost. To swim in it is to commune with our past. To drink from it is to shed tears with us, and so join in our grief. Would you drink with me, Albrecht?"

Albrecht stared into the water. It looked more like honeydew than water, nothing like salty, sorrowful tears.

The Last Battle

This was surely some sort of Ivory Priesthood thing, and Tvarivich, born under the crescent moon, was the high pooh-bah of that secretive order. They were obsessed with the mysteries of death and the Underworld, places not natural to most Garou, who knew that their ancestor spirits lived not in the Abodes of Death—places reserved for humans, mainly—but in the Summerlands of the spirit world. He didn't know what game Tvarivich played here, but he knew that to deny her request would be a serious insult. "Sure," he said. "I want to know what you guys go through here."

Tvarivich dipped her hand in the water and brought it to her mouth, drinking with closed eyes. She shuddered and her mouth trembled. When she opened her eyes, they glistened with wetness and she no longer smiled.

Albrecht reached his own hand into the water. It felt warm. He cupped it in his palm and brought it to his mouth. It tasted odd, like nothing he'd drunk before. If anything, it was an absence of taste, a brief numbing of the tongue. As soon as it passed his throat he was wracked by a deep, terrible loneliness, a feeling of abandonment. He barely kept a sob from escaping his lips and shut his one good eye to hold back the tears. As he opened it again, the light in the grotto seemed brighter, and he knew with a strange surety that he was not alone, that he was never alone, no matter the odds assembled against him. His ancestors waited, along with those who had fallen fighting beside him, in the spirit world, in their tribe's true home. But more than this, he felt the bond between his packmates, the powerful ties between himself and Mari and Evan. Distance did not matter; only loyalty, which spanned all spaces and times.

"Do you understand?" Tvarivich said, her voice soft and cracking.

Albrecht looked at her and saw not a political rival who had to be won over through games of diplomacy, but a fellow Garou, one of Gaia's own, trapped like him in a dying world that no longer wanted them. He knew his perception was some sort of trick caused by the water, but he also knew it was true. Tvarivich, by sharing this water with him, showed that she disliked politics also, and wanted to meet him as an equal, to let them communicate without pretense or ploys, one Garou leader to another.

"Yeah, I get it," he said, nodding.

She moved away from the pool, toward the passage through which Albrecht had entered. She stopped and placed a hand on Lord Byeli's shoulder, and he lowered his head in deference. She then looked back at Albrecht and gestured toward the exit with a tilt of her head, and left the grotto.

Albrecht followed, Lord Byeli and Erik falling in behind him. The two wolves remained, sitting beside the wall and watching without comment.

Leaving the grotto, but still in the spirit world, Albrecht could now see the water spirits sliding up and down the waterfall, slim, tenuous snakes with odd smiles and sparkling eyes. They slithered down his fur as he went through the water, tumbling down into the widening lake.

Tvarivich stepped from the thin path onto the grass, waiting for Albrecht to join her. He could now see that what Broken Talon had said about the giant fir tree was true: it towered past the bowl of the sky and into the realm of the stars.

"How old is that thing?" Albrecht said as he reached Tvarivich's side.

She shrugged. "Older than our most ancient grandmothers, I suppose. It has always been here." She wrapped her arm in his and began walking, following the edge of the lake as it bent around toward the river. Her gesture was purely friendly and royal, an act of communal, not personal, intimacy.

"So," she said, "the world turns and here we are, two leaders of the Silver Fangs, long sundered by time and distance, now reunited. House Crescent Moon and House Wyrmfoe, allies again."

"Yeah, all together now, to quote the Beatles," Albrecht said. "Thanks for having me over. You know, you're welcome in the North Country Protectorate any time you'd like."

"It would be interesting to see America. I understand that your packmate, Evan Heals-the-Past, is a Wendigo? I have met so few of that tribe. They fascinate me. As do their cousins, the Uktena."

"Well, most of them are probably more fascinating from a distance than up close. They don't like us 'Wyrmcomers' much. But they're damn good warriors. Evan's not typical for most of the tribe, although he's not exactly alone among them either. He's trying to get us all to work together, despite what's happened in the past."

"Much like you and I. We, too, need to put aside any problems from the past and seek our future together. Our tribe will be stronger united under two powerful rulers, rather than a hundred petty kings."

"Ooh, I sense revolution in the air. It's one thing to dream it, Tamara, another to achieve it. We're a tribe of alphas, each trying to stay on top. It's never been easy to get Silver Fang kings to pal up with one another. It usually requires pretty bad times to cement alliances under a few of us. It's one thing for you to gather the Silver Fangs—hell, the other tribes for that matter—under one banner here in Russia. It's not going to be easy spreading that banner over Europe or the States. Hell, I barely have contact with the Midwestern Silver Fangs, let along the West Coast ones. It's just too much territory to cover."

"Freeing Russia from the Hag was not easy. But it had to be done. The same here. If we do not forge a global alliance of Silver Fangs, we can never unite all the tribes together. What if the final times come upon us now? We are weak and scattered. We would fall like leaves defeated by the coming of winter."

"Don't get me wrong; you're right that we need to get everybody's act together. But I have a hard enough time winning the hearts and minds of the tribes in the New York area, let alone worldwide. It's going to take more than you and me, Tamara."

"I know. That's why we need to ally with the Margrave."

"Konietzko? He's good, I'll grant him that. But I don't like his vision; too bleak." Albrecht held up his palms when he saw the frown on Tvarivich's brow. "I know, I know: if I went through half of what he's had to, or even a quarter of what you've had to, I'd be thinking differently. But I do think differently, and that's the problem. Yeah, we do need to have better ties with Konietzko, but we gotta be careful here. He's the kind of guy who's all too ready to steal the show. We can't have a Shadow Lord dictating to a Silver Fang."

"Dictating, no. Consulting and making decisions on a council, yes. With you and I united, we could easily keep Konietzko's own ambitions in check and ensure that our own are forwarded… with his aid."

"I wasn't expecting this. I figured you and I'd be parleying on how to trade moon bridge privileges, loans of pack assistance and spirit pacts. Here you are talking about some sort of global—what exactly? A council?"

"No, a triumvirate of true rulers, who would lead the other tribes against the Wyrm all over the world. It wins now because we are scattered, because we have no central rulers to bring tactics against it. We won here in Russia because we had such a rule. I took over and demanded complete loyalty. Once it was achieved, all the tribes followed my rule, and we moved against the Wyrm as one hand, not five disconnected fingers. It proved our victory."

"Look, I admit that what you did was remarkable, but you lived in remarkable times. Each tribe saw that it had more to lose on its own than by following you. How do you aim to get Garou the world over to believe in the Silver Fangs again? They think we're nuts and past our prime."

"So I hear. They speak disrespectfully of us in other lands. You and I will have to teach them otherwise."

"By what, threatening them? That only goes so far. Believe me, I know the value of a well-timed challenge, but it doesn't always work. Especially against the Wendigo and Uktena, those tribes you're so fascinated with. They don't show throat for anyone but their own."

They reached a ford in the river, where a line of stones had been piled, allowing an agile Garou to step across in a few bounds. Tvarivich went first, and Albrecht followed. On the other side, a large ring of standing stones formed a ritual area. Albrecht could see spirits—bird, hares and some other small animals—watching him from the nearby woods. He turned to watch as Byeli and Erik followed him across.

"Here," Tvarivich said, standing in the center of the circle, her arms spread wide, "is where I accepted the allegiance of the Russian tribes in our war against the Hag. Here is where our tribe's power was made whole again." She looked at Albrecht with utter seriousness. "The Margrave is doing the same, Albrecht. He consolidates rule among the European tribes. Already, many of the tribes involved in the Jo'cllath'mattric war are behind him, including the Jarlsdottir and the Fenrir. If we do not become a counterforce, his will be the ruling voice in the coming years. His howl alone will command the legions of the Apocalypse, to our ancestors' eternal shame."

Albrecht walked into the circle, his head down, hands behind his back. He paced around it, walking clockwise. "I hear you. I understand the threat, if you can call it that. If he can unite the tribes at all, that's a good thing, regardless of what it means for our tribe. However, I know the American Garou won't follow him, at least not all of them. He's too old school."

"Which is why I need you, Albrecht. You can appeal to them; they will follow you. When faced with the choice of Konietzko and I, they will prefer you. If you were to join us...."

Albrecht stopped and looked her in the eye. "Us? Is it 'us' already? You've already teamed up with him, haven't you? He knows he can't win over Russia's tribes; only you hold their loyalties. He didn't kill the Zmei—you did. His best bet is to share power with you. That gives him old-style Silver Fang cred, but at his beck and call."

"Not *his* call—mine. I *chose* to ally with Konietzko. We shall lead together, deciding the course of the Garou Nation jointly."

"I get it. It's already been decided. You two are gathering the world's forces, tying them into a nice ribbon and bow, and delivering them as a present to yourselves."

"You speak of this as if it's a bad thing," Tvarivich said, her voice cold now and tinged with anger.

"I'm not sure what it is. That's the problem. I've been kept out of the loop, a last-minute invite to the party. You need me to deliver the rogue tribes, those who will never fall in with an old country agenda, but who might be willing to follow me, 'cause I don't exactly fit the stereotype. But I'm just supposed to plug these forces into the grid and stand beside the throne, being out-voted by my partners. And that's what'll happen, too. You know it. My style won't mesh with yours or Konietzko's, so I'll be the odd man out, overruled and out of luck."

Tvarivich fumed, her eyes slanting. She crossed her arms over her chest. "You are being cynical. We are not tyrants. Of course you will have an equal voice. Do you think we are stupid? If we spurn you, we lose the support of the tribes under your banner. I did not invite you here to insult you, Albrecht, but to win you to a great and noble cause."

"Okay, I grant that maybe I am being cynical and quick to see the bad rather than the good. It would be nice to have a central command structure. We are at war, after all. But dropping this on me like this, when it's already been decided, is not the best tactic to win over a rogue, you gotta admit."

Tvarivich smiled. "True. I see that now. I am too used to others giving in to my will. I believed our plan was too good to pass up, and that you would jump at it regardless of hurt feelings. I apologize. Yes, you heard me, but you will not hear it many times from me."

"Well, that takes the cake. I can't go away mad with a rare apology from Queen Tamara Tvarivich; they're collector's items. Look, Tamara, I gotta think this over.

It's a major new step, not just for me, but for anybody who'd fall in behind me."

"Of course," Tvarivich said, coming closer and placing her hand on Albrecht's shoulder. "I do not mean to rush you. You may stay as long as you wish. Enjoy the caern. Perhaps it will speak to you and deliver you wisdom helpful for your choice. The ancestors come here and whisper on the winds, as does mighty Falcon himself. Perhaps he will come to you and ease your burden with advice."

"Yeah, maybe he'll do that. He's done it before. Thanks, and I'll stay a bit. I do want to see the caern. However, about that answer. I can't give it without first going home and getting the lay of the land there. A lot of folks are depending on me to do right by them, and they've given me that trust because I don't abuse it. I've got to ask them what they want."

"What they want should be to follow a valiant leader wherever he goes."

"That's old style. In America, we do it new style: democracy. No, that doesn't mean they get to vote on everything I say. It means I don't abuse my power by forcing them to make major changes without consulting them first."

"Ah. I think I understand. Again, I apologize for not involving you. We are not much used to Western style democracy here. We follow our leaders and trust them."

"Where I'm from, trust needs to be earned. It's not awarded by fate or birth, no matter how much our tribe doesn't like that."

Tvarivich grimaced and looked away. "You speak as if I have not earned trust, but only seized it like a bauble."

"Whoa, not what I meant at all," Albrecht said, palms up. "I'm just saying, the new world's a lot more independent. People make up their own minds about whether to follow a leader. My position gets me heard, but it doesn't guarantee the other tribes will lay their lives down for me."

Tvarivich nodded, and smiled again. "Then stay and think it over. Come to me with any questions. Ask anything you like of my people. I will instruct them to answer you with complete candor. I want you by my side, Albrecht, not as a pawn or bringer of armies, but as a friend. I will need your vote against Konietzko more than he will seek mine against you."

Albrecht nodded. Tvarivich left the circle and walked back along the lake toward the grotto beneath the waterfall. Albrecht stood still for a while, thinking. He looked up into the trees, at the majestic mountains, searching the sky. He didn't see what he was looking for, so he dropped his gaze and began to leave the circle.

A black wolf stepped from behind a standing stone, blocking his way.

"Nightmane?" he said. "How long have you been here?"

Nightmane's four-legged form grew until she stood on two human legs. She stepped aside so as not to impede his way. "I arrived before you did, following a train of spirits who wished to show me the circle."

"So, what's your advice? You heard her. Should I join up or stay out?"

Nightmane shrugged. "Only you can answer that question for yourself."

"Boy, you're a lot of help." Albrecht scowled and walked past her; she followed just behind him.

"I am a seer, not a politician. You must ask yourself what are the consequences for accepting and what are they for refusing."

"Yeah, I know," Albrecht said, grinding his right fist into his left palm. "Being left out of such a power trio could be pretty harsh, but playing drums to their lead guitar and vocals might be just as frustrating. Besides, I'm not even sure a central command is what we need. I want it myself sometimes, but that might be the part of me talking that wants everything to always behave the way I want it to. The world doesn't work like that."

"The world is changing, my king. The spirits whisper of it. Old alliances are shifting and new nations are on the rise. You must decide for yourself what your role will be."

Albrecht turned to look at her. "Yeah, I know. I got a big decision to make, and it ain't easy. If you know of any spirits here that can, well, chime in with their two cents, ask them to do so. Okay?"

"I will spread the word." Nightmane tilted her head in a slight bow.

Albrecht had reached the spot where Lord Byeli and Erik waited patiently for him. He walked around in a slow circle, taking in the view. The river rushed passed him down the gentle slope of the valley, rumbled down another waterfall, and then disappeared into the mountains. Forests covered most of the valley floor. To Albrecht, it seemed truly primeval and pristine.

"Well, I guess we'd better step over to the physical world," he said. "There's probably a meet-and-greet from the sept waiting for us."

"My lord?" Byeli cocked his head. "I could not hear what you and the queen talked about, but you seem concerned. Is there anything I can help with?"

"Aw, let's put that heavy shit aside for now and meet some tribemates." Byeli frowned. "Later, Byeli," Albrecht said. "I'll explain it all later."

Byeli's eyebrows rose, but he nodded, accepting Albrecht's offer. Albrecht stared into the lake water, watching it clamor around the banks, channeled into the rushing river, white foam cresting the tops of the short-lived waves. The moonlight sparkled across its surface like silver dust. He reached out his spirit, felt for the physical world, and readied himself to step across the velvet curtain.

A crack of thunder shattered his concentration.

He shot a glance upwards, at the topmost branches of the mighty fir tree, and saw the tail end of the lightning bolt and the frantic flames it ignited.

"Holy shit!" he yelled.

"No!" Nightmane cried, frozen in shock. Other exclamations erupted all around them, the screeching of birds, the roars of animals and the shushing rush of the trees themselves, spirits reacting in anger to the attack on their sacred center.

"What the hell just happened?" Albrecht said, his gaze darting between Byeli and Nightmane. Byeli stood with his mouth agape, incredulous at the enormity of the blast. As he watched, a giant branch wreathed in flames fell, tumbling through the vast sky to crash on the ground.

"Snap out of it!" Albrecht yelled.

"Something terrible in the Aetherial Realm!" Nightmane said. "Something in the heavens has attacked the caern."

"What? A Wyrm creature? Where is it?"

"Not a mere creature—an Incarna."

Albrecht stared upwards, searching the starry heavens. He could see no sign of the attacker—no spirits of any kind, but then he didn't really know what to look for.

"It is gone," Nightmane said. "It was not an assault. It was an omen. A sign of dread days to come. We are not safe here. We are not safe anywhere...."

Chapter Three:
No Tomorrow

Garou began to appear, stepping across the Gauntlet from the physical world to the spiritual realm, growling and angry, searching for the enemy who dared strike their home. The first ones across were obviously shamans, clad in robes, thick coats or their natural fur, all painted with pictograms representing spiritual alliances. They were quickly followed by warriors in battle form, claws ready and jaws gnashing, their snouts sniffing for the presence of the Wyrm.

Nightmane barked to them, telling them that the threat had gone. It had only been a warning, an omen in the heavens of ill times to come. The shamans gathered about her, growling among themselves, occasionally calling out to various nearby spirits, who answered in the strange spirit tongue like distant, barely heard music to Albrecht's ears.

Albrecht saw Tvarivich, still dripping wet from the waterfall, join them, demanding answers in Russian. Some of the shamans answered her, and a small argument began, with some pointing to the top of the wounded tree and others gesturing to the caern as a whole.

Albrecht sauntered over, about to inquire what the hell was going on, when a falcon swept overhead.

Tvarivich's head snapped up to stare at it, and her ear cocked to catch its cries. She heard something Albrecht couldn't, some important communiqué, and then immediately disappeared, leaping across the Gauntlet into the physical world.

"This can't be good," Albrecht yelled back to Byeli and Erik, and vaulted himself across the Gauntlet. He was made for fighting, born under the full moon. He was never as good at world-hopping as a crescent moon, so his journey was far from instantaneous. The Gauntlet felt like rubber for him, and he pushed against its resistance, slowly bending it out of shape, tearing a hole through which he could pass. By the time he appeared in the physical world, Tvarivich was already across the river and standing in the ritual circle, a shimmering, silver portal of light floating in the air before her.

Down the tunnel of light revealed by the moon bridge, Albrecht could see a man running toward Tvarivich. As he got closer, Albrecht could discern his features: long, black hair, a black, billowing cloak and gray shirt and pants. An insignia painted in blood glistened on his chest—the cross-hatched claw marks of the Shadow Lords tribe.

He leapt from the open moon bridge and landed on his knees, bowing before Tvarivich, breathing heavily—he had obviously run long and far. The shimmering light vanished behind him, leaving only night. Albrecht blinked to adjust his eyes and entered the circle, standing behind and to the right of Tvarivich.

The man had caught his breath and began to speak in Russian, but Tvarivich interrupted him. "English. Or Garou. Our guest must also hear this." She gestured toward Albrecht, and the man raised his eyebrows. He bowed his head to Albrecht and returned his attention to the Queen, speaking English with a Balkan accent, not Russian.

"Queen Tvarivich, my lord the Margrave Konietzko sends his greetings and apologies at the dire news I am to convey. He bids me warn of the terrible happenings in Europe. The Wyrm moves against us on many fronts. Its assaults are terrible and random. It has caught many septs by surprise. So many creatures… they come from places unknown."

Tvarivich shot Albrecht a worried look and then glanced at the smoking heights of the fir tree. She placed her hand on the messenger's shoulder. "Stand, brave Garou. Give me your name, and you shall have water and food as you deliver your tidings."

The man stood, nodding. "I am Yorgi Firedancer, Ragabash of the Smoking Tower Sept in Budapest. The first attack came three days ago, in Poland. A nest of banes who many thought had been defeated long ago. This was followed by a horde of creatures who appeared in the Balkans, fomori who ate everything that moved. Then, in Germany, a nexus crawler. Many died defeating it."

"Who is behind these attacks?" Tvarivich said. She motioned over an old woman who carried a tray of food. Yorgi eagerly ate the berries and slices of raw meat.

"They come all at once," he said, juice dribbling down his cheeks. He slurped a cup of water and handed it back to the old woman, bowing briefly to her. "These enemies, they are not related. They simply appear and attack, with no plan other than destruction. The Margrave sent messengers to all septs, warning of further attacks. The first messenger sent here did not return.

Bill Bridges

The Margrave also sent war parties into the Umbra, searching for answers. They returned with rescued spirits, who screamed of terrible happenings across the realms, from deep in the Umbra. They speak of monsters unleashed from ancient chains, as if all unbound at once. These things roam freely, drawn to the Earth and Gaia's flesh, seeking to defile it."

Tvarivich looked at Albrecht, a stricken look on her face. Albrecht stepped forward and looked Yorgi in the eye.

"Is there any clue at all about some central force behind this?" Albrecht said. "Some asshole who might be freeing these banes?"

"Yes. The fomori in the Balkans did not die without divulging certain secrets. They came from the Scar, the dread realm of the Umbra lost to corruption. The spirits likewise speak of the Scar, and say that all the creatures' trails through the airts lead back to that pit."

"Holy Gaia," Albrecht said, teeth grinding. "The Scar's spitting out monsters like there's no tomorrow. Just what we need."

"Don't you see?" Yorgi said. "That is what the Margrave says: 'There is no tomorrow.' The time is upon us. Now is when we must all rise together, to form an army so mighty even the Wyrm will quake. We must march upon the Scar, and there defeat the Wyrm's forces before they can corrupt Gaia."

"Now hold on," Albrecht said, shaking his head. "That's jumping the gun. Just because a Wyrm realm is mass-distributing creatures doesn't mean the end is nigh."

"I am not so sure, Albrecht," Tvarivich said. "The heavens have spoken, striking the heart of my caern. Why now? Why are all these horrors coming from one place?"

"That's only conjecture," Albrecht said. "It *could* be unrelated. They could be coming from all over."

"Even worse! It could be the first wave of a greater assault. We dare not fail to respond to this threat."

"My lady," Yorgi said, dropping to one knee, head bowed. "The Margrave requests that you join his army, bringing as many troops as you can spare. He will march upon the Scar and destroy all remnant of the enemy. He asks: Will you fight by his side, and help to lead the troops?"

Tvarivich said nothing. She took a deep breath, her eyes closed, and appeared to utter a silent prayer. When she opened her eyes, she stared at Albrecht with a steely resolve. "Will you join us, King Albrecht? The moment is here. I had hoped we would have years to build our world alliance, but the Wyrm has sniffed us out and made the first move. It knows that, should we join as one, it cannot stand before us. It moves to destroy us while we are scattered. Come with us, Albrecht. Lead the army in the Final Battle, shoulder to shoulder with the Margrave and I."

"Wait, wait," Albrecht said, pinching his brow with his hand. "This is coming too quick and fast. The Wyrm's never acted this quickly and with this kind of organization before. Believe me, I've fought the Defiler Wyrm's servants, and they're unified all right, but they're subtle, no way given to loosing rampaging monsters. That's more the Beast of War's style, and I can't believe *it* could ally troops to this degree."

"To doubt is to risk destruction," Tvarivich said, opening her arms wide, incredulous. "Do you think the Margrave lies?"

"No! Hell no, I didn't say that. I'm just saying that this isn't necessarily *it*—the Big One. It sounds pretty bad, and even worth fighting with an army, but I don't think we should draw defenders from all over to follow it to the Scar—that might be what it wants. Defenseless caerns, taken down by a vicious rearguard that slips in as soon as we all charge off into the Umbra. *That'd* be your Apocalypse, Tvarivich."

Tvarivich cooled, nodding. "Yes, there is wisdom in what you say. I shall not draw all my soldiers from the caern. But I will fight this battle. Even if it is not the last, we must show our strength, demonstrate to the others what we can achieve when led by united rulers. This is the moment we've needed—the clarion call to bring the other tribes to us."

Albrecht shook his head. "It's too easy. It's gotta be a trap of some kind. Don't you see, luring you and Konietzko away from Earth? It's perfect. And if you add me into the bargain, what then? If we fall, there's no one left to unite anything. Even if we survive, that still leaves us far from home. No, Tvarivich, the final battle won't be fought in the Umbra—it'll be here, in the place the Wyrm most hungers for… on Gaia's green soil."

Tvarivich nodded slowly, sadness in her eyes. "I wish it were true, Albrecht." Tvarivich sighed. "But I do not think so. If I had been as cautious as you during the long night of the Hag's rule, we would never have freed the Mother Country. We must be bold, and thrust ourselves into the heart of our enemy's lair. If we slay its heart, we kill its limbs. I will march with Konietzko, and destroy our enemy where it breeds. I would be proud to have you with me, but I do not condemn you if you decide otherwise."

Albrecht looked into Tvarivich's eyes. "I can't, Tamara. As much as I'd like to fight beside you, I have to go home. If these creatures are roaming the Umbra and popping up all over Europe, Gaia knows what's happening back in the States. I'm needed there. If things are calm—and I sure as hell hope so—I'll gather an army and meet you in the Scar. It can't hurt to have two fronts, right?"

Tvarivich smiled. "I hope to see you there. It is a good plan. Your fresh forces might well aid us in our greatest need."

Albrecht clasped her hand and she reached out and pulled him to her, in a great, grasping Russian hug. She then released him and turned to address the Garou who had been gathering at the edge of the circle. "Call everyone in! Prepare for war! I leave with thirty soldiers before tomorrow's moon!"

The Garou began to move, running toward their lairs to gather fetishes and provisions for the long march. Others gathered to discuss who would stay and who would go.

Tvarivich motioned over the Gatekeeper, the small man who had opened and closed the moon bridge by which Yorgi had arrived. She turned to Albrecht. "When your party is ready to leave, Ivan will open a bridge for you. Tell him the words he needs to get your caern's totem to open the gate, and you will be home before we have departed for war."

"Thanks," Albrecht said. "I won't say goodbye. We'll see each other again, and soon."

Tvarivich smiled and walked away, gathering to her a group of hardened warriors, including Broken Talon, whom she led away to discuss war plans.

Albrecht sighed and looked around for his own group. They had gathered into a single circle, waiting for him by the river's ford. Lord Byeli and Nightmane stood nearby, watching him. He walked over to them. "Well, looks like our moot's been cut short. We gotta go. I hate to do it, but I can't abandon my own at a time like this."

"No one shall make that claim," Lord Byeli said. "Any that try it shall answer to my claws first."

"And my fangs," Nightmane said. "We cannot go with you, O king. Our place is here, with our queen."

"I understand," Albrecht said. "It was great having you as my guides. And thanks for standing up for me."

Lord Byeli put his hand on Albrecht's shoulder. "Remember the lessons I taught you about our tribe's history. Draw on their wisdom when troubles descend."

"I will," Albrecht said, clasping his hand. "I won't forget." He turned to nod at Erik, who then led the rest of the crew, all eleven of them, toward the ritual circle. The Arrow's Fall pack sat nearby, watching them. They had traveled together for nearly a week, and had made friends. The pack let out a group howl, answered by all of Albrecht's soldiers. The Howl of Departing. Albrecht joined in, as did Byeli and Nightmane.

Albrecht gave a final wave and then turned to jog to the front of his company. Derick Hardtooth, one of Albrecht's Theurges, spoke to Ivan, giving him the words he needed to open a moon bridge from the caern of the Crescent Moon in the Ural Mountains of Russia to Albrecht's own North Country caern in Vermont. The shimmering, silver portal appeared in the air, and Albrecht stepped into it without hesitating, followed immediately by his soldiers.

As soon as they were all on the wide bridge, which arched upwards at a gradual slope, its horizon covered in mists, the portal closed behind them. Mists engulfed the ground off the pathway, but brilliant stars shone in the night sky above, a clear view of the Aetherial Realm.

Albrecht frowned. Far away in the sky, but seemingly larger than he remembered when he saw it last, a red star loomed close to the horizon. The Eye of the Wyrm, the baleful omen that had appeared in the heavens a few years ago. It now looked more like a small moon than a star. The others noticed this also, for a hushed growl ran throughout the group. Albrecht grunted a command, a call to discipline, and the warriors formed more tightly into their marching order.

Albrecht walked close to the head of the troupe, preceded by Goldflame and Birchbark, who scouted ahead but within sight. He cursed his luck. Damn that Konietzko, he thought, always looking for the *moment*, the singular battle that would elevate him above all heroes before him. He was going to drag a lot of Garou out to a far realm, risking caern defenses, all on a conjecture. And worst of all, he made Albrecht seem like the wuss for not going along with it. That's how the other tribes would view it. Brave Konietzko, seizing the moment, showing his colors as a true leader. *Colors, hah!* His fur was black as the moonless night. Albrecht's and Tvarivich's was stark white, the sign of true breeding and purity, the sign of true alphas.

Albrecht's anger at the Margrave hid a greater anxiety—that the assaults from the Scar were truly worldwide, that they harried his protectorate back home. But no messenger from his sept had come, and the moon bridge had opened right away—both good signs. Maybe the troubles were isolated in Europe. If so, he could follow up on his promise and arrive at the Scar with a staggering army, enough to knock the Margrave out of the history books.

Albrecht shook his head and chided himself. This was no time for ego. He could pat himself on the back once it was over, once everything was steady again, not before. He'd been a real bastard once, right full of himself. His exile had rubbed some humility into him, though, even if the exile was undeserved, the unjust punishment of his own ego-mad grandfather, the previous king. Slinking around by himself on the streets, taking succor from Bone Gnawers, was enough to wise Albrecht up real quick. He looked back on those times now as a trial, a seasoning that made him more fit to be what he was today, to deserve the relic he bore on his brow.

The Silver Crown had shown many times in the past that it did not long suffer fools to wear it. Previous kings had gone mad or come to bad ends, but the Crown survived them, eventually coming into Albrecht's hands. He always strove to be worthy of it.

The ground beneath Albrecht's feet shook and he halted, reaching for his klaive. His warriors immediately assumed defensive positions, looking about, searching for any sign of what caused the quake.

"Hardtooth!" Albrecht said. "Is that supposed to happen?"

"No, my king," the shaman replied. He was staring off into the mists ahead of them, clearly perplexed. "Umbral quakes do not reach to the heights we scale. This is… strange."

"All right. Everybody proceed ahead. Keep marching, fully alert. I want eyes on all sides."

He heard assenting grunts throughout the company, and the march resumed. A few moments later, the ground shook again. This time, they didn't halt, but kept moving. No one saw any sign of its cause.

The scout Birchbark came running back to the group, panting. "Banes! On the bridge ahead!"

Albrecht growled, his form growing, white fur sprouting, snout stretching. His growl gained depth and pitch as his vocal cords shifted. "How's that possible? It should repel them!" He drew his grand klaive and sped up his pace until they could all see the figures ahead, far off in the distance, silhouettes in the mist. Goldflame crouched on the path, watching the enemy, waiting for the king to arrive.

"They have not seen us," he said as Albrecht came near. "They are trying to sever the bridge, with tools I cannot see clearly."

"Can't let that happen," Albrecht said. "This is our only way home. All right, form up. On my word, we charge." He waited a few seconds as his warriors took their positions, weapons drawn or claws unleashed, waiting for Albrecht's signal. He threw back his head and howled from the pit of his stomach, and the Garou shot forth.

The banes—squat, broad dwarves who looked as if they had been covered in hot asphalt—leapt up from their work, scattering to and fro, unsure how to respond. Their eyes were like tiny pieces of gravel, black as the void, and their mouths were like sewer holes. Albrecht's howl, however, had chilled them to their ephemeral marrow. Some, meaning to flee, ran the wrong way, and saw the horde of Garou charging at them. They slammed into one another trying to turn around and run the other way.

A few, however, remained composed and set themselves against the charge. Their steely eyes glinted, giving off an aura of malice. Less-experienced Garou might have paused, but Albrecht's soldiers were the cream of the crop. They noted the evil eye aimed at them but sloughed it off, their fury more powerful.

Albrecht had never seen banes like these before. They apparently had some degree of control over their black flesh, because spikes began to grow from their arms—crooked, sharp knives of ebony, dripping with black goo.

Albrecht hoped it wasn't poisonous, but it couldn't be helped. His crew would just have to avoid getting hit. The first wave of his warriors struck the forefront of the banes, the confused ones, and scattered them like shale underneath a bulldozer. As Garou claws and klaives struck them, they shattered into a hundred pieces. A howl of triumph went up from the Garou.

Then the warriors hit the line of bane defenders, the ones who hadn't flinched at their charge. These guys didn't go down so easily. They seemed to be melded with the bridge, unmovable. The Garou leapt on them, trying to bring them down with force and size, but the creatures didn't budge. They lashed out at the attackers with their black, gooey spikes.

A few warriors howled in pain, flinching back as they clutched wounds sizzling with the heat of the toxic tar. Others ignored the burning touch of the corrupted asphalt, fueled by their rage, and tore into the banes with all their power. They managed to snap the limbs off some of them, leaving them with no means of attack, but the others responded by charging closer. Every footfall melded the tar banes once more with the bridge, giving them expert purchase.

Albrecht reached the battle line and swung his klaive at one of the banes in motion. Its stumpy head rolled off its torso, along with the tops of its arms. The thing emitted a moaning gasp, like gas escaping a sealed container. Albrecht's follow-up blow shattered the rest of the body.

"My lord!" Hardtooth cried from somewhere behind him. "It's a trick! They distract us from the others, who are tearing apart the bridge!"

Albrecht looked ahead, past the line of defending banes, and saw a group of smaller banes chiseling with their spikes into the bridge, pulling up whole sections of it like linoleum. As the silvery substance was torn, cracks appeared, spreading across the width of the bridge. The banes took advantage of these to chisel faster.

"Everybody!" Albrecht yelled. "Ignore the banes—get across the bridge before it breaks!"

He leapt over the shards of his victim and rushed toward the growing tear. The banes went into overdrive, grabbing Garou and holding them tight, preventing them from moving. Albrecht halted to stab his klaive into a bane who wrestled with a Garou warrior. This, coupled with the blows the warrior delivered at the thing's head, brought the bane down. Albrecht rushed on, slashing at the smaller banes crawling on the path, trying to get them to halt their mad tearing.

He turned to see that most of his warriors were stalled, some held by a foot or arm, slashing away at their grapplers. He looked down at the bridge, and knew it would be too late. The cracks were growing as he watched, stretching across the entirety of the width. Five Garou were with him, ready to get across, but he couldn't abandon the others. Moon bridges were supposedly inviolate, but these banes proved otherwise. Those few times he'd heard of where a bridge had been been torn apart resulted in disaster for its travelers. They could be flung anywhere in the Umbra—or worse, they could fall forever, never coming to rest, as some dire legends told.

He howled in rage and rushed back to the struggling warriors, hacking left and right at banes, shattering arms, legs, torsos. Within minutes, the large banes were decimated and the Garou were free. As Albrecht turned back to lead them across, a creaking noise split the air and the bridge began to shift sideways, separating from its other half.

"Shit!" Albrecht said, kicking one of the small banes off the bridge and into the mist. "Hold on! Everybody get hold of one another and don't let go!" He sheathed his klaive and grabbed onto Hardtooth, who grasped Goldflame, and so on, each warrior holding on to another. Albrecht had no idea what would happen next.

The bridge fell away from its severed half, the far side already fading from existence like moonlight blocked by a dark cloud. They plunged into the mists, feeling the cold wetness blanket them. A sense of falling, but in no direction—up, down, sideways, they couldn't be sure which. Albrecht could feel Hardtooth being torn from him, so he grasped tighter.

His leg impacted hard ground, followed by the rest of his body. The blow knocked the air out of him. He sucked in as much breath as he could and crouched, looking around. Hardtooth sprawled next to him, arm still wrapped around Albrecht's elbow, trying to get his breath.

Albrecht heard other warriors grunting and could see shapes in the mist. But it wasn't the same sort of mist anymore; this was more like a thick fog, more… mundane. He sniffed the air, smelling mud and marsh. He hoped for an instant that maybe they had landed on Earth somewhere, but the sudden noise off to their right signaled someplace different. It sounded like the barking roar of a dinosaur from *Jurassic Park*.

"Goddamn it," Albrecht muttered. "We're in some sort of realm," he said aloud. "Pangaea, maybe."

"No," Hardtooth coughed, rising. "Not Pangaea. The smell is all wrong. I don't know this place."

Albrecht nodded. "You're right. It smells... well, odd. Can't put my finger on it." He looked around again, trying to make a head count. "All right, gather round. We missing anyone?"

The warriors circled their king, still holding on to one another. They said their names, one by one, but one name was missing. "Birchbark?" Albrecht said. "Anybody seen her?"

Erik hung his head. "She could not reach us before the collapse. She fell without us."

"She could be anywhere then. All right, first, we'll assume she's near. On the count of three, everybody give me a loud howl, and be ready in case something else besides Birchbark answers." He counted off three fingers, taking a deep breath with the last one, and then let loose a deep howl, joined by the entire group. The sound thundered off into the fog, and they each stood silently, ears cocked to hear an answer. None came.

"Maybe she can't hear us, or maybe she's not here at all," Albrecht said. "We'll head out and try to find our way out of this place, wherever it is. Keep your eyes and ears open for any sign of her."

The others hung their heads, realizing that there was little they could do. They followed Albrecht as he set out, his nose guiding him to the smell of trees in the distance.

Albrecht didn't say anything, knowing he needed to put forth a steadfast image to his troops, but he knew as well as they that they were lost, maybe beyond getting found. He hated leaving a warrior behind, but knew there was nothing he could do about it. Garou had been dumped into strange realms before, some of them never heard from again. He gritted his teeth. He wasn't going to let that be their fate. He'd head for steady ground, get his bearings, and use every trick in the inventory to figure out how to get out of the realm and back to Earth.

He just hoped they could do it while there was still something to come home to.

The Last Battle

Chapter Four:
The Most Ancient

The land glowed even in darkness. Snow covered everything under the night sky, shining dimly as if it had soaked up the daylight and now slowly released it again, light with no heat. Snow to the farthest horizon.

A shape moved in that immense whiteness, a lone wolf stumbling on three legs, dragging a fourth, leaving a trail of paw prints and blood. It stopped every now and then, standing still but for the weak quivering of its legs, and looked behind it, ears cocked. Seeing and hearing nothing but the wind, it limped onward.

Occasionally it fell, its crumpled legs buried in the snow. It waited a few moments, mustering itself, and then stood, moving again, ever onward. On the horizon, it saw a dark, unmoving shape, tall in the featureless flat of snow. The wolf continued limping, toward the shape. As it came closer, it could see the rocky places beneath the cliff overhang, unmantled by the snow. And it saw the dark opening in the rock, the mouth of the cave.

It limped to the edge of the dark hole, listening. Wind whistled within, down deep passages in utter darkness. It put one foot within the hole, but then hesitated, whimpering. It looked back along its trail and saw the dark stains here and there, where its wounds had opened over and over again, spilling more blood. A trail any hunter could follow. It bent its head low, skulking, and entered the cave.

It felt instantly warmer. The wind shuffled through the hole and past the wolf, but with nowhere near the force it mustered on the flat plain outside. The wolf crept forward cautiously, testing each step. It couldn't see anything in the complete gloom, and sniffed, seeking any trace of a scent. There—an old hint of wet fur, leading down. The wolf stood taller, straightening its legs and neck, and continued on, following the slight, vague scent.

It bumped into the walls as the passage twisted to the left and right, sloping always down. The scent grew stronger, no longer a trace. Its source lay somewhere ahead.

Hot air brushed the wolf's fur and it halted, shivering, a whine almost escaping its mouth. A faint rumbling sound, somewhere ahead, preceded the bursts of hot air. An overpowering scent—something huge, old and warm.

The wolf limped forward until it could sense the furry bulk before it, mere inches away from its snout. Cautiously, the wolf nudged the shape and stepped back, cringing.

Nothing happened. The hot air continued to rhythmically blow, the low rumbles echoing in the chamber around the wolf.

The wolf crept forward and nudged harder. Before it could step back, a huge paw swept out and pinned it to the ground. The wolf yelped in pain as its back left leg—the wounded leg—twisted painfully. But it kept still, whimpering, as a massive muzzle inches from its face sniffed the air, sucking in roaring gusts. A deep, bass growl escaped the thing's throat, seeming to shake the walls of the cave.

The wolf whined again and twisted under the massive paw, its belly now facing the muzzle.

The paw slowly released its pressure, lifting away from the wolf.

The giant shape moved, and a loud scraping sound tore the air as its claws struck the cave floor. An almost articulate growl rumbled from its throat and light burst into the cave. A small shining orb, like a miniature moon, hovered in the air above the beast, lighting the cavern with a dim, silvery glow.

The wolf whimpered again and bowed its head before the huge, prehistoric cave bear, whose mysterious eyes looked down from a looming height. The massive bulk—at least ten times the size of the wolf—began to shift and reform its contours and features, growing smaller, into the form of an old human woman, still large by human standards, her limbs rippling with muscle. Her brow jutted over her eyes and squat nose, and hair grew in places unusual for a woman. Along the Neanderthal's arms, chest, stomach and legs, faded tattoos danced in the dim light as her muscles shifted.

She looked at the wolf on the floor before her and grunted. Then she spoke, in a tongue no longer known to any of its original speakers' modern descendants. "Well, pup? Why have you come?"

The wolf rolled over, standing on its three good legs, its fourth bent beneath it, and also shifted forms, becoming a middle-aged Native American man, thin and weak, wearing only a loincloth. He spoke in the ancient language of the bear-woman. "Most Ancient of Bears," he said, bowing, "I beg you: The Heartsplinter is free."

The bear-woman grunted, shaking her large head. "I have had bad dreams. I am not surprised." She closed her eyes and seemed to sigh, a deep grumbling sound. "Has the time come?" She nodded. "I shall use the last of my ten thousand years, and then sleep the Eternal Winter."

She leaned forward, gripping the man's mangled leg in her two large hands. She bent her head over his wound and began to lick it with her coarse tongue. The sight would have been odd had she been in bear form; it was odder still in her human form. As she scraped her tongue across the red slash marks—wounds caused by sharp claws—they began to heal. The scars remained prominent, but the wound was gone. Even the muscles and tendons of the leg grew strong, restored to health.

The Garou watched this with a look of wonder and awe on his face. He had not asked this boon of her; she had given it unasked and with no more bother than a mother tending to a child.

The Most Ancient of Bears rose up, muscles rippling, and walked down the passage through which the wolf had come. The Garou, still limping on his healed but tender leg, followed her. As they came out of the cave, the woman seemed not to feel the biting wind, which cut through the man's skin like claws. He shivered and watched as the woman sniffed the air with her large nostrils, her sense of smell strong in human form. The Garou saw her fingers moving, as if counting, and knew that she used her spirit gifts.

The bear-woman turned her head to the south, away from the direction the wolf had come. "It has already moved past us. You must rouse your people. What of your packmates?"

"Gone," the Garou said, head hung low, a sound of despair in his voice. "All the banetenders of the North are slain."

The bear-woman nodded, accepting this news with disappointment but no surprise. "I will catch it and hold it as long as I can. You must bring as many of your kind as you can. My kind are scattered and broken. This fight will be yours."

She fell forward, her hands outspread, her form growing as she fell. Two huge paws hit the ground, and she shook her entire giant, furred bulk, her snout upraised to the night sky, as if nodding to the stars. A low grumble tumbled from her throat, a prayer to the Powers, becoming a mighty roar as she leapt away from the cave and vaulted across the snow unimaginably faster than a creature her size should have be able to move.

The Garou watched her go. When he could no longer see her, he finally shifted back to wolf form, protected again from the wind by his fur. His leg was greatly improved, but he still could not put his full weight on it. He walked slowly toward the south, following the bear's trail, testing his legs to regain his rhythm. When he was sure that he could handle it, he broke into a run, heading south to seek his own kind.

Chapter Five:
Northern Shadows

A twig snapped in the distance. Evan Heals-the-Past, his bow half drawn, darted his eyes in the sound's direction, looking for any sign of motion. The woods were still. He opened his mouth and made a strange, twittering sound. Far off to his left, a similar twitter answered him. Evan bent down low and moved slowly forward, following the faint tracks through the underbrush. He had taken only three steps when the buck broke and ran from the thick brush, suddenly visible, its body crashing through branches.

Evan stood, drew his bow to full, and aimed at the vanishing deer. He loosed the arrow and heard the beast crash to the forest floor, thrashing. He could no longer see it through the autumn leaves, but its sound was unmistakable. He ran forward, his legs transforming from human feet to wolf paws, his torso dropping and his front hands—now also paws—hitting the ground at a run. His bow vanished into an ephemeral haze, becoming an intangible thing of spirit, ready to reappear when he again shifted forms.

Evan, now a wolf, came upon the dying deer. They locked eyes, the deer's stare imparting an ineffable, ancient message. Evan leapt forward and tore the deer's throat out with his jaws. He then reared his head back and howled.

Answering howls broke from the woods to the left and right, growing louder as Evan's fellow Garou approached. Evan licked at the steaming blood coming from the open throat, and grumbled gestures of thanks to the departing spirit. He bent his whole body before the beast, looking almost as if he prayed beside an altar of sacrificial flesh.

Two Garou broke through the foliage from different directions at nearly the same moment, a raven-haired Native American man and woman, both wearing jeans and brown leather jackets decorated with medicine wheels. They watched Evan, waiting for a sign. He let out a snuffling sound and raised his head, stepping away from the kill. The two Garou stepped forward. The man bent down while the woman lifted the carcass onto his broad shoulders. Once the weight was well distributed, the man nodded and began walking east. The woman playfully rubbed the fur on Evan's shoulders.

"Good job," she said. "Maybe you aren't so white after all."

Evan shifted into human form, a young, dark-haired Caucasian man, wearing jeans, a T-shirt and hiking boots. He smiled as he moved to follow behind his departing kill. "It's not about skin, Quiet Storm. It's about spirit."

Quiet Storm said nothing, but nodded skeptically, smiling. She followed behind him.

The colors of fall foliage burned brightly in the orange light of the setting sun. Already, many leaves had fallen, coating the forest floor in places, making it very hard to move silently through the woods. That had been part of the challenge. Modern humans had little idea of how to walk silently through the dried leaves littering the forest floor. A true hunter—a true Wendigo Garou—could move unheard and hunt unseen in such an environment. Evan had done so with ease. He had proven himself to his new friends among the Winter Wolf Sept.

Evan was not a typical Wendigo; his Native American blood was thin, diluted many generations ago. As far as he could tell, he was what they would call one-thirty-second Indian. By United States government rules, you had to be one-eighth to be considered full blood. Anything more than one-sixteenth and even most Native Americans thought you were a pretender. But it wasn't his Native credentials that truly mattered—it was his Garou blood, and that had bred true.

The Garou "gene" was considered recessive, so far as any Garou bothered to think in terms of modern DNA and genealogy. It could skip many generations before breeding a true Garou. Evan's family hadn't been considered Kinfolk—close breeding stock—for generations; he was one of the many lost bloodlines of Garou. Common among European tribes, especially after the immigrant diaspora to America, but not so common among the Wendigo, whose diehard tribal ways meant that most breeding was kept well within known families of human Native tribes or wolf packs.

It wasn't easy for those who discovered their heritage without the support of a Garou community. When Evan underwent his First Change, the Wendigo weren't there to aid him. Instead, the Black Spiral Dancers showed up, following a prophecy about him. By happenstance—or fate—Evan literally bumped into King Albrecht (then "Lord" Albrecht), and the resulting quest not only revealed a piece of Evan's identity but helped

Albrecht redeem himself from the depression of his exile. Since then, they'd been packmates, along with Mari Cabrah, who had also been drawn into Evan's Legacy Rite.

"So, Snow Skin," Quiet Storm said with a smirk as she caught up with Evan and walked beside him. Her nickname for him wasn't exactly fair, considering that Evan's complexion was actually slightly darker than the average white's. "When's King Albrecht going to come up here? Isn't he interested in the Wendigo?"

"You know he is," Evan said. "But he's got tribal business in Russia. He'll be back by the end of the month."

"Uh, huh. So, Russia takes precedence over Canada?"

"C'mon," Evan said as he shook his head, still smiling, "you know as well as I do that Aurak Moondancer's invitation didn't come until after Albrecht had already accepted Queen Tvarivich's."

"So why's your other packmate not here? Mari?"

"Doesn't anybody tell anybody anything around here? I explained all this when I arrived. But you were out staring at your reflection in a still pond somewhere, I suppose." Quiet Storm's smile grew wider, but she didn't look at Evan, keeping her gaze on the path ahead of them. "She's back in New York, doing a favor for the Silver River Pack. Something to do with a factory in Jersey, someplace pumping out toxins."

"Silver River Pack? Isn't John North Wind's Son one of them? He should be here, too! It's not everyday you get a Wendigo moot with septs from all over the East. And it's not every tribal get-together where we invite non-Wendigo like your packmates."

"They'll come when they can, Quiet Storm. And John's first duty is to his pack, as you well know."

"Well, I suppose. *You're* here, at least."

"Thanks for the glowing endorsement."

Quiet Storm looked at Evan, examining him before speaking again. "Is it true what they say about you?"

"I don't know," Evan said, looking at Quiet Storm with raised eyebrows. "What are they saying about me?"

"That you're favored by the ancestors. They say the ancestors revealed the past to you during your Rite of Passage and marked you for a future quest."

Evan shook his head in exasperation. "They sure say a lot of things. I don't know about that kind of stuff. Yes, the ancestors did show me a vision of the past during my first rite, and clued me in about healing the rift between Garou tribes, the debt of blood between our kinds. But I don't know anything about a future quest."

"Don't the ancestors speak to you, and tell you what is to come?"

"No. I haven't seen or heard from them since that rite. I know lots of Wendigo and half-moons who have council with the ancestors, but I don't. They don't seem to listen to me. Maybe it's my white skin."

"Well, for someone they don't talk to, they sure talk *about* you. Every elder knows who you are. They all think you're destined for something. Otherwise, why would you, just a kid when you had your rite, have become packmates with the king of the Silver Fangs? I think that's why your skin's white—to show the spirits your link to the pure-bred Fangs."

"That's quite a theory there. But my fur's not white. It's gray."

"Aw, you're getting literal. The spirits don't think that way."

They came into a large meadow through which a small stream meandered in the deepening twilight. The Native man who carried the deer bent down to drink, cupping water in his palm and bringing it to his mouth.

Evan joined him. "Thanks for offering to carry my kill, Flint Knife, but I can take the load the rest of the way."

"No," Flint Knife said. "I keep my word. I said that if you could actually get a kill out here, I'd carry it all the way back in human form. I keep my end of the bargain."

"I'm not saying otherwise. I just want you to know that I don't hold you to it. You've proved your honor."

"I'll prove it when I walk into the village carrying the deer." He stood up, grunting. It was an awfully long way to walk with a heavy deer carcass on your shoulders. If he was in the stronger "cave man" form, it wouldn't be such a hardship, but human form was a true challenge, even for someone as muscled and hardened as Flint Knife.

As Flint Knife adjusted the carcass for the next leg of the journey, he froze, surprised, and squinted downstream. "There's somebody there," he said.

Evan followed his gaze and saw a shape, lying half in, half out of the stream. "It's a wolf!"

Evan ran over to the wolf and could see its thin ribs rising and falling slowly. Its eyes were closed, its snout almost submerged in the stream, only the tip of its nostrils above water. The wolf's hindquarters bore a strange glyph, burned into the fur. This was no mere wolf, but a Garou.

Quiet Storm appeared by Evan's side, and bent down—still in human form—to sniff the strange wolf.

"I don't know him," she said. "But he's got old blood dried in his fur. Not all of it his."

"I don't see any open wounds," Evan said. "A few scars, but nothing that would knock him out. He must have dropped from exhaustion."

He helped Quiet Storm to pull the wolf from the water, dragging him fully onto the shore. The wolf's eyes fluttered open and he blinked at them, confused. He weakly tried to stand, but collapsed, whimpering.

"We should get him back to the village, to a healer," Quiet Storm said, looking at the wolf with pity.

"All right," Evan said. "I'll carry him." His form shifted, growing larger, uglier, muscles rippling on his now-broad, brutish frame. He picked up the wolf and settled him on his shoulders, similar to the way Flint Knife carried the deer, and then stood up, looking to Flint Knife. "Look, this guy's hurt. We shouldn't waste time. Why don't you switch to a stronger form, so we can move faster?"

"No," Flint Knife said, his face a mask of expressionless stoicism. "If I fail to keep up, just leave me behind. I'll stick to my promise."

"But maybe this guy was attacked by something," Quiet Storm said. "It could still be near. We can't risk splitting up."

"If he was attacked, we'd know it," Flint Knife said. "Just go. I'll be behind you."

Evan shrugged and began jogging. Quiet Storm ran ahead of him, leading the way back to the village.

● ● ●

A howl of pain escaped from the old weather-beaten, aluminum trailer. Evan grimaced, sitting outside the mobile home on a folding deck chair, waiting for word of his patient's condition. Quiet Storm paced nearby,

The Last Battle

nervous. She looked up at the sounds of people greeting someone down the road, and saw Flint Knife finally enter the ramshackle village, huffing and puffing. He dropped to his knees and let go of the deer carcass, holding a fist up in triumph. Evan smiled.

Fellow Wendigo and Kinfolk gathered around him, slapping him on the shoulders or punching his arms, congratulating him. A small group took the deer carcass away to be gutted and prepared for dinner. The Wendigo turned toward Evan and nodded at him, a stoic but heartfelt expression of praise for his catch. Evan couldn't help grinning wider.

The trailer door opened with a rattling creak and Aurak Moondancer motioned Evan inside. He got up and Quiet Storm followed quickly behind him, even though she hadn't been directly invited.

Inside the dark, incense-fogged room, an old woman leaned over a bed where the wolf lay on his side, eyes open and head rolling in delirium. The woman waved an eagle feather over him, creating eddies of incense, and mumbled in a Native tongue.

"He is from the North," Aurak said. The old man sat down on a wooden chair, watching the wolf. Aurak's long white hair descended almost to his waist, spread out over his buckskin shirt. Only his shoes were modern, some brand of Nike rip-offs. "An Uktena. His wounds are Wyrm tainted. The worst of them on his leg was healed by spirit gifts, but his soul rots from an unseen poison. The thing that did this is unknown to me."

"Will he be okay?" Evan asked, standing near Aurak. Quiet Storm moved past him to get a closer look at the wolf.

"I cannot say," the old woman said. "He is tired. I do not know if he has the strength to live. I do what I can."

The wolf suddenly barked and shifted forms into human shape. He was a Native man, middle-aged, his black hair streaked with white. He wore nothing but a loin cloth. His hand shot out and grabbed Quiet Storm's wrist. He looked at her with intensity, his saliva frothing as he spoke.

"Banetenders!" he said in English. "Cries-at-Sundown, banetender." He gestured to himself. "I am the last."

Aurak stood up. "What wounded you? How did you travel here?"

"It escaped. We guarded it. That was our duty, from ancient days. In secret, to watch the cage." Cries-at-Sundown closed his eyes tightly, as if trying to shut out the light of a memory. "It killed them all. The Red Star, low in the sky. The bane broke its bonds. It is free!"

"What is it?" Aurak said. "What is free?"

Cries-at-Sundown moaned in anguish, as if the enormity of events were too much for him to bear. "The Talon! The Fifth Talon!" His eyes rolled manically, as if seeking something that was not there. "I am the last. It killed them all. None can bind it again."

Aurak frowned, greatly disturbed. He sat back down, letting out a tired breath.

"*She* goes to fight it. She gives us time, time to gather. Little Brother must not fight alone...."

"She?" Evan said. "Who is *she*?"

Cries-at-Sundown stared at Evan, puzzled. "Who...?"

"He is Evan Heals-the-Past, a Wendigo," Aurak said.

Cries-at-Sundown's eyes opened wide. "The Heartsplinter! It comes for you! It..." He began to cough, rolling on the bed in pain. The old woman chanted loudly, waving her hands in the air. The coughing subsided, but Cries-at-Sundown was too exhausted to continue speaking, and passed quickly back into deep sleep.

Aurak stood up and left the small trailer, motioning to Evan and Quiet Storm to follow him. He picked up his walking stick from where he had leaned it against the side of the trailer and began to draw circles in the dust, thinking to himself. Evan and Quiet Storm stood quietly, waiting for him to speak. Finally, he raised his head and looked at them.

"This is terrible news. The banetenders hold ancient secrets and know where the oldest and most powerful of Wyrm beasts are bound, those that were too powerful to slay. There is a legend of the Five Talons of the Wyrm, the claws broken off in battles by our ancestors. They became monsters and roamed across the land, causing havoc and destruction. One by one, they were trapped and bound, kept hidden in the Earth, watched over by the Uktena. Their secret magics knew how to make the monsters sleep and how to keep the bonds tight."

"Is it true?" Quiet Storm said. "Is one of the Talons free?"

Aurak didn't answer. He looked down at the scribbles he had drawn in the dirt. "We must call a council, and prepare to fight this monster." He walked away from the trailer, heading toward the center of the village. Quiet Storm, her face stricken, ran in the opposite direction to tell her packmates.

Evan felt alone for the first time since he'd arrived at the sept. They'd made him welcome, and even though they teased him about his heritage, they seemed to genuinely respect him. But now, in the face of this crisis, he was a stranger. He had no packmates to run to.

He sat down on the dirt and waited.

• • •

They brought Evan strips of deer meat roasted over the fire and called him back with them to the fire pit where many of the tribe were gathered. Wendigo warriors, shamans, lorekeepers and scouts stood or sat, none of them speaking, all of them watching Aurak Moondancer with wary expressions on their faces. The old sept leader stood throwing dust and ashes into the fire, creating odd clouds of mist that seemed to glow. Evan thought he saw pictures in the clouds, but couldn't be sure.

Gathered beyond the circle, poking their heads from trailers or tents, the human Kinfolk watched and listened.

Evan sat down next to Quiet Storm and her pack, and she gave him a brief, guilty smile before turning back to watch Aurak.

Finally, the old Garou stepped away from the fire, sighing. He sat down on a log, grimacing with arthritic pain. He looked down at the ground and spoke, his voice deep and loud.

"Bad times have come. A monster runs loose, escaped from the North. It is old, very old. Older Brother has watched it for many ages, keeping it tied up. Now it is loose. It is one of the Talons of the Wyrm."

A growl traveled through the ranks. One warrior stepped forward. Evan recognized him: Painted Claw.

"The Narlthus? That was defeated!"

Aurak shook his head. "No. It is another. There are five talons. The Narlthus was but one."

Evan thought he remembered that name. It was a Wyrm creature that threatened New York about ten years ago. He didn't know the full story, but he now seemed to recall mention of the Talons before in reference to the Narlthus.

Painted Claw said nothing more and stepped back to his place. Evan couldn't be sure—many of his tribemates had a practiced stoicism—but the warrior looked worried.

"I know very little of this creature," Aurak said. "The Talons were captured so long ago—soon after the Three Brothers came to this land. One of the Uktena charged with guarding the Talon lies dying. I will try to learn more from him, but until then we must prepare to hunt this creature, to destroy it before it kills too many people. It will be weak after its long captivity, but it will still test the power of every Garou here. We may not be enough."

"Then let us go now!" Flint Knife said. "We must find its trail and chase it!"

Growls of assent came from all quarters. Evan stood up.

"Wait," he said, stepping forward. "The banetender, he said something important." He looked at Aurak, whose face gave no clue as to what he was thinking. "He said 'Little Brother must not fight alone.' We need allies."

"Yes," Painted Claw said, stepping forward again. "We should call the Uktena. Perhaps they know how to bind it again."

"He also said no one could bind it again," Evan said. "The Uktena aren't going to be enough. We need the other tribes. Surely among all of them, we can find the power needed to stop this thing."

Painted Claw growled in anger. "The other tribes? The Wyrmcomers brought the worst of these things here! They can't be trusted to stop them." He shot a glare at Evan. "We know your history, Heals-the-Past, and how you want the tribes to work as one. It cannot be done. Blood spilled cannot be poured back into the veins."

Evan almost spoke but stopped himself. He was a guest here, and had no desire to create bad blood between himself and one of the sept's mightiest warriors. There were many in the tribe who did not respect Evan's mission to heal the rift between Garou tribes, and Painted Claw was clearly one of them. He looked at Quiet Storm to see if she would speak for him. She watched Painted Claw and chewed her lower lip, but said nothing.

Aurak spoke next. "This thing was here before we came. It is that old. We trapped it with the help of Middle Brother, but he is now gone. Heals-the-Past speaks wisely."

"But the other tribes are far away in New York!" Painted Claw said. "Even if we could spare the time, they would refuse to come such a distance! It is foolish to wait for them."

"And yet," Aurak said, "we should wait. Evan will go to the South, to summon help, and return in three days' time with an army. This will show us the true merit of the other tribes. We will be a force unseen in the North for ages."

Painted Claw bowed his head, accepting Aurak's decision, although clearly not happy about it. "I will gather a war party. It leaves in three days... with or without aid from the South." He glanced at Evan with suspicion and skepticism, and then left the circle.

Evan looked down at Quiet Storm, who tried to smile for him but didn't seem to have the power. Aurak stood and motioned Evan to him as the rest of the Garou turned to leave. The council was closed. Now was the time to prepare for the hunt.

Evan joined the old man as they walked from the circle to a nearby grove, where Lame Paw, the

Gatekeeper, lived in his old tent. They waited for Lame Paw to return, for he had been at the circle like the others and had stopped to speak to his packmates. Aurak looked Evan in the eyes, an uncommon thing among his tribe. He patted the young man's shoulder lightly.

"You must show Painted Claw and his band that they are wrong. The other tribes must come. Cries-at-Sundown did not speak lightly. I fear it was prophecy, not advice. Bring the others to our aid, Heals-the-Past."

"I will," Evan said. "Don't worry. Even they wouldn't be so hard-headed as to refuse. If this thing isn't stopped here, it will come for the other tribes next."

Aurak nodded. Lame Paw arrived, shrugging his shoulders. He set about the ritual for opening a moon bridge. He knew the destination, the same from which Evan had come: Central Park in New York City. The Sept of the Green.

When the silvery radiance unfolded in the small glade, Evan stepped through the portal without a word. He had learned over the years that his tribemates, like many Native Americans, were far less verbally demonstrative than the average American. The value of silence was well recognized and words, when they came, were carefully weighed. Even those spoken in passion by warriors such as Painted Claw were spoken from the heart.

But there were no words worth speaking now. It was a time for action.

Chapter Six:
Trouble All Over

The factory stank of death and chemicals. Mari Cabrah wrinkled her nose and tried not to breathe the stench. Her eyes darted about to catch a glimpse of any enemies who might still lurk in the seemingly abandoned industrial warehouse on the New Jersey shore. Her ears perked up at what sounded like people talking in next room. Mari crouched down, her thickly muscled, olive-skinned body moving smoothly, making no noise in her green fatigues and Chinese martial arts slippers. She crept slowly and carefully to the edge of the large docking ware-house and edged her head partway around the corner to get a glimpse.

Three men—clearly factory workers, judging by their overalls with the Tao Chemicals logo—stood around an open drum, dipping their hands into it and bringing up handfuls of greenish sludge. They eagerly devoured the foul liquid, moaning with pleasure as they slurped it down, as if they were connoisseurs at a caviar-tasting contest. Mari looked closer and saw the scabrous warts on their hands, arms and necks. As they opened their mouths to swallow the gunk, she saw the barbs on their oversized tongues.

She had been right: fomori. The factory had once been crawling with them. But now, on the day she and the Silver River Pack had arrived to clean it out, it was practically abandoned; only these three workers remained. Her rising rage almost caused her to jump forward and take them out immediately, but she knew they had information she needed. She'd have to make sure they couldn't escape before confronting them.

Mari crept quietly back into the room from which she had come and from there back down the long hallway to the front offices. She stepped into a room full of filing cabinets and desks. The plant bosses had disappeared quickly, so quickly they didn't care what incriminating evidence they left behind.

Julia Spencer, a well-dressed woman in her mid- to late twenties, looked up from a desk where she was going through a computer's data files. "Find anything?" she asked Mari in her curt British accent.

"Yeah," Mari said. "Three fomori."

Two heads poked out from behind the rows of file cabinets. One was a wolf, the other a Chicano girl.

"Say what?" the Chicano said. She wore oversized baggy pants and a tight muscle shirt. "There're still some of those bastards here?"

The wolf growled and padded over to stand by Mari, looking up at her, obviously waiting for some sort of order or call to action.

"Where's John North Wind's Son?" Mari said. "I want to surround these guys before they know we're here. I need someone quiet."

"I'll get him," the Chicano girl said, running into the next room and down a hall. A few minutes later, she came back with two men, one a Native American, the other a shy white guy with a knit hat pulled down low over his ears. "So, let's go," she said.

"Okay," Mari said, "here's what I want to do: Big Sis," she pointed to the Chicano girl, "you come with me to cover the main exit. John and Storm-Eye," she looked at the Native American and the wolf, "you creep around back to cover the docks. That's where they'll try to run when they see we've blocked the exit. Julia and Cries Havoc," she looked at the shy young man, "I want you two in the Umbra, in case these guys have some way of stepping sideways. Everybody got it?"

They all nodded.

"Good. Let's go."

Mari headed back down the hall and into the packing room foyer, Big Sis following close behind. John and Storm Eye went the other way, heading for the side exits that would take them to the docks. Julia and Cries Havoc stayed in the room, each shifting from material reality to spiritual substance, beyond the Gauntlet and far from the reach of mundane senses.

As Mari and Big Sis approached the dock room, they heard an argument among the fomori.

"Hey, you fuck!" one of them yelled. "Who says you get the last bite? I'm the supervisor here!"

"Screw you," another one replied. "You wear the suit, but I'm older and more experienced. I get the prime pick."

"The fuck you do," the third said. "You may be able to grow a barbed tail and two more arms, but that don't impress us. That barbed-tail shit don't mean nothing to armored skin!"

Mari and Big Sis poked their heads around the corner and saw each man taking off his jumpsuit, each displaying some freakish, mutated feature. The last one to speak did indeed have armored skin, thick folds of carapace that had appeared like rolls of fat underneath his jumpsuit. Another one was now completely naked, with a long, whitish tail jutting from his buttocks, a cluster of sharp barbs on its swaying end. He had four arms; the two extras extended from his ribs.

The third fomor laughed, pointing at the tailed one. "Thinks he can take us both, huh?" he said, sharing a smile with the armored one. He unzipped his suit and revealed a slick, slimy layer of gelatin that coated his skin. He rolled some off into his palm, balled it like a snowball, and raised it back, ready to hurl it.

Big Sis moved forward, but Mari held out her hand, halting her. She shook her head, still watching the fomori.

The slimy one threw his ball at the tailed one, who barely dodged it. It slammed into the wall behind him with incredible force and immediately burned a hole into it, its acidic sizzle crackling and echoing through the empty dock room. The tailed one leapt forward, grabbing Slimy with all four arms. Three of the arms couldn't grip the slippery surface, but one latched onto the guy's wrist and held tight, at which point the tail lashed over his head onto Slimy's back. The barbs broke skin and the victim screamed in pain.

"Okay! Okay, goddamn it! Fucking poison! Hurts like a bitch! Let go!"

The tailed one released his prey and the guy fell in a heap, clenching his jaw and shutting his eyes tight, pounding the floor with his fists to distract himself from the pain.

The armored fomor looked at his felled comrade and shrugged his shoulders, clearly telling the tailed one that he wanted no part in the drama.

Mari stepped forward, clucking her tongue loudly. The two standing fomori spun around, surprised. The one on the floor spat through gritted teeth.

"Dissension in the ranks?" Mari said. Big Sis walked in behind her, shifting into battle form. As impressive as her hulking, wolfish form was, Mari, still in human form, seemed more threatening. "Maybe we can give you something to unite against. Or maybe we can beat the shit out of you, after you tell us where the hell your bosses went…."

The two fomori turned and ran, leaping through the open dock port and onto the dock planks below. Wolf howls erupted to their left and right, and Mari and Big Sis could hear them yell in surprise and anguish. The third fomor, trying to rise but still wracked by pain, started to cry.

"Please," he said, holding up his palms as if to show he had no weapons, gobs of acidic slime still dripping from his skin. "Please, I don't want to die. I just worked here, that's all. I didn't asked to be changed into a… a monster."

"But you sure enjoyed it anyway," Mari said, towering over his kneeling form. "You seem to have adjusted to eating Wyrm toxins, even fighting for leftovers. I'll tell you what: I'll make it quick and painless if you tell me what I need to know."

The fomor began whimpering. Big Sis came up behind him.

"Fuck this!" she said, looking at Mari. "Let's string out his guts real slow and paint the walls with his blood!"

"No!" the fomor cried. "I'll tell you! The owners, they just left. They did what they planned and then said the heat was getting too hot. They didn't show up yesterday. We were the only ones who came in today, hoping we'd still have our jobs. You don't understand: I don't like eating that shit—I have to, or I'll die. They addicted us to it."

"You said they had a plan," Mari said. "What was it?"

"Oh, that. They infested the New York sewer system with a bunch of pig things. Sludge spirits or something. Sent them out yesterday, in barrels on a tugboat."

"Tugboat?" Big Sis said. "Like the one that sank yesterday?"

"Exactly the one that sank yesterday. That's how they were released, where no one could see them."

"Shit," Mari said. "How many?"

The fomor looked confused.

"How many things are loose?!" Mari said, pulling back her fist.

"Thirteen! That's all! I swear it!"

Terrible animal growls and screams erupted outside. The slimy fomor covered his face, shuddering.

"Please… just do it," he said.

Mari nodded to Big Sis, whose claws cleanly sliced the fomor's head off with one swipe. The stump sprayed whitish-gray goo in a ten-foot high torrent for a few seconds, but then lost pressure, dribbling to a slow ooze. The body thudded to the floor, unmoving.

"I hate fomori!" Big Sis said. "Gross motherfuckers!"

"They were once normal men," Mari said, walking to the open door to peer outside.

"Yeah, no better," Big Sis said, following Mari.

John and Storm-Eye stood over the bodies of the two fomori, kicking them to make sure they were dead. The one with the barbed tail had three of John's arrows sticking from him; the fatal shaft jutted from his eye. The armored one apparently had no armor on his legs— an eye-level attack for Storm-Eye. Mari could see the terrible jaw marks on his calves.

"Let's drag them in here and burn the bodies," Mari said. "Then we've got to get to New York."

"And do what?" Big Sis said, a look of disgust on her face. "Crawl through a bunch of sewers looking for pig monsters?"

"No. We're going to warn Mother Larissa and let your fellow Bone Gnawers take care of it. Leave the sewer work to the children of the Rat totem."

• • •

Traffic was a bitch, but it always was. Julia's SUV finally pulled over to the curb by an entrance into Central Park. Mari opened her door and leapt out before the car came to a complete stop.

"Mari!" Julia said. "Hold up a moment. I can't park here. I'll let you off, along with anyone else who doesn't want to help me find parking," she said, looking coldly at her packmates in the backseat, "and meet you at the caern. Okay?"

"I have to get to Larissa pronto," Mari said. "See you in a few!" She slammed the door and turned to leave.

"Wait!" Cries Havoc said, climbing out of the back passenger-side door. "I'm coming with you."

Mari stopped and waited, clearly impatient, for him to close the door and join her. She had been a trying passenger the whole trip over the bridge. Too much waiting and too little action. As soon as he reached her, she headed off into the park with a power walk that had him jogging to keep up.

Julia pulled away from the curb and drove off into the thick stream of cars. The others stayed with her, probably fed up with Mari's griping about slow traffic and glad to be rid of her for a while.

Mari led Cries Havoc deep into the park. They passed couples walking, kids playing Frisbee, men and women jogging or walking dogs, gangs of black or white males hanging out listening to loud boom-boxes and even a few people reading quietly by themselves on park benches. Of course, the homeless were everywhere, ignored by most people but given quick nods of respect by Mari. Some looked at her confused or angry, but others winked back or nodded solemnly.

Finally, they reached a well-wooded area, a camping ground for the homeless. Makeshift tents of cardboard and hanging blankets spread out across lawns between the trees. Mari leapt over a tall curb and walked up a small hill toward a large cardboard refrigerator box. She rapped her knuckles loudly against it.

A head poked out of a square hole, a curious-faced old wino. When he saw Mari, a grin broke across his cracked, weathered features. "Hey, Ms. Cabrah! Watchoo doin' here?" He crawled out of the hole and stood up, his head reaching only to Mari's shoulders.

"Hey, Fengy," Mari said. "I need to see Mother Larissa. It's important. Is she in?"

"Oh, yeah," Fengy said. "She's gotta be here, what with all the weird reports comin' in."

"What reports? What's going on?"

"Who's your friend?" Fengy said, lifting a chin in Cries Havoc's direction.

"Oh," Mari said, looking slightly embarrassed. "Fengy, this is Cries Havoc of the Silver River Pack."

"No kiddin'! I heard of them. You're those cubs that went up against that Jo'cllath'majjiggy, ain'tcha?"

Cries Havoc looked like a spotlight had been thrown on him. He didn't like it. "Um, yeah. Jo'cllath'mattric."

"Wow, you kids're celebrities!"

"Fengy," Mari said. "Larissa? Remember?"

"Oh, yeah. C'mon, follow me. I'll take ya right to her." He turned to lead them farther up the hill, motioning them along behind him. Without looking back, he continued speaking. "So, where's the rest of your pack, Mr. Havoc? They comin' too?"

"Yeah, they're on their way. They had to find parking."

"Parking? Shit, they coulda checked with us. We gotta number of tricks for leavin' cars nearby where they won't get towed."

"Oh? Well, maybe next time." Cries Havoc said, looking at Mari with a "can't-you-distract-him" query on his face.

Mari smiled. "Fengy, what's with these reports you mentioned? What's going down around here?"

"A whole lot of shit hittin' the fan is what," Fengy said as he ducked under a tangled bush, its branches so low to the ground that Mari and Cries Havoc were forced to get down on their knees to pass through it. "But you can ask Mother yourself."

Beyond the bush was a circle of pristine lawn, surrounded by more thick bushes on all sides. In the center, two women sat by a shopping cart filled to the brim with clothing. One was a truly ancient looking woman dressed in a motley collection of Salvation Army chic; she slowly knitted a needle and thread through a buttonhole on a ratty old jacket. The other woman appeared to be in her mid-fifties, but was quite stocky and well built, wearing a black-leather trench coat and boots. Her hair was long and black, but with a pure white streak descending from either side of her forehead.

The old woman looked at the visitors with one skeptical eye, then smiled. "Ah, Mari Cabrah," Larissa said, putting aside her knitting and standing up on creaky old bones. She held out her arms for a hug. Mari came forward and let the woman wrap her arms around her. "Been too long, child. You don't come by enough."

"I'm very busy, Mother," Mari said. "You know that." Mari looked at the other woman, a quizzical expression on her face. "Loba? What brings a Silver Fang here? Albrecht's the only one of your kind who usually comes out this way."

"Oh, don't paint me with that tired old brush, Mari," Loba said, standing and offering her hand, which Mari took. "You know my work takes me all over."

"How's that going? Any inroads?"

Loba shook her head, looking down. "Nothing. It's as if my enemies have disappeared. The Seventh Generation is more subtle than ever—if it even still exists. I can't tell anymore. But at least they've loosened their clutches on the children. I've saved nine kids from the Defiler's clutches in the past few months."

"You do good work, Loba," Mari said, putting her hand on Loba's shoulder. She knew that Loba had long waged a battle against an enigmatic conspiracy, a sect of Wyrm cultists who specialized in compounding the trauma of victims of psychological and physical abuse. For many years, few other Garou believed such a conspiracy even existed. "Nobody else wants to admit it, but those kids would grow up to be real monsters if it weren't for you. Keep up the fight."

"Thank you, Mari. But what about you? What brings you here?"

"Well," Mari said, looking at Mother Larissa, "I've got bad news."

Larissa shrugged her shoulders and walked over to Cries Havoc, patting his shoulder. "Who doesn't, girl? I've heard it all these days. Here, child," she said to Cries Havoc, "why don't you sit down and rest a spell with old Mother Larissa? I know who you are. I recognize them horns under that hat of yours. No, don't be surprised; I doubt other folks can figure out that's what they are, hidden and all. But Mother's got a good eye on her."

Cries Havoc smiled and removed his hat, revealing two curving ram's horns on his forehead. His birth disfigurement marked him as a metis, a half-breed born from the forbidden union of two Garou. He could only be himself among other Garou, but was usually judged harshly by his fellows. Mother Larissa seemed completely nonjudgmental. He sat down next to the cart and helped her lower herself back onto her sofa cushion.

"Mother," Mari said, squatting down to look her in the eyes, "Cries Havoc's pack and I just busted up a Pentex factory. Problem is, they'd already done their job. There are thirteen pollution banes of some sort crawling around in your sewers."

"Only thirteen?" Mother said, waving her hand dismissively. "Best news I've heard all week. They'll have to wait in line, behind the fomori on Wall Street, the scrags in the Bowery, and the Black Spiral Dancers in the Bronx. Girl, there's a boatload of hell breaking out all over the city."

Mari frowned. "What's going on? Why so many assaults at once? Are they coordinated?"

"Not that I can tell. None of these folk seem to know one another. The Black Spirals weren't happy to hear about the scrags—seems they got in the way of their own plans. But we're on it—my boys and girls are mopping things up with help from the Glass Walkers. Those skyscraper wolves told me something even more vexing than banes in the sewers, though. They say the Leeches are gone. They done up and disappeared. They ain't hunting no more. Now, they've always been real tricky and hard to find, but the Glass Walkers keep an eye out for them, sharing the same territory and all. But now it's like they all burnt up one morning and didn't even leave the ashes behind. My own scouts, they say that even the ugly ones who live down under are gone." Larissa shook her head, as if she'd finally heard it all. "Imagine that."

"There's got to be some mistake," Mari said. "They've got some new plan, some new way of hiding from us. If they can cover their own corrupt scent from spirit senses, they're going to be harder to find. But I can't believe they're completely gone. Vampires have always preyed on cities."

"I was just telling Mother," Loba said, "that I'm hearing reports of weird events going on upstate. I just drove here from the Finger Lakes, on my way back to Vermont, and they're talking about bad things going on in Europe."

"Europe?" Mari looked worried. "Any word from Albrecht yet?"

"Not that I've heard. I'll know more when I get to the caern tomorrow. They should have heard something from him by now, assuming all has gone well."

"He could be in real trouble...."

"I wouldn't worry about Albrecht. I know you're his packmate, but I think the king can take care of himself. He's got a retinue of our best with him. That's what worries me, actually. Since they're not home to guard the caern, who knows what's happening in the North Country. I've got to get back there and find out." Loba stood up.

Fengy, who had stood back by the bushes and done his best not to be noticed, coughed. Larissa looked up at him, eyebrows raised. "Mother," he said apologetically, indicating the bushes behind him, "they're saying out there that someone just came through the moon bridge, from way up north."

Larissa stood up and threw her knitting onto the ground with disgust. "Darn it all, nobody gives me time to digest nothin' anymore! When he, she or it gets here, let 'em in. And it better be good!"

Fengy nodded and slipped out under the bushes. Mari looked at Loba, who returned the look and nodded. She made no motion to leave, clearly intending to stay and find out who the visitor was.

Fengy came back through the bushes, smiling and cackling. "This way, this way," he said to someone behind him. A figure on his hands and knees crawled under the bushes and quickly stood up as soon as he was through. As he rose to his full stature and began to brush the dirt off his knees, peering about in the dim glade to see who else was there, Mari rushed forward and wrapped her arms around him.

"Evan!" she cried, practically lifting him from his feet.

"Mari!" he said, surprised. "What are you doing here? I thought you were in Jersey...."

Mari put him down. "And you were supposed to be at that important Wendigo moot. What happened? Why are you here?"

Evan's smile vanished. "It's not good, Mari." He noticed the other Garou, and bowed to Larissa. "Mother, thank you for receiving me. Loba, it's good to see you. And Cries Havoc, you look great. Where are the others?"

"Parking," Cries Havoc said. "They should be here soon."

Mother came over and hugged Evan. "Of course we'll accept a moon bridge bearing you, boy! You've shown us nothing but respect from your First Change. You're always welcome here. Now, tell me what's going on. I hope it's not worse than what's happening here or elsewhere."

Evan looked confused. "Uh, oh. I don't like the sound of that."

"Don't worry about us. Just tell us what you came so far for."

"A Talon of the Wyrm. It's free."

Larissa moaned and almost collapsed. Evan and Mari caught her and eased her back to her seat. Loba's face became grim, and her eyes had a faraway look, as if she was absorbed in thought. Cries Havoc looked confused.

Evan continued. "It killed the Uktena banetenders guarding it and now runs free, heading south. The Wendigo are gathering a war party to hunt it, but they can't do it alone. We need help from the other tribes."

Larissa rocked back and forth, shaking her head. "Oh, Gaia, I wish I'd never lived so long to see this day. It's hitting us on all sides, with all it's got. Spreading us thin, splitting us up. That damn fool Wyrm's gonna get us all in the end."

"Don't say that, Mother," Loba said, her words icy. "I've fought its tricks and strategies all my life. I'm not going to let it fool us now. And neither are you."

Larissa nodded. "I hope so, Carcassone. I really do. Oh, Evan, I'd do anything I could to help you, but I can't spare any people. I just got done telling your packmate here just how many fires we're all trying to put out ourselves."

"You don't understand," Evan said. "The last banetender. He had a prophecy—that the Wendigo couldn't fight it alone. I've got to get the other tribes to help."

"I know. I know you do. And I'll put out the word. Maybe there's still some packs out there, those who don't answer to anyone, who'll gather 'round you. But it'll take a while. You go to the Finger Lakes. That's where you need to go, to get the others to listen to you. The Black Furies and Children of Gaia will help, and Alani Astarte will call the others all in. When she calls, everybody's got to listen. Most of them don't care what an old crone like me says, but they'll listen to her."

"That's not true, Mother," Mari said. "You've got a lot more respect than you think among the Garou tribes."

"And all of it grudging at best. No, you get to the Finger Lakes and send out the call. I'll do what I can here, but I can't make no guarantees. You go, and you go now. Hurry." She shooed Evan away, pointing to the bush under which he'd crawled to get to the glade. "Take a moon bridge there. And you go with him Mari. Packmates need to be together in times like these."

"We'll come, too," Cries Havoc said. "My pack, that is. As soon as they get here, I'm sure."

"Thanks for the vote of confidence," Evan said. "But you better talk it over with them first."

"Are you kidding? John North Wind's Son can't turn his back on his tribe and we can't turn our backs on him. Of course we'll go."

"I'm sorry, Evan," Loba said. She grasped his hand with urgency. "I would come, if I could. But I have to get back to the North Country. With Albrecht gone, who knows what's happening there. I… I've got to go." She bowed quickly to Larissa, nodded at Mari, and then flung herself through the bushes, not bothering to crouch or crawl.

"That's a woman with a mission," Larissa said. "Something's haunting her, more so than usual. But then, I guess it's time we came face to face with all our own demons." She pointed again at the bush. "Go! Get out of here! Time don't wait for none of us!"

Evan gave her a weak smile and then dropped down to crawl out of the glade, followed by Mari and Cries Havoc. Fengy already waited just outside the circle of bushes.

"You get yourselves over to the moon bridge," Fengy said. "I'll put the word out throughout the park to herd the Silver River Pack over there as soon as anyone sees them. And, uh, good luck." He started to put his hand out, but then got flustered and ran off, grabbing each homeless person he passed and whispering in their ears.

Cries Havoc sighed and pulled his cap back on, covering up his horns. "I sure hope Julia found a long-term parking lot."

Chapter Seven:
First Steps

Loba's Ford Ranger pickup squealed into the parking lot in front of the Morningkill Estate, leaving tire marks as she spun it into a tight space between two BMWs. She could see the wince on the nearby security guard's face, followed by the sigh of relief when it became clear that she hadn't nicked or dented the perfect paint jobs on the Beemers.

Loba swung the door open, almost slamming it into the adjacent car, and jumped out of the cab, flinging the door closed again behind her with a loud, metallic *thunk*. She stormed over to the mansion, the huge home built from the Vermont marble quarries that had made the family fortune—the fortune that Loba's own kinfolk also had a piece of.

She paid only bare attention to the two Silver Fangs standing by the porch, both smoking expensive cigars. They nodded at her but clearly hoped she wouldn't do something so gauche as to actually acknowledge them and force them to strike up a conversation. She walked past them and into the huge foyer.

"My lady Carcassone," said a middle-aged man with a shock of white and gray hair. He came down the large staircase, dressed in an immaculate white suit. "You are back from your travels."

Loba's frown disappeared for a moment as she nodded at the man. "Lord Abbot, it is good to see you. Has there been any word from King Albrecht?"

Abbot's tightened features were all the answer she needed, but he spoke nonetheless. "I am afraid not, lady. We had expected... something by now. A moon bridge opened briefly between our caern and the Crescent Moon in Russia, but it... closed before any travelers arrived. Our attempts to reopen it have been unsuccessful."

Loba shook her head and put her hand on her forehead, rubbing her left temple. "This is not good, Abbot. I've just seen Mari Cabrah and Evan Heals-the-Past in New York. There's bad news from up north. A Talon. A goddamn Wyrm Talon is loose. I think you had best prepare the sept to defend the caern at the highest level of alertness."

Abbot's face whitened. "I thought all the Talons had been... bound or destroyed."

"Legend says they were. This one *was*... until a few days ago."

Abbot's hand tightened on the banister. "We have already called in what defenders we can. Our seers have noted dire omens. At least we now have a form to put to our fears." He paused for a moment, as if trying to figure out how to say something, but then just held up his hands and spoke frankly. "What's going on, Loba? We're hearing word of attacks on Silver Fang septs as far away as Chicago. The king should be here."

"I don't know," Loba said. "I wish I knew. There are many terrible things afoot, there and upstate. And Europe. It could be even worse there. I don't know." Loba looked Abbot straight in the eyes. "I have to go, Thomas. I have a duty to fulfill."

"A duty? Your duty is here, with your tribe."

"You don't understand," Loba said, shaking her head vigorously. "I've spent years—hell, decades—working against my foe. I won't have that work torn down in a single night. No, I have someone who needs me more." She turned to go, heading for the door, still speaking. "I'm sorry. I'll come back when I can."

Abbot said nothing for a few moments. Then, before she disappeared from his sight completely, he spoke. "Go with Gaia, Carcassone. I pray we meet again, in this life or in the Summerlands."

Loba did not hear him.

• • •

It was well past twilight when Loba turned off the state road and onto a dirt lane that wound into the thick woods. She shut off her headlights, driving slowly in the dark. She concentrated and her eyes shifted, becoming wolfish. She could see better now, her pupils drawing in more light. After traveling a half mile, she stopped and shut off the engine, and then stuck her head out the window, listening. After a few minutes of silence, broken only by the night sounds of insects and other creatures making their way through the woods, she shifted the transmission to four-wheel drive, started the pickup truck again and continued down the lane.

When the dirt trail ended, she continued on into a meadow, taking a smaller, less traveled lane on the far side. A light could be seen in the woods ahead. She stopped the car and shut off the engine.

Slowly, trying to make as little sound as possible, she crept from the cab and slipped into the woods. She moved slowly towards the light, taking a circuitous route that kept her moving in a crooked path more perpendicular to the light than directly towards it. Every now and then, she stopped and listened, her arms hanging loosely at her sides, standing in a half-crouch.

She could see the outline of the house now and the porch lamp that lit it. She crept to the edge of the woods, waiting, watching for any sign of movement. The interior of the house was dark, except for a manic bluish light reflected through heavy drapes in a room on the ground floor. She stepped forward, ready to break from the cover of the woods, when she heard the faint snap of a twig behind her.

She spun around, instantly shifting into white-furred battle form, clawed arms up and ready to slash. With a look of shock, she tumbled over as a wolf barreled into her legs. It leapt back as soon as she was down and nipped at her legs, a painful bite that nonetheless failed to break the skin.

A heaving, hot breath hit her face and a shape loomed over her head, a snout inches away from her ears. It growled low, a query.

Loba smiled and shifted back into human form. She sat up and looked at the large, golden wolf. "You've gotten better, Johnathon Strongheart. I never even heard you—or Liza. I assumed you were both inside."

"Ha!" a voice said from behind her. The first wolf now looked like a young woman, dressed in jeans, T-shirt and sandals, with long braided hair. "With the racket your truck makes? Loba, we heard you even before you hit the meadow. We've been tailing you since then."

"I thought I was careful," Loba said, standing up. "But I was sloppy. I'll have to do better."

"Hey," Strongheart, the golden wolf, said as he shifted forms, becoming a blond, well built, athletic male clad only in jeans. "Don't beat yourself up. We've been practicing. There's been some creepy stuff going down around here lately."

Loba frowned. "Why didn't you call me?"

"Chill out," Liza said. "Nothing happened. Just weird talk among the spirits is all. They're spooked, but say there's nothing going on nearby. It's something happening deep in the Umbra."

"I know," Loba said. "Attacks from all over. Ancient things breaking their bonds. That's why I'm here. How is he?"

Strongheart motioned to the room with the blue light. "Playing video games. He loves them. Keeps him from fidgeting. I've never seen a kid with so much excess energy."

Loba smiled. "Well, as long as he channels it constructively. That's what we're here for. To make sure he uses it well."

The two Garou exchanged glances. Then Strongheart headed over to the house. "C'mon. He'll want to see you."

As Loba stepped on to the porch, a floorboard made a loud creaking noise. Loba glanced at Liza, one eyebrow raised.

Liza smiled. "Another safeguard. Just in case anyone got this far without us knowing about it."

Loba smiled and followed Strongheart through the door into the front hallway. The living room opened off the hall, and she could now hear zapping and screaming sounds. She stuck her head around the corner and saw a twelve-year-old boy staring slack-jawed at a TV screen, his hands furiously working a video game controller.

"Hello, Martin," she said.

He turned his head, looking annoyed. His face exploded into a smile when he saw her. He dropped his game controller and launched himself at her, barreling into her legs and hugging her tight. "Loba!"

She hugged him back. "How have you been, kiddo? They treating you right here?"

He looked up at her, scrunching his face into a frown. "Yeah, I guess. It's boring! When are we going to do something? I'm sick of sitting here listening to stories. I want to kick some Wyrm butt!"

Liza rolled her eyes and went into the kitchen. Strongheart walked past them into the living room and sat on the couch, crossing his legs.

"What have I taught you, Martin?" Loba said. "Violence comes only from necessity. You must learn to control your rage, to use it as a tool. Never let it use you."

"Yeah, yeah," the boy said, letting go of Loba and flopping down on the floor. "But it's so boring! Can't we go someplace? I never get to see anybody."

"Well, perhaps. How would you like to travel to the Umbra? To the Aetherial Realm, to see the stars?"

"Would I!" Martin said, rocketing up. "When are we leaving?"

"Tonight," Loba said, glancing over at Strongheart, whose eyebrows rose. "Go get some things. You'll need to pack for a long journey."

"All right!" the boy yelled as he vaulted upstairs. Loba could hear the thunderous sound of his footfalls as he careened off the walls in the upstairs hallway and into his room.

"The Aetherial Realm?" Strongheart said, incredulous. "What's going on, Loba? That's too long a journey for him. Too dangerous, especially with what the spirits are saying."

"I've no choice," Loba said. "Events have overtaken us. Too many omens, portents and dire affairs. I can't wait any longer. He's of age for his Rite of Passage. He can do it."

"Can he?" Johnathon leaned forward. "He still has so much rage in him. Liza and I can barely teach him the basics of serenity. He will get hurt. And he will hurt others."

"Who among us doesn't? We all bear this curse, some more than others. He will prove all his detractors wrong. I know it."

"On what faith? I agree that he has much potential. I have seen it. But I have also seen his anger. He has potential for madness as well."

"No!" Loba growled, staring at Strongheart with fury. "I refuse to believe it. I rescued him. I raised him through his early years." Loba looked down, dropping her shoulders, easing her tension. "I appreciate all the help you and the Children of Gaia have given us, but I won't hear any more talk about some damn prophecy of doom. I've seen into his heart. I know what he will become, given time."

"Your crusade is blinding you, Loba," Johnathon said, sitting back against the couch cushions. "Not every child can be saved. In some, the wounds are too deep."

"Wounds? The wounds of his birth? Is he to be condemned simply because of his unfortunate nativity? Bullshit! Remember, all these years only I saw through the Defiler's tricks to figure out its plot. Everyone—even you, Strongheart—denied it. But I was proven right in the end."

"And that's why I've aided you, Loba, and the boy. That's why I've given my trust and effort so far. But… he's not ready."

"We don't get to choose that anymore. The last Talon of the Wyrm is loose. I cannot allow Martin to become its instrument."

Strongheart said nothing, but his face revealed his fear.

Liza coughed. She stood at the end of the hall, half-way in the kitchen. She held a tray with three steaming mugs of tea. She didn't meet Loba's eyes as she walked past her into the living room and put the tray down on a coffee table.

"You might as well have something to drink before your journey." She picked up a mug and sipped it. "We'll go with you."

Strongheart looked surprised at this announcement, but then nodded.

"No," Loba said. "I do appreciate your offer, but I want to attract as little attention as possible. Besides, you two are needed in the north. Mari Cabrah and Evan Heals-the-Past are gathering the tribes, to help the Wendigo hunt the Talon. They're gathering at the Finger Lakes. You should go there tomorrow. They'll need all the help they can get."

Strongheart and Liza said nothing, pondering silently. Loba walked over, picked up a mug and began to sip it.

"Why the Aetherial Realm?" Liza said. "What's there for him?"

"Sirius Darkstar," Loba said. "If anyone knows Martin's fate in the coming days, it's him. I don't know what to do next. I need answers from on high."

Strongheart let out an exasperated sigh. "But the prophecies you despise about Martin come from that realm as well as the ones you heed. Why do you think you can trust them now?"

"Because everything's falling apart," Loba said, throwing up her hands. "I can't take him to the north. They'll hate him there, and blame him for their troubles. And he will come too close to the enemy. I need to find the will of Gaia. Darkstar will know it."

A rumbling noise from upstairs grew louder, and Martin practically tumbled down the stairs, dragging an almost-bursting backpack. "Can we go? Can we go now?"

Loba laughed. "Hold, boy. I need to gather things myself."

Martin looked annoyed. "Couldn't you have done that while I was packing? Sheesh!"

Loba rolled her eyes and shook her head, still smiling.

"I'll get some provisions," Liza said. She put her mug down and headed back to the kitchen.

Strongheart stood up. "Let me at least loan you my travel tent. You might need it."

Loba nodded her thanks and touched his shoulder as he left the room. "So, Martin," she said, turning to address the boy. "We've got a very, very long walk ahead of us. I don't want to hear any complaints about it. All right?"

"Yeah, yeah. Let's just go." Martin suddenly got an excited look on his face. "Can I wear my real form? Please?!"

"Once we get into the Umbra. Not before."

The boy threw his fist into the air in a gesture of victory. "They never let me wear it here!"

"There's a reason for that," Loba said, turning as she heard Liza exit the kitchen. Liza carried a satchel with food and a full waterskin. She handed it to Loba with a gentle smile and walked over to tussle Martin's hair as if he were an eight-year old. The boy wiggled away from her, annoyed.

Strongheart came back up from the cellar, bearing a large hiker's backpack. "It's got a tent and two bedrolls," he said as he handed it to Loba.

"Thanks," Loba said. "Thank you both." She held out the food satchel. "You carry this, Martin. Time to pull your weight."

His initial look of annoyance transformed to one of pride at her last words, and he took the satchel and slung it over his shoulder.

"It'll be easier to bear once you change forms," Loba said. She turned to look Liza and Strongheart in the eyes, smiling. "We will meet again. Soon. And I will come bearing good news."

"Let it be so," Liza and Strongheart said in unison, clasping her shoulders. They released her and stood back.

She walked to the door and opened it, holding it wide for Martin. "You first."

Martin shot past her and out onto the lawn. "Which way?"

She pointed down the dirt driveway, toward where her car was parked. "That way. To the meadow. We'll step over there."

Martin ran off into the woods and Loba followed, walking at a steady pace. Liza and Strongheart watched her go.

When she reached the meadow, Martin was turning around in circles. What the Children of Gaia had said about the boy's excess energy was clearly true. "Okay," Loba said. "Stand still. Hold my hand. We're stepping over."

Martin came over and wrapped his hand in hers, for once managing to stand still. Loba reached out her spirit and tugged them both past the Velvet Curtain between worlds, drawing them into the Penumbral reflection of the earthly meadow in which they had just been standing. Here, in the spirit world, it looked even more beautiful, its small wildflowers all in bloom.

"Yes!" Martin yelled, and began to shift forms. He grew hairy and tall, shooting upwards until he towered over Loba in his wolfman body. His native breed form.

Loba wondered once again at how a metis, an incestuously bred Garou child, could possess no deformity. All metis had handicaps of one form or another, whether it be Cries Havoc's ram horns or some other moon calf's club feet. But not Martin. He had no handicaps. Indeed, his native form was a prime model of what a Garou warrior should be. The incongruity chilled Loba when she thought about it, and she knew why others feared the boy, why so many evil prophecies had been spoken about him, why they derisively called him the "Perfect Metis." But she also knew that the unknown was not necessarily bad, that the Wyrm could never produce such beauty as she saw in this child. His purpose was surely not for evil but for the greater good of Gaia. He was a sign of victory, not defeat.

She pointed to the west, toward a thick tangle of bushes, beyond which could barely be seen the faint gleam of a moon path. "There. That's where we're going."

Martin ran over to the path, and Loba jogged behind him. He was still energetic, but seemed to have normalized somewhat now that he was in his native form. He would surely tire her out on this journey, but she'd suffered greater challenges than ferrying a metis child to a distant realm.

"Slow down, Martin," she said. "We have a long way to go. We've got to pace ourselves. We mustn't be too tired to hear the song of the stars once we arrive."

Martin forced himself to walk slower and smiled at Loba. He appeared truly happy, and Loba hoped they could remain that way. She looked up into the sky and felt a shadow pass over her heart as she caught a glimmer of red brightness on the horizon, but then it was gone.

She prayed grimly that she was mistaken, that she had not just seen the Red Star flicker as she took her first steps on the path into the night sky.

Chapter Eight:
Guided by a Star

The Pole Star glimmered brightly in the night sky over the mountains of western China. The vast industrial development that afflicted the nation had not yet made it to these peaks; there were no artificial lights to compete with the distant suns. It seemed that a thousand stars gleamed in the limitless expanse, a vista denied to most city dwellers.

Antonine Teardrop sent a prayer of thanks to Gaia for her bounty, still clear and unchecked here in the Purest Resolve Monastery where he had first learned to harness his powers as a Stargazer, the Garou tribe of mystics. Here he had mastered his rage and disciplined his body and mind, and here he had learned the secrets of the stars from the caern's totem patron, Vegarda, the Pole Star. The movements of the stars revealed fates, and he had come to know something of their oracular language.

He stood on one leg in the temple square on the highest peak of the mountain, his other foot resting against his knee, his hands joined in a mudra of remembrance, a sacred hand gesture that could, with the proper mantras, unlock distant memories from his younger days. He had spent the last week in silent meditation, honoring the memories of the temple's chief abbot, who had just passed into the eternal dream realm, shedding his mortal, transitory form. Antonine pondered once more the gift of shapeshifting, how it made literal and real what to a human was abstract and ideal. All forms were transitory, changing in time. A werewolf's was simply more obvious about it. A wonderful teaching tool that too few Garou made use of.

He opened his eyes to thin slits and watched the new abbot as he performed his martial meditations, stepping in circles, following an ancient, spiral pattern written in his mind. It was the secret bagua written on the stomach of the Great Tortoise. Ages ago, the Tortoise had revealed the sixty-four hexagrams of the I-Ching to the Yellow Emperor of China, who had seen them written on the Tortoise's back. He had not seen the extra symbols on the stomach; only the Stargazers knew those glyphs. The new abbot, Persimmon Cloud, now danced them in his internal martial arts form.

Antonine had traveled far from the Catskill Mountains of New York to visit the old temple, to pay homage to its deceased abbot. He welcomed the distance it put between him and the world and all the projects and duties he had there. As an elder, he had obligations to the Garou Nation. Unlike the rest of his tribe, he still pledged himself to aid the other tribes, refusing to give up on them. With the ceremonies of the past week, the bawn had been shut, and even spirits were barred from interrupting the rituals. Now, as the abbot danced, he carefully opened the wards once more and revealed the temple to the physical and spiritual world.

Persimmon Cloud's long, silk robes flowed as if borne on the wind. The yellow phoenix so elaborately embroidered on his back and sleeves seemed to fly in circles, hovering around the Garou as if it were alive. Antonine blinked. The phoenix turned to stare at him.

He cocked his head in curiosity and watched as the fiery, feathered bird broke away from the abbot's robes and glided over to him, swirling about him in a spiral, its flickering yellow flames hypnotic, dulling Antonine's sharp mind. He closed his eyes and breathed deep, trying to remain alert, and opened them to another world.

The phoenix hovered above him and to his left, pointing with its wing toward the horizon, which roiled with dark smoke. As Antonine peered at the thin, distant shape the spirit seemed to indicate, his vision shot forth, like a camera zooming forward on a helicopter, until the shape came clear: a thin obsidian and green-flecked tower rising above a plain of fire, wreathed in shadows cast by unseen entities.

Antonine felt a numbing dread in his stomach as he realized what tower this was, and he watched unblinking as his vision plummeted through its windows and down, down its dark-boned stairs into the pit below, lit by faint balefire. A path led into the horizonless darkness in ever-widening spirals. Antonine lurched and tried to awaken as his vision was tugged down the path, around its grim twists. He felt a scream growing inside him as he resisted the utter, maddening despair it awoke.

Then he was deeper along the path, bypassing whole sections of it. The vertigo was gone—he saw as if from a television screen, watching images from the past accompanied by no smell, sound or touch.

A growl escaped his disciplined throat when he saw *her*, the huge, leather-clad bitch from Alamogordo. Zhyzhak. The she-wolf cracked her whip at the mists around her, beating them back, tearing tiny chunks of ephemera from the banes that could not escape her reach.

They parted for her, but tried to draw her to the side or to cloud her vision with their forms. She hurled them aside or simply walked through them, peering through some sort of thick monocle held firmly in her left eye.

Antonine looked closer and saw that it was part of a compass, and that she looked through its magnifying lens. It was a fetish, judging from the pictograms carved around it.

Confused, he turned to look over his shoulder, to the source of the dim light by which he viewed Zhyzhak's march, to the Phoenix totem hovering there.

"What is this?" he asked.

"The doom of the world," it said.

"How can this be?" Antonine said, his eyes wide, brow furrowed. "I saw the Temple Obscura and the Black Spiral Labyrinth. She dances it, and yet overpowers its guardians. She marches heedless of its twists and whorls, making her own path to its center. How can this be?"

"She, like you, is guided by a star."

Antonine felt another lurch of fear but ignored it, as his long years of training had taught. "The Red Star. Her fetish allows her to navigate by it. Brilliant."

"Where one goes, another can follow."

The rush of revelation Antonine felt upon hearing those words was broken by the pain of his body hitting the ground. He blinked and opened his eyes, and saw once more the night sky of China. Persimmon Cloud rushed over, a look of concern on his face. Antonine sat up and motioned that he was all right.

Persimmon Cloud looked at him curiously, waiting for him to speak.

"Phoenix came to me," Antonine said, standing up. "He gave me a vision. A chance for us to overcome a terrible wrong."

"The Phoenix is not known for forthright answers," Persimmon Cloud said, crossing his hands over his belly. "Are you sure you saw this correctly?"

"I think so. Would you accompany me below, to speak with the other monks? I want to tell you what I saw. Perhaps your combined wisdom can reveal flaws in my interpretation."

"Of course," the abbot said, leading the way down the long stairway that wrapped around the mountain toward the monastery quarters below.

● ● ●

Antonine sat on a reed mat, watching the six gathered monks. He had just told them his vision; now he gave them his interpretation.

"Zhyzhak has discovered a means to thread the labyrinth, to surpass the Ninth Circle and reach the heart. As our tribe teaches, the Weaver's web entraps the Wyrm, driving it mad with rage. But where is this web? It is all around us, but like all ideas, it is given expression in certain forms. The one form that is most representative is terrible and maddening to behold, for it is the Black Spiral Labyrinth, the single thread that leads from Malfeas straight to the Weaver's victim, the Wyrm itself.

"But none can trace its convolutions without losing all reason. The Black Spiral Dancers worship the Wyrm's corruption and, in an attempt to emulate it, they dance the Labyrinth, losing their minds along the way. Only those truly strong of will can overcome the tests confronted with each step on that path, tests administered by banes and other high officials of the Wyrm's cultic hierarchy.

"This hierarchy is none other than the Wyrm's own need made manifest. The only way to reach it, to free it from its bounds, is to pass beyond all reason, for even a bare spark of logic has something of the Weaver in it, and hence cannot overcome the Weaver's illusory web. Only something unraveled from that web can escape it and reach its center, where the Wyrm thrashes.

"This is what the Wyrm seeks, what it wants above all else. This is why the Black Spiral Dancers seek madness: Their master begs it of them, although they do not suspect the true reasons for it. They believe they will be rewarded with power, but their true purpose is to pass the test of the final circle, the Ninth Circle, and so reach their master's very presence. Those few who have taken this test of the final circle have failed."

Persimmon Cloud spoke. "How is this true? Is it not said that the dread general who rules in Malfeas gained his rank by passing that final test?"

"Indeed, so it is believed by the Wyrm's faithful, perhaps even by that general himself. But in truth, he failed. His punishment was worldly power, condemned to struggle to maintain it for endless years. The Black Spiral Dancers do not see that what they most desire is the reward for failure."

"And what if he had succeeded? What then?"

"I believe he would have encountered the Wyrm in its true presence. He would have been completely mad, without any reason, acting on instinct alone. And what is a Garou's deepest instinct?"

A young monk raised his head, a look of sorrow on his face. "Rage."

"Indeed. But then his rage would have unleashed an assault on the bonds of the Wyrm, on the twisted cocoon. Pure, unadulterated madness versus calcified logic. Perhaps… perhaps the Wyrm would have been freed at last."

"And so freed," Persimmon Cloud said, "it would have destroyed the world."

"It would finally have brought the corrupt world age to an end, to begin a new *kalpa*, a new world of purity. The Wyrm is the Great Devourer, eating not only flesh but ideas. In times of balance, its eating transformed stagnant energy into the rich manure from which new life and ideas could spring. A macrocosmic reflection of each living thing's digestive cycle, the most intimate form of communion—eating another being and returning his raw substance to the world.

"In its imbalanced state—the only state we have ever known in this lifetime—it hungers endlessly and yet is denied its feast. Old forms remain, undevoured, rotting the universe. Its minions devour things in mimicry of the Wyrm. But they pervert that act, birthing only new horrors. Horrors begetting horrors."

The monks nodded, understanding.

Persimmon Cloud sighed. "Do you believe Zhyzhak will succeed where Number Two failed?"

Antonine was silent for a while, and then spoke. "Yes… and no. Nothing good can come from her victory. If she is not beyond reason when she passes the Ninth Circle, she will free the Wyrm only to turn it toward her own, ego-driven ends. She will not serve the greater good of the universe, but will serve herself, driving the corrupt age into an endless abyss from which no new world can arise."

The monks were quiet for a time, pondering what had been said. Finally, Persimmon Cloud spoke. "What can we do? What is the meaning of the Phoenix's last words to you?"

"*Where one goes, another can follow,*" Antonine said. "I believe there is a chance… an opportunity for me to follow her trail. She does not confront the circles in the traditional manner and leaves a broken road behind her. If I can reach that road, I can follow her past the final circle, to the heart of the web."

"But it is madness to dance the Labyrinth. You will lose all sense of your way and forget your purpose. If you survive, you will become a terrible general of the Wyrm and a great foe to us."

"There is that risk. But if Zhyzhak succeeds unopposed? Is my risk any greater than the risk of inaction?"

Persimmon Cloud sighed. "Beset by poor choices in all directions."

"I think there is a chance that, once she beats down a door into the Wyrm's heart, I can slip through that door and turn her march into our victory. She is strong and powerful, a cunning foe, but she will be blind to the truth of the Wyrm, seeing it as an entity to serve. She does not perceive it as a caged animal, but a demonic overlord. She will not think to free it, and that will give me a chance to break its bonds before she realizes my goal."

"Very risky. And even if you succeed, the world will end. You assume that it is doomed either way."

"There is, of course, a chance that I'm wrong. I will have to be open to that possibility, to perceive all that I see as it *is*, and not act from ideology. If, after considering the evidence of my travels, it appears that my freeing the Wyrm is not the right answer, then I shall instead concentrate all my energies on destroying Zhyzhak."

"But what if your doubt at the last minute is part of its trap? Perhaps a fixed ideology is required as the only armor against its aura of despair. Our tribe's virtue of questioning may prove to be a weakness before such a presence. Either way, it means your death. You cannot return from such a journey beyond all boundaries of the real and unreal."

"I accept that. There is no other choice."

Persimmon Cloud nodded. "Then I have something to give you, to prevent a long and deadly journey to Malfeas."

Antonine cocked one eyebrow in curiosity, but said nothing as the abbot stood and went into his quarters. He soon returned with an object wrapped in white silk. He placed it on the floor before Antonine and bid him unwrap it.

Antonine pulled away the layers of silk to reveal an old brass *dorje*, a Tibetan thunderbolt scepter—a meditation tool symbolizing the foundation of the Wheel of Time.

"This is a sacred relic of our tribe, rescued from the fallen Shigalu Monastery. The previous abbot kept it safe, and it now comes to me. I give it to you. Its power is such that it may transport you bodily to Rirab Lhungpo, Mount Meru, the center of the universe. Once there, if you succeed in a *korwa*, a circumambulation of the mountain, you can step anywhere in space that you desire—even to Zhyzhak's very footsteps."

Antonine bowed to the abbot. "Words can't begin to express my thanks and relief at this gift. Getting to the Temple Obscura without a pack of Garou to protect me was surely the most problematic part of my plan. But now I can proceed alone."

"As it must be. Others will only draw attention. Phoenix revealed his vision to you alone. Tonight, after you have eaten your fill and Vegarda once more takes to the sky, you shall meditate by the moon pool and there begin your journey to the Center of the World."

The other monks bowed to Antonine and he bowed back. They stood one by one and left the room, leaving him alone to ponder his uncertain path.

Part Two:
Calling Down Curses

The Wyrm made itself manifest in
the towers and the rivers and the air
and the land, and everywhere
its children ran rampant,
devouring, destroying,
calling down curses of every kind.

—*The Prophecy of the Phoenix*, "The Seventh Sign"

Chapter Nine:
Circling Prey

Zhyzhak gnashed her teeth and wiped the sweat from her hairy brow. She halted her inexorable march and took a deep breath. The constant nagging of the banes and the need for continued vigilance, lest the path itself beguile her, began to wear on her, causing her to stop more often to catch her breath. She paused to stare again at the smoldering red orb above the horizon. Seen through her special lens, its rays burnt away the deceiving mists around her, making her direction clear. Even when the path steered itself astray, she could force it back to its true direction.

She reflexively snapped her whip to the side and heard the squeal of a bane that had been sneaking closer. It covered its eyes with its reptilian hands and skittered away, mewling.

The first five circles had presented only the barest of challenges, easily swept aside by her whip or circumvented by viewing through her fetish lens. Besides, she had danced those circles before when she had fought to attain rank and prestige in her tribe. They had the cumulative effect of tiring her somewhat, but it was nothing she couldn't handle.

The Sixth Circle, upon which she now stood, had a special challenge of its own, one she had never before experienced. The Sixth Circle was said to be the test of corruption, the crucible she must endure to prove her own taint.

The mysteries of the Labyrinth were not always revealed through encounters with creatures or places; they often instilled strange thoughts and desires, memories not one's own but which had a forceful pull nonetheless. The conflicted emotions and ideologies had to be confronted just like any bane challenger. Zhyzhak now suspected that the doubts she had begun to entertain were not so much her own as those the Labyrinth whispered to her soul.

None of the other Black Spiral Dancers back at the Trinity Hive had ever shown the pure resolve and twisted determination she had. Her dedication to the caern and Grammaw were unblemished in their raw, pestilent decadence. Her fervor rubbed off on the others, especially her hand-picked soldiers, but none could exceed her certitude.

Except White-Eye.

Cursed, traitorous White-Eye-ikthya. His strange utterances always confused her, but left her—along with any who heard him—convinced that he was right, even if his words made no sense. He had that sort of legendary wisdom that held true beyond evidence or faith. No proposition could unseat him, no argument of rage could sway his unerring interpretation of the Wyrm's wishes. Dancers came from all over to hear his quiet but assured statements about the Wyrm—statements even the dreaded Maeljin Incarna could not aver. White-Eye had seen the Wyrm's birth into materiality, its brief flowering into the world when the very first atomic bomb had been dropped in New Mexico. The poor wolf had seen it, been blinded by it, and now saw depths and dimensions invisible even to the Malfean Lords of Corruption.

And Zhyzhak had to cater to this high priest of doomful revelation. Leader of her Hive, she nonetheless had to bow to this ancient, wizened saint, a wretch barely able to hunt for himself. She hated it, but feared him.

Zhyzhak stepped forward once more, planting her foot on the twisting path as if trying to pin it down, to keep it from slithering in new directions. She grunted and cracked her whip again, this time only at the air, at the image of White-Eye-ikthya.

His words came back to her, haikus and aphorisms, words of wisdom meant to open her heart further to the heart of corruption. They had muddled her mind but left her breast swelling with pride and newfound purpose, a demented, chaotic urge to convert the gifts of Gaia to the excrement of the Wyrm.

But now, as those words rang once again in her head, she understood their true meaning, a dawning realization long overdue, and she screamed in anger—a deep, primal wail, the bereft cry of a child abandoned and betrayed by her despised but secretly loved father.

She had been duped. They'd all been duped. She saw, with the harsh balefire light of the Labyrinth's insight, that everything White-Eye said was a lie. He had cleverly tricked them into believing they served the cause of corruption, when in fact, by following his subtle hints and declarations, they had only stalled that cause. He had spent years in their midst, using the language of faith to goad them into a battle here, to forestall a fight there, to plunge themselves into foolhardy dilemma or to delay necessary actions. All in the guise of a prophet, one whose vision could not fail for it had been stolen and returned a thousand-fold by the Wyrm itself.

Zhyzhak's screams turned to tears and pitiful wailing as she realized what a fool she'd been—what fools they'd all been.

In her despair, she almost stumbled, and in so doing, nearly stepped from the path. At the last moment, instinct—or providence?—saved her. She saw through wet eyes that the green glow had nearly deserted her feet. In an instant, rage blossomed in her breast, drying her tears and sending her leaping back onto the labyrinthine path.

She crouched low on all fours, as if holding the path down by sheer weight. She turned her head, searching, until she finally found what she sought: the crimson blotch in the sky. She let out a long breath and smiled, and then began to cackle loudly.

It had nearly won. She had almost failed the test of the Sixth Circle, had almost failed to live up to its ideal of corruption. She knew that what it had revealed about White-Eye was true—he had indeed fooled them for years, and in so doing, set back the cause. But she didn't care about that anymore. She only cared about going forward, about moving on to meet her Master.

She slowly stood and raised her hand high, bringing the whip down hard, sending its crack echoing throughout the empty expanse on all sides. Then she marched forward and heard the moans erupt around her as the banes both cheered and cried at her victory.

The next circle was the seventh. Its test was loyalty. She sneered at the thought. Her loyalty was to herself; she couldn't possibly fail *this* one.

As she came to a new bend in the path, the ground shook beneath her, an undulating rumble like something passing beneath the soil. She knew that feeling, and felt a pang of regret. She looked ahead and saw to her right, off the path, a hole in space, opening into a desert twilight.

She peered closer and her chest tightened, her breath freezing. There, in the desert, *her* desert back home, Grammaw Thunderwyrm had surfaced. She had plowed her way out of the cave and now thrashed about in the open air of the canyon, her horrible sores visible in the pink light.

Instinct almost doomed Zhyzhak then, as she barely caught herself from leaping into the hole, rushing to comfort her beloved Grammaw. She forced herself to close her eyes and continue down the path, her legs weak from betrayal.

A howl broke out in the desert, joined by others. Not the ululating warble of her hive-mates, but the cursed call of the Gaian Garou. She spun around and saw the packs of warriors descend from the canyon walls onto Grammaw, driving spears and claws into her flesh, using her open sores to circumvent her armored carapace. Grammaw thrashed and let out a low, bass rumbling wail, a plea for help.

Zhyzhak screamed and ran in the opposite direction, covering her ears and letting the whip trail loosely behind her. The terrible pain of betrayal dug a raw wound in her spirit, but she knew the challenge of the circle—the test of loyalty. Not loyalty to Grammaw or even herself. Loyalty to the Wyrm and the Wyrm alone.

After what seemed nearly an hour, she slowed her mad dash—always keeping to the path—and limped weakly forward. She was empty now, void of any attachment to her old Hive, to her fellows, to the Thunderwyrm that had nurtured her as she lived in its Umbral guts.

Zhyzhak walked alone, bereft of any companions, alone forever more.

In her numb despair, she failed to notice the perfectly quiet wolf that loped along behind her, keeping her just within sight. It stopped when she stopped and moved when she did, mirroring her own movements exactly as if well practiced in precise footwork, a creature of grace and poise shadowing a hulking beast of hate and greed.

• • •

"If I so much as see a single other spirit, I'm killing it," King Albrecht said in disgust, wiping off the ephemeral blood that clung to his grand klaive.

Normally, spirits didn't leave such a mess behind, but none of the creatures he and his entourage had fought in the last twenty-four hours were normal. Things he'd never seen or heard of before were crawling from the Umbral woodwork, skittering over moon paths they should be afraid of, invading realms they didn't belong in.

He glanced down the moon path ahead, waiting for signs of his scouts. Just off the path, a cave led into a glade, a sylvan realm of natural bounty. He could smell the water and fruit from here, but dared not send his whole crew in, not without first getting a report. Things had a habit of not being what they seemed ever since the moon bridge had collapsed.

They had finally found their way out of the dinosaur realm, a place full of sound and fury that, in the end, signified nothing—no encounters or true obstacles. They'd heard numerous dinosaur spirits, but had glimpsed precious few of them. Then they had exited the sub-realm, walking through a thick bank of fog and coming out onto a moon path in the shapeless zone between realms, where Luna's crescent light waxed towards fullness.

That had been a relief—finally seeing the moon. Where Luna shone, they had power and fortitude. Her power extended to the glowing moon paths, the only sure trails through a shifting and trackless wilderness of raw spirit.

They marched on, following a direction their shamans hoped would lead them home. On two different occasions, they'd investigated nearby realms, only to withdraw when attacked by unknown spirits, unformed shapes that only occasionally seemed to develop fleeting features, as if deciding what to become.

Tired from their long march, they needed rest, and Albrecht preferred to find someplace allied fully to Gaia. Even the moon paths were proving too crowded, judging from the disturbing tracks they kept finding.

The glade promised that place of rest, but hostile creatures—again, not banes, but strange spirits—barred their way. The amorphous things floated beside the entrance, their bodies composed of brilliant gases with internal fires that resembled small suns.

"All right, I'm in no mood for this," Albrecht said. He turned to Hardtooth. "Tell me why I shouldn't kill these things right now. They're blocking our way."

Hardtooth peered at the spirits and emitted a high-pitched moan. The gases spun in place, but made no sound.

"I think they are celestial spirits," Hardtooth said. "From the Aetherial Realm. Perhaps the ephemeral shadows of unborn stars. It is extremely unusual to see such things here, far from the night sky. Perhaps they have been trapped here by similar moon bridge collapses."

"Okay, this is way past weird," Albrecht said. "I no longer give a damn why or how, I just want them to step aside so we can pass."

Hardtooth shrugged. "They do not answer my appeals. I'm not even sure they understand the spirit speech."

"Let's see if silver gets them moving," Albrecht said, stepping forward and brandishing his grand klaive. As he neared the spirits, they twirled frantically, warning him away. He kept coming. At the last moment, as he drew back his sword, they floated upwards and away, drifting off into the Umbral sky.

Albrecht nodded. "At least someone's still got some sense. All right, way's clear. I want scouts in there now."

Goldflame and Eric Honnunger ran past Albrecht and crept into the cave mouth that led to the glade. Moments later, they stuck their heads back out and barked an okay.

Albrecht sheathed his klaive and turned to address the group lined up behind him, standing but obviously tired. "All right, let's go. But be on your guard."

He turned again and led them to the cave. He could see the sunlight coming from within; the cave lasted for maybe fifteen feet before opening into a valley. He slipped through and came out into a fresh, pure breeze that ruffled his white fur. The sound of a trickling stream behind a bank of lush green foliage proved that the promising smell of water had not been false. Trees all around, as far as he could see, were bursting with fruit—apples, oranges, even bananas. The ecology was completely off, but it all seemed perfectly natural here. It was indeed a Gaian glade, and a good one.

He howled a quick yap of joy, echoed by his warriors, and sauntered forward to plop down by the stream, submerging his snout in its cold flow. He sat up and shook the water off, revitalized by its bracing wetness.

"Dig in, everybody," he said. "Drink up and eat now; we can't stay here forever."

The group spread out, lapping up water from the stream or reaching up into the trees to pluck large, juicy apples, berries and even nuts. Some of them laughed, unable to maintain their serious veneer, and Albrecht joined them, his own deep chuckling giving them all permission to put their woes aside for a short time.

He shifted to human form and lay back in the grass, stretching out, exulting in the chance to relax all his muscles. Somewhere in the distance, a songbird sang. He smiled and closed his eyes, listening to its chirps.

The melodious notes suddenly stopped, followed by complete silence. Albrecht frowned and opened his eyes. Across the stream from him, Erik Honnunger, still in wolf-man form, sniffed the air and growled.

"Wyrm scent!" he yelled.

Albrecht instantly leaped up, metamorphosing into his broad-shouldered, fur-covered battle form as he jumped the stream and drew his klaive. His warriors fell into combat positions around him, everyone's senses alert to the source of the foul odor.

Albrecht smelled it now, the rot of decay. It drifted in from deeper in the glade. They should back out now, return to the moon bridge, and continue without a hitch. But he knew they *couldn't* do that. If Wyrm taint fouled this place, it was their duty to eradicate it.

He motioned a group of warriors on his right forward. They moved ahead through the bushes, cautiously searching. He signaled the left wing to move and they curved around and forward, intending to catch whatever the enemy was in a pincer. Albrecht and the small group around him planted themselves, ready to receive anything that decided to run toward them when confronted with the two flanks of Garou.

A low series of summoning barks carried over the wind, and Albrecht headed forward. He broke into a small clearing, in the center of which stood a huge yew tree. The base of the trunk was hollow, its core long since rotted away, replaced by a gaping hole from which came a greenish, flickering light. Albrecht immediately recognized it as balefire, the poisonous

Wyrm light. Judging by the overwhelming scent emanating from the hollow, they'd found the Wyrm taint.

The two flanks gathered on either side of the tree, waiting on word from Albrecht. He marched up to the edge and peered within. A spiraling hole into the ground could be seen within, large enough for two Garou to walk abreast. A hard packed dirt path led downward.

Hardtooth approached. "My lord, it appears to be a hellhole. These two realms impinge upon one another."

"Is this recent?" Albrecht asked.

"I cannot tell. I assume that, since the glade seems to lack any corruption, whatever denizens may exist below have not yet ventured forth. Whether this is because they are unaware of the hole, or due to some unseen barrier, I do not know."

Albrecht nodded. "Doesn't matter. We're not going in it. Normally, I'd do what I could to plug it, but we just don't have the time or resources." He could see the relief on his warriors' faces and in their posture. They were good, dedicated soldiers, but they wanted to get home. "All right, then. Let's go back the way we came, slowly and cautiously. Back to the moon path."

He stepped back and felt suddenly weightless for a moment as the ground collapsed beneath him. Then he was falling through a roof of tangled roots and dirt, down into a cavern below. The whole meadow had collapsed, and all the Garou fell with him, plummeting into a brackish brown river.

Although the water broke their fall, some of them accidentally sucked in some of the fluid, and spent the next few moments thrashing and coughing as the vile liquid burnt their throats.

Albrecht recovered immediately upon hitting the water, and bounded to the shore. From there, he reached out and dragged Garou to the relative safety of the bank. A screeching sound erupted in the distance, down a dark passage, accompanied by a thrumming roar. Seconds later, a horde of bats exploded into the cavern, descending on the Garou, some of whom still struggled in the river.

Albrecht slashed his klaive cleanly through the air, chopping down three bats with one stroke, and deftly stepped aside as two more bats dove for his head. They were large, hairy, bony things, their wings tattered and fleshy. But their teeth were huge and sharp, and they didn't need eyes to home in on their prey.

Albrecht barked a command. Three Garou stopped their assault long enough to call upon their spirit gifts, scribbling imaginary pictograms into the air, ignoring the bats landing on their shoulders. Before the things could bite, the pictograms took effect, spelling a threat to the bats. They took wing and scattered, as if pressed away from the pictogram makers by gravity. The effect extended beyond the Garou and kept the spirits at bay from most of Albrecht's crew, except for those few still in the water.

Albrecht yelled another command. One of the warded Garou waded into the river, bearing his mystic wards with him. The bats, pressed away before its power, fled to the far side of the cavern.

Before Albrecht could reform his soldiers' ranks, a coughing howl rang out from the passage and a horde of creatures charged forth—corrupt and tainted glade spirits, animals that crawled and dug through the earth. Giant badgers, voles and ants, swarms of beetles and snakes slithered and skittered across the floor with uncanny speed. All of them were warped and diseased, some of them ten times their normal size, with warty hides bursting through their fur, carapace s and scales.

As they hit the warriors surrounding Albrecht, it became clear that the warts were mystical. Claws skidded off them. The creatures overwhelmed the line and brought the Silver Fangs to the ground, leaping over them to charge Albrecht, as if they sensed he was the key prey.

Without a moment's hesitation, Albrecht swung his klaive and beheaded a gigantic badger in midair as it sailed at him. Its body exploded, spraying noxious gore in all directions. The gobbets sizzled as they hit Albrecht's armor, and he could feel a wave of pain as droplets singed bits of fur.

Something tugged at Albrecht's leg. He looked down to see scaled coils wrapped from his ankle to his knee, quickly tightening. He shoved his claw between the coils and yanked, tearing away chunks of snake flesh. The creature's head shot toward him, but he brought his klaive up in time, allowing the snake to skewer itself on his blade.

He heard the tortured growls of his soldiers as they suffered the acidic blood of their foes, and he stepped forward to hack at a giant beetle the size of a small tank. He slipped in the slick snake's blood and hit the ground, his klaive clattering from his grasp.

He looked up to see a swarm of carapaced larvae descending on him.

● ● ●

Zhyzhak stopped. Her hackles rose; there was something behind her. It wasn't a bane, or at least not a normal one, she was sure of that. Something trickier.

She kept moving, pretending to have paused only to get her bearings. The thing moved closer. She could hear its careful tread behind her as it tried to place its steps in accord with hers to muffle its sounds.

Zhyzhak spun and leaped at the thing, grasping it by its torso and slamming it into the ground. It struggled, yelling for truce, but she refused to let go, placing her full weight on it and pinning it down. She looked into its face and saw a beautiful man with flaxen blond hair and full lips.

There came another sound from nearby, also from where Zhyzhak had come. She snapped her head in that direction to look, but saw nothing, save what might have been a slight movement that swiftly vanished. She turned to look back at her prey, who now smirked at her.

"You cannot destroy *me*," he said, in a voice far too deep to be a normal man's. "I am your deliverer."

Zhyzhak frowned and growled, thrusting her jaws next to the man's throat. "Who the fuck are you?" she yelled.

"I am the Prince of Enigmas, the Master of the Eighth Circle. I can be your enemy… or your ally. You must choose."

"This some sort of trick?" Zhyzhak said.

He laughed but said nothing further.

Zhyzhak stood up, releasing the man, and walked away, peering through her monocle to regain her course.

"Wait," the man said as he rose and dusted off his black Edwardian suit. "I came to warn you."

Zhyzhak stopped and turned to look at him, her eyes suspicious slits.

"Believe it or not," the man continued, stepping closer with one hand out to her, "I want you to succeed. You have come this far. Maybe you are the one we have long waited for. The savior."

Zhyzhak spat. "Liar!"

"Indeed, no. I speak true. I wish to help you win through this circle's test, and so continue on."

"Ha! You're the master of this circle! Why not just let me pass?"

He shrugged. "I do not make the rules. I am as trapped by my role as you by your desire, your urge to power."

Zhyzhak reached out and clawed his cheek, opening a bloody welt that stained his immaculate white collar. He didn't even flinch.

"I can show you your obstacle, the being that stands in your way." He gestured to his right, off the path, toward a glimmering hole in space, a rent like the previous window into Zhyzhak's desert home.

Zhyzhak peered into the window and saw a cavern. A pack of creatures, twisted nature spirits of various sorts, encircled a white-furred Garou, who lay sprawled on the ground. Nothing moved. It was as if time stood still, as if she looked at a picture, but one with incredibly realistic detail. She sucked in her breath when she saw the simple, unadorned silver band that circled the white-furred Garou's brow.

"Albrecht!" she cried, stepping forward. Then she stopped, staring suspiciously at the man. "A trick!" She raised her arm, ready to bring down her whip on him.

He held open his palms, as if to show that he had no weapons. "No trick. It is he, the king of the Gaians, your mortal enemy."

"Why isn't he moving?"

"You see a glimpse of time, a moment of choice, which I offer you in return for a promise."

"Promise? What the fuck do you want, asshole? Spit it out!"

"I want you to kill Albrecht. In return, I'll get you straight to the Ninth Circle."

Zhyzhak stared at the fallen king, who looked angry but overwhelmed. If she did nothing, he would be engulfed by the creatures, and perhaps be wounded or killed. That last thought drove a dagger of envy through her heart— she deserved to deliver his death, not a pack of mindless beasts. She grabbed the man by his collar and shook him. "He'll die anyway!"

The man chuckled. "Do you really believe that? He'll make mincemeat of them. He's not alone. He's got an elite guard ready to jump in. I need you to kill him before his guard can get past the creatures."

Zhyzhak looked again at the frozen moment of time. It was tempting. She looked at the Red Star, and then at the path underneath her feet. She threw back her head and laughed. Then she slowly walked around the window, with its view into Albrecht's predicament, and dragged the edge of the path with her foot, forcing it to realign itself. It resisted, but by this point, she had beaten it into submission often enough for it to give in. She could forge its direction in any way she desired, even straightening it from its convoluted spirals if she so desired. She wondered for a moment what would happen if she did, but decided that now was not the time to experiment, not with her hated enemy so near, so close to her claws.

The man looked on uneasily, clearly unnerved at her ability to reposition the Labyrinth's pathway, a sacred, mysterious artifact from prehistory. She no longer cared if he spoke the truth. Her power over the path was enough.

Once she had placed the path underneath the window, she readied herself before it and then jumped through, screaming in rage.

• • •

Before the larval horde could reach Albrecht, a terrifying wail wrenched the air, so loud the king squinted and covered his ears.

Suddenly a new shape loomed in front of him, a huge, black-clad Black Spiral Dancer. Before he could react, tearing pain exploded in his chest, shoulders and snout at once, followed by a sharp crack. He then saw the whip fly back, ready to snap forward again, and realized what had hit him.

He knew his new foe's identity as soon as he heard the whip-crack. Her wail alone was unmistakable. Zhyzhak.

He leaped to the side, missing the lash by millimeters, and rolled into one of the oncoming creatures, another badger, knocking its four legs out from under it. He kept rolling, trying to get as far away from the whip as he could.

The fallen badger, as big as a wolf and foaming at the mouth, lay between him and the mad bitch, buying him the time he needed. He concentrated, shutting out the distraction of his senses, and drew on the secret bestowed on him by a Luna moon spirit, calling on the sacred power of the moon itself. His fur began to take on a metallic sheen and he felt his muscles strengthen as they changed from flesh to silver. He rose up from his crouch, his body fully reforged, a thing of moon metal.

Zhyzhak leaped over the fallen badger, ready to dig her claws into Albrecht's abdomen, when she noticed the change.

It surprised her just long enough for Albrecht to knock her arm aside and rake his own claws against her hide.

She hissed and jumped back, the wound boiling from the touch of silver, agony playing across her face. Albrecht moved in to swipe again, but she threw her hand forward and flung a hot, green-glowing ball of fire at him, conjured in an instant by her own gifts.

He couldn't dodge in time. It glanced off his shoulder, sending sparks flying. He grunted in shock but felt no burning; the silver protected him.

Zhyzhak backed up, trying to gain distance, where she could use her whip and keep him at bay, but she failed to notice the Silver Fang warrior behind her. He had beaten past one of the huge ants to thrust a spear at her. It grazed her back, causing her to leap forward in surprise, slashing back behind herself with her claw as she did so. Her assault scraped the warrior's snout. He cried out in pain.

Albrecht didn't hesitate to take advantage of her imbalance. He leaped in and grabbed her, wrapping his arms around her torso. He was big for a Garou, but she was bigger still. Once more, he called on his spirit gifts. The silver fur on his chest burst into flame, suffused with the solar power of Helios.

Zhyzhak screamed, more in anger than pain, her leather bodice smoldering where the burning fur singed it. She leaned forward and clamped her jaws on his ear, her strength ungodly, far more than a match for Albrecht's. The touch of his silver ear was pure agony, but she wrenched her jaws and tore it off.

Albrecht fell back, dazed for a moment with the pain. Zhyzhak grabbed him in an iron grip and drew back her free hand to slice his throat—and then stopped. She glanced back at something over Albrecht's shoulder and her wolf-face contorted with even more rage and hate—something Albrecht would not have guessed possible.

She turned her thrusting blow into a sideswipe, knocking Albrecht aside and to the ground, and leaped forward through the ephemeral spirit window he could now see was floating in the fetid air of this hellhole. A mist-shrouded realm lurked beyond it, but the window was closing fast.

She spun around, growling, as Albrecht rose and blinked through the window, astounded by its appearance and her sudden escape.

"You're mine, Albrecht!" she yelled. "I'll come for you, with the armies of Malfeas behind me!"

Before the king could deliver a retort or give chase, the window closed.

• • •

Zhyzhak spun and ran toward the beautiful man.

Looking over Albrecht's shoulder at the very point she was ready to finish him, she'd seen through the man's trickery. She'd looked into the window through which she'd come, and seen the mist-covered darkness lit only by the faintly glowing path… the path that was slowly creeping away from the window, reasserting its own pattern. The beautiful man, the Bane of Enigmas, had smiled, pleased with himself. He'd known the path would resist her will once she ceased to concentrate on it, and delivering her King Albrecht, her worst enemy, was exactly the way to distract her. Now he would pay.

But the Bane of Enigmas blithely sidestepped Zhyzhak's charge, his form already fading into nothingness. He simply laughed and shrugged, and then was gone.

Zhyzhak pounded the ground in rage, but then lay spread-eagled upon it, catching her breath. Her abdomen hurt and still bled; the wound refused to seal. Her tongue also hurt, burned by silver. She gritted her teeth and stood up, kicking herself mentally. She had been a fool, underestimating the tricks the circle wardens would play to keep her from her goal. She would remember that and be more wary with the next circle. The last circle. The worst of them all.

She shifted into dire-wolf form and loped forward on all fours; it caused less pain in her guts. She would remember this wound and who had delivered it. As soon as victory was hers, she would stand by her vow and come for Albrecht, with the fury of the Wyrm itself in tow.

• • •

Albrecht's warriors finished killing the last of the corrupt nature spirits. They had lost three of their own in the melee. They numbered only eight now.

The bats, upon seeing the last of the creatures fall, fled back down the passage from which they had come.

Albrecht, clutching the remains of his ear, which had finally stopped bleeding, stared at the spot where the window had been, looking at it from all angles. Hardtooth also examined the now-empty space.

"It is gone, my lord," Hardtooth said. "No sign of its ever having existed. I have no idea what place it opened upon."

"It was weird. Misty, dark. A snaking green trail, glowing like balefire. I could see it looping around in the distance. For just a second, the sight of its tangled path made me dizzy, sick."

Hardtooth raised his eyebrows. "It cannot be...." He frowned, shaking his head. He looked at Albrecht and seemed to notice his shredded ear for the first time. "Sire! Your ear! Let me heal it." He stepped forward and placed his palms around Albrecht's wound.

"Mike Tyson's got nothing on that bitch," Albrecht muttered, looking down while the shaman used his spirit powers to mend the ear.

Hardtooth stepped away, a look of concern on his face. "It will no longer bleed. I could not make it whole again."

"It's pretty ugly, I'm sure," Albrecht said. "Another scar to go with the rest." He squinted, looking at something on the floor. "What's that?"

A tiny scroll, the size of a single finger joint, rested in the dirt above Albrecht's footprint.

Hardtooth bent down to examine it. "Strange. This doesn't look like it belongs here. It was dropped after your battle, for it lies on your footprint."

"Be careful. Could be a trap."

Hardtooth sniffed it without touching it. "It does not smell of the Wyrm. If anything, it smells like… saffron. The sort of scent one smells in a temple." He looked up at Albrecht. "With your permission…?"

"Hold on," Albrecht said, and whistled. The others gathered around, weapons ready. "Okay. You can check it out."

The shaman picked up the scroll and unfurled it with his claws. As he did so, it grew in size, becoming as wide and long as a newspaper, revealing painted Garou pictograms. Hardtooth's eyes widened as he read it. "I… I can barely believe it."

"I've had well enough suspense already…" Albrecht said.

"Of course, my lord. The scroll is a messenger talen. It claims to be from Antonine Teardrop, the Stargazer elder."

"Antonine?! Where is he?"

"It reads: 'I follow Zhyzhak's steps upon the Black Spiral Labyrinth.'"

At that, a number of the Garou hissed and growled. Albrecht held up his hand, silencing them.

"'If she succeeds, Gaia is doomed. I must ensure she does not. I beg you: Return to your packmates. Pray that Gaia endures.'"

Albrecht snatched the scroll and read it himself. "Is that it? Is there anything else?"

"No, my lord. It was written hastily by a spirit at Teardrop's bidding."

"If he walks the Labyrinth," Eric Honnunger said, "he's doomed. If he falls to the Wyrm, they'll have a powerful elder to use against us. He is a fool."

"I knew the Stargazers couldn't be trusted," Goldflame said.

"Shut up," Albrecht said. "I don't know what's gotten into his head any more than you do, but he's done right by me too many times to deserve that kind of second-guessing. Quit griping and get over to that incline out of here, back to the glade. We're getting back on that moon path and we're not stopping till we're home."

He rolled up the scroll and stuck it in his belt, then marched over to the path leading upward to the hole in the tree trunk above. The light of the glade shone down through the massive rent in the roof where the ground had collapsed, lighting his path as he came once more into the sunlight.

Chapter Ten:
Pledged to the Cause

"The Dawn Rover Pack pledges itself to this cause," said the slim, young boy, his head and shoulders swaggering as he pointed out his three packmates, also young teens, a ragged group of ex-skateboarders and videogame junkies turned Garou.

Evan nodded, hiding his deep disappointment. These were raw cubs, not even adults by human standards, untried Bone Gnawers all. They'd each had their Rites of Passage, but from what he could tell they'd gotten off easy with barely a challenge. He looked at Mari, waiting for her to give them some acknowledgment or encouragement, but her scowl showed she would have none of it. He turned back to the boy.

"Great," Evan said with a weak smile. "You can bunk in the common room for now. We leave tomorrow. Cries Havoc will introduce you to the other packs."

"How many others are here?" the boy said eagerly. "How many do we fight with?"

"Two packs," Evan said, unable to hide the sour tone in his voice. "Six Garou. Ten, now that you guys are here."

The boy looked startled, as if he'd just been told the big game had been canceled. He looked back at his fellows, who glanced nervously at one another. Then he nodded, raising his chin again.

"Then we've got a true challenge at last," he said as he turned to lead his pack down the forest trail to the large cabin that served as the bunkroom for the gathering Garou.

When he was out of earshot, Evan groaned. Mari put her arm around his shoulders.

"It will get better," Mari said. "The word hasn't had time to travel yet. More will come."

"More like that?" Evan said, gesturing at the departing gang of kids. "That's all we need: the Children's Crusade. Sweet Gaia, the Wendigo are going to lynch me. What was I *thinking*? That I could single-handedly gather a force capable of tackling a Wyrm Talon? Why didn't you stop me?"

"Enough," Mari said, poking him in the chest with an index finger. "Quit selling yourself short. You know that the troubles are causing the low turnout. Otherwise, we'd have more Garou than we could count, all itching for a long-overdue fight. We do the best we can with what we've got."

Evan threw up his hands. "If Albrecht were here, we'd have the whole northeast mustering."

"I'm not sure even he could rouse them in these conditions. But he's not here. Not yet."

Evan looked at Mari, his face stricken with concern. "What if he's not back before we have to leave? What if we have to go fight this thing without him?"

Mari shrugged. "Then he misses out. His loss."

"Seriously, Mari. What are we going to do?"

"Soldier on, Evan. We do the best we can. Now come on. Let's check in with Alani and see if any of the heralds from the other septs have arrived yet." She walked down the trail toward the lake, dragging Evan by his wrist.

• • •

"Damn it!" Julia cried, slapping her laptop computer with her palm. "I can't get through. There's a blockage I just can't circumvent."

"What do you mean by that?" Cries Havoc said. He moved to stand behind her, peering over her shoulder at the computer screen. "The ISP is down?"

"No, I mean something's preventing me from hooking up with the London sept," Julia said with her clipped British accent. "Every time I get a connection, it's severed or freezes."

"What could cause that sort of thing?"

"Net spider," she replied with a frustrated frown. "It's like there's a horde of them swarming the sept. I don't like it one bit. I need to get home, make sure they're okay."

"Run out on us?" Carlita said, putting down her music magazine and sitting up on her bunk. "We gave our word to Evan, your highness. You can't back out on that. Besides, if they're under attack, what the hell do you think *you* could do? If the place is swarming with net spiders, you're not getting in without getting caught. Not unless you've got some kind of net bug spray I've never heard of. Give it up, girl. Things are screwed up all over."

Julia sat back in her chair and gritted her teeth, holding back tears of anger and frustration. Cries Havoc stepped around and sat on the edge of the desk, catching her eye.

"She's right, Julia," he said. "There's nothing you would be able to do. I'm sure they're fine—they're top notch Glass Walkers. A net spider attack's nothing to them. A temporary denial of service is all. Right?"

"I guess so," Julia said, her shoulders slumping. "Maybe I'm overreacting. It's just… well, it's not easy being an ocean away from your sept in times of trouble."

"Tell me about it," John North Wind's Son said. He sat on a bunk with his legs crossed, watching the new, younger Garou packs who'd gathered across the large common cabin, their bunks lined up against the far wall. "I had to put up with all that crap in Europe, remember? Not exactly the Pacific Northwest."

"You're right, of course," Julia said, standing and stretching. "I *am* being a drama queen. I admit it. But it's still not easy."

"Why don't you get your mind off it by helping me organize the packs over there?" Cries Havoc said. "They haven't been fully introduced to one another yet."

"I guess I should," Julia said. "*I* don't even know them all yet. Right, then, let's go say cheers." She pushed her chair away from the desk and headed across the room, followed by Cries Havoc. Carlita lay back down on her bunk and resumed reading, while John, unmoving, watched them go. Their pack's alpha, Storm-Eye, was outside, roaming the Finger Lakes bawn and woodland.

As Julia approached the line of bunks where ten young Garou milled about in three distinct groups, she clapped her hands loudly. Once she'd gotten their attention, she surveyed the group.

"All right, let's line up here, shall we?" she said. "So I can get a good look and get to know you, right?"

The young Garou grumbled but fell into a single line that stretched across the row of bunks. Julia walked to the end of the line to her left, where a girl of Middle Eastern descent slouched uncomfortably. She was obviously shy, and wore loose-fitting khakis, walking boots and a thin shawl around her neck.

"And who are you?" Julia said.

The girl looked at Julia but did not lift her head. "Uhm, I'm Shazi. Uh, Shazi Windwhistler."

"Let me guess. You're a Silent Strider."

"Yeah. I guess my ethnicity gives me away, huh?"

"No, I could tell by that tattoo you try to hide under your shawl. I don't know what it means, but I recognize an Egyptian hieroglyph when I see it."

"Oh. Yeah. Uh, it means 'sandstorm.'"

"Where are you from?" Julia said, crossing her arms.

"I was born in Egypt, but my parents moved to Buffalo when I was five. I... had my First Change last year. I'm fifteen. It was pretty rotten."

Julia nodded. "Not many Striders here in New York, as I understand it. Who helped you out?"

"Oh, there are some here. They wander through." She clearly did not want to reveal her mentor's identity.

Julia shrugged and moved down the line to the teenage boy standing next to Shazi. He was black and wore a new pair of jeans, perfectly clean running shoes and a button-up shirt. Julia looked him up and down. *Obviously middle class*, she thought. *The lack of tribe signs is odd, though.*

"All right, I give up," she said. "What tribe are you?"

He looked surprised and gave her an admonishing smirk. "I'm a Glass Walker, like you."

Julia raised her eyebrows. "Oh, really? You don't look it."

"My equipment got fried on our last action. Me and the gang here," he gestured to Shazi on one side and a large redheaded kid on the other, "ran into bane trouble. Lost my prize PDA-cell phone getting rid of it."

"Sorry to hear it, uhm…?" Julia said, clearly waiting for the Glass Walker to give his name.

"Feedback," he said, smiling, proud of himself.

"If you need help making a new fetish, Feedback, let me know."

"All right! Let's do it!"

"Later, when we're done here. Okay? First, who's your friend?" Julia indicated the redhead. "And what's your pack's name?"

"Jacky Brokentooth," the redhead said. "Fianna. And we're the Open Road Pack. Wanderers all."

"Wanderers? How far have you gotten?"

Jacky frowned, as if she'd made an unfair social foul. "Across the state so far. But we're just getting started."

"Well, pleased to meet you, Open Road wanderers. I'm glad you're with us. We'll need all the muscle and brains we can get." Julia moved down the line, to the next pack, also three in number. All beefy white males in their late teens, they looked like American football players and dressed alike in jeans, T-shirts and sports shoes. One of them had a klaive hanging from a makeshift sheath on his back.

"Let me see if I remember your name," Julia said. "The Vanguard, right? Get of Fenris?"

"You got it," the one with the klaive said. He seemed to be their leader. "I'm Jim Jurgens, this is Al Krupp and that's Fred Berger."

"Not very Garou-like names. Haven't you earned monikers yet?"

"Yeah, we each got one of them, but they sound sorta silly. They call me Broadshanks. Al's known as Ironpaw and Fred's called Runestone. Among our tribe, that is."

"Okay, you guys are football players, right? New to this whole thing?"

"Yeah, we were all on different high school teams across the counties. It was kind of weird to all be having our First Changes at the same time, but it also works, if you get what I mean. Like fate, you know?"

"Why are you here? Why not with the other Get in the Adirondacks?"

"Well, we were sent to New York to look for an old fetish that somebody'd seen in a pawn shop when we heard the call. We're not detectives, ma'am; we figured coming up here to fight was a better way to serve Fenris than going from pawn shop to pawn shop looking for an old hammer."

"Glad to hear it. Oh, and please, don't call me ma'am. I may not be a teenager anymore, but I'm nowhere near old-maid stage yet." Julia stepped down the line to the new pack, the one that had just come in today. "Dawn Rovers?"

"That's us," a young boy said, stepping forward slightly. He wore baggy pants, Doc Marten boots and a T-shirt depicting some sort of hip-hop group. "Me, Tommy D, and the others: Sasha Sharpeye, Dweezil, and Loper."

Sasha Sharpeye was a small girl with a surly look that showed she'd had more rough living than most her age. Dweezil was a white kid, dressed similarly to Tommy D, his pockets filled with a Gameboy, an MP3 player and junk food. Loper was clearly a lupus, a Garou born as a wolf, but he had worn his human form ever since arriving at the Finger Lakes caern. He looked like a homeless kid with no sense of hygiene.

"Good, good," Julia said, nodding politely at them. She turned to address the whole line. "Well, I'm sure you all heard the introductions. I'd like you each to spend the next few hours getting to know one another. Find out the others' capabilities. You'll be fighting together, so this is important. Don't be shy. Others will be coming and I expect you all to take the initiative and introduce yourselves when they arrive. By the time we leave tomorrow, you need to all have some idea about how to react when we're attacked. Know which among you are the warriors, and which the tricksters. Plan accordingly." She turned to Cries Havoc, who had followed quietly behind her during the line review. "Anything to add?"

"No, you covered all the bases," he said. "If you guys need anything, let us know. We're over there," he motioned to their own bunks across the room. "Thanks."

Julia and Cries Havoc went back to join their own packmates. The ten Garou cubs now mixed together, members from different packs going to greet members of other packs.

"How'd it go?" Carlita asked, sitting up and putting her magazine aside.

"Well, at least they're talking to each other now," Julia said. "They're so damn young—younger than *we* are. I hope Mari knows how to lead them into action; they're not used to taking orders."

"Are you kidding? You think any of them has the guts to question an order from Mari? Hell, I don't got those kind of balls."

Julia smiled and chuckled. "What kind do you have?"

"Shut up, girl! It was just an expression." Carlita threw her pillow at Julia, who didn't bother to dodge it and fell down onto the bunk, laughing.

* * *

"The Shadow Lords will pledge no packs to this enterprise," the dark-haired herald cried, his eyes scanning the faces of the gathered Garou in the light of the flickering bonfire. Clouds partially concealed the half-moon, but all the Garou there could see quite well in such light. The Shadow Lord wore a flannel shirt, workpants and boots. He looked like a redneck day laborer, complete with five o'clock shadow. His eyes, however, had the cunning of a predator.

"Not a single one?" Evan said, standing across the circle from the Shadow Lord. "Why not? Care to explain, or do we assume cowardice?"

The Garou hissed but smiled, seemingly glad that Evan had not backed down easily. "We have none to spare. The Minions from the Black Lacquer Box are free; we must hunt them down before they insinuate themselves into our dreams."

Evan frowned and looked down at Mari, sitting to his right. She shook her head; she didn't know what he was talking about either. "Who are these Minions?"

The Shadow Lord spat into the fire. "I expected that all the tribes here would forget. Only the Shadow Lords remember. It was the tribe of thunder who recaptured these banes when the Silver Fangs set them free many decades ago. They were brought to these lands in an ancient box created by Baba Yaga. The white-furred fools released them and only our cunning tracked them down and returned them, one by one, to the box. Since then, our tribe has safeguarded it against further meddling."

"So what happened? How'd they get loose again?"

"If we knew the answer to that, we would be one step closer to trapping them back in their cage. Until then, we need all our packs to hunt the shades and capture them before they can migrate into the dreams and minds of all Garou."

Evan nodded, accepting the inevitable. "If this is your answer, I must accept it. I am sad not to have the Shadow Lords by our side. It is our loss."

The herald's eyes narrowed. He had not expected a compliment to accompany his report and clearly suspected its sincerity, but he bowed and stepped aside, seating himself outside the light of the fire.

A huge woman next to him stood up and marched up to the fire, looking around to catch the eyes of all in attendance: Evan, Mari, the Silver River Pack, the packs of cubs and the resident Black Furies and Children of Gaia, gathered around their leader, Alani Astarte, an old black woman.

"The Get can send no further aid," she said. "I see that three of our own have already pledged their services to your cause." She scowled at the Vanguard pack, the three football players, who simply blinked, unconcerned at her annoyance. "May they earn great glory in your service. Our tribe is beset by Black Spiral Dancers, crawling forth from their holes in the Adirondacks. We sealed these long ago, but they have found a way to open them; they harry our packs at all hours. We are preparing an assault on their underground caverns. We need all our strong arms. None can be spared to aid the Wendigo in the north." She said this last with a degree of contempt, as if the idea were repugnant even if she could send warriors.

Evan spoke. "Do you understand that the Black Spiral Dancers will only be strengthened if the Talon is not destroyed? That your expedition might be in vain?"

"I think the reverse, boy. Our action prevents the Dancers from going north to aid this thing. It lessens the forces arrayed against you. You are lucky that we undertake this task."

Evan sighed, throwing up his hands. "If that is how you see it, I won't argue. I can't deny that the Dancers pose a threat. I don't know their numbers. I do know that a Wyrm Talon is one of the greatest enemies ever unleashed on Earth. This one might still be weak from its long captivity. That gives us a chance. The strength and courage of the Get might be what we need to succeed. The Wendigo can track it and hold it, but I can't guarantee we can slay it without Fenris's children."

The woman said nothing for a few moments, and seemed ashamed at her own words. "You speak well, Heals-the-Past. I wish I could fight beside you, but our elders have chosen our path. It is our duty to follow it, no matter what maw we march into. The Vanguard will prove themselves for you, and so honor our whole tribe." She sat down again and sulked.

A man sitting next to her then stood, dusted himself off, and stepped forward. He was portly, with a huge, blond beard knotted into five tails, and wore a ceremonial kilt.

"It breaks my heart to bring more bad news to your moot, young Heals-the-Past," he said. "But the Fianna can send none of their own to aid you. We're needed—every man of us—at Niagara Falls. The banetenders in the north weren't the only ones keeping beasts at bay. The Niagara Uktena are having a terrible time of it, and we're oathbound to aid them. Unless, of course, they say otherwise." He looked to his left, to the last herald, waiting for some sign or gesture.

The man, a middle-aged Native American, slowly stood up. He stepped up beside the Fianna herald. "Our need is dire. Three monsters from before the European tribes came to these lands now struggle against the wards that trapped them in ages past. If they should break those wards, our sept will need all the Garou it can get to bind them again. But we are also pledged to Little Brother, the Wendigo, and cannot deny their need. We ourselves cannot go, but we release the Fianna from their oath and allow them to send one pack of their own, should they choose to do so." He stepped back and took his seat.

The Fianna herald smiled. "It is my great pleasure to announce that the Fianna *will* send you a pack. I cannot say who they are—that's up the elders—but I'll get them here by tomorrow morning, before you head out."

"It's a great relief to hear it," Evan said, nodding solemnly. "With the Fianna by our side, we'll keep our spirits up. And thank you, Great Horn," he said, bowing to the Uktena. "I am grieved to hear the troubles at your sept, and sorry that Elder

Brother cannot fight beside Little Brother again, but your generosity has given us the Fianna. Thank you."

He looked out at all the Garou gathered and saw that there was no one left to speak. The four heralds—the only ones to answer the call—had all delivered their messages. He stepped back and bent to sit down when Storm-Eye, in her natural wolf form, jumped up and paced forward, circling the fire.

"No good!" she growled, her Garou words rough and limited in her wolf form, communicated and accented as much by gesture as articulate growl. "We go fight great evil. Only cubs with us. Where are Stargazers? Red Talons? Why nothing from them?"

Evan stepped forward again. "I know your frustration, Storm-Eye, but the tribes have done their best. Antonine Teardrop is gone, traveling in the Far East; there are no other Stargazers here to speak for his tribe. The Talons, as you know, are few in number here in New York. Surely, some from Canada will join us at the Winter Wolf Sept."

Storm-Eye didn't stop her pacing. She turned her gaze upon Alani Astarte. "Why no Furies? Why no Children of Gaia?"

Alani stood up and looked at Storm-Eye with a gentle expression, taking no insult. "The Finger Lakes is a haven. It will become even more so in the coming days, when the troubles get worse. It is the strongest caern in the region, the only one powerful enough to regularly forge moon bridges overseas. We must defend it with all our strength. We have none to spare."

Behind her, a Garou stood up. "Elder? May I speak?"

Alani looked surprised and nodded. The Garou stepped forward, wending past those who sat in front of her, until she finally stepped into the light of the fire. She was of average height, with dark hair and loose-fitting clothes, and had an aura of arrogance about her.

"I wish to go with the Talon fighters. My pack—Athena's Shield—wants to go. All five of us. We know we are needed here, Alani, but we are also needed there. Can we not choose our own means of renown?"

Alani frowned. "Without your strength, Delilah, and the wisdom of your pack, the caern might not withstand an assault."

"And if the Talon makes it this far south? Can it stand then?"

Alani said nothing.

"Then let us go with them. Let us bolster their ranks. Let Pegasus and Unicorn cry to the other totems that their children were not afraid to risk their homes and their lives in the struggle against evil. Let us claim victory for Gaia together!"

Alani did not respond but closed her eyes, thinking. She hummed a quiet tune that no one could clearly hear, and then opened her eyes again. "If it must be so, then let it be so. I shall not deny the Fates. Go, Delilah, and all of Athena's Shield with you."

Delilah bent down on one knee before Alani, a silent gesture of thanks and respect. She then stood and motioned her pack forth. From the crowd, four Garou came forward, all of them women dressed in modern clothes, but each clearly more than cubs, for they walked with the assurance of Garou who had seen war before. Delilah led them to stand before Evan and she bowed her head to him.

"Athena's Shield pledges itself to aid the Wendigo, to slay the Talon. In the name of Gaia."

Evan bowed back. He looked at Mari, smiling, who also smiled, an uncharacteristically large smile. He thought he saw a tear in her eye, and turned back before he could embarrass her by acknowledging it.

"We are proud to have you, Athena's Shield."

The gang of cubs broke into a cheer, full of pride, camaraderie and relief that they wouldn't be fighting alone.

Storm-Eye threw back her head and howled, joined immediately by her packmates and Evan. Mari howled too, and Athena's Shield likewise. Soon, even Alani joined, followed by all the rest of the Garou in attendance, including the heralds.

Had there been any Wyrm creatures skulking nearby, they would surely have fled the victorious cacophony.

Chapter Eleven:
The War Party

A horn sounded in the distance. Evan, sitting by the lake in the dim mist before dawn, cocked his head and listened, waiting. The horn sounded again, this time closer. Evan frowned and stood, looking at the group of cabins where the sept lived. Nobody else was up and about yet, but as he watched, Garou poked their heads out of doors and windows, listening for the horn.

The Fianna herald came loping down the trail that led to the guest cabins, a smile on his face. He saw Evan and veered to meet him. "I told you! The Fianna are coming and it's a quite a pack they've sent!"

Evan smiled and grasped the large man's outstretched hand. "I hear the horn. Who blows it?"

"That would be the Black Bellower, hardiest of our Galliards. If he comes, his pack comes with him: the Boar Spear, a mighty band of hunters. I must say, young Heals-the-Past, I'm surprised. The elders are sending our best with you. The Uktena won't be happy to lose them, but then, they'll want to keep the Wendigo happy, too, I suppose."

"I've heard of the Boar Spear," Evan said, his smile growing wider. "They outran the Wild Hunt."

"That they did," the herald said, "that they did. You're in good hands with them."

"I can't tell you how relieved I am to know it. You've got my—"

"Tut, tut," the man said, holding up his hands as if blocking the words, "none of that, now. We know it already. Some things don't need to be said. Now, let's get your war party gathered. The Spear won't want to wait around once they've arrived. Judging from the sound of the horn, they'll be here within the hour."

Evan could already see more Garou coming out of the cabins, readying themselves for the journey. "Then I better see what I can do to make sure everybody's ready." He shook the herald's hand one more time and then hurried down the trail to his own cabin to get his backpack.

Before he reached it, he saw three Garou coming from a side trail, the one that led to the parking lot. One of them he recognized, a local Child of Gaia, one of Alani's aides. The other two were strangers. One was a strongly built man, about six feet tall with blond hair, jeans, boots, a button-up khaki shirt, and a wide-brimmed hat. The other was shorter, about five feet tall and slim, with jeans, white shirt, sandals, and brown hair braided down to her waist. They waved at Evan; he walked over to greet them.

"Evan Heals-the-Past?" the blond stranger said, offering his hand with a smile.

"Yes." Evan shook it. "And you are?"

"Johnathon Strongheart. And this is Liza," he said, indicating the woman. "Children of Gaia. We came to join your expedition at the suggestion of Loba Carcassone."

"Loba?" Evan said, excited. "Is there news from the North Country Protectorate? Is Albrecht back yet?"

"King Albrecht? I don't know. I'm sorry. We saw Loba before she left on a mission of her own. She didn't say anything about her sept."

Evan's face fell.

"Hey," Liza said softly, trying to cheer him up. "I'm sorry we're not Silver Fang kings, but we've been around the block a couple of times. We can help out."

Evan, embarrassed, smiled and nodded. "Oh my gosh, I'm sorry. I didn't mean it that way at all. You can't even begin to imagine how relieved I am to see some experienced Garou join us. We really, really need you. It's just that, well, I was hoping to hear from my packmate. He hasn't sent any word at all."

Strongheart frowned. "That's not like the Silver Fangs. I'm sure there's a good excuse. Should we delay departure until a herald arrives?"

"No," Evan said, his shoulders sloping. "We can't wait any longer. The Wendigo need us. We leave within the hour. I... Look, thanks for coming. We'll have more time to talk once we get to the North."

"Go do what you need to do," Liza said. "We don't need babysitting."

Evan sighed. "Glad to hear it. The problem is, some in our war party do."

Evan turned and went into his cabin before Strongheart and Liza could ask him what he meant by that. They shrugged and let their fellow tribemate lead them to the caern center where the packs would be gathering.

Mari sat on top of a closed trunk, watching Evan as he entered and began stuffing shirts and pants into his already overstuffed backpack. Her own full backpack was on the floor by her feet. She knew him too well not to see his tension. She didn't have to guess at the cause.

"Let it go, Evan," she said. "We can't worry about Albrecht now. We've got an army to lead."

"What if he's dead?" Evan said, fiddling with his pack, trying to get everything to fit. "What if he was killed in Russia? Gaia knows what's going on *there*."

"He's not dead. You know that. There's a reason he's not here. We don't know what it is, but it's a good one. He wouldn't shirk us on this."

Evan looked up at her in surprise. "Of course he wouldn't. It's not that. It's... I don't know if we can handle something this big without him. He's a king, for Gaia's sake. Remember Jo'cllath'mattric's cave? We need a war leader like him, Mari. He's the only one all the tribes will listen to."

"They respect you, too, Evan. You don't see it, but everyone else does. They trust you."

Evan hung his head. "They think I'm chosen by the ancestors. It's ridiculous. They're expecting great things of me but I'm just going to let them down. I'm not a full-moon warrior, Mari. I can't lead a war party."

"Leave that to the Wendigo. You've done your part: getting all of these Garou together. And you'll keep them together, because that's what you do. Leave the military tactics to the experts. You do the real job—making sure the tribes can join together without fighting each other. That's work enough."

Evan nodded. He sat for a few minutes, silently pondering, and then stood, shouldering his pack. "Now or never."

"Now," Mari said, also standing and lifting her pack. "Definitely now."

• • •

The war party gathered at the caern center. The cubs were all there, although judging by their deep, sleepy yawns and the red eyes they couldn't stop rubbing, some of them looked like they weren't used to getting up this early. Clearly, the Silver River Pack had taken on the task of rousing them and getting them outside in time.

Athena's Shield also stood ready, joined now by Johnathon Strongheart and Liza, who knew the two Children of Gaia members of that mixed pack. The tribal heralds stood to the side with Alani Astarte, watching, curious to see how well these disparate packs could blend.

Evan and Mari arrived and stood in the center. Mari arranged the party's marching order, placing the Silver River Pack to guard the rear, with the cubs in the center and Athena's Shield in the vanguard, behind Evan and Mari.

Nearby, louder than before, the horn rang out once again, this time with a note of finality. Soon, six Garou in human form entered the clearing, keeping to a loose but defined marching pattern. They were all obviously Fianna, the Garou of Celtic stock, for they literally wore their allegiance on their sleeves and clothing, woven with Celtic knotwork and spirals. They each bore a short klaive and two of them had fine yew bows. The bowmen were redheads, while the rest had black hair. All were in their late twenties.

The Garou who walked in the middle of the oval formation wore black and bore a silver horn engraved with detailed scenes from Fianna legend. He broke from the formation and walked over to greet Evan and Mari, after nodding and winking at the Fianna herald.

"I recognize you two," he said, "packmates of King Albrecht. The famous Mari Cabrah and Evan Heals-the-Past. I'm right glad to meet you. They call me the Black Bellower, but my friends can call me Tom."

Evan smiled and offered his hand, which the man took and shook heartily. "I hope that means we can call you Tom."

"It certainly does," Tom said, with a broad grin that Evan couldn't help liking. Tom raised his hand to his brow in an exaggerated salute. "Reporting for duty with the Boar Spear Pack, the Fianna's finest in all of this land."

"Pleased to have you with us," Evan said.

"I noticed your formation," Mari said, "and I've heard that you guys are all expert scouts."

"You've heard right," Tom said, his right eyebrow rising, waiting for the question she was sure to ask.

"Can we have the Boar Spear form around the entire party? To be the vanguard, the sides and the rear? Or is that spreading you too thin?"

"Not thin at all! We're used to spreading out over distances, and we got all manner of calls and howls to alert one another. So, yeah, you've got a good eye for these sorts of things, Ms. Cabrah. We'll be glad to be your escort."

"Well then," Evan said, turning to scan the line. "I guess there's no reason to wait any longer. Let's move out."

Tom nodded and motioned to his packmates, pointing to where each should go. They all headed for their assigned posts, spread out equidistant around the line, which marched two by two. The party was now twenty-eight strong in all, seven packs (including Evan and Mari's), a much better number than Evan had begun to fear they would leave with, but with a worrisome potential for disunity. So many packs representing so many tribes, most of them strangers to one another. Garou were not renowned for their ability to work well with other tribes; this task would be a real challenge.

The party filed up the trail to the moon bridge point, where the sept's Gatekeeper opened a bridge to the Winter Wolf sept, speaking across vast distances through spirit intermediaries. With no hesitation and no farewells to the Finger Lakes sept, the war party marched onto the bridge and into the North.

● ● ●

Evan stepped from the moon bridge onto ice and snow. The village had clearly suffered a snowstorm since he had last been there. Three Garou waited nearby, watching as the war party stepped from the bridge: Aurak Moondancer, Painted Claw and a young man dressed in a thick robe with the sign of the half-moon upon it. They said nothing to the arriving Garou but simply watched them with expressionless faces.

Mari marched the party forward until they had all cleared the bridge and then called a halt. She looked over at the Wendigo greeting party and their blank faces, and then looked at Evan, frowning.

Evan walked over and bowed to Aurak. John North Wind's Son broke away from the end of the line and joined him, also bowing to Aurak, whose eyes betrayed a slight smile upon seeing him.

Aurak stepped forward and looked over the newly arrived Garou. "I thank you for coming," he said. "We have prepared a lodge for you. Food and water waits for you there. Gleaming Tree will lead you."

Gleaming Tree, the young half-moon, turned and walked down a trail, not waiting to see if he were followed. Evan nodded at Mari, who barked a wolfish growl at the war party. They followed her down the trail, keeping their formation, leaving Evan and John behind with the two Winter Wolf Wendigo.

Once the group was out of sight and hearing, Painted Claw growled a long, rumbling grunt of annoyance. Aurak held up his hand and Painted Claw fell silent, but he glowered at Evan and John.

"There is a war council waiting for us," Aurak said. "Please join us." He walked down the trail, followed by Painted Claw, who looked back to make sure that Evan and John followed. They looked at one another, shrugged, and fell in behind the two older Garou.

At a fork in the trail, Aurak led them to the left. The tracks in the snow revealed that the war party had been led to the right; Evan could smell smoke from a distant fire in that direction. Their own trail led them to a wooden cabin covered in snow, its windows blocked by tautly stretched animal hides. Aurak bent to enter the low doorway. Painted Claw gestured for Evan and John to enter before him, which they did, also bending past the low entryway.

A central fire lit the dark room, along with what little daylight came through the translucent hides stretched over the windows. Wendigo sat in a circle around the room. Aurak crossed the hall to take a place reserved for him. Evan and John recognized the places meant for them, along an empty bench to the right of the entrance. As he sat down, Evan could see the nearest Garou in the gloom: Quiet Storm nodded and smiled at him. He smiled back.

Painted Claw dropped a flap of hide over the door, blocking the chill outside breeze, and took his own seat in the middle of the room on the far side from Evan and John.

Aurak shook a turtle-shell rattle three times and all the Garou prayed in silence. Then the old man spoke. "We have spent the days preparing for a long hunt. We have gathered food and water and prayed to Gaia and the ancestors for guidance. Now that you have returned with the other tribes, we can depart."

Painted Claw let out a gruff, angry bark. Aurak sat back, saying, "We may speak freely here. We are among friends."

"Friends *here*, yes," Painted Claw said, rising to stand and survey the Garou gathered there. "But not in the guest lodge. They are strangers. Cubs, even! A mangy band of pitiful Garou. Is this the best Heals-the-Past can do?"

There were murmurs around the room. The rest of the lodge members were clearly disturbed by Painted Claw's news.

Evan spoke without standing, his voice calm. "There are terrible troubles throughout New York, events you wouldn't believe. Black Spiral Dancers, fomori, banes—evil creatures loosed from all directions. Every sept is under attack. This is unlike any time we have ever known. The other tribes have done their best to aid us and given us what packs they can."

"Then where are their warriors? Their shamans? I saw a group of curs escorted by a handful of Garou who might— *might*—be called warriors. But I will wait until they prove themselves before judging them such. Where are the Uktena? It is an outrage!"

Evan stood up. "The Uktena struggle to maintain the bindings on three monsters. They cannot come, but they released the best Fianna pack in the northeast to aid us, at the risk of their own peril. We have the famed Boar's Spear Pack as scouts."

A murmur traveled throughout the room. Even here, in the far Canadian north, some had heard of the Boar's Spear.

Quiet Storm stood up and looked straight at Painted Claw. "Clearly, Heals-the-Past has fulfilled the prophecy. He has brought many of the tribes to fight with us, more than we could gather with our own words. That is enough."

"Enough for what?" Painted Claw said. "Enough to have a representative of each tribe die at the hands of the Talon? Good! Our blood spills together! Our sacrifice is even more in vain! We should have been hunting this thing by now, taking it down ourselves. Instead, we have waited. For what? Children!"

"You speak as an Ahroun warrior, as is well," Quiet Storm said. "I speak as a Ragabash advocate, and I say they are enough. What do the other Ahroun say? What do you say, Flint Knife?"

All eyes turned to watch Flint Knife, who did not reply immediately. He let out a few consternated breaths and finally spoke: "We shall see. There is nothing to be done for it now. We must leave. Soon."

Most of the Garou in the dimly lit lodge nodded. Painted Claw sat down again. Evan also sat, followed by Quiet Storm. John North Wind's Son stood up.

"I am also a full moon," he said, " and I say that you are all arrogant." Many of the Wendigo looked at him with surprise and a few growls of anger. "You have lived a long time in a place untouched by troubles. I have not. I have fought in New York and in Europe, side by side with the other tribes. I know how they fight and I know their renown is earned just as ours is, with blood, honor and wisdom."

Painted Claw rose to rebut him but Aurak stood first. Painted Claw sat back down, in deference to the elder. "Many times I have been called to aid the other tribes. Rarely have I asked them to aid us. Perhaps they could have sent more, perhaps not. I do not know. I believe Evan speaks true; his voice is one to heed. As I have seen, the other tribes did answer. They are here to fight beside us. We must put aside our anger at what has not come to pass and be thankful for what has come. Tonight, we will hunt. We abandon our village and our families, but there is no other way. We must find the Talon and end its days." He sat back down and the room fell silent. After a while, he spoke again: "Let us go and greet our new allies and eat with them, so that we are strong for the hunt." He stood up and headed for the door.

Everyone nodded and rose to follow. As Aurak passed Evan and John, he motioned them to walk with him. The rest of the lodge fell in behind them. As they walked, Aurak spoke again. "I am sorry to tell you, but Cries-at-Sundown, the banetender, has died. Our medicine could not help him; he lost too much from his wound, more than anyone could heal. The Talon's poison ate at his spirit. It is good he died before it could finish its meal. He is free now."

Evan nodded, sad at the news. It was yet another heartrending development in a series of bad happenings.

● ● ●

At twilight, the war party left the village, each member loping through the snow in wolf form to speed travel. The Wendigo, following the whispers of spirits and their own scouting parties, had divined a suspected location for the Talon, three days to the north. They would need speed to catch it before it veered again.

Fifteen Wendigo joined the party, jointly led by Aurak Moondancer, the most experienced shaman among them, and Painted Claw, the highest ranked warrior. Following the Wendigo tradition, Aurak would lead until they found their prey, after which Painted Claw would become the War Chieftain. Flint Knife and Quiet Storm were among them. Only three Wendigo were left behind to watch over their Kinfolk, all of them too old or too disabled to make the long run across the tundra.

They split the band into two divisions, one to range across the material world and another smaller group to scout the spirit world. Each division had a balanced representation of moon auspices and certain Garou in both groups were designated as heralds, those who would quickly fetch the other group if the need arose.

Shamans called upon hunting spirits to aid them, beings expert at tracking or who could provide spiritual powers. They also brought an array of fetishes to help find their prey and flush it out of hiding if need be.

Most of the non-Wendigo Garou were soon in awe of the Wendigo's hunting prowess, surprised at how quickly and efficiently they tracked the Talon across a vast range of featureless tundra. Its direct tracks had not yet been encountered, but rumor of its passing came to them by way of spirits or was brought on mystical winds.

Despite this newfound respect for the Wendigo, however, the tribes chose to remain somewhat segregated, each pack keeping mainly to itself, despite Evan and the Silver River Pack's attempts to draw them out of their uncomfortable shells and mix with the others. The interactions between the volunteer packs and the quiet Wendigo were few and far between.

On two different occasions, Evan had to break up fights. One was between the Vanguard Pack of Get of Fenris and two Wendigo tale-keepers, arguing over whose tribe was tougher. The tension was thick and everyone could feel the hairs rising on their napes as the arguing Garou's rage rose to the surface. Evan managed to soothe them both, getting them each to concede a virtue of the other (the Wendigo's enduring stoicism and the Get's unquestioning fury).

The other fight was worse, this one between Loper of the Dawn Rover Pack of Bone Gnawers and Feedback, the Glass Walker. Claw strikes were exchanged, and Mari had to leap in and knock the fighting cubs' ears before they would stop and listen to Evan's command to cut it out. It was clear that if Mari had failed to intervene, Painted Claw would have, with a much worse outcome for the cubs.

It began to seem to Evan that nobody wanted to join together, that everyone had come seeking personal glory and didn't care for any sense of group unity or purpose. When confronted with the hard work of compromise and task sharing, even the Fianna proved recalcitrant. They were affable enough most of the time, but when asked to undertake some duty—such as ensuring the cubs didn't fall behind, or ranging far out to one side or the other—they seemed to take it personally and begrudgingly.

More surprising still was the increasingly poor attitude of the Silver River Pack. Evan had assumed that they, of all the Garou here, were dependable and ready to sacrifice for the greater good. They'd earned renown for it before. But now, they seemed on edge, gruff and annoyed whenever they had to work too closely with any of the other packs, especially the Wendigo. Even John didn't seem to want to have much to do with his own tribe. True, they weren't his septmates, but they were fellow Wendigo. His cold aloofness rivaled that of Flint Knife.

On the evening of the second night, as they called a halt to their roaming and began to build a camp, Evan approached Aurak, who sat in wolf form by the edge of a snow bank, panting. He was older than all of them, and had a tougher time keeping up with the rigorous run. When he saw Evan approach in human form, he also assumed that shape, smiling at the young Wendigo.

"Elder," Evan said. "I'm worried about the war party. I've seen dissent in the ranks before, but the sheer distance between tribe members here is… well, it's getting insurmountable."

"And grows worse the farther north we go," Aurak said, unsurprised at Evan's concern.

"Yes. Over time, we're not coming together so much as coming farther apart."

"It is not the *time*, but the *distance*. We are getting closer to the Talon."

Evan's eyes widened. "Is this something the Talon's *doing* to us?"

Aurak shrugged. "I do not know. Something is causing it. It is not normal. I know my sept well and they do not act in accord with our ways."

Evan nodded. "Neither does the Silver River Pack. I figured the other Garou were always like this, but maybe not. Maybe we're all succumbing to something, some power."

A terrible growling broke out nearby as two wolves tore into each other in a fierce fight for dominance. Evan leaped up, looking for Mari or Painted Claw, but saw that they both watched the fight with indifference.

"Stop it!" Evan yelled, shifting to battle form and rushing toward the two embattled Garou.

Mari seemed surprised at this and then ran over herself, likewise shifting to her wolfman form. She and Evan each grabbed onto a different wolf and tugged them away. As soon as the wolves lost contact with one another, the fight went out of them. One of them was a Wendigo, a wolf-born Garou; he shook the snow off his fur and padded away. The other shifted into human form; it was Ironpaw, one of the Get of Fenris. He looked ashamed and tired.

"I think we should keep the packs apart for now," Evan said to Mari, as she released Ironpaw from her grip.

"That's probably a good idea," Mari said, cuffing Ironpaw on the ear as he walked away. He bent his head and clutched his ear in pain but did not cry out. As they watched him walk away, he suddenly fell over, blood spreading out over the snow beneath his head. Moments later, a loud, echoing crack carried across the tundra.

"We're under attack!" Mari yelled, staring at the bullet hole in Ironpaw's head. The shot had killed him instantly. If he had been in any other form than his natural, human form, he might have had a chance, but it was too late for him now.

Howls erupted throughout the nascent camp as Garou shifted into battle form and scattered across the tundra, seeking the source of the shot.

"No!" Evan cried. "Don't spread out! We've got to keep organized!"

A roaring exploded in the air behind him and he spun around to see a snowmobile barreling straight at him across the snow. Two men in paramilitary fatigues straddled the bucking and thudding vehicle. A flash of light from one of their hands heralded a burning sensation in Evan's shoulder. He screamed in pain as the silver bullet exited from his back.

He fell to the ground, dazed, as the snowmobile shot straight at him.

The Last Battle

Chapter Twelve:
Death's Door

Evan writhed in pain as he rolled to the side, desperate to move from the snowmobile's path. The oncoming vehicle veered toward him. He felt faint, about to pass out. Knowing no other option, he dug his finger into the wound and twisted. The searing pain wracked his body. He lost all sense of anything but pain. Pain and anger. Rage erupted from deep in his belly.

• • •

The snowmobile driver laughed as his sleek machine barreled at the fallen Garou. He imagined the Garou's guts splattering across his windshield. Instead, the snowmobile wrenched to a sudden halt and he went flying, crashing into a snow bank.

He crawled from the thick bank and shook his head, dizzy. He saw his snowmobile, upended in the snow, its front fender completely crumpled. He stood up, trying to get his bearings, when he felt a sudden warmth in his belly, which then spread down the front of his legs. He looked down—a huge, furred and clawed hand jutted from his torso, covered in his own steaming blood and intestines.

He moaned in fear and sudden pain as the claw withdrew, tugged back through him and out the entry wound in his back. He collapsed onto the ground, dead before his head hit the snow.

The snowmobile's passenger, trying to stand on a broken leg, screamed in fear as he saw his partner fall. A hulking, gray-furred Garou stood behind him, its hand glistening wet with blood. Its feral eyes turned to meet his own. He brought his pistol up and fired madly. The thing was insanely fast. Before he could re-aim, it appeared at his side, slicing downward. His forearm cleanly detached from his elbow and thumped into the snow. He stared in shock at the stump and then saw the massive jaws closing on his head. A sickening crunch followed and he slumped lifeless to the ground.

• • •

Evan shook his head, his rage subsiding, his awareness returning. He smelled blood and snow and had vague memories of combat. He surveyed his surroundings and saw the two dead men, each dressed in parkas with a prominent corporate logo: ARC OIL. His nose wrinkled, not at the stench of their steaming brains and guts, but at the logo: a Pentex subsidiary. A corporation beholden to the Wyrm, pledged to destroy the Earth for massive profit.

His head snapped up, fully alert, as gunshots erupted nearby. The roar of more snowmobiles surrounded him; he scanned about to see their fast shapes rushing past to his far right and left. He saw the shapes of Garou leaping and slashing at human passengers. He moved to join them but stopped and clutched his shoulder in pain. The silver bullet had almost killed him.

He felt a hand on his back and heard a soft whispering in his ear, a familiar chant. Aurak Moondancer stood beside him, healing his wound. The spirit power flowed from his hand. Evan's blood rhythmically beat with the cadence of the chant, until nearly all trace of the wound was gone. Only a small scar remained.

Evan clutched Aurak's hand and let out a wolf grunt of thanks. He rushed to join the others. He could see Mari next to an overturned vehicle, choking a parka-clad man with two hands while she kicked another in his groin. As he doubled over, she raked his face with her toe claws. He cried in pain and covered his eyes as his partner gurgled and struggled against her iron grip.

Evan ran up and severed the screaming man's spine with one slash. Mari smiled and drove her fingers into the other one's skull, tired of waiting for him to die. She dropped his lifeless body and pointed across the snow.

"There are least fifty of them," she said. "In all directions. *Pentex*."

Evan could see other dead bodies, all human, none of them Garou. "They don't seem very good at this."

"They've got silver bullets and aren't afraid of us, but that's it." Most people reacted to werewolves with mind-numbing terror—ancestral memories from the long-ago days when Garou hunted men. These fomori had been immunized to that, it seemed.

"So we disarm them first?"

"Exactly."

Evan nodded and ran off toward a streaking snowmobile. Its passenger pointed a submachine gun at members of the Dawn Rover Pack, who were busy attacking the riders of another downed vehicle. Evan leaped and sailed over the vaulting snowmobile, his front claws snatching the gun as he passed overhead. The disarmed human stared up in surprise and slapped the driver on the back, screaming for him to get out of there.

The driver accelerated and skidded away. Too late. Mari dropped to all fours, bolted forward and rammed them from the side, toppling the snowmobile over. It skidded through the snow, slowing to a halt. The passengers leaped up and tried to run, but Evan was already on them. His claws hamstrung and then eviscerated one of them and his jaws rent the other's throat.

He spat the blood from his mouth. He hated committing such slaughter but had long ago come to accept that anyone who was foolish enough to work for Pentex was way beyond help or redemption, at least once bullets flew. These poor humans were out of their league, but neither he nor any Garou there could afford to spare them at this stage.

As he turned away to seek another foe, he noticed a strange movement out of the corner of his eye, a sharp twinkling that was gone as soon as he turned to look for it. But he knew what it was and where it had gone. He concentrated and reached out, merging his spirit with the greater world that existed beyond, and stepped over the barrier into the Penumbra.

The snowscape looked exactly the same, perfectly in accord with its material counterpart. A number of Garou—the expedition's Umbral scouts—chased several flitting and swooping winged creatures. Their unearthly scales and feathered wings seemed out of place with their insect-like forms: multi-faceted eyes, multiple legs and pulsating, striped stingers.

Evan saw one of the creatures flapping away from where he had just appeared. He jumped up and snatched it from the air before it even realized he was there.

The bane struggled in his hands, screeching and pecking at him, twisting and trying to wriggle free. He clutched it hard, denying it any opening, withstanding its painful pecks and giving it no leverage to use its stinger. He shook it hard and it finally ceased its struggling.

He looked around and saw Crying Bird, a Wendigo shaman, pacing nearby in his native wolf form, watching the skies for more signs of the banes. Evan whistled. The wolf snapped his head in his direction, and then ran over.

"What are they?" Evan grunted.

Crying Bird barked an undulating growl at the bane in Evan's hands, speaking in spirit speech, commanding it to answer. The thing screeched in response, although it clearly didn't want to; it was compelled by the shaman's power.

"Banes made by Pentex," Crying Bird growled. "They know we hunt. Send them from base nearby. Possess human leaders." He growled again at the bane, and it reluctantly screeched. The wolf barked in anger. "Fomori! We must return!"

Evan crushed the bane in his hands, piercing it with his claws. Its ephemeral substance dissolved. He watched as Crying Bird faded into the material world, and then followed behind.

● ● ●

Mari looked around for Evan. His scent was gone. His tracks ended in one place and went no further. She knew where he'd gone and prepared to follow him, when something barreled into her and knocked her down.

A massive scaled tail wrapped around her waist, pinning one arm, and lifted her from the ground. She traced its length and saw that it sprouted from the torso of a humanoid figure, covered in a thick, leathery carapace, with four other tentacles whipping through the air. Its human jaw opened to reveal rows of sharp teeth and it croaked in a horrible imitation of laughter as it flung Mari down, driving her head into the hard, frozen earth. The snow barely blunted the impact.

She took a deep breath, dazed for a moment, and shifted to wolf form, slipping from the tentacle's grip before it could tighten to bind her now-smaller shape. She vaulted forward, shifting into black-furred battle form again, and slashed at the tentacle with all four claws. Its blood spurted out green and acidic, but she managed to sever the tentacle from its stump with another concerted slash.

A claw raked her back, opening up deep furrows, but she twisted and kicked her attacker with her toe claws before it could move. The thing's carapace kept her from penetrating skin, but the force of her blow knocked it back.

"Ferectoi," she spat, and launched herself at the imbalanced fomor. It dodged aside with a surprising burst of speed and she skidded in the snow past it. As she spun around to charge again, a wolf appeared in the material world, stepping sideways from the Umbra.

The fomor's three remaining tentacles shot forth and grabbed the wolf before it could react. With incredible strength it ripped the surprised Garou limb from limb. The wolf's howl was cut short as its body dropped to the snow in three pieces.

"No!" Mari screamed and jumped onto the fomor's shoulders. Her jaws clamped onto its head and her claws dug under its shoulder plates, seeking weak, unprotected flesh. It thrashed about, trying to knock her off, moaning in pain as her teeth slowly penetrated its head plates, bringing forth trickles of green blood. Her claws found what she was looking for and dug in deeper, tearing into muscle and bone.

The fomor's tentacles wrapped around Mari's neck and yanked, flinging her five yards away. Her body slammed into a snow-covered rock. She immediately righted herself and charged back again.

Between her and the fomor, a shape shimmered into view, materializing from the spirit world. She skidded out of the way just in time, barely missing Evan.

Tentacles wrapped around Evan's head and waist and began to squeeze. Mari heard bones cracking. She ran toward the tentacles and paused, scrutinizing them and calling upon the insight of the spirits. She drew back her claws and slashed at a single area where all the tentacles intersected—the weak spot her powers had revealed. All three tentacles broke apart, spurting green blood. The stumps flopped about in agony.

Evan dropped to the ground, breathing deeply, sucking in the air the tentacles had denied him.

The fomor leaped onto an abandoned snowmobile, kicking aside the human bodies next to it, and roared off across the tundra. Mari shifted to wolf form and took off after the fleeing vehicle.

As she ran past John North Wind's Son, she howled for assistance. He shifted into wolf form and joined her, followed by the entire Silver River Pack, which had been busy killing more Arc Oil commandoes. They now ran together, chasing after the snowmobile. The vehicle gained speed, steadily increasing the distance between them. But Mari kept running, following the trail left by its tracks. The Silver River Pack struggled to keep up.

• • •

Evan's entire body throbbed but he could feel it knitting itself back together again as he caught his breath. He surveyed the scene around him and saw Garou slowly gathering together as they killed the last of the humans. At least fifteen snowmobiles lay scattered across the tundra in ruins.

The human dead must have numbered at least fifty, although it appeared to be more. They all wore the same parka uniforms, each emblazoned with the Arc Oil logo.

He saw the severed body of Crying Bird, who had preceded him through the Gauntlet into the material world, and he also saw the bodies of three more Garou: a Child of Gaia from the Athena's Shield pack, another Wendigo, this one a half-moon named Swift Talker, and Ironpaw, the Get of Fenris who had been the first to fall.

He went over to Crying Bird's body and bowed down beside it, praying to Gaia that the shaman's spirit would rest with his ancestors. He saw once again the brief twinkling, as if something darted into the Umbra. Growling, he stepped sideways after it.

The Penumbra was nothing like it had been mere moments before. A green mist veined with purple streaks covered the ground, pooling up in vortices near four different areas, places that corresponded to the bodies of the dead Garou in the material world.

Evan was alone. The Umbral scouts had already shifted into the material world to aid the battle.

Evan growled and struck his claw against the closest vortex, the one surrounding the empty place where Crying Bird had been. It recoiled as if alive and retreated. A voice spoke from behind him.

"You must chase it from our spirits, before it can devour us."

Evan turned to see the shadowy form of Crying Bird, a hazy, ephemeral wolf. He stood not five feet away, but looked as if he were at the end of a far tunnel, unreachable.

Evan turned to watch the mist coil around the other Penumbral anchors to the dead. He rushed over to each of them, chasing the mist away with claws and fang. He could feel nothing as he touched it, but it shot away from his contact as if in pain.

The mist receded to the horizon and hung there, as if waiting for Evan to leave so it could creep forward again.

"It will return," another voice said. Evan now saw three ghostly forms, the shades of Ironpaw and the two other fallen Garou. "The ancestors call you, Heals-the-Past," Ironpaw said. "Open your heart to them."

Evan felt a chill down his spine as the hair on his nape rose. These were the departed spirits of recently killed Garou. It was almost unheard of to encounter such ghosts, for their spirits usually went to the lands of the ancestors or the totems, where they chose to either become patrons for future generations of Garou or to serve Gaia in some other way unknown to the living. Some, however, were corrupted upon their deaths and remained behind to become banes. But these four shades did not appear to be malevolent or tainted.

He shuddered as he looked at them. The Silent Striders were said to delve into the mysteries of death but there was only one of that tribe among the war party, and Shazi was too young and inexperienced to break open the barrier between the living and the dead. There was another group, however, that sought the mysteries of the afterlife, a sect within the Silver Fangs called the Ivory Priesthood. Queen Tamara Tvarivich of Russia was their leader, and they supposedly uncovered secrets even the ancestors would not reveal.

Evan winced as he remembered Albrecht. His packmate had gone to Russia to meet Tvarivich. Were these weird apparitions tied to Albrecht's journey? If so, they showed no signs of it.

"Why are you here?" Evan said, his voice a whisper.

"The door is open," Crying Bird said. "The time has come. The past is unchained. Those who came before speak through us."

"Will you listen to what they have to say?" Ironpaw said with uncharacteristic dignity and solemnity, as if he had grown a thousand years old since his death. As he spoke, Evan thought he saw another figure behind him, a standing shape with a crooked staff, but when he focused his eyes, it was gone.

"Yes," Evan said without hesitation.

The world shifted. The landscape changed, metamorphosing to match a different environment. Trees shot upwards, creating a pine forest in mere moments. The moon rose and set and the faint light of dawn perched on the horizon.

Evan stood amid the forest, the apparitions with him, watching over a low hill, as if waiting for someone. Moments later, a pure white dire wolf crested the rise, limping down a deer trail, coming toward Evan but oblivious to his presence. His leg bore a recent wound and around his neck a strange twist of green vine held a small stone, a dull, black crystal that seemed to weigh him down.

Evan stepped aside as the wolf loped past him, never registering his presence with its eyes or nose. As the wolf departed, Evan reached out and brushed its tail. His hand went through it; it was an intangible echo of the past.

Evan looked at Swift Talker, the dead Wendigo, and saw that she still watched the hill. He saw a new shape appear there, a Garou with a crude spear. When the spear-bearer saw the limping dire wolf, she halted and growled a warning. The dire wolf stopped and turned around, taking a defensive posture.

More Garou came over the rise, all in their battle forms, lining up to the right and left of the spear-carrier. They stared threateningly at the dire wolf.

"What will you tell them?" the spear-carrier said in gruff voice.

"The truth," the dire wolf said, with a voice more articulate than usual for the dire wolf form. "How the Stone Fist Pack turned on their brothers and sisters, how they slaughtered them instead of accepting their just submission."

"You will turn the others against us," the spear-carrier said.

"They will do what they must," the dire wolf replied.

"Then we cannot let your howl reach their ears."

The dire wolf hunkered down, its eyes slits. "You would dare attack your king?"

The spear-carrier seemed to hesitate, looking at the nervous faces of her fellow Garou. She snarled and turned to stare into the dire wolf's eyes. "We need no more kings!" She hurled her spear at him; it pierced his left shoulder.

The white wolf howled in rage and pain and charged the Garou, who scattered like pups before an angry alpha. The spear-carrier met him head on, crashing into him and hurling both of them to the ground. They snarled and swiped at one another, rolling back and forth across the snowy pine needles, each opening terrible wounds in the other.

Then the spear-carrier's jaw locked on the white wolf's throat and refused to let go. The dire wolf flung her about with all his might, but couldn't dislodge her. His blood sprayed in all directions, staining his fur red. He stumbled and fell, breathing shallowly as his life drained from him. He whimpered and lay still.

The spear-carrier released her hold and howled with victory. The other Garou gathered around her, presenting their necks. She roughly rubbed all of them with her snout and then snatched the black crystal stone from around the dead wolf's throat.

"The Binding Stone," Crying Bird whispered to Evan. "He was the last Guardian of the Talon, before there were tribes."

The spear-carrier sniffed at it, smiling. She rolled it around in her clawed hand, looking at it from all angles. "So this is his power…."

One of the Garou, the smallest among them, whined and backed away. "That is king's magic. Leave it be."

The spear-carrier growled at the Garou and took a step toward him. He sidled back, away from her, head bowed. She held it forth for him to see.

"How do *I* gain its power, Crescent Moon?"

"Its power must never be called upon. Many died to bind it; many more will die if it comes free."

The spear-carrier barked in anger and slashed at the shaman, who dodged from the claw and ran into the forest.

"King's magic!" the spear-carrier cried. "I killed the king. His magic dies with him."

The spear-carrier dropped the stone onto the ground and picked up a rock. She raised it high and brought it down upon the stone with all her might. The stone cracked and exploded, throwing the spear-carrier back into a tree with enough force to split the trunk, sending the upper bole crashing into the woods behind her.

A green mist seeped from the shattered crystal, purple veins growing into tendrils as it spread out across the forest floor, wrapping around the confused and scared Garou, who whined at the fallen, unconscious body of the spear-carrier. The mist curled around her and crawled into her nostrils. The spear-carrier's eyes opened and she stared at her Garou underlings.

She stood up and fetched her spear from the dead king's side. Her pupils glinted green in the growing light of dawn; the whites of her eyes were streaked with purple veins. She hissed at the Garou and motioned them forward along the path, down the direction the king had traveled.

The mist followed them, clinging to their fur. As they padded away, Evan could see something red and pulsing moving amid their feet, but it was covered by mist. They soon disappeared into the primeval forest.

"The first king-slayer," Ironpaw said.

Evan shivered. The mist was the same he had seen in the Penumbra. "The mist. It's the Talon, isn't it?"

Crying Bird nodded.

Evan swallowed hard, bolstering himself. "It's all around us. It isn't a day's march away. It's *here* already."

"Possessing them all," the dead Child of Gaia said. Evan wished he knew her name. "Imprinting them with its violence."

"I'm confused. Did it cause the king to die?"

"No," Swift Talker said. "Garou rage killed the king. The act of king-slaying shaped it, gave the unbound spirit a new form."

"I don't get it. It's a Talon. It's supposed to be a monster or something, at least according to the legends."

"The Talons are *our* monsters," Crying Bird said. "They are given life by the Wyrm, but the form they take and the powers they wield are shaped by Garou fear. In every age, every time a Talon is freed, it takes the form that freed it. In all ages, this has been the form of betrayal and distrust. The power of murder."

"That doesn't make sense. The one that's free now, *it* killed Garou this time, the Uktena banetenders. They didn't kill each other to release it."

Crying Bird shook his head. "It has been free since the king-slaying you witnessed. The Uktena only captured its heart. Its tendrils have always touched the descendants of those who participated in that slaying."

"So it's been affecting Garou all this time? Since when? When was the king-slaying?"

"Before the Pangaian Moot. Before the Litany. It is the Heartsplinter, the wound that will not heal, the scar that tears apart siblings. It festers in all Garou hearts, hidden by rage. It cannot cause hate, but it empowers it, turning petty disputes into vendettas."

Evan felt his legs weakening with the enormity of the revelation. "I can't fight this. Nobody can."

"You are the Healer of the Past. You must set things aright. You must atone for your ancestor's wrongs."

"How?! How do you fight bodiless mist?"

"Strike at the heart."

Evan moaned in anguish. He turned to address the apparitions but they were gone. The Penumbral snowscape, now empty of pine trees, stretched to the featureless horizon in all directions. A green mist roiled in the distance, hovering, waiting for him to leave.

Chapter Thirteen:
Burying the Past

Mari thundered across the tundra, ignoring the increasing pain of growing fatigue in her limbs. In the far distance, she saw the tiny speck of the fomor, moving quickly away from her. Judging from the sheer amount of humans it had mustered, Mari figured that the Pentex base must be nearby. She had to catch the fomor before it could gather reinforcements.

The Silver River Pack followed behind her, lagging by fifty yards, with Storm-Eye in the lead. The wolf-born Garou was more used to running for long periods than the others but even she felt exhaustion setting in; Mari could tell by her and the others' occasional faltering steps. She didn't allow herself to speculate on what would happen if they were attacked in force before they could recover.

Far ahead, the fast-moving figure came to a stop. Mari felt a thrill rush through her nerves as she put on more speed. With her enhanced wolf eyes, she could see it flailing its limbs, thrashing at something. The snowmobile. It had broken down or run out of gas. The fomor turned to look at the chasing Garou and then broke and ran, hurrying in the same direction as before, but now on two feet.

It was only a matter of time. Where before the fomor had slowly gained speed and distance from them, now they gained on him, much faster this time. The wolves' four legs and physique, designed for the chase, easily outdid the fomor's two legs. What's more, his wounds were beginning to tell on him; he soon slowed, huffing and puffing.

Then the horizon lit up. A huge fireball erupted from the earth, gusting into the air, its heat sending forth a hot wave of air that even Julia, the straggler of the group, could feel on her fur.

The force of the blast knocked the fomor over. Mari blinked and kept running.

The massive cloud of flame and smoke billowed outward, darkening the sky. Mari sniffed the air. Burning oil. The base must be ahead; it was probably an oil refinery. Something had just caused it to explode.

She was maybe two hundred yards away from the fomor. He staggered up and ran again, dropping from sight. Mari realized that the ground ahead fell sharply downwards, creating a valley that she hadn't seen from afar. She kept running and closed the distance in seconds.

She skidded on the edge of the incline and slowed just enough to judge the landscape before committing to it. Then she slid down the slope, following the fomor's footprints.

Ahead, spread out across what looked like a mile-long crater, a number of aluminum sheds belched smoke from their interiors, all their windows and doors broken out. A giant skeletal tower in the center of the crater seemed to melt before Mari's very eyes, the raging fire bursting up beneath it from a hole in the ground.

But that wasn't the most shocking view. The snow was black with soot; here and there, wherever the soot had not yet settled, blood covered over the floor of the crater. Human bodies—more Pentex employees—lay strewn about, slashed to pieces by some massive clawed hand. Mari could see even with a bare glance that the five-clawed hand that made those wounds was bigger than any Garou she'd ever seen.

The fomor stood at the edge of the base, less than twenty yards from Mari, trembling with shock or rage—Mari couldn't tell which from behind. It clearly had not expected this.

Mari shifted into battle form and halted a few yards away, bringing both her hands up and pointing her claws at the fomor. Her initial intention for the chase—to stop him before he could alert his base—was no longer relevant, but she certainly didn't intend to let him live.

The fomor turned and hissed at her, stepping forward to fight. She snarled and let her claws fly. They shot from her fingers like wasps and swooped at the startled fomor, angling toward his soft sides, where his carapace was weak. They tore into his flesh, embedding themselves deep.

The fomor gasped, surprised and indignant, and fell dead. His body kicked up a cloud of blood and ashes as it hit the ground.

The Silver River Pack trotted over to Mari, looking around, sniffing for any live enemies. Mari wriggled her bloody fingers as new claws began to grow. The process itched a little, but that was a small trade-off for such a powerful boon from the wasp spirits.

"What the hell happened here?" Julia said.

"Something attacked them," Mari said. "Something big."

"Where?" Storm-Eye said, sniffing deeply. "Can't find."

"I don't hear or smell anything, either," Mari said. "But I've got a theory. Come on, grab on to me."

The Silver River Pack immediately understood her intentions and each of them reached out to grasp an arm or tuft of hair. Mari pulled them all with her across the Gauntlet, into the spirit world.

The landscape was the same scene of carnage but instead of dead humans, the ephemeral remains of banes smeared the blackened ground. The fire still burned, for the sheds and tower had presences in the Umbra.

"That's not right," Julia said. "It's not easy getting new buildings to show up in the Umbra. It usually takes Pattern Spiders to do that."

"I don't see any sign of Weaver work," John North Wind's Son said.

"But a lot of Wyrm," Cries Havoc said. "All over. That's not natural fire."

The fire glowed green in the Umbra. It was weaker than in the material world, but still guttered in a giant crater.

"Balefire," Carlita spat.

"Don't get any closer," Mari said. "It's poisonous."

"And radioactive," Julia added. "Highly mutagenic. The sooner we leave, the better. We're in no shape to shut that down. We need spirits for that."

"All right, let's skirt the perimeter," Mari said. "Maybe we'll find some clues to our mysterious benefactor."

They nodded and followed her as she walked around the complex in a wide circle. They could see that the buildings radiated out from the central tower. Pipes from the tower went into each shed, some of which were clearly barracks while others looked administrative or lab-oriented. The compound looked like an oil operation, but something else was clearly going on here.

"They're mining Balefire," Julia said. "Drawing it from that pit in the Umbra and transferring it to the material world through some sort of technology."

"What the hell for?" Carlita said.

"To create fomori, I suppose. Maybe some special banes, too. Look at these bodies." Julia kicked one of the bane corpses with a clawed toe. "They usually dissolve, reforming in a Hellhole somewhere. Not these ones. They're truly dead."

"They look like some sort of wasp-bird hybrid," Cries Havoc said.

"Shh!" Mari said, holding up her hand for them all to be silent. They quieted and listened with her, straining their ears to hear. Mari pointed away from the complex toward the edge of the crater. "Over here. Breathing. Some sort of animal. It's faint, though."

She walked cautiously in the direction toward which she had pointed, motioning for the Silver River Pack to fan out behind her in both directions. Cries Havoc and John went to the left while Carlita and Storm-Eye went to the right. Julia stayed with Mari.

Mari stopped and pointed at a trail of blood mixed with the fallen soot. It led up an incline, over the lip of the crater. She followed and slowly raised her head above the lip, eyes searching for signs of movement. The trail of blood curved around a large embankment. The breathing sound was louder now, coming from behind the embankment.

Mari led the Silver River Pack up over the edge and they spread out across the snow, approaching the embankment from two directions. Mari, Julia and Carlita took the right, while the others went left.

As she came to the edge, Mari crept around it slowly, trying not to startle whatever lurked there. She stopped, shocked at what she saw, and raised her hand for the others to halt. Then she stepped cautiously forward.

A giant, prehistoric-sized bear lay against the embankment, its body shredded by a thousand tiny cuts, blood slowly pooling from the wounds. Its breathing was like a huge bellows, although a deep rattle betrayed that the beast was dying.

Its eyes weakly opened as Mari approached, and then closed again. It seemed to collect its strength and then rose up, sitting and leaning against the embankment, its eyes open once more. It was clearly female.

As the bear settled herself, Julia sucked in a startled breath. Sitting, the bear's head still rose above their battle forms by a foot or two.

"Step near, wolf-children," the bear said.

Storm-Eye stepped forward, unhesitating, reverently. She bowed to the bear, who smiled and gave a faint nod in return.

Mari cocked her head, confused. She looked to the rest of the Silver River Pack, but they each shrugged. They didn't know who the bear was, but Storm-Eye seemed to know.

"I have only a few breaths left of all my years," the bear said. "I wounded the Heartsplinter. It cannot strike directly, but it will poison your people's hearts against one another. As it strikes at your hearts, so must you strike at its."

The bear wheezed horribly and closed her eyes again, withstanding a wave of pain in her lungs. She breathed deeply a few times and then opened her eyes again. She scanned the Garou and settled on Mari, staring intently at her, as if readying a challenge.

"When I am gone, take one of my teeth. Make a string of my sinew, and hang the tooth from it. Follow where it points and make your stand there." She coughed up a gout of blood, which spilled across her chest. "No time. No time. Reach into my fur, below my ear."

Mari stepped forward, carefully. The bear did not move, waiting. Mari reached behind the ear she had indicated, her left one, and ran her fingers through it. The fur was thick and deep, but she felt something hard tangled within it, like a nut.

"Yes," the bear said. "That is it. Cut it free from my fur. I have carried it all my years. When all is over, you must bury it in the earth, in the place to which my tooth guides you."

Mari nodded and yanked at the fur, severing it with her claws. It took a moment, but the hard shell came free. Mari held it up, rolling it in her palm, and then placed it in her pocket.

The bear growled loudly, her eyes searing into Mari's. "Do not forget! Nothing else matters." She winced and caught her breath, then looked at each of them. "Step forward. I must… cleanse you of the Talon's taint."

Cries Havoc looked nervously at Mari, but she nodded at him. He stepped forward and the bear licked her massive, coarse tongue across his face. He stumbled back, looking disoriented. He shook his head and glanced at the others, smiling, nodding to them.

One by one, they each stepped forward, Mari also, and let the bear lick her tongue across their faces, like baby cubs being cleaned by their mother.

When she was finished, the bear let out a low moan and her head slumped. Her eyes slowly closed and her throat let out a chilling rattle. Her breathing halted and she moved no more.

Storm-Eye howled with grief. She formed her anguish into the ritual Howl of Departing, an honor to lost heroes. The others joined in. They didn't know whom they eulogized, but they had all been moved by the bear's majesty and grace, and Storm-Eye was clearly distraught.

Once the howl died down to echoes across the snow, they all looked at Storm-Eye, waiting.

The wolf loped forward and rubbed her snout against the bear's paw, as if seeking to be stroked. She turned to look at her packmates and Mari.

"We have lost her. Most Ancient of Bears. Oldest of Gaia's children. Last of those to see the Dawn."

John North Wind's Son let out a cry of anguish. He shut his eyes, holding back sudden tears, clenching his fists. "I heard the legends. I didn't know… I didn't think they were true."

Mari slowly nodded, remembering. "I've heard that, too. The oldest of the Gurahl werebears. She's supposedly a thousand years old."

Storm-Eye growled. "Older. Oldest of all."

John nodded. "She hibernates through many centuries, long enough that people think she's gone for good. Then she shows up again for a short time, before sleeping again. It's been so long, I thought… I didn't expect to encounter her. Not like this."

"We've got to bury her," Mari said. "Away from this place."

Mari walked over to the large body and bowed before it. "May your spirit find its way to the Great Cave of your people, who have long awaited your coming." She stood silently, praying for the Most Ancient's spirit.

Then Mari stepped forward and wrapped her arm underneath the bear's right shoulder. "All right, she's going to be heavy. I'm going to need you all to join in here. I think our combined strength can manage it."

The Silver River Pack gathered around. Each chose a portion of the body to grasp for lifting. Mari counted to three and they heaved. Even with their full might they had trouble raising the huge bulk. Nonetheless, they managed it. Mari motioned out across the tundra, away from the Pentex base, and they began to march, carrying their sacred burden.

After half an hour, once the smoke plume could no longer be seen, Mari called a halt. They carefully lowered the body and each dropped to the ground, muscles relaxing, breathing in deep.

"She's the biggest thing I've ever seen!" Cries Havoc said.

"No," Carlita said. "There's a lot bigger. But none of them are working on our side."

"Okay," Mari said, catching her breath. "Let's take five. Then we shift her back to the material world with us. We'll dig a grave there."

"Would she really want a grave?" Julia said, looking at Storm-Eye.

"Yes," John said, answering before Storm-Eye could. "The Gurahl are very ritualistic. It is said that they taught humans their first religion—bear worship. The most ancient human graves are associated with bear rites. For all we know, she's the one who taught our human ancestors to know their ancestor spirits."

Storm-Eye grunted and shook her head. "No human ancestors."

"Your Garou blood has *some* human legacy," Cries Havoc said, "whether you want it or not."

Storm-Eye grunted again and turned away from the conversation.

After a few more minutes of silent rest, Mari signaled that she was ready. They gathered around the body again and this time followed Mari across the Gauntlet, back to the material world, clinging to the Most Ancient as they did.

They scanned around them. Blank tundra lay in all directions.

"It won't be easy finding our way back," Mari said.

John snorted. "You've got to be kidding me. City slickers."

Mari smiled. "Ah, yes, we have a Wendigo with us. I'm sure you can find your way around in a featureless snowscape, but we can't."

"Then just follow me. When we're done here, that is." John looked at the Most Ancient's body with sorrow.

Storm-Eye clawed at the dirt. It was hard-packed, tough to dig into. "Long time for dig."

"Maybe we should look for rocks," Julia said. "Build a cairn."

"Yes," John said. "That would be traditional for this place."

They split up and circled around, seeking rocks underneath the snow. Mari stayed with the body, guarding it in case any creature appeared seeking to despoil it. She undertook her duty, the last request of the Most Ancient.

Mari opened the bear's jaws and reached in. She tugged with all her might and finally loosened a tooth. She pocketed it and went down to the legs. Slowly, carefully, and with respect, she began cutting out a long, leathery sinew. It was as strong as steel cable but as flexible and thin as a thread. She tied it around the tooth and hung it around her neck.

After a while, the rest returned with armfuls of rocks and began piling them around the bear. Their Garou strength allowed them to haul large pieces of shale; after an hour, the massive body was completely covered in rocks, a small mountain on an otherwise empty plain.

They stood, heads bowed, each praying silently.

Mari looked at John, who nodded and shifted into wolf form. He ran off across the tundra. Mari shifted into wolf shape to follow, as did the rest of the Silver River Pack.

They ran as fast as they could, searching for their fellow Garou, hoping that nothing more had occurred in their absence.

The Last Battle

Chapter Fourteen:
Tomorrow We March

Mephi Faster-Than-Death looked down from the high mountain pass and surveyed the tents and the moving figures of wolves, men and shapes in between that filled the wide valley below. He stopped and took a breath, leaning on his cobra-headed staff. He tried to estimate how many Garou were gathering below but soon gave up—there were far too many to count or to even approximate. The Margrave's army was indeed mighty, the largest Mephi had ever seen with his own eyes. He felt a twist of apprehension in his guts at the thought. *So this is really it, as the Phoenix revealed.*

Mephi shook his head sadly and continued onward, down the spiraling path, into the valley. *I hate being the bearer of bad tidings…*

A fierce cawing erupted above his head. He stopped to watch three crows circling on high, watching him.

"It's okay," he yelled. "Konietzko knows me!"

The birds cawed again and wheeled away, swooping into the valley, landing outside a large tent in the center. Mephi could no longer make them out at this distance, so he kept walking, his staff over his shoulder.

As he finally reached the valley floor and walked out onto its black soil, two large Garou stepped from hidden clefts to either side of him, each pointing a sharp spear at him.

He raised his hands, still clutching his staff. "Hey, guys. I already told the crows I'm a friendly."

"Who are you?" one of them said.

"Mephi Faster-Than-Death. Silent Strider. I helped the Margrave out during the Jo'cllath'mattric troubles. Remember?"

They lowered their spears but showed no signs of happiness at seeing him. "We remember you, wanderer," one of them said coldly. He looked Mephi over from head to toe, from his long dark ponytail to his leather duster, faded jeans and well-worn hiking boots. His eyes stopped for a moment when they saw the golden bracelets on Mephi's wrists, visible beneath the duster's sleeves. He seemed to be judging Mephi and didn't much like what he saw, but he nodded anyway. "You may enter."

"Great," Mephi said with a sarcastic smile. "Now, can you tell me which tent is the Margrave's?"

"In the center of the encampment. It is obvious."

"Right. Well. I'll just be heading over that way. See ya." Mephi began walking, looking back at the guards to make sure they were okay with his stated plan. They had already disappeared back into the dark clefts. He shrugged and headed into the mess of tents and mingling Garou.

From what he had seen on his downward trek, the camp was laid out in a giant half-circle, radiating from a central tent—the one to which the crows had flown. He figured that was the Margrave's HQ. Behind that tent was a huge field, probably for assembling the troops. In front and to the sides of the tent, lines of tents with lanes between them radiated out in semi-circles. Flags and banners flew from the tops of some tents. He hadn't been able to make them out from afar, but now he could use them as a guide, for many bore the pictograms of a tribe or a renowned sept.

As he wove through the lanes, he dodged a number of fights. Garou tumbled and wrestled with one another, occasionally drawing blood, until one or the other submitted and accepted the other's dominance. This many Garou couldn't gather together in one place without such fights erupting. It was best to let them play it out as needed.

In avoiding the struggling warriors, he slipped through a few tents, stepping over bunks and sleeping bags and some carefully wrapped and stored fetishes. He spent no time examining them, knowing that his witnessing them alone might get him accused of being a thief. So he kept moving, trying not to draw attention to himself. Luckily, most of the Garou here were busy watching the packs work out their pecking orders, seeing which would ultimately prove the leaders when the war party finally had to march.

Of course, issues of individual rank among pack members would be the main determinates. Those of equal rank, however, had to figure out where they stood with their peers. As Mephi could clearly hear, it wasn't just combat that determined dominance. A number of gamecraft challenges were also being declared. He wanted to stay and listen to a few of them, but his business was more pressing. He kept on, heading for the center.

Many packs were single-tribe packs but a surprising number were multi-tribal. That meant the banners, declaring the tribal leaders' tents, weren't the sole representation for those tribes. A *motley army*, he thought. *This'll be a trick to lead. But if anyone's up to that challenge, I suppose it's the Margrave.*

He finally broke through the circles and arrived at the main tent, marked with the crosshatched claw marks of the Shadow Lords. It was a huge military tent, the kind used to house a large logistical operation. The sides were all tied down, concealing the interior. One of the crows who had spied him in the pass sat on top of a pole, watching him now as he crossed the lane toward the entrance.

A Shadow Lord stood by the tent flap, dressed in old style, Eastern European royal garb. He watched Mephi through half-lidded eyes.

"Greetings," Mephi said, offering the man a half-bow. "I am Mephi Faster-Than-Death. I have come with news for the Margrave."

"He expects you," the man said, pulling back the flap.

Mephi nodded and went in.

Five Garou gathered about a central table, pointing out features on a map. The room was full of tables, chairs and weapons. Most of the posts were empty; only the five Garou were present. Three of them, two men and a woman, turned to watch Mephi, while another woman spoke with a large, white-haired man dressed in black furs. The man's eyes darted up and looked into Mephi's. His face showed no recognition, but Mephi had the distinct impression that he had been seen and known.

"Margrave," Mephi said, kneeling on one leg and bowing low.

"Faster-Than-Death," Konietzko said. "It is good to see you again."

The other Garou whispered among themselves, watching Mephi.

"Don't all talk at once," Mephi said, standing again, with a smile he hoped was taken as deprecating. "No need to go all out on my account."

The Garou became silent, watching him with calculating glares.

"Ahem," Mephi said. "I come bearing news, Margrave. It's about King Albrecht, and… larger matters."

The Margrave's head titled back slightly, a sign that Mephi figured would have been a double-take in anybody else. He turned to the woman with whom he had been speaking.

"Summon Queen Tvarivich," he said.

Without any hesitation, the woman nodded and walked past Mephi, exiting the tent. The Margrave turned to the others.

"We shall continue our strategy later. I need scouts to find that moon path first. If it can't be found, I need Theurges to forge it."

Mephi raised his eyebrows. Getting shamans to command Lunes into making moon paths meant something was important enough to risk pissing off the mercurial moon spirits.

The Garou nodded and left the tent, whispering among themselves again.

The Margrave motioned to a wooden chair. "Please sit, Mephi. You have traveled far, I can tell."

Mephi took the offer and eased into the seat. It felt good to finally relax his leg muscles. "Thank you, Margrave. It's greatly appreciated." Beside the chair was a small table with a pitcher of water and three wooden cups. "May I?"

"Of course. Help yourself to anything you need. After you have delivered your message, I will arrange for your dinner." Konietzko sat down on a large wooden chair with a high back, set with rubies and black opals.

The tent flap opened and Queen Tamara Tvarivich entered. She wore a white cape with furred edges and a black leather jacket, pants and boots. She nodded briefly at Konietzko and stopped in front of Mephi, who began to rise. She motioned him to remain seated, then picked up a nearby chair and pulled it over, sitting down herself.

"It is very interesting that you have come at this time," she said, looking at Mephi curiously.

Mephi waited for her to continue, but she said nothing more. "Really? Why's that?"

"First, tell me about Albrecht. Is he all right?"

"Well, that's just it. Nobody knows. He still hasn't returned to the North Country Protectorate. They said his moon bridge collapsed before he arrived."

Tvarivich hissed. "I suspected as much. We could tell on our end that something happened, but we didn't know if he made it back before that. And nobody has sighted him in the Umbra?"

"No. He's MIA. The North Country asked me to see if you'd heard anything, but the Jarlsdottir was sure you hadn't. I just came from her sept."

Tvarivich, her brow furrowed, looked at Konietzko, whose own face betrayed no emotion. "I fear the worst. If

Albrecht doesn't come with reinforcements, we must go with your initial plans. They are more... fearsome."

"We do not need King Albrecht to achieve victory," Konietzko said. "His forces would allow for fewer casualties, but we will win nonetheless."

"Curse these times," Tvarivich said. She looked back at Mephi. "What do you know of the mysteries of Garou death, Silent Strider?"

"Me? Not much. Everybody is convinced that my tribe's all obsessed with death, but that's because our ancestors aren't..." Mephi paused, a sour look on his face. He seemed to be remembering something, a bitter experience. "They're not available to us. You guys can contact yours; ours are gone."

Tvarivich nodded. "Yes, I know. I am the head of the Ivory Priesthood. We seek to learn the secret of death, the mystery of overcoming it, as learned by the First Wolf, the Silver Fang who rescued Gaia from death."

"Yeah, I've heard that legend. Funny how every tribe claims the first wolf." Mephi held up his hands in a truce gesture as Tvarivich frowned. "I admit, your tribe's probably got the best claim. No contest there. But why ask me about this stuff? It's somewhat of a sore subject at the moment."

"You are the only Silent Strider in the encampment. I was curious if you had felt the door open."

"Door?"

"A door into the path the ancestors travel between death and recovery in the ancestral realms. A secret path, one no living Garou has yet traveled. My order has sworn to walk upon this path and return to tell of it."

Mephi looked at Tvarivich, as is if sizing her up. "Are you sure that's wise? If no Garou goes there except in death, maybe that's what Gaia wants."

"Like everything else since the First Dawn, Gaia's purposes with death have been perverted. Our order seeks to restore them."

"Now? You've got nearly your entire sept outside, living in tents, waiting for a big battle. This doesn't sound like the time to go adventuring down paths no Garou was meant to know."

Tvarivich sighed and looked down. "Yes, and that vexes me. Why has this door been opened *now*? I sensed it and have divined that it is open, but it is far from here. I fear I shall never know the answer to the one mystery I have always sought. But such is our fate. Mine is the battle. So be it."

Mephi looked at Konietzko as she said this and saw him nod slightly, as if glad to hear where the queen's allegiances lay.

"Look," Mephi said, turning back to Tvarivich. "You've got something my tribe doesn't: connection with your ancestors. Some of us would give anything for that. Believe me. But Gaia comes first. Why do you need to go looking for something you already have?"

Tvarivich frowned, but didn't seem insulted. "Not all our dead return as ancestors. There are many mysteries to be uncovered. What if their spirits are trapped, as perhaps your ancestors are? How would we know it unless we seek out these mysteries?"

"I had the chance to break our tribe's curse," Mephi said. "Wepauwet, a powerful spirit, claimed to have discovered the way. I refused it. Why? Because of this." Mephi gestured to the tent around him. "It's coming. Now is not the time to pursue personal quests. We've got to put all that aside. For Gaia's sake."

Mephi stood up and faced Konietzko. "I didn't just come with news about Albrecht. I came to tell you about my vision, the reason I turned my back on our ancestors."

Konietzko leaned forward, fascinated. His silence was clearly a cue for Mephi to continue.

"Phoenix took me up in her claws. I saw what is to come, the horrors that are even now beginning. The Red Eye. The Apocalypse."

Konietzko's eyes became thin slits. "And what did Phoenix show you of our fate?"

"It hasn't been written yet. I saw the world die because no Garou fought for it. If we fight, we can change that."

Konietzko stood, nodding. "So I am right. Our army shall decide the outcome of our long war."

Tvarivich stood up and faced Konietzko. "So we march upon the Scar then? Without Albrecht?"

"I see no other strategic option," Konietzko said. "Their army gathers there and grows stronger by the day. The latest scouting party to return claims they number over five hundred already, while we are but three hundred strong. We cannot wait for them to destroy caerns with an attack. They will not expect us to march on their own demesne. The surprise will be ours."

Mephi felt a chill pass up his spine. The Scar. A terrible realm of utter corruption in the Umbra. Not only was it a long march from here, it was one of the most hellish places imaginable. The enemy would be strongest there. Even surprise might not gain them much. He understood now why the Margrave wanted moon paths, to deliver the army to the Scar without alerting its forces.

"Then we should not wait any longer," Tvarivich said. "I go to prepare my forces. Will you call a general muster?"

"Yes. All the troops shall gather onto the field by first moon. There we shall address them, you and I together."

Tvarivich turned and left the tent with only a slight nod toward Mephi.

Konietzko walked to the table with the map. Without looking at Mephi, he spoke. "My steward shall provide you quarters. You will need to rest. Another long journey begins tomorrow evening."

Mephi bowed but wasn't sure the Margrave saw it. He picked up his staff and left the tent.

• • •

Mephi sat upon a rock outcropping above the field, along the mountains that bordered it. He looked down on the teeming masses of Garou gathered there, lined up into units by pack, sept and tribe. The Margrave and Queen Tvarivich stood on another outcropping to his right, far enough away that all the eyes below were directed away from Mephi, something he was glad for. He didn't want three hundred pairs of eyes on him.

He munched on a leg of lamb and swigged a flask of beer. He'd been starving ever since he'd arrived earlier, but hadn't let himself admit it until his work was done. Now, he caught up by chowing down on as much meat as the camp cared to provide. After the muster, he'd crash out on a bunk the Shadow Lords gave him, in a tent with some of the Dawntreader's Children of Gaia.

The Dawntreader himself was here, leading those of his sept who chose to fight, which was more than Mephi had figured would come. Most Children of Gaia were pacifists, willing to fight defensive battles but rarely committing to all-out war. Not because they were cowards, but because they believed the Wyrm fed on such slaughter.

The Margrave's steward stepped forward and howled, a deep, resonant sound that quieted everyone on the field below. Mephi was impressed; the guy had some serious pipes. No wonder he was Konietzko's favored tale-singer.

The Margrave stepped forward now and surveyed the crowd, nodding satisfactorily, a gesture Mephi could tell was a better morale booster than any speech he could give.

"Tomorrow night we march," Konietzko said. The crowd responded with a hundred growls and grunts. "We face an army great in size, greater than our own. But they shall lose. We shall be victorious. Why?" He waited, as if seeking an answer from below. Before one could come, he spoke again. "Because we are Garou. Let them have ten for every one of us; they shall still lose."

A massive cheer broke out, nearly deafening. The Margrave waited for it to die down before speaking again.

"Our destination is the Scar. Our trail is by moon path. Each unit has at least one Theurge to keep the path, so that none shall fall behind. My marshals shall brief each unit and make clear every Garou's role. He who refuses to follow can leave tonight. If he is still here tomorrow and still refuses to heed, he shall answer to my jaws."

Another cheer broke out, this more scattered, taken up only by Shadow Lords, Get of Fenris and a few other hotheads.

The Margrave stepped aside as Queen Tvarivich stepped forward.

"I shall lead the first wave," she said. "The Silver Fangs shall draw first blood."

A new cheer erupted, this one louder than the last, although many of those who cheered before stayed silent. Mephi shook his head. The usual divisions between the tribes were apparent even here. It was a pity. The Margrave and Tvarivich had done a surprising job of coordinating their efforts so far, better than Mephi would ever have given them credit for. And for the Margrave to give the Fangs the first charge—unheard of among most Shadow Lords! That, more than anything else Mephi had seen yet, was a clear sign that the Margrave was a true leader. No group could possibly decide the battle from a first charge, not against these odds. They would gain much glory, but the victory would be decided by the Margrave, leading for the long haul.

Mephi stood up and worked his way back down the mountain toward his tent. He meant to hit the sack and get some sleep before the crowds blocked the lanes and the inevitable final dominance challenges began.

● ● ●

The march was a long one. The Margrave's marshals estimated it would take them five days to get to the Scar, using the moon path route they had devised, adopting existing paths and using fetish-bound Lunes to create new ones as needed. Supposedly, their circuitous route would keep the enemy from knowing they were coming. That didn't stop them from having a number of sorties on the way.

Various Wyrm creatures were on the prowl, coming far deeper into the Gaian realms than Mephi had seen before. Most of them were surprised to find a giant army of Garou there; these ones didn't last long or cause any significant casualties. Others fled upon seeing them, which caused a worse problem. The Margrave had already designated a number of packs as hunters sent to chase these runaways down before they could alert the Scar army, but it took them a long time to make their way back to the army and so further divided their forces.

Following the Margrave's request, Mephi acted as a messenger up and down the line, delivering the marshals' orders to certain units as needed. It gave him something to do during the march and kept him moving. He didn't like to get too cozy with any one pack or unit in particular. That always made it harder to leave when the time came for him to roam again. He, like many in his tribe, was a loner, something the other tribes thought of as indescribably sad. Nonetheless, they respected his tribe's skills as unequaled heralds.

At the end of the fifth day, they called a halt and camped in a glade realm that was almost too small to accommodate them. This would be the last chance for rest before reaching the Scar tomorrow. They were lucky to have the glade, uncorrupted despite its proximity to the Wyrm realm. Mephi wondered if its appearance was the doing of Tvarivich and the Margrave's shamans. There were some powerful shamans in the army, and he wouldn't put it past them to find the one pure place in a landscape otherwise abandoned by Gaian spirits.

He had no trouble sleeping; he rarely did. One thing that his tribe learned well was to take rest where and when they could, for they never knew when the next chance would come. He didn't envy the restless warriors, too eager for the fight to sleep deeply.

Upon waking, Mephi felt a pang of wistful regret. The glade could well be the last respite he saw, should he be slain in the fight. His place wasn't to go charging in, but it would be dangerous enough for all of them; nobody's claws would remain unstained.

The army moved out, leaving the glade behind, watching as the landscape became more and more twisted, rotting and reeking with raw corruption. The moon was gibbous, waxing toward full. A full moon would have been a great boon to the Ahroun warriors, but it couldn't be helped. At least the Galliard tale-spinners like Mephi had their moon; the stories told would be good ones.

The Margrave called a halt when the moon reached its highest peak in the Umbral sky. The moon path curved ahead, entering a bank of roiling fog. The boundary of the Scar. Past this point, the enemy would surely sight them. They rearranged their ranks, sending the scouts to the rear and the Silver Fangs to the fore, and waited for the Margrave's signal. Every single Garou wore the battle form.

He silently raised his arm and then brought it down. The army charged forward without a single howl, intent on the silent hunt, meaning to take down as many of their enemy as they could before the alarm was raised.

Mephi was with the scouts in the rear and could not see the charge hit the enemy, but he heard the howls of victory as it did. Terrible wails and screeches reverberated back to his ears, the screams of the enemy. In the far distance, a series of warbling howls announced the presence of Black Spiral Dancers.

The battle was on.

In a surprisingly short amount of time, Mephi and the rear column advanced into the boundaries of the Scar. Dead fomori, scrags, psychomachiae and Black Spiral Dancers lay in all directions. Strange hoots and calls rang out from all sides as more of the Scar's army responded to the attack. Unsettling shapes moved in the mists close to Mephi and the rear guard, coming closer.

A snorting roar broke out behind him. Mephi spun in time to see a herd of corrupted boar-like creatures charging at him, their skulls stripped of skin, revealing bone, tendons and huge, lidless eyes.

Mephi called upon a secret a jackrabbit spirit had taught him and leaped into the air, vaulting over the herd and landing well behind it. The herd scattered, seeking new targets. Mephi ran at them from behind and slashed at their hindquarters before they realized he was there. Two pigs went down squealing but three spun around and rushed at Mephi, too quick for him to leap again.

Tusks tore into his right leg and nearly knocked him over, but he slashed down at them, severing one pig's head from its body and cracking the ribs of another. Before the final one could charge again, Mephi clubbed it with his staff, breaking its neck.

He limped forward, leaning on his staff, surveying the field. Fellow Garou were mopping up what remained of the herd. The landscape was a blasted, blighted ground, dotted with sharp ridges, bubbling geysers and stinking pools of stagnant liquid.

As Mephi cautiously put weight on his wounded leg, he noticed the landscape changing. Nearby Garou stopped moving and stared, turning around in all directions, growling uneasily. The stagnant pools dried up, replaced by cracked and desiccated fens of dead, brown grass. The ridges flattened, creating a broad plain that stretched as far as the eye could see, sprouting with scraggly weeds.

The sky went from purplish twilight to dark, slate gray, a bank of black storm clouds growing on the horizon. There was no longer any sign of the moon path.

A Theurge shaman ran over to Mephi, looking around with an apprehensive face. "Do you realize where we are?" he asked in a hoarse whisper.

Mephi looked around again. He saw no identifying marks. "No."

"We're no longer in the Scar. This is the Battleground realm. We're on the Plain of the Apocalypse."

Mephi's mouth fell open, speechless. He tried to put words together to express what he felt, but none came. The revelation was too chilling—and perfectly in line with the vision Phoenix had shown him. He looked around. Others had also realized what he had and were reacting with worry or exultation. "I've got to see the Margrave," Mephi said.

He concentrated, trying to remember what the cheetah had taught him. He strapped his staff to his back and dropped to all fours, running with a great burst of speed, even with one leg injured. He shot past Garou warriors who stood in the blood of their slain enemies, staring about in curiosity, and aimed for the Margrave's command unit, which was wreathed with the toughest Ahroun guards. They recognized him and let him pass. He slowed as he approached the Margrave, who listened to the hurried reports of his marshals. He turned to look at Mephi, holding up a hand to silence the talking marshal.

"The Plain of the Apocalypse!" Mephi said.

Margrave's eyes became slits. "So I was right," he said, looking at his marshal.

The marshal looked at Mephi. "How can this be? We were at the Scar for sure. There's no mistake!"

"It's in the prophecy!" Mephi said. "The last battle will be fought on the Plain of the Apocalypse, in the Battleground. *This* is it. The last battle."

"No," the Margrave said, "It is our final *victory*, where we defeat our enemy for good."

The line of Ahroun guards broke to admit Queen Tvarivich and a number of her Silver Fangs. She had a nasty scar running down her shoulder to her stomach; if it pained her, she showed no sign of it. "Is it true?" she said. "Is this the field of Apocalypse?"

The Margrave nodded. "Where are they?"

Tvarivich pointed across the plain to a line of moving figures on the far horizon. "There. They're on the march. We had them in our claws, damn it! They just disappeared, and then here we were. And now they're back, fully prepared for us."

Mephi looked at the approaching army, stretched in a line across the horizon. They far outnumbered the Garou. He couldn't clearly see their composition but he made out an unreal mixture of different shapes and forms: fomori and banes of many types, led by hooting Black Spiral Dancers.

Chapter Fifteen:
The Plain of the Apocalypse

"Form up! Position Stormcrow!" the Margrave Konietzko yelled, leaping onto a rock where the Garou army could see him. He gestured with his klaive toward the approaching Wyrm forces. "They march! We will meet them with all lines in place! Form up!"

The marshals ran throughout the ranks barking orders to pack leaders, who commanded their packmates to take their places according to battle plans laid out days before. Position Stormcrow meant that two wings would spread in lines to either side of the central command group, with the fiercest warriors along its front edge and shamans behind them ready to unleash a storm of fetish-bound spirits. The wings would then spread, "flapping" outward as the warriors advanced on their spirit-beset foes.

The Garou hurried to take their places, jostling one another to get through. The Margrave's Shadow Lords waded into the fray, pushing Garou here and there, ensuring that each got to his assigned position.

Mephi limped toward the leftmost wing. Konietzko looked down at him from the rock. "No, herald. I need you here," the Margrave said. "You must bear my commands to Tvarivich once we have been separated."

Mephi nodded, glad to be given an important role. Dangerous, certainly, but also weighty, a worthy honor. He headed to join the Margrave's personal pack, the beak of the Stormcrow. Tvarivich's Silver Fangs formed the Stormcrow's talons, ready to lash forward and advance deep before pulling back again to strengthen the line against reprisals.

He could see details among the approaching army now. It was like a casting call from the Garou's worst enemies list: fomori of innumerable breeds, including ferectoi; bitter rages, banes that fed on Garou anger; hideous crab-like dratossi; carapaced ooralath hounds; Wyrm elementals, most of them balefire furmlings that were essentially floating pieces of napalm; psychomachiae, with their diverse collection of blades, scalpels and fangs; and scrags, spirits of murder, resembling a host of psycho killers and more bestial creatures. Mephi couldn't make out other shapes and figured they were among the many unique creatures the Wyrm birthed in realms beyond human and Garou ken.

Behind them, leading them with howls of anger and threats, marched the Black Spiral Dancers. They wore their battle forms, marked by hideous deformities—bat wings, ears and snouts, or mismatched limbs from different animals. Their ululating cries sent a shiver through Mephi. They seemed supremely confident, more so than usual even for these insane werewolves.

Mephi looked at Konietzko. The Margrave stood tall and severe, unmoved by the warbles and gesticulations of the oncoming army. Mephi felt a wave of pride melt away his trembling and knew that, whatever the outcome, it would be noble. The Margrave had that effect on others. Mephi knew that some of his aura of confidence was due to his Shadow Lord spirit gifts, but most of it came from the Margrave himself. He was a supreme elder of the Garou; it was impossible not to be impressed just by looking at him.

Tvarivich stepped beside the Margrave and pointed out a figure in the rear ranks of the Wyrm army. "Do you see him? That is Charvas Yurkin. He was once a Get of Fenris from Moscow. He served the Hag. We thought him killed."

"He commands the army," the Margrave said, nodding as he assessed the distant figure. "He is perhaps more powerful than when you last knew him."

Tvarivich spat. "He will still fall beneath by mace."

"Do not get so eager yet. He is deep in their ranks. We can't risk a sortie that far. Not yet."

"I will hold my rage for him," Tvarivich said, spinning around to meet up with her Silver Fangs. "But he will succumb sooner than you think."

The Margrave did not reply. Mephi watched his eyes dart across the enemy line, sizing them up, hatching adjustments to his own battle plan. The Margrave leaned over and spoke to a marshal, who immediately ran into the right wing and exchanged the positioning of ten Garou, re-dispersing them throughout the line. The Margrave nodded, pleased. Mephi tried to scan the enemy line to figure out which foes the Margrave had adjusted their forces to meet, but it was all a jumbled confusion of screaming monstrosities to him.

The Wyrm forces were less than a hundred yards away. The Garou stood still, waiting, ready to move or receive the charge based on the Margrave's orders. Konietzko nodded to a group of Shadow Lords near him and they spread their arms, howling. Their cry echoed across the sky. Storm clouds instantly gathered overhead, opening to disgorge a torrent of rain upon the Wyrm army. Lightning forked down to pierce seven fomori, electrocuting them on the spot. Their bodies dropped, trampled by the onrushing forces.

Five furmling banes, the floating masses of glowing balefire, writhed and tried to hide beneath the nearby soldiers, burning them as they did so. The rain battered at their shapeless forms, eroding them, washing pieces away into the mud. A panicked mass of fomori broke from the line, burned by the furmlings' attempt to seek shelter, running back towards the rear. The Black Spiral Dancers howled and leaped forward, their jaws snapping at the deserters, forcing them back into the line. Two of them refused and were cut down by claws.

The corrupt army slowed, unsure now. The Black Spiral Dancers waded into the lines, barking and slashing at the hesitant Wyrm creatures, forcing them to move again.

Konietzko looked off to his left, catching the eye of a commander there, and nodded. The commander howled to his pack and the air shimmered before them. A shape took form, large and horned and astride a great horse, followed by smaller shapes, white with red-glowing eyes. The horseman vaulted across the field toward the Wyrm forces, a huge pack of slavering hounds following in his wake.

Mephi stared with wide eyes. He had never seen the Wild Hunt before. The most accomplished among the Fianna could summon that chaotic force and unleash it on their foes. The hunt tore into the line of Wyrm creatures, the huntsman slashing with his huge spear and the dogs tearing at flesh with their sharp teeth.

A large swatch of creatures went down, startled by the spiritual force's sudden charge. A horde of other beasts moved in to fill the line, falling with fury upon the hunters, tearing the dogs limb from limb and unhorsing the huntsman, who was soon lost beneath a mountain of creatures clamoring to destroy him.

While the enemy was distracted with that ploy, the Margrave unleashed another. From the Stormcrow's right wing a grand howl went forth, answered by loud growls coming from the sky. Mephi saw ghostly wolves forming there, running down to join a charge led by the Get of Fenris. The fabled Hordes of Valhalla, answering the call of their totem kin.

The horde of Garou and spirit wolves hit the line of Wyrm creatures like a tank driving through a crumbling wall. Many creatures fell before the onslaught but others recovered quickly and moved in.

The Black Spiral Dancers rushed forth, three packs responding to the Garou's rash attack. They slashed and gnashed at the Fenrir, grappling and slipping in the sloshing mud beneath the torrential downpour. The Valhallan spirit horde spread deep into the enemy lines, breaking their formation and causing chaos, but the wolves were soon cut down. The Get could advance no further, but the Black Spirals could not push them back.

The Margrave nodded, once more, unleashing the Stormcrow's talons. Tvarivich's Silver Fangs leaped forward, smashing into what remained of the enemy's center, tearing down banes and fomori like grass before a lawnmower. Blood and ichor sprayed across the field, mixing with the falling rain to stain the pure white fur of the Fangs. The ground became a muddy mound of mangled bodies.

The Black Spirals whistled and hooted, giving a preset command, and the Wyrm army drew back, its broken left line falling back to form a box with its still intact right line. The Fangs and the Fenrir tore into the stragglers, decimating them.

Konietzko howled, his roar echoing across the field, causing even those creatures who had not yet fought to shiver. Tvarivich cursed but heeded the command, calling her warriors back. They retreated, slipping back into the Garou line, resheathing the Stormcrow's talons. The Fenrir likewise retreated, although with greater reluctance, forming again within the right wing.

Mephi tried to count the losses. Seven Fenrir dead with eleven badly wounded. Three Silver Fang dead with nine wounded, none severely. An incredible accomplishment, given that the Wyrm fallen had to number nearly a hundred. The Wild Hunt and the Valhallan horde were gone, but they were merely spirit manifestations; they could not be destroyed permanently.

Mephi almost held out hope for a quick battle, but he sobered as he watched the Wyrm forces reestablish themselves. The Garou were still outnumbered three-to-one at least, assuming the Wyrm-spawn had no tricks up their sleeves, such as spirits of their own to summon. Mephi hoped that their summoning had already taken place, that this army was the extent of their forces.

Mephi's balance wavered for a moment, and he leaned on his staff to center himself. He looked around and saw other Garou suffering similar problems. Some had fallen. Their comrades helped them to rise only to risk toppling themselves as a second massive tremor shook the ground. Mephi felt his stomach lurch, not just from the tremor but the awareness of what was coming.

The ground to his left burst open. Garou fell into the gaping hole. Some scrambled to maintain purchase on the fast eroding edge while others leaped free of the collapsed earth. Screams came from the pit and a gray, warty tentacle whipped up and out, thrashing the Garou as they tried to climb up from the crumbling lip.

Mephi cursed and looked to Konietzko. The Margrave's anger clearly simmered in his eyes but he was otherwise expressionless. He growled and swept his hand at a group of Garou in the right wing, and they charged toward the hole. The Margrave howled again and Tvarivich's forces once more vaulted forward, crashing against the Wyrm force's sudden advance. The Black Spiral Dancers had timed their charge to take advantage of the ground's collapse.

Mephi crept as near as he dared to the hole and peeked in. As he feared, the massive open maw of a thunderwyrm clamped shut, trapping fallen Garou in its throat. They must have lost nearly twenty Garou. He leaped forward and grabbed onto those still struggling, helping them escape the pit.

The dispatched contingent surrounded the circle and began to growl, each tearing a fetish from a vine around their necks. Their lack of other accoutrement told Mephi their identity: Red Talons, the feral tribe, all of them wolf-born. They released their fetishes simultaneously, accompanied by a buckling of the earth.

The ground swelled up, sealing the pit. Before it closed completely, Mephi could see a horde of rocky earth elementals battering at the thunderwyrm's snout, beating it back down the hole and cracking open its hide.

"Mephi!" Konietzko cried. Mephi snapped his head toward the Margrave and ran to him. Konietzko pointed out across the field, where the Silver Fangs were fighting against the Wyrm advance. "Get Tvarivich back here! She can't hear my howls!"

Without hesitation, Mephi dropped to all fours and ran across the field into the fray. *Finally, something to do!*

He weaved under combatants, barely dodging the blows of tentacles, pincers and knives, his speed boosted by spirit powers. He skidded up short to avoid barreling into an Ooralath hound but failed to completely avoid its jaws. Teeth clamped onto his tail and he yelped as he shot forward, the beast's fangs tearing a piece of his tail off. *If that's the best meal they get out of me, I'm doing good.*

He leaped across a mound of fallen scrags and landed behind Tvarivich, who spun around and glanced at him before turning again and focusing on the Black Spiral Dancer leader, who clearly saw the queen and worked to move his personal guard toward her, itching for a fight.

"Tvarivich!" Mephi yelled. "The Margrave commands you to withdraw!"

Tvarivich shot an angry look at him. "No! I will kill Yurkin! Once he falls, their forces will splinter!"

"The Margrave has other plans!" Mephi said, reaching out his hand to grasp Tvarivich's shoulder. She spun around and clubbed him with her mace. He reeled and fell, his jaw rattling. Tvarivich stood over him, breathing heavily, rage smoldering in her eyes. She hefted the mace and hesitated, trying to control her fury. She threw back her head and howled, the call to withdraw.

Silver Fangs ran over to form up around her and Mephi and then worked their way back, parrying the blows of the Black Spiral Dancers and fomori who beset them. Mephi limped next to Tvarivich, who fumed, staring back at Yurkin, who sneered at her from afar.

Mephi clutched his jaw, which had barely missed being dislocated. He knew, however, that as mighty as her blow had been, she'd still held back most of her strength. He was lucky to be alive.

As they melted back into the Garou line of defense, the Wyrm forces stopped short of engaging the full line. Tvarivich grasped Mephi's shoulder.

"I apologize, herald," she said, brows furrowed. "My urge for vengeance overcame my senses."

"Hey," Mephi said, wincing as he worked his jaw. "We all know the cost of rage. No need to explain."

Tvarivich gave him a crooked smile. "You are a bold soul, Faster-Than-Death. Return to the Margrave and seek his next orders."

Mephi nodded and limped back to the center amid Konietzko's pack. He scanned the line, trying to catch up on what had happened while he was fetching Tvarivich. He groaned in dismay as he noticed the left wing. It was folded back, tightened for defense after withstanding a charge against the line, weakened after the thunderwyrm's assault.

The Margrave seemed unconcerned. He ordered the entire formation to retreat slowly. When the Black Spiral Dancers saw this, they cheered and pushed their forces forward, sending a ragged, uneven charge against the Garou. They hit the Stormcrow and the wings parted to admit them. Fomori, scrags and psychomachiae charged exultantly through the line of defense, spreading out amid the scattering Garou ranks.

The Margrave howled and the trap was sprung. The Theurges held up their fetishes—black crow eggs—and smashed them on the ground. Smoke billowed forth, engulfing the attackers. Mephi heard a cacophony of cawing and screaming and saw the edges of the smoke shimmer with the shapes of wings and beaks. The real stormcrows were free.

The Wyrm forces tried to retreat, running in all directions. Dark clouds of smoky crows clung to their heads, pecking at their eyes and tearing their scalps with sharp, ephemeral claws. The Ahroun moved in, tightening ranks once more to prevent the creatures' escape, and began mowing them down in droves.

A snarling growl rang out across the field. Mephi shot his glance back at the Margrave in time to see him charge forth, his Shadow Lord guard tearing into the Black Spiral Dancer packs that had come too close, overconfident of victory.

The Shadow Lords hacked at the deformed werewolves, who fell like saplings before machetes. The Dancers, beset by a force more powerful and disciplined than they, resorted to their favored tactic. One by one, the deranged wolves howled and screamed, all vestiges of their sanity burnt away by the raw power of rage. The warriors went berserk, their rage overcoming all reason, becoming mindless, brutal monsters.

Against any other foe it would have been terrible. But the Shadow Lords, masters of manipulation and under-handed rule, had long ago learned the trick of turning such mad fury to their own ends.

The Margrave halted and gestured to his guard, who called on their storm lore and directed the berserk fury of the Black Spiral Dancers against their own tribe mates. Lost in frenzy, the Dancers had no idea that they now tore into one another. Each exulted in the raw sensory thrill of the kill, believing themselves to be tearing their enemy limb from limb, when in reality they eviscerated their brothers and sisters.

The Shadow Lords held back, waiting for the foes to deci-mate themselves. The Margrave howled again and unleashed Tvarivich's forces. The Silver Fangs shot forth, heading around the snarling, gnashing gang of Dancers caught in their own rage and drove into the next line of banes and fomori.

The Margrave howled again and the Stormcrow forma-tion broke, becoming the Raging Storm. Packs separated and shot off across the field, engaging the enemy in small units, spread out and impossible to focus against with any significant force. All the battle lines were down; now it was a grand melee.

Mephi kept close to the Shadow Lords, within earshot of the Margrave. Charvas Yurkin, the Wyrm army's general, veered away from Tvarivich's forces and aimed now for the Margrave. His elite guard had remained sane; they did not resort to rage, recognizing it for the suicidal move it often proved to be. Yurkin clearly understood now who the true leader of the Gaian forces was and directed his guard to intercept Konietzko.

The Margrave smiled and Mephi knew he had been expecting this. He had expertly maneuvered the enemy into this moment, this personal fight. The two forces moved slowly across the battlefield, drawing closer to one another. The berserk Dancers were nearly all dead, only a few of them still fighting. The Margrave ignored them. One of the other Gaian tribes would finish off what was left.

Mephi peered through the battlefield. Tvarivich was far off, still driving into the enemy, oblivious to the Margrave's coup. She wouldn't be happy to have revenge stolen from her.

The rain fell lightly now, more of a faint mist, although certain areas of the field still suffered stronger downpours. The eye of the storm seemed to follow the Margrave.

Yurkin halted fifty yards away, gathering his guard around him. He chortled and drew a large piece of slate from a leather pouch. Mephi squinted and saw that it wasn't slate—it was some kind of scale from a huge creature. Yurkin whipped his hand back and flung the scale forward. It spun through the air like a giant Frisbee and clattered against the breast of one of the Margrave's guards. It exploded as soon as it touched him—not with a conventional bomb blast but something far more terrible.

A rent in reality gaped there, growing huge within seconds. It drew all features of the landscape toward it with incredible force, like a blown-out airplane window at high altitude pressure. Garou, dirt, dead bodies and even the storm itself were sucked into it.

Mephi dug his staff into the ground and held tight, feeling the tug of sideways gravity as it attempted to draw him into the hole. Within moments, the tugging stopped and a huge, barbed shape appeared where the hole had been, a massive insect squeezing forth from its nest. Mephi moaned and scrambled backward, searching around desperately for the Margrave.

Bill Bridges

The nexus crawler stepped forward, its armored head pivoting on its long neck. The air shimmered around it and transformed into a poisonous cloud.

The Margrave howled in anger, yelling for all troops to retreat and re-form.

Yurkin's laugh rang out across the battlefield and he howled for his troops to charge. His own guard surged forward, rushing toward the retreating Margrave.

The nexus crawler, seemingly blind and responding only to sound, shot its giant pincers out, spearing two of the Black Spiral Dancers as they rushed past. As it gestured, the air warped around it, sending out waves that washed over the rest of the Black Spiral Dancers. As each wave hit them, they screamed and transformed, their flesh-and-blood bodies becoming malformed clay, the mud of another reality entirely.

Yurkin howled in anger and retreated before the waves of warping reality could touch him.

Mephi joined the Shadow Lords, staring at the nexus crawler. It was the biggest Mephi had ever seen—the biggest he had ever even heard of in myth. The sheer range of its reality-warping power was tremendous—nothing could get near it without succumbing.

The Margrave growled at his guards and they pressed back further, while he, along among the Garou, stepped forward, heading for the nexus crawler, klaive drawn.

"Is he nuts?!" Mephi yelled. "Stop him!"

The Shadow Lords ignored Mephi and pulled him back with them in case he was foolish enough to follow the Margrave.

As Konietzko approached the outer waves of the thing's power, he pulled a medallion from beneath his armored breast, yanking it from its chain. He kissed it and cried out to the winds. Mephi made out the word "Grandfather," but nothing else.

The storm clouds concentrated above the Margrave, pooling into a single, thick mass. It descended from the sky and wreathed Konietzko, hiding him from sight behind the roiling, lightning-filled cloud. The storm mass moved forward, past the waves of improbability, marching toward the nexus crawler.

The beast sensed its coming and stepped forward, pincers flailing, seeking prey. The storm leaped towards it, engulfing the nexus crawler. A terrible screech rang out. Beneath its grating tone, Mephi could hear a deep-throated howl.

Mephi peered into the cloud, seeking some sign of the Margrave, but saw only lightning and blackness. A sharp pain in his right shoulder brought him back to full awareness of his immediate surroundings. He threw up his staff in time to block the second blow of the clawed fomori. He twirled the staff around and smacked the creature on its neck, knocking it over. Then he snapped down with his jaws, crushing its skull.

The Shadow Lords around him fought the new wave of fomori, slashing and biting in all directions. Many of the Lords had already fallen.

Mephi glanced around the battlefield and his heart lurched. A roaring line of reinforcements spilled across the field, slamming into the Garou packs and driving them down or back.

The ground shook and Mephi looked again at the cloud. It was tattered now, pieces missing. The Margrave hung from the nexus crawler's neck, his klaive buried in the thing's breast. His right leg was gone, speared on the creature's pincer.

Konietzko reached up into the thing's jaws and yanked its tongue out. It screeched in pain and slashed at him, opening up a vicious wound in his back. The Margrave shoved his arm into the mouth and the thing spasmed, trying desperately to throw the Garou off. Konietzko drove his arm deeper, using his other arm to prevent the jaws from closing completely. He howled, summoning a burst of strength, and yanked his hand back, dragging a piece of brain clutched in his claws.

The nexus crawler imploded. The shockwave of slamming air deafened Mephi and most everyone else on the battlefield. The crawler was gone, its manifestation withdrawn. The Margrave's body lay on the battlefield, unmoving.

Mephi shot forward, arriving at the Margrave's side within seconds, before Konietzko's own guard had made it half the distance. He bent down and saw Konietzko's chest rise and fall weakly. The Margrave's eyes fluttered open.

"It is over for me," he said. "My wounds can never heal."

"No!" Mephi said. "Healers are on the way now."

Konietzko shook his head. "Nothing can heal what that thing did."

Mephi sucked in his breath as he saw the wound Konietzko indicated. There was a large hole where his guts should have been. It was impossible that he had even stayed alive this long.

Tvarivich thumped down next to Konietzko, panting from her long run across the field. She stared in horror at the wound.

Konietzko smiled. "You must lead in my place. Finish this." His eyes closed and his breath stopped.

Tvarivich hid her eyes beneath her arm, sobbing. A howl of anguish erupted around them as the Shadow Lords cried for their lost lord.

Tvarivich stood, staring across the field at the approaching forces. The Garou were terribly outnumbered. She snarled a command at her Silver Fangs, their numbers much fewer than before. They rushed over to surround her and Mephi, prepared to throw back any attack.

Tvarivich grabbed Mephi by the shoulder and yanked him up him, staring into his eyes. "You must leave," she said. "Go to Albrecht. Tell him what happened here. He's the last line of defense."

Mephi broke from her grip and glared fiercely at her. "Hell, no! This isn't done yet! I can't sing of a victory I didn't witness!"

Tvarivich stepped forward and shook him. "Fool! There's no victory here! We're all going to die! But we will die fighting, taking every last one of them down with us. You, however, will not be here. I need a herald to warn Albrecht, to tell him what happened, and you're the only one capable!"

Mephi, astonished by her icy anger, stepped back, shaking his head. "I *can't* leave—none of us can. The rules of this place—it won't let any of us out until we've won or lost."

Tvarivich nodded impatiently. "You can't leave by moon path or bridge, no. That is why you must follow the Margrave." She advanced menacingly toward Mephi.

"You're going to kill me?" Mephi said, refusing to back away, standing tall. "I'm a Silent Strider, damn it! None of my kind comes back to tell the tale!"

"Kill you?" Tvarivich said, startled. She stopped and stooped on her knees, pulling a vial from her pouch. "You can't warn Albrecht if you're dead. I need you to *follow* the dead."

Mephi shook his head and spread his arms out. "What the hell are you talking about?"

"The doorway into the paths of the dead," Tvarivich said as she uncorked the vial. A dim light escaped from within, shimmering. "It is still open. The spirits of our slain walk through it. I cannot see it or them, but I sense this. And you," she said, looking straight into Mephi's eyes, "have a connection to this door, even if you cannot sense it."

Mephi bent down next to Tvarivich. "What is that stuff?"

"Water from the Pool of Sorrows, the tears of our ancestors. Come closer." Mephi bent forward and Tvarivich wiped the shimmering liquid over his forehead. He shut his eyes and she rubbed his lids with the wetness. As she did, she muttered an invocation under her breath. "Part the mists, ferryman, reveal the river. In Charon's name, let it be so."

Mephi opened his eyes and blinked. His jaw dropped open in astonishment as he scanned the field. Shadowy figures stood beside the bodies of the fallen, guiding the shades of the dead Garou to rise and step through portals of dark mist. Mephi recognized the figures immediately. They turned to watch him with curiosity.

"You… you're real," he said, rising, gripping his staff.

The nearest figure approached him, leaving the Margrave's body. He wore the Crinos battle form, with a long, thin snout and tall, upraised ears. An Egyptian head-dress, golden armbands and a shepherd's staff, curved into a crook along the top, were his only accoutrements.

"How… how did you get here?" Mephi whispered.

"Mephi Faster-Than-Death," the Silent Strider said, "You are my scion. My loins birthed your kin long ago, in lands far from your own."

Mephi looked down at Tvarivich, who looked back at him with an inquisitive look on her face. He realized that she couldn't see the other Silent Strider; only he could.

"How can this be?" Mephi said. "My ancestors are gone."

"Gone?" the Strider said, cocking its head. "No. Unseen, but never gone. Our duty is to the dead, and so we are never seen by the living. Until now."

"Why now? Why me?" Mephi gripped his staff tighter.

"The door has been opened by the ancestors' decree. Only three times before has this happened; the fourth will be the last. The door cannot close until one among the living has made his choice. The Ivory Priestess's power—secrets stolen from the dead—has opened your eyes to us. This is forbidden. And yet… I sense that you might still serve the ancestors' purpose."

"How? Who is this 'one among the living'?"

"Come," the Strider said. "The dead depart and we must guide them." The Strider walked slowly back toward the misty portal over the Margrave's body, waiting for Mephi.

Mephi looked back at Tvarivich and clutched his staff tighter when he saw her swinging her mace at a Black Spiral Dancer. The Wyrm army had broken through and he had not heard them. He felt a cold shudder shoot up his spine as he saw a Black Spiral Dancer step *through* him from behind, oblivious to Mephi's presence. Mephi was intangible.

"You have already taken the first step," the Strider said. "Now finish the journey."

Mephi walked to the portal, tears welling up in his eyes as he watched Silver Fangs fall beneath the tide of Wyrm forces. Tvarivich had pummeled her way through and now traded blows with Yurkin. Mephi paused, waiting to see the outcome. The Strider's hand reached forth from the portal and pulled him into complete darkness.

Chapter Sixteen:
Empty Caern

"Hold, boy!" Loba yelled. "We must stop to rest." She bent down on the moon path, unhitching her backpack.

Martin, a few yards ahead, shook his fists. "Again? But I'm not tired!"

"I am," Loba snarled. Martin hung his head sheepishly and walked back to sit beside her. "It's not far now. Don't worry, we'll be there soon. But if we are attacked again, I need to have all my strength."

Martin furrowed his brow, staring at the wound on Loba's left arm. The claw marks had not yet healed and occasionally burst open again, causing Loba more blood loss.

"I'm sorry, Aunt Loba," Martin said. "I wasn't quick enough."

"Not you. Me." Loba sighed, wincing as she examined the wound again. "I let the bane get too close."

"Yeah, but that's because I poked my head where I shouldn't have." Martin pouted, his chin resting on his hands.

"Enough recriminations. What's done is done. We'll have to outrun them next time, as we have with the rest of them." Loba reached into her pack and pulled out the water flask, taking a tiny sip from its nozzle. She offered it to Martin, who shook his head and kept sulking.

Loba looked around, searching for signs of any other predators. The Umbra had been insanely crowded on the first leg of their journey, with both ally spirits and enemy banes roaming seemingly at random. A few had decided to snack on them. Most of these she beat into submission easily enough, but one had gotten its claws into her, literally. Since then, she'd run from future encounters. She couldn't risk Martin getting hurt.

The boy had performed incredibly well so far, with strength and skill she had not possessed at his age. His rage, however, still proved a problem. He had lost control of it twice and chased off after the banes, causing Loba to hunt him down and hold him still until he grew calm. That hadn't been easy; he was quite the firecracker.

The moon path curved on ahead through featureless terrain. They were far from any known realms here, except— she hoped—the one they sought: the Aetherial Realm where the star spirits dwelt. She had come here twice before, once with Antonine Teardrop and once by herself. The paths had changed somewhat—no surprise there—but it was proving to be a far longer journey than she remembered.

"If the entryway isn't beyond the next bend," she said, "we'll have to turn back and find a different route."

Martin sighed. "I thought you knew the way."

"The way sometimes changes." Loba stood up, shouldering her pack. "All right. Let's go."

Martin hopped up and skipped down the path, an endless reservoir of energy. Loba didn't know where he got it from.

As they rounded the bend, stars began to appear in the sky, faint and distant, seen through a haze. Loba breathed a sigh of relief. "Not far now. Follow Vegarda."

"Who?" Martin said, scrunching his brow.

"Vegarda, Incarna of the North Star," Loba said, pointing at a shard of brightness in the dark. "She's the brightest one in the sky. Although she's not very bright right now…" Loba had never seen such a haze before. She scanned the sky, trying to count the stars. They were so few. She halted as she noticed a large red glow near the horizon. The Red Star. It was closer than she had ever seen it.

The moon path gradually rose in height, rising into the sky and passing through clouds that smelled of rain. It led toward a tall, silver tower.

"What's that?" Martin said, pointing to the tower.

"Our destination. The spirit-orrery of the Sept of the Stars." Loba breathed a sigh of relief. *Almost there.*

As they broke through the cloud layer, Loba looked down over the realm. She gasped and halted, grabbing Martin.

"What is it?" Martin said, worried.

"This can't be…" Loba whispered. Broken shards of moon bridges jutted into the sky, some leaning precariously, ready to collapse. Moon bridges were supposed to last only as long as a single journey. These had become calcified husks, broken and crumbling at the foot of the realm. Unheard of. "Hurry," she said, pressing Martin forward.

They rushed up the moon path to the front door of the tower. It hung open.

Loba stopped and listened, gesturing to Martin to be silent. She heard nothing from within. She crept forward, peering into the doorway. No sign of movement. She stepped through.

The bottom floor foyer was empty. A wrought iron stairway spiraled upwards, stopping at each level of the tower. The very top, the observatory, could be seen from below. The stars winked brighter through its massive domed lens.

"Come on," she said to Martin and began climbing the stairs. She stopped at every level, listening, but no sound greeted her. When they reached the top, she leaped onto the dais and scanned around the tower, across the starscape, which was magnified through the tower-top view.

A group of people walked down a moon path far off in the distance. Loba peered closer and spoke to the walls of the orrery. "Farther." The spirit in the lens responded and magnified her view, bringing the party into close-up.

A robed man led the group of five, each wearing loose tunics or robes. They talked among themselves; Loba could not read their lips. She cursed.

"They're leaving," she said. "Abandoning the place."

"Why? Are they afraid of me?"

As soon as Martin spoke, a woman among the distant group stopped and perked up her ears, which transformed into the furred ears of a wolf. She turned toward the tower, listening.

"Call to them!" Loba cried.

"Hey!" Martin yelled. "We're here! Please don't leave!"

The woman, her eyes closed, spoke. The others halted, turning to look back at the tower. The leader stepped forward, as if he could see Loba and Martin, and motioned to them, summoning them down the path.

"Come on," Loba said. "They'll wait for us!" She and Martin ran down the flight of stairs. They rushed to the far side of the tower and saw the beginning of the moon path. As soon as they stepped upon it, it seemed to draw them closer to the distant party. With but a few strides, they arrived.

"Loba Carcassone," the leader said, bowing politely.

"Altair," Loba said, also bowing. "Where are you going?"

"Where only we can go. It is what we have prepared for all this time."

"I don't understand," Loba said. "I need your help. Martin needs your help. He must have his Rite of Passage. He must find out who he is. Where is Sirius Darkstar?"

The blind woman stepped forward, reaching for Martin. He took her hand and she smiled. "You have done wonders with him, Loba. I no longer get the visions. Perhaps they were wrong after all…"

"Not all of them, Moon-Sister," Loba said, smiling. "He'll live up to the good prophecies."

"Perhaps," she said, ruffling the boy's hair. He wiggled free, annoyed, but said nothing.

"Altair," another woman said, stepping up and touching the old man's elbow. "We should not tarry. The time draws near."

Altair nodded. "I respect your mission, Carcassone, but we cannot help. The stars call to us. Prophecies spoken long ago now unfold."

"The other Garou will try to kill Martin," Loba said, snarling. Martin looked at her, worried. "He must know his destiny."

"That is unclear to us," Altair said, a sorrowful expression on his face. "Since the boy was born to Garou parents, his lack of deformity has sparked many prophecies. He is thought to be both Destroyer and Messiah. None can say which, although perhaps the lord of Uranus knows. Ruatma claimed to possess special prophecies about the boy. He once spoke of him as the Shadow Queen, although Martin is male. Omens are more things of dream, where we are truly metamorphic, where even our sexes can change. But Ruatma is distracted now. Greater matters impinge."

"What's going on?" Loba said. "The moon bridges. The desolation. Where is everybody?"

"The spirits have already departed, joining their broods," Moon-Sister said. "The Red Star grows brighter. Its time is nigh, its power ready to be unleashed."

"Even death walks abroad, calling to the living," Altair said. "My sept must join the Planetary Incarna to fight this baleful eye. You cannot be a part of this battle."

"Why not?" Loba said, stepping forward with palms out, pleading. "Maybe this is why glimpses of Martin's destiny are seen here and nowhere else. Maybe he belongs in this fight."

Altair shook his head. "He cannot travel the star paths. His essence would not deliver him to those subtle realms. We have spent decades perfecting our own so that we might reach the outer roads. His destiny remains on earth."

A black man stepped forward. "Evan Heals-the-Past has gathered an army in the North. They fight a Talon of the Wyrm."

Altair frowned. "Canopus, we cannot reveal these things."

Canopus shot a glare at the old man. "It's way too late to worry about propriety with the spirits, Altair." He turned back to Loba. "I think you should take the boy there."

Loba shook her head. "I know about that, but it's too dangerous for Martin."

"Dangerous?" Canopus said, eyes wide. "You march the boy all the way here, *alone*, and don't call that dangerous? Of course the fight is dangerous! It's never easy for Garou, Loba. You want to know the boy's destiny? All Garou destiny is revealed in a fray."

"No," Loba said, shaking her head. "They'll turn on him, blame him for their troubles. The Talon will use him."

"I want to go!" Martin said. "If Evan's there, King Albrecht will be there too!"

"Not even he can save you from a Talon!" Loba snarled.

"I want to go," Martin said, low and growling, as if gearing up for a challenge.

Moon-Sister stepped forward and put her hand on the boy's shoulder. He seemed startled and looked at her, then hung his head. "You will do what you think most fit, Loba. And you, Martin, will heed her. She has brought you farther than you can know. You must go a little while farther with her."

Martin nodded, sulking.

"Tell her," Canopus said, looking at Altair.

The old man grimaced but nodded. "Carcassone. I have long kept my counsel to myself on many matters; it is the will of the spirits. But I will reveal this: Sirius Darkstar departed many weeks ago, seeking to unravel a thread of fate woven around this boy. He has not returned. If you can find Darkstar, you might find the answer to Martin's destiny."

Loba nodded, clenching her fists. "How do I find him? Where do I start?"

Altair paused, looking at Canopus, reluctant to reveal more. When the old man stayed silent, Canopus spoke. "There is one place he might have gone. Before joining our tribe, he was born to the Uktena in New Mexico, to a sept that has suffered much tragedy. It is possible that he went to consult… an old septmate."

Altair frowned and shook his head. "Speak no further. That way lies only evil."

Loba growled. "Tell me. I don't care where it leads. I *must* take Martin to Sirius."

Canopus closed his eyes, seeming to pray, and then spoke. "I fear he has gone to consult White-Eye-ikthya, the prophet of the Wyrm."

Loba hissed. Altair lowered his head in shame. "Do not go, Loba. I fear that Darkstar is lost to us."

Loba shook with frustration, eyes tightly shut, cursing her fate. When she opened her eyes again to look upon the Stargazers, they were mirrors of cold resolve. "We go to New Mexico. If Sirius is in trouble, we will aid him. If he is lost to us, we will kill him."

Canopus nodded, watching her with sorrow. "Then follow this path as it forks to the left. It is the way Sirius took when last we saw him."

Loba nodded, wrapping her arm around Martin. He stood unmoving, worry creasing his brow. "Thank you. I'm sorry for my impatience. I've waited so long…."

Moon-Sister stepped forward and hugged Loba. "We know. Do not think that the totems are unaware of your sacrifices." She released Loba and turned to walk down the path.

Altair nodded and followed her, as did the others. They walked down the moon path, taking the right fork where the path split, rising into the vastness of space.

Loba grasped Martin's hand tightly. "Come. We follow the left fork."

Martin nodded, still silent, and followed Loba down the moon path without complaint.

• • •

The giant bonfire threw manic shadows across the mesa. The Uktena Garou danced around the fire, calling to spirits, gathering an army on the other side of the Gauntlet. The gatekeeper, an old Navajo woman, chanted an ancient song in the Garou tongue. It told of a pathway through the Umbra to the North, to where Little Brother lived. It was a prayer for permission from the spirits that guarded the path to allow Older Brother to walk it once more, to reunite with Little Brother.

Loba perked up her ears, motioning for Martin to listen. They hid behind a rock outcropping in the New Mexico desert, close enough to watch and listen but just outside the bawn, where the warders did not search. The Uktena were so involved in their war party preparations, they no longer seemed to care about caern defense. Loba felt a pang of fear as she realized that they were abandoning their caern.

As they watched, the Garou shifted across the barrier between worlds, disappearing in small groups until only the gatekeeper remained. She fell silent and sat still for a while in the quiet desert, and then she too stepped sideways and departed.

Loba stood up and walked into the empty caern. Martin cautiously followed her. Ever since they had met with the Sept of the Stars, he had been quiet and calm, as if his rage had been quelled by their worry.

"This is unbelievable," Loba said, looking around the camp, lit by the still burning bonfire. "All this way and no sign of Sirius."

"I'm sorry, Aunt Loba," Martin said, anguish in his voice.

Loba turned to him. "There is nothing to be sorry for. They were small-minded and ignorant."

"But if I hadn't come, they would have talked to you and answered your questions about Sirius, instead of attacking us." Martin kicked a rock into the fire. "I'm no good."

"Not true!" Loba growled. "People have spread lies about you out of spite. The Uktena believed them rather than the evidence of their senses or my own pledge of honor. Besides, we interrupted some sort of burial rite. We must have broken a spirit taboo of some sort."

Martin said nothing. He sat down and stared into the fire, with his elbows on his knees and his chin in his palms.

They had camped out alone in the desert for two days, avoiding the Uktena patrols that had searched for them. Only the fact that the Uktena were distracted by their departure preparations allowed them to avoid the hunters in their native home. The strange burial rites they had held for the dead elder—rites Loba and Martin had interrupted while the old Garou's body was consumed by weirdly colored flames— seemed to be the last duty the Uktena owed the caern.

Loba caught a faint scent on the mild breeze, almost hidden by the burning smells from the fire. She stalked to the nearby cave that marked the entry to the caern's center. A shape lay in the cave, unmoving. It appeared to be a wolf.

Loba moved slowly forward, sniffing and peering at the figure. He smelled of blood and disease, but not the rot of death. He still lived. She growled a challenge and saw the shape start as if awakened from sleep. The wolf whined and crawled forward, revealing massive wounds up and down his body.

Loba choked back a sob and leaped to his side, clutching him to keep his horrendous wounds from opening as he moved. "Sirius!"

Sirius Darkstar coughed up blood, trying to speak. "Loba... Wh... White-Eye... he *knew*."

"White-Eye is evil!" Loba said, sobbing. "Why, Sirius? Why did you come to him?"

Sirius shook his head weakly. "No. White-Eye Uktena. Always Uktena. Died with honor. Killed thunderwyrm." He coughed up blood. "I tried to fight. Too many wounds. I forbid them wait for me. Knew you'd come. White-Eye knew the shadow...."

Sirius's eyes darted across the clearing and stopped when he saw Martin. Loba looked back at the boy and frowned. Martin stood stock still, as if frozen by fear, staring at Sirius with a strange expression. She looked back down at Sirius.

"What happened?"

"*She* is in him!" Sirius growled.

Loba frowned, unsure if she understood what he had said. "Who?"

Sirius barked as a claw slashed out at his throat. Arterial blood sprayed over Loba; she barely noticed. She was already in battle form, spinning to gut Sirius's attacker. She froze before her claw could strike, horrified.

Martin stood directly before her, panting in battle form, Sirius's blood dripping from his claw.

Sirius croaked something low and weak. "The Shadow Queen…"

Loba stared at Martin. His face was wracked with conflicting emotions, worry and anger fighting for dominance. Anger won. He stepped back, smiling, baring his teeth and raising his claws.

Loba hunched over, growling. "Who are you?"

Martin laughed, but it was not his voice. It sounded more feminine, older. "I'm the very thing you have always fought."

"You're a bane!" Loba said, advancing. Martin took a step back from her. "Get out of that boy's body or I'll tear you out!"

"He and I are one. His parents were damned—puppets of the Seventh Generation, your worst enemy. His body is the culmination of generations of treachery. It is my host."

Loba's body began to fade, shifting into the Umbra, from where she could attack the possessing spirit. Martin growled and parted the Gauntlet like a curtain, arriving in the spirit world just as Loba stepped through.

She stared in surprise at him. Martin had never exhibited such spiritual control before. She scanned him, seeking signs of the spirit that inhabited him but saw none. She growled again.

"You won't find me. I'm coiled too deep. As I said, the boy and I are one. I was entwined with him before he left the womb. *I* am the reason for his purity. I shaped his body to perfection, hiding the hole in his soul where I sleep."

"Martin!" Loba yelled. "Listen to me! You've got to resist her! Throw her off!"

Martin laughed, an old woman's cackle. "He can't hear you. When I'm awake, he sleeps. When he is awake, I watch. Your open heart took him in and saved him from those Garou who suspected the truth about me. Ironic, no?"

"I'll kill him if I have to," Loba said, approaching Martin slowly, hunched over. "To get to you."

Martin frowned, snarling. "The boy has one gift I did not give him. A legacy from his Garou genes. They'll be your death!" Martin howled and leaped forward, his claws slicing through Loba's left arm, severing it completely. His speed astonished her.

Loba screamed in rage. Her raw fury at the sudden wound battered at her resolve, trying to take over. She clutched the severed stump and leaped back, gritting her teeth, using the focus of the pain to block out the rage.

Martin was clearly completely out of control, consumed by his own prodigious fury. She couldn't afford to succumb.

Martin sniffed her out and charged again, moving faster than she thought possible. She barely ducked out of the way, slashing him as he went past.

He wheeled and fell upon her, his rear claws tearing away at her thighs, his front claws digging into her shoulders.

Loba cried out in pain and shut her eyes, concentrating, focusing her falcon lore. She opened her eyes and spoke in a deep voice: "Be still."

Martin immediately let her go and stood slack jawed, watching her warily but moving no further.

She limped away, leaving a trail of blood. She needed a Theurge, someone expert in controlling spirits. If the Shadow Queen had spoken truly, it might not be possible to extricate her from Martin. They might both have to die to save Martin's spirit.

She squinted at a sudden red glare. The Red Star broke through the Penumbral clouds, painting the desert red. As its light hit Martin, he broke from Loba's spell and leaped forward again, a claw slicing open her throat with one clean swipe.

Loba stumbled and fell, breathing heavily, her strength gone. She howled in pain.

Martin hesitated, blinking, watching her clutch her throat, trying to stem the tide of blood. His eyes softened and he dropped to his knees.

"Aunt Loba!" Martin cried in his own voice. "What happened? Don't die!"

Loba stared in surprise at the boy as she collapsed, unable to sit any longer. Her blood flooded out of her and into the Umbral clay.

Martin rushed forward and cradled her, rocking. "No! Sirius! You did this to her!"

Loba shook her head, trying to deny his accusation, trying to speak. Only air came out. Her eyes fluttered and closed. Her body went limp.

"Nooo!" Martin cried, leaping up and running around the clearing, trying to catch some scent of the foe that had killed her. He smelled only Loba and himself. Sirius was subtle, able to hide his scent.

He hunted in ever widening circles. Frustrated, he stepped over the Gauntlet and hunted in the physical world, this time catching Sirius's trail, which led him into the cave. The wolf lay dead.

Martin sat down, confused. If Sirius was dead, who killed him? The same being that had killed Loba?

He broke down crying, great howling sobs that echoed from the cave and across the desert. There was no one to hear them.

• • •

Martin patted down the grave dirt with a shovel he had found in the cave. He bowed his head, praying for Aunt

Loba's spirit. He dropped the shovel and walked away, toward the fire pit.

He shifted to wolf form and stepped sideways. There, stretching away to the North, was the moon path the Navajo woman had sung about. It had not yet faded. He began to run, heading North to join King Albrecht's army.

Chapter Seventeen:
The Cage

Antonine Teardrop padded silently on all fours, walking beside but not upon the green-glowing path. He couldn't risk Zhyzhak seeing his silhouette. The Black Spiral Dancer was well ahead of him on the path; she had been increasingly wary and cautious after her encounter with the Eighth Circle's warden. Antonine had to fall back farther behind her, even though he risked losing her at times.

The mists that billowed around him, passing between him and Zhyzhak, might have thrown him off her track, causing him to take one of the many false paths branching away from the main trail. But Antonine knew his tribe's special lore, taught to them by the spirits of the wind. It allowed him to see through impeding substances and illusions, to perceive something as it truly was. Mists, fogs and even darkness were no barrier for his far sight.

He had watched as Zhyzhak stopped now and then, catching her breath and resting. The march was taking its toll on her. Few had ever gotten this far and only two were said to have passed the test of the next circle, although Antonine believed that they had in fact failed it.

Zhyzhak looked around now and then, screaming at the void. It took Antonine a while to realize that she was interacting with shapes or sounds that he couldn't see, things that were not truly there. The Labyrinth's tricks were beginning to work on her.

Antonine knew with a sense of dread that he now existed beyond the boundaries of space and time. He and Zhyzhak walked a realm of ancient, primordial power, one lacking any literal form or substance—everything here was pure metaphor. Zhyzhak saw shapes and heard sounds because she expected to see and hear them. She could not imagine a place without such substances, a place of pure abstraction.

Even Antonine, schooled for decades in the mystical training of his tribe, had trouble interpreting this place's reality. It shifted randomly—or at least, it seemed to be random. He wondered what the Wyrm would actually look like when—*if*—he actually encountered it. Would he be able to perceive it as it was, a force of nature so powerful as to be nigh unimaginable? What did the very concept of entropy look like, anyway?

Antonine frowned as he padded on, keeping sight of Zhyzhak ahead. The Wyrm would be cloaked in imagery, of course, not because it wore such a substance of itself but because limited, mortal beings such as he and Zhyzhak could not perceive it any other way. His own mind would paint it with shape and substance, a mind desperately trying to encompass a power beyond conception.

He wondered: Would Zhyzhak see the same Wyrm that he did? They were both Garou, beings of matter and spirit, born of Gaia. Would this racial tie cause them to share a consensual illusion when encountering the Wyrm? It would be interesting to see.

Antonine halted, dropping to the ground. Zhyzhak's loud yelling echoed through the mist. He peered past the shifting clouds to see her crack her whip. Something stood in her way and she seemed prepared to attack it.

• • •

"Get the hell out of my way!" Zhyzhak yelled.

The hydra before her did not move. Its nine snakeheads floated in the air, sinuously curving around one another, examining Zhyzhak from all angles. It sat on its haunches, large muscular legs armored in golden scales. Its wings unfurled lazily, stretching and then folding again.

Zhyzhak raised her whip.

"We are the Warden of the Ninth Circle," the nine heads said, their combined sibilance hissing across the empty landscape.

Zhyzhak adjusted her blow before it landed, cracking her whip to the side, missing the leftmost snakehead by a bare inch. She stepped forward, examining the creature. "So?"

"This is the Circle of Deceit," the hydra said. "You must betray the Wyrm's truest servant."

"It's not me!" Zhyzhak cried. "Ha! Point him out! He dies!"

The snakeheads all turned to look at a portal in the mist revealing the blasted, fiery landscape of Malfeas. At its center, upon a throne on a high tower, sat a large, heavily muscled Black Spiral Dancer, his fur carved from head to toe with blasphemous pictograms. His eyes darted from side to side, watching all that took place in the duchies below.

"The general of Malfeas," the hydra said, its heads watching the portal. "The only being to pass our test who still lives."

"Him?" Zhyzhak said. "I kill him, then rule Malfeas?"

"Exactly," the hydra said, all eyes watching the general. He sniffed the air suspiciously and turned around in his chair, looking for something. He seemed to sense that he was being watched. "He fears you. He knows someone will usurp him eventually. He is weak. If you strike now, you can take him."

Zhyzhak howled and cracked her whip. Instead of reaching through the portal, it slashed across the snakeheads' necks, severing six of them. Blood hosed out of the six stumps.

The hydra stumbled and its three remaining heads spun to stare aghast at Zhyzhak.

The Black Spiral Dancer stepped forward, howling with laughter. She looped her whip around the frantically moving necks and tugged tightly, yanking them together into a single bunch, trapped by the barbed strands of the whip.

"Circle of Deceit, idiot!" Zhyzhak yelled. "That means *you* die!" She yanked the whip again, like pulling the cord on a lawnmower or boat engine, and the three heads fell from their stumps.

The hydra's body hit the ground and dissolved. Its blood spread out in a widening pool. Wherever it touched the path, the glowing balefire dimmed and went out, extinguished. The mists dissolved, taking the portal into Malfeas with them.

Zhyzhak stood on a dark, empty plain, all signs of the Labyrinth gone. Only a single feature appeared before her: a grimy manhole cover on the ground where the hydra's body had been.

Zhyzhak stepped forward and reached down, slipping her claws through the tiny holes. She yanked the iron disk up and threw it aside. Its clang reverberated across the emptiness. A flickering orange light escaped from the hole, suggesting fires burning somewhere below.

Zhyzhak crawled down the rungs into the sewer hole.

● ● ●

Antonine let out his breath. He'd held it for nearly five minutes, trying desperately not to draw attention to himself. As soon as the Labyrinth shut down and the mists disappeared, he feared that Zhyzhak would see him, even crouched as low as he was. But she hadn't bothered to turn around and look behind her.

He stood slowly, cautiously, watching as her shadow disappeared and the full stream of light spilled from the sewer hole.

He padded forward, disappointed. He had hoped the test would be subtler, more convincing. Most of the others who'd made it this far had fallen for it. The challenge was to kill a manifestation or great servant of the Wyrm. Victory meant taking that being's place, with all the power and privileges that came with it.

But that was the trap. Worldly power. It was cheaply given and cheaply won. The victor, who had fought so hard to reach this last, final test, would easily succumb to its lure, little realizing that the true power still lay beyond. Or that was the theory. Antonine knew that no true Garou elder would have fallen for the hydra's ruse. Perhaps the Wyrm was now so desperate for help that its banes could no longer pose a convincing challenge.

Zhyzhak had properly turned her deceit against the warden and so won through to the Wyrm's lair. But did she realize that the challenge was not over yet? The only true deceit worthy of the Ninth Circle was to betray the Wyrm itself.

Antonine had to get to the Wyrm before she did. Zhyzhak had broken the rules by using the fixed Red Star to guide her path. She had arrived with some measure of her sanity—her own will and purpose—intact. If she had succumbed to rage by now, she might very well free the Wyrm and return the balance. This was the deep irony of the Black Spiral Labyrinth's true purpose: not to corrupt but to free, to systematically drive any aspirant mad so that only instinct prevailed when meeting the Wyrm—an instinct for rage and destruction.

Zhyzhak would not attempt to free the Wyrm. She would try to destroy it, mistaking it for yet another test. She would act not from instinct but from deliberate cruelty and desire for power. Its freed manifestation would be formed from her hate and lust. She would control its march of destruction; under her insane will, it would not serve Balance, but Corruption.

Antonine reached the open sewer hole and peered down. Rungs led into a large tunnel flowing with water and muck. Antonine shifted into battle form and climbed down the ladder.

If he could beat her to the Wyrm, he might be able to free it, allowing it to resume its natural role as the Balance between Order and Chaos. It was the goal his tribe had always sought. In the lore of the Stargazers, the Wyrm was not monster but victim, trapped in the Weaver's cocoon of twisted logic—the very concept of the selfish, limited Ego given form. As with everything at this level of reality, forms were merely metaphors made manifest. Spider webs were symbols for the convoluted, entrapping processes of Ego consciousness, which had long ago choked the natural, instinctual order. If the instinct, the universe's Id, could be freed from the suffocating dictates of a super-ego gone mad, the Balance would return and a new world would rise from the ashes of the old.

Heresy, of course, to the rest of the Gaian tribes. Antonine himself felt the gnawing of doubt as he climbed down into the sewer. What if his tribe was wrong? What if the Wyrm really was a horrid beast whose unleashing could only spell a final doom for Gaia? He shook his head. Even the other tribes acknowledged that the Wyrm was once a force of Balance, that its role had been perverted. What once was could be so again. He had to believe that. The only other option was unremitting, unending fighting, life versus death. There had to be a way to transcend such opposites.

As he reached the last rung, Antonine dropped the rest of the distance into the tunnel. It stretched in two directions until it dead-ended in T-intersections. The slimy water flowing past his knees felt warm and clinging.

He sniffed the air, seeking sign of Zhyzhak's scent. The odor of the muck overwhelmed any other smell. He looked around for footprints but the water covered any sign of them. She could have gone left or right, and from there down one of four directions.

Antonine focused, willing his eyes to pierce the illusion around him. He knew it was false, an image conjured by the Labyrinth. He sought to perceive the true Labyrinth beneath. The sewer walls faded away, replaced by twisted and knotted whorls of spider silk, ancient and rotting.

He looked carefully and saw a single silver line running through the threads, following a convoluted path back and forth and around other threads. The legendary Silver Spiral that led to the heart of the Weaver's cocoon, slipped into the tapestry by Gaian spirits as the Weaver frantically wove her web. The Great Spider failed to notice the single thread and wove it like any other into her work. It would now lead Antonine straight to the Spider's ancient prey, the insect caught in her trap—the Wyrm.

Zhyzhak, blind to the thread, lost in the illusion of the sewer tunnel, might take a series of wrong turns and become delayed, giving Antonine his one chance. He thanked Gaia for her bounty and headed to the left and then right, following the faint gleam of silver hidden in the pale, yellowing tapestry that surrounded him.

● ● ●

Zhyzhak roared in frustration, banging her fist against the slime-drenched stone wall. She had not counted on this. Her fetish no longer worked; the Red Star could not be seen. She had no idea where to go. The passages led to more passages that led to still more passages. She doubted she could even find her way back to the manhole again.

She stopped and wracked her brain. Mental gymnastics were not her forte. She had risen to power through strength and unremitting savagery. She relied on her thralls to figure out the details. She could really use Slatescrape-ikthya now; he'd be able to puzzle out this maze.

A distant, faint clanging sound reached her ears. She cocked her head in its direction and listened. Nothing.

She broke into a run, tearing through the corridor toward the source of the noise. She didn't know what had made the sound, but it was her only clue. She paused at another intersection, listening for a repeat of the clanging.

There—to the left, another clang, this time closer. She vaulted down the tunnel, turning as it bent to the right, and skidded to a halt as the tunnel ended in a hundred-foot drop.

The tunnel mouth opened out before her into a vast room where multiple tunnels met, heading in directions that seemed unnatural, the perspective all wrong. For a brief moment, it looked as if webs covered the room. Zhyzhak shut her eyes and shook her head to clear it. Her brain began to hurt. She opened her eyes again slowly and peered down into the cavernous chamber.

Hundreds of drains emptied liquid sludge into the center. It pooled on the floor before whirling down an unseen drain.

Another clang rang out, this one loud and just below. Her eyes shot to its source: a towering, rusted, slime-strewn gate with six huge bolts holding it shut. It looked designed to admit a giant. A figure moved down there, struggling with all its might to open one of the bolts. Three bolts were already undone.

Zhyzhak squinted at the figure and finally made him out. She gaped incredulously at it. A Gaian Garou. A cursed, stinking, goddamned Gaian Garou—*here*, in her Labyrinth. She growled, her rumbling consternation traveling across the room and down to the ears of the Garou.

The Garou's head snapped up. He looked straight at her, a scowl on his face, and then redoubled his efforts to move the fourth bolt.

Zhyzhak screamed and leaped from the tunnel mouth, falling toward the Garou. He easily sidestepped away from her. She careened into the gate and bounced off it, splashing into the sludge, stunned. She had never hit anything so hard in her life. The gate seemed to be made not of rusted metal, but of *hardness* itself.

She shook her head and snarled, rising and advancing on the Garou.

He looked over his shoulder at her and blinked. She could tell he had called upon some wretched spirit gift, a power the spirits taught to his kind. Zhyzhak put on a burst of speed and snatched the Garou's neck, yanking it down and throttling it.

Except she only grasped air.

Her empty claws clutched nothing. She looked back up and saw the Garou continuing to push away the fourth bolt. It slid open with a reverberating clang.

Zhyzhak screamed and leaped at the Garou again. He evaded her grip once more; her claws again slashed through empty air. He climbed the open bolts to reach the higher ones.

Now she had him. Perched high up as he was, he had no room to maneuver. She carefully climbed up behind him and snatched his ankle, tugging him free. Again, she grabbed empty space. The Garou was not where she had thought he was.

Zhyzhak pounded the gate in anger but pulled back as her fists throbbed in agony. The hardness of the gate again. What the hell did it hold? What possible force was it designed to bar?

Zhyzhak froze, realization dawning. The Wyrm. Her lord and master waited beyond that gate. She had but to open it and…

That made no sense. If the Garou was trying to open the gate, that couldn't be good for her or the Wyrm. Did it have a weapon she couldn't see? Some fetish with which to destroy the Wyrm?

He couldn't be allowed to continue, but she couldn't get hold of him to stop him. Maybe words would delay him.

"Garou!" she cried, still clinging to the gate, below his climbing figure. "What the hell are you doing?"

He didn't respond. How dare he ignore her!

"Listen to me, scum!"

He paused, looking down at her, a frown on his lupine face.

"Why?!" she yelled. "Why are you here? Why do you open the gate?"

He watched her silently, seeming to measure whether he should speak or not. He made his decision. "I followed you here, Zhyzhak. Your trail was obvious."

"Impossible! No Gaian can walk the Labyrinth without taint!"

"You destroyed the Labyrinth behind you as you went," he said, shaking his head, surprised at her ignorance. "It had no power over me."

Zhyzhak growled, angry at herself for her lack of awareness. "How long?"

"I caught up with you around the Fifth Circle. I've shadowed you ever since."

"Why? You think you can destroy the Wyrm?" Zhyzhak couldn't help barking out a laugh as she said this.

"Free it." The Garou turned away from her and began to climb again, reaching for the fifth bolt.

Zhyzhak stared at him, confused. Why would he try to free it? What sort of trick was this? She wracked her violent brain but saw no solution. She had won the Ninth Circle, hadn't she? By slaying its warden, she had won the right to abase herself before the Wyrm and beg a boon.

Or had she? It was the Circle of Deceit after all. Perhaps she was the deceived. Maybe this Gaian was just another trick of the place, designed to confuse her. If it sought to free the thing behind the gate, then surely her goal was to destroy that thing.

Yes! The thing behind the gate was the answer. It was the true manifestation of the circle's test, not the warden. If she killed it, she would win.

She peered between the bars, looking into the deep gloom beyond for some glimpse of the creature. There, in the muck, chained to the far wall, was a coiled snake. It appeared to sleep, although parts of its body jerked and thrashed as if it experienced a nightmare. The thing was thin and weak, obviously starved. The chains held it tight and chafed its scales. It sat on a bed of its own dead skin, shed over a period of years.

She smiled wickedly and opened her mouth, heaving her stomach in and out, stoking the bellows that the Green Dragon totem had given her when she first pledged fealty to it. She coughed forth a stream of green flame. It shot across the length of the cell and into the snake, who awoke instantly, screaming and writhing, its chains rattling as it tried to escape the blistering fire.

Something heavy crashed into Zhyzhak, knocking her from the gate. She plummeted into the water and smashed into the floor, her submerged mouth gulping in a gout of sludge.

The Garou straddled her, his claws flaying her hide. Only her leather fetish saved her, armored with spirit powers. As he tore the last of the leather aside, ready to drive his hand into her chest, she rolled over, throwing him off.

She understood now: As long as he didn't attack her, she couldn't touch him. But he had broken his own spell by hitting her.

She leaped up from the water, surfacing in time to see the Garou climbing again for the bolt. She leaped again, slamming into him before he could get halfway up. She grabbed him by the neck and squeezed, using all her strength to crush his windpipe. He gagged, weakening. Instead of struggling to fight her grip, his eyes roved up and down her body, searching for something. Zhyzhak laughed at the ridiculousness of it.

The Garou reached out a single finger and pressed it into her rib. She spasmed, releasing him and flapping backwards, her limbs out of control. The pain overwhelmed her for a moment and she almost lost awareness, her rage rising to respond to the threat. She snarled and resisted the urge, realizing that this foe was no normal Garou.

She looked up and saw the Garou just as the fifth bolt clanged open.

She spat into her palm and summoned her power, transforming the spit into a glowing ball of balefire. She flung it at the Garou and hit him between the shoulder blades. He howled in agony and fell, splashing into the water.

Before he could recover, she coughed again, sending a gout of flame in his direction. It burned his fur and he rolled in the sludge, trying to extinguish the fire.

She unwrapped her whip from around her waist and snapped it at him, its barbs biting deep. He was weak— cunning, perhaps, but no match for her strength. He surprisingly dodged her next blow but came too close to her in doing so. She lashed out with her claws and tore away a piece of his thigh.

He limped away, breathing heavily, cringing from the pain all over his body. He glared at her and began to speak. Before he could get out a single word, she snapped her whip again. It slashed open his forehead and he collapsed. His labored breathing echoed throughout the room but he had stopped moving, his eyes closed.

She stepped up to him, ready to end it with a raised claw, when the furious clanking of chains from the cell distracted her. She turned to peer into the cell and saw the snake slipping from its bonds. She howled in anger and ran to the gate.

She snarled, calling upon a simple power taught to Black Spiral Dancer cubs. She poked her head through the gate and kept pushing, squeezing her body through the small opening. Her bones melted to allow her egress, reforming as soon as she was free of confinement on the other side of the gate. She oozed her entire body into the room and marched over to the snake.

It writhed, dancing to avoid her. She shot a claw forward and snatched its head. Without a moment's hesitation, she bit the head off and crunched its skull to pieces, swallowing them down.

It tasted awful. She spat out a scale and picked another from between her teeth.

She walked back to the gate and squeezed her way through it again.

The fallen Garou opened his eyes weakly, watching her warily.

"Take that, fucker!" Zhyzhak barked. "I killed your friend!"

"You devoured the Devourer," he said, weakly rising on wobbling legs. "Now you will always be hungry. Not even the entire universe will satisfy you."

Zhyzhak cocked her head. "What the fuck are you—" She gagged as something thrust up from her stomach into her throat, fighting its way into her mouth. Her jaws were pried open and a massive snake's head slithered out as she uncontrollably vomited it up.

It kept coming. Yards and yards of snake, growing as it hit the water, coiling and circling the room. And still it came, bursting forth from within her, growing ever larger, sprouting wings and hundreds of arms.

It looked back at her, its eyes sparkling with malice.

A tail finally slithered from her mouth and she finished belching the beast forth. The tail grew a large fin, which traveled up the dragon's length, fanning out over its head.

Then it bowed to her, waiting her command.

Zhyzhak stared at it, stunned. Then she laughed, great roaring guffaws. She understood now. She had won. She was more powerful than the Malfean general or the Dukes of Malfeas. Her reward was power unrivaled in history. She commanded the Wyrm's supreme manifestation, the ancient dragon of destruction.

"Get me back to Malfeas!" Zhyzhak cried.

The dragon spread its wings and the ceiling burst apart. Above, the ruins of the Temple Obscura crumbled to the side, the tower cracking into pieces as it hit the ground. From the open crater, Zhyzhak squinted up into the storm-wrought sky of Malfeas.

For a bare moment, the dragon disappeared. A vast swirling vortex of energy roiled in its place. Every imaginable destructive force—fire, lightning, crushing earth and sharp ice—gathered into its single point. It drew her vision in, sucking at her sight with its awesome gravity. Then it exploded outward, spreading across and beyond the horizon.

She barely noticed a movement at the corner of her eye. She spun and saw the Garou scrambling up the wall, almost to the top already, rushing to escape. She almost let him go. If he could get through Malfeas, then let him warn his brethren about her, to tell them about her new power. But then she remembered the humiliation he'd put her through.

"Devour him!" she snarled to the Wyrm.

The dragon's snout shot out and swallowed the Garou whole in one bite. Zhyzhak began to cackle, but it became a growl as she saw the Garou's face just before he disap-

The Last Battle

peared into the dragon's maw. She snarled, confused. He had displayed no fear, none of the bowel-loosening terror she wanted him to suffer. The bastard's final insult to her was to smile and whisper a word she had barely heard. What was it? She struggled to understand the sounds. *Chimera?* One of the Gaian's cursed totems. The fool had called out to his totem at the last. Pitiful. She would eat this Chimera herself.

"Bring me my army!" she yelled.

The dragon spread its wings again and shot into the sky. It hovered just below the clouds, where every being in Malfeas could see it. It opened its huge jaws and roared.

Part Three:
The Last Days

These are the last days.
May Gaia have mercy on us.

—*The Prophecy of the Phoenix*, "The Seventh Sign"

Chapter Eighteen:
Bane Arrows

"You've got to believe me," Evan said, pacing back and forth in front of a snow bank a few yards from the center of the camp. "I saw it—a giant mist engulfing the whole area, pervading everything. The Talon is *here*. Now."

Aurak sat with his back against the snow bank. He nodded his head slowly, digesting what Evan said. He held a compress to a wound in his stomach. One of the Pentex commandoes had shot him with a silver bullet. It was nothing life-threatening, but Evan could see that it was painful. Aurak had insisted that his fellow shamans see to the wounds of the others before he would allow them to use their mystical powers on him. Their spiritual energy had limits, and he felt it was necessary that all the warriors be healed first, despite Painted Claw's insistence otherwise. The War Chief felt that Aurak was more important but had been unable to sway him.

If worst came to worst and another attack began, Aurak could call on his will to ignore the pain—a power known to the Wendigo. But he knew that would tax his mental reserves so he frugally chose to suffer the pain for now.

"Crying Bird's vision is strange," Aurak said, grimacing as he shifted his weight from one side to the other. "I have heard legends of a few heroes who walked the Path of the Milky Way, the road our ancestors take to reach Gaia after their deaths, but they are old and say very little about that road."

"I've never seen a Garou ghost before," Evan said. "It's pretty chilling. I've heard of human ghosts, though; they're supposed to be cursed, not like our ancestors. Our ancestors return to us as spirits, part of the natural cycle, *after* they've taken their place in the ancestral realms. Crying Bird and the others…." Evan shook his head, shivering. "Their spirits hadn't departed yet. They waited to show me the vision."

"They were not yet part of the ancestors' realm," Aurak said, nodding, "but they did the bidding of the ancestors. The ancestors chose you long ago—perhaps from before your birth—for a special task. I think the Heartsplinter is your task. It is your nemesis, the thing that prevents you from bringing together our tribes."

"Then why won't anybody else listen to me?" Evan said, throwing his hands up in frustration. "You're the only one who believes me about what I saw!"

Aurak nodded and looked over at the rest of the camp. Painted Claw paced by the fire, scowling, talking with his warriors. He occasionally shot an angry glance at Evan but then turned away, purposefully distracting himself with some other affair: a report from the perimeter guard or a request from a wounded warrior.

"It is the Talon," Aurak said, sighing. "It distracts them and does not allow them to hear your words."

"Why do *I* see it?" Evan said. "I expect *you* to see it— you're an elder. But I'm not that strong yet. And I'm not even a Theurge."

Aurak frowned. "But I cannot see it. I only know it by what you tell me and by the strange behavior of the others."

Evan stopped his pacing and looked at Aurak. "But… I thought you could sense its presence."

Aurak shook his head. "Sense it? No. I read the clues in our people's behavior. I suspected it was here, or at least somewhere close. Your vision only confirms my suspicions."

"Then again—why am I the only one who can see it? Is it because of the ancestors? Did they give me some power?"

Aurak shrugged his shoulders. "I do not know. You are meant to confront it. That I know. You and the Heartsplinter are connected in some way. Cries-at-Sundown knew it as soon as he heard your name. Perhaps the ancestors worked for many centuries to bring your spirit forth so that a champion would exist here and now to fight it."

Evan shook his head. "Then why didn't they warn me before now? Why spring it on me out of nowhere?"

"Sometimes, to speak of a thing is to give that thing power over you—or to alert that thing. If the Heartsplinter knew you were near, would it have come this way? Maybe it would have gone west or east instead, and caused havoc among those who could not see it and so could not fight it. Secrecy is a type of power, for us as well as the Wyrm."

Evan shut his eyes and buried his face in his hands. "I don't know what to do."

Aurak leaned forward. "Think about what you have experienced in the past: Your pack discovered the Defiler Wyrm's servants. What is the lesson the Defiler teaches? Wounds that remain untreated do not heal and become infected. It infected the spirits of many Garou."

Evan knew the Wyrm's three aspects: the brutal Beast-of-War, the ever hungry Eater-of-Souls and the secretive, supremely corrupting Defiler. "Loba Carcassone found out about the Defiler Wyrm's minions," Evan said. "The Seventh Generation cultists. Loba's a tribemate of Albrecht's. Nobody believed her but him. When he became king, he made everybody else see the truth by getting them out in the field to fight them."

"Good. It must be confronted, like the Heartsplinter. But where does it hide?"

Evan frowned. "It's not hiding. It's all over the Penumbra. But only I can see it."

Aurak shook his head. "That is not what I mean. Where has it hidden all these years? You said that the banetenders only bound its heart. That means the rest was free. Why was it not discovered?"

Evan thought for a minute. "It's called the Heartsplinter because it hides in our hearts. Not literally, though. I guess that means it masks itself with our emotions."

"And what is the strongest of those emotions?"

Evan's jaw clenched. "Rage. It hides behind our rage. That's why we can't see it. Anytime its actions might reveal it, they're misinterpreted as rage—aimless anger."

"Our rage is its camouflage. Rage is our pain at Gaia's wounds but it is also the means by which we block that pain. It keeps us from looking within. All our anger is sent outwards. We miss what is hidden inside. That is how the Defiler Wyrm gets its power. The Heartsplinter does the same."

Evan sat down, tired. "So it's using our rage against us. Probably even making it worse. Obviously, giving in to rage is out of the question; it probably has power over Garou who are lost in frenzy."

"We must think of the bane as two aspects," Aurak said, leaning back, his eyes watching the night sky. "The bane itself, one of the five Talons of the Wyrm who was bound by the banetenders—*this* is its heart. Then there is its *power*, capable of reaching far beyond itself, creeping into the hearts of Garou and enhancing their anger. It does not *possess* Garou like a normal bane does; it uses its power from afar to unleash their rage and help them bring about their own destruction."

"If it can do that when bound, what can it do *now*, when it's free?"

"It can make us destroy ourselves," Aurak said, looking back at Evan. "It has used its power to keep the tribes angry at one another, to prevent reconciliation. Your task is to achieve that reunion between lost brothers and sisters. You are its nemesis. You must each confront the other."

"How?" Evan cried, spreading his arms out. "It's a formless mist!"

"No," Aurak said, waving a finger at Evan. "It cloaks itself with mist. Somewhere within is its heart, the thing the banetenders bound. You must find that and strike there."

Evan stood up. "Then I need to go back into the Umbra. That's where I can see it." He reached over his shoulder and lifted his bow. "Will my arrows even stop it? Only three of them are bane arrows."

Aurak thought for a moment, sighing. "I think all your arrows will hurt it. You are the Healer of the Past; it is the wound. In your hands, arrows are knives with which to cut out its poison." Aurak grunted and leaned forward, gripping his staff. He then stood up, wavering unsteadily for a moment before catching his balance with the staff. "I am going with you."

Evan shook his head. "They need you here. Besides, you can't see it."

Aurak raised his eyebrows. "So? That did not stop me from figuring out more about it than you."

Evan hung his head. "Yeah. I'm really out of my league."

"No," Aurak said, smiling. "That's not what I meant. I just want you to give an old man some credit now and then. I may not be able to see it, but I can figure out its tricks. I've been around a long time, you know. Garou don't get as old as me without some cunning."

Evan smiled. "I've got to say, I'm relieved to hear it. I didn't want to do this alone."

"Do what alone?" Painted Claw said, appearing behind Evan. He had moved so silently that Evan hadn't noticed him. Aurak seemed unsurprised.

Evan turned to face him. "I've got to go into the Umbra and fight the Talon. Aurak has decided to accompany me."

Painted Claw frowned. He opened his mouth and then shut it, as if trying to think of something to say. He shook his head and crossed his arms. "I don't know what you're talking about. The scouts have not reported anything."

Evan sighed. This was the same response he'd gotten earlier. It was as if Painted Claw's brain disconnected whenever he mentioned the Talon.

Aurak stepped forward. "Evan and I are going to scout the Umbra. If we're not back before dawn, come look for our bones."

Painted Claw's eyes widened. "Bones? Don't be malicious, grandfather. Our warriors will protect you if anything comes near. If you must step over, that is your decision. But we need to break camp and move at dawn, or else the Talon will outrun us."

Aurak shrugged.

Evan didn't bother to correct Painted Claw, to remind him that the Talon was already here. He asked, "Has there been any word or sign of Mari and the Silver River Pack?"

Painted Claw looked away, scanning the dark horizon. "None yet. I am sure they are well. We cannot risk sending warriors out to follow their trail."

Evan hung his head. "I know. It's just…." Evan looked up at Painted Claw. "Well, I know you're doing your best. Thanks." He hesitated for a moment and spoke again. "If she comes back, tell her where we've gone."

Painted Claw nodded, frowning again, as if he suspected their jaunt was more than Aurak was letting on. He clearly didn't remember Evan's explanation about the Talon.

Aurak waved his hand at Painted Claw impatiently and began to walk away, leaning on his staff. Evan joined him and the two walked away from the light of the campfire.

"Hold on to me," Aurak said. "It is time."

Evan grasped Aurak's sleeve and, before he could blink, his next step landed in the Umbra, in the spiritual landscape of untrodden snow. Aurak was a powerful Theurge; his ability to part the Gauntlet outstripped even Mari's.

The green mist covered everything now, hovering in all directions around the campsite. Evan nocked an arrow.

"It's all around us," he said. "It's as high as knee level. I can barely see through it."

Aurak looked around and shook his head. "I see nothing but snow. And yet... I sense a wrongness here."

Evan scanned the ground, trying to see through the drifting waves of green fog. "In my vision, I saw something moving between the feet of the cursed Garou. It must have been the heart."

"Be careful," Aurak said. "The Talon has proven itself to be subtle. It might—" Aurak howled in pain and clutched his leg.

Evan saw a red, fleshy thing skitter away from Aurak, hidden beneath the mist layer. He drew his bow and shot at the thing before it could disappear. His arrow barely missed it, digging into the ground with a *thunk*. The mist recoiled from the arrow, leaving a blank, swirling window around it. Then the arrow faded away, as if pulled from the spirit world. Evan frowned.

Aurak groaned and fell over. Evan dropped his bow and caught him before he hit the ground. He eased the old Theurge down. Aurak's eyes were tightly shut and his hand clenched the staff tightly, muscles taught from pain.

"It bit me," he said through gritted teeth. "On the leg."

Evan examined the wound. It was a nasty tear, obviously made by a jaw with sharp teeth. The purple wound festered with poison. Evan groaned and pulled out his knife, cutting into the wound. He bent over and sucked at it, drawing the venom into his mouth and spitting it away. It burned his tongue.

Aurak's breathing grew labored. His closed eyes twitched, wracked by a fever. Evan opened Aurak's pouch and pulled out a compress. He placed it on the man's forehead and prayed to the healing spirit bound within it. The spirit awakened and spread its vigor into Aurak.

Aurak's eyes fluttered open briefly and then closed. His breathing grew steadier, but he fell unconscious.

Evan looked around. He wanted to take Aurak back to the material world, where the Talon couldn't bite him again, but he was afraid to leave. Bringing a wounded Aurak back might make Painted Claw try to prevent Evan from returning to the Umbra.

He fished in Aurak's bag. The old shaman must have a fetish that could protect him. He pulled out a stag's horn and looked carefully at the pictograms painted on it. He had made an effort to learn the pictograms that Garou used when writing down their oral lore. Luckily, these were pretty standard. The bound spirit's name was listed; that was enough information for a half-moon like Evan to use.

He summoned his power and called to the spirit, asking it to fulfill its duty. The mist around Aurak parted as a shape appeared. Four hooves dug into the snow and a snort of icy breath heralded the arrival of the stag spirit.

Evan smiled. "Watch over him. Keep the ground around him clear."

The spirit snorted again and bent its head to rub its antlers in a circle around Aurak's body. Again, the mist parted, not recoiling as before, but moving aside slowly, more annoyed than repelled. It left a blank, open area where

Aurak's body lay. The stag circled the space, tramping its hoofs hard into the snow, demarking its territory.

Evan grabbed his bow and stood up, nocking a new arrow. He set out, moving through the mist, circling the area in search of the fleshy heart. When he neared the center of where the camp would be in the material world, he saw a flash of movement. He loosed an arrow instantly. It thumped into the snow and the recoiling mist revealed a quickly vanishing creature.

It looked like a throbbing red heart, torn from the body of a large animal, its ventricles trailing behind it. Along its center Evan caught a glimpse of yellowish spikes—rows of teeth. It seemed to move along the ground through sheer force of will, tumbling across the snow without leaving a trail. Its path was erratic, as if it were limping. As if it had been wounded.

Evan pulled another arrow from his quiver and noticed that the last arrow had disappeared, gone like the first one. He tried to figure out what that meant. The sudden sound of a Garou howl startled him from thought.

Flint Knife stood a few paces away from Evan, gesticulating wildly in his battle form, teeth gnashing and head spinning, his nose sniffing the air. Evan could tell by the way he moved that he wasn't in control—he was berserk, consumed by rage. One of Evan's arrows jutted from his shoulder.

Flint Knife caught Evan's scent. He howled and charged forward. Evan broke and ran, running in a spiraling circle, trying to evade the onrushing warrior. Flint Knife halted, sniffing again, trying to relocate his quarry.

The Garou warrior's rage blinded his reasoning. Evan could evade him by slipping around and doubling back on his own steps. Flint Knife's senses seemed sharp, but he was clearly confused by Evan's maneuvers. Evan crept away, low and silent. Flint Knife howled and ran off across the tundra, away from the campsite.

As he watched him go, Evan caught the heart's movement again. He let fly another arrow. This one glanced off the heart, bringing forth a tiny spurt of blood before embedding in the ground. As the mist recoiled, the arrow disappeared.

Evan waited, fearing what might come next. Another howl broke out nearby. One of the Boar Spear's Fianna stumbled around, howling and growling, clutching Evan's arrow in his thigh. He, too, was lost to rage, hunting for any scent or sound of his attacker.

Evan crept away and kept as far from the Fianna's senses as he could. Every time he shot an arrow through the mist toward the Heartsplinter, he realized, it somehow struck a Garou in the material world. The wound drove them over the edge, igniting their rage and bringing them instinctually to the spirit world, seeking their foe. How could he strike the Talon's heart without first hitting every Garou in camp?

More howls broke out and five Wendigo Garou appeared, stepping across the Gauntlet. Evan frowned. He hadn't shot any more arrows. These Garou weren't wounded but they were frenzied, lost to rage like the others. Evan frowned. *What's going on here?*

The Garou spread out, sniffing for prey. Evan backed away, moving farther from the center of the mist. He saw a movement beneath the newcomers' feet—the heart hid among the throng. He took careful aim and shot another arrow. At the last minute, one of the Garou moved, stepping in front of the arrow. It penetrated his torso, sparking a howl of anger. The Garou vaulted toward Evan, tracing the trajectory of the arrow's flight even in his maddened state.

Evan ran to his right but slipped in the snow. The sound of his fall—even muffled by snow—alerted the enraged Garou's ears. The Wendigo landed on Evan's back, claws tearing at him.

Evan struggled to throw the Garou off him, his back-pack and quiver protecting him from the brunt of the claw damage at the cost of some of his arrows, which snapped under the powerful blows. He cried out, summoning his spirit gifts. A sudden wind slammed into the maddened Wendigo warrior, knocking him over and making him howl in pain. Evan leaped up and ran, out across the tundra, away from the mist.

The other enraged Garou heard him and homed in, charging directly at him.

He fumbled in his quiver for an intact arrow and nocked it as he ran. He twisted around and let it fly at the lead Garou, who took the arrow in his neck. The Garou tumbled over, thrashing, and yanked the arrow out. It wouldn't stop him for long. Most of Evan's arrows were normal, not designed to damage werewolves.

Evan doubled back around, trying to figure out where to go, and barely ducked away from a slashing claw. Flint Knife was back, mere inches from Evan. He must have heard Evan's footfalls.

Evan shifted to dire wolf form and barreled into him, knocking the Garou over. Without losing stride, he kept running. He needed his four legs to outpace the others, who had dropped to all fours in their less agile battle forms.

A shape darted up ahead, moving at an angle to inter-cept him. The Fianna.

Evan veered away, running perpendicular to the camp. Whatever he did, he had to make sure that none of the Garou came anywhere near Aurak. The stag spirit could only hold off enraged Garou for a short time. Some of the Garou kept running in a straight line, having failed to hear his course change, but two seemed to sense it and veered toward him.

A new Garou appeared before him, stepping over the Gauntlet, howling in frenzy. He sensed Evan's rushing presence instantly and launched into him, knocking him over.

Evan rolled and leaped on top of the Garou before it could get its superior weight on him. Jaws gnashed and claws swiped at him, tearing open wounds in his rear legs. Evan's jaw clamped on the Garou's throat and shook, spilling blood across the snow. He realized that he was chewing into Broadshanks, one of the Get of Fenris.

The fight seemed to go out of the boy and Evan released him, jumping away to avoid the rush of other Garou, who had heard the growling and teeth snapping. He felt awful when two of the Wendigo tore into Broadshanks, mistaking him for Evan in their rage-addled state, but he couldn't do anything to prevent it.

He ran.

Flint Knife appeared beside him, also in dire wolf form. His jaws clamped onto Evan's right front paw. Evan went down, howling in pain, as Flint Knife released him to move in for a better bite on his neck. Evan writhed, trying to get free, but the Garou was on top of him now, his jaws lowering.

A new howl broke out nearby, deep and angry, carrying across the tundra. Flint Knife paused, confused for a moment even in his frenzied state.

A white wolf plowed into him, knocking him away from Evan. Four more white wolves ran past, colliding with the Wendigo and Fianna. A sixth newcomer, a white-furred Garou bearing a large hammer, moved to block the enraged Garou's access to Evan.

Evan got to his feet, looking around wonderingly. Three more white-furred Garou moved to surround him, protecting him on all sides.

A new howl broke out, loud and triumphant, chilling even the frenzied Garou, who stood whimpering, unsure where to run.

Evan almost wept in relief as he recognized it. He broke from the Garou who had protectively encircled him, shifting back to human form as he ran. He threw his arms around King Albrecht's chest.

"Hey, kid," Albrecht said, smiling as he wrapped one arm around Evan, hefting his grand klaive with the other. "Didn't I tell you not to go around picking fights with more guys than you can handle?"

Chapter Nineteen:
Return to the Ancestors

Evan released Albrecht and looked at him, wide-eyed. "How did you find me?"

"Are you kidding?" Albrecht said. "With all the racket these guys are making?" Albrecht gestured at the frenzied Garou with his klaive. His Silver Fangs had chased them off to a distance and now stood in a line, ready to repel them if they charged again. The raging Garou ran in circles, confused.

"That's not what I mean!" Evan said. "You were in Russia!"

"Took a while to get back," Albrecht said with a shrug. "But we made it." The king stared at the frantic werewolves, who howled and paced in a circle, sniffing at the air. "I don't know what's going on here, but those guys should've come out of their trance by now."

"It's the Heartsplinter," Evan said, looking at the enraged Garou with a worried expression. "It's all around us. I've got to find its heart and kill it." Evan scanned the area, looking for signs of the crawling heart.

Albrecht frowned and looked quizzically at Evan. "I don't see anything. You say it's around us *now*?"

Evan nodded, groaning. "Only I can see it. Aurak sensed it, but—ohmigod! Aurak!"

He spun around, searching for the old shaman's body. It was still where he had left it. The stag spirit stomped the ground, marching in a circle around Aurak's body, threatening anything that even looked in its direction.

Evan ran over. Albrecht followed him with three Silver Fangs closely behind, Derrick Hardtooth among them.

"He got bit by the Talon," Evan said, leaning down over Aurak. The stag stepped aside for him, but snorted and bellowed as Albrecht approached. Albrecht stopped a few yards away, respectful of the spirit's duty.

"I think I got the poison out," Evan said. "But I can't be sure."

Hardtooth spoke to the stag in a tongue Evan couldn't understand. The stag lowered its head and stepped aside for the Silver Fang Theurge, who bent down on his knees beside Evan, examining Aurak. He placed his hands over the old man's body and used a spirit power to heal the wound.

"There is still poison in him," Hardtooth said. "I cannot remove it. We must hope his spirit can fight it."

A howl broke out nearby, joined at once by all the frenzied Garou. They charged suddenly, aiming at the source of the voices they heard.

The Silver Fangs leaped forward and met the charge. They fell into a rolling, gnashing, barking tangle of limps and claws, blood spilling across the snow.

"I've got to find this thing now!" Evan cried as he leaped up, nocking a new arrow.

Albrecht put his hand on Evan's shoulder, halting him. "Where's Mari?"

Evan groaned. "She chased off after a fomor. She hadn't come back when Aurak and I stepped over." He swallowed hard, hoping that she hadn't been a victim of his arrow assault on the Heartsplinter. What if she'd come back to the camp only to find a bunch of maddened Garou out for blood? He shook his head, forcing himself not to think about it. "I've got to catch the heart, Albrecht. It's our only chance. I think it's wounded. Something hurt it before I found it. Otherwise, I don't think I'd be able to hit it."

Albrecht looked at him for a moment, silent. Then he nodded and released his shoulder. "Don't let anyone get near Evan!" he yelled to his warriors.

Evan ran toward the fighting Garou, searching the ground for the heart. He suspected it would use the commotion to hide and try to strike at the Garou from close by. He felt of flush of triumph when he saw it, creeping under the feet of a Silver Fang. He raised his bow and shot. The arrow impaled it right in its middle, pinning it to the ground. A terrible screeching sound clawed at Evan's ears. Even Albrecht and the others heard it; Evan could see them clutch their ears to block the sound.

He ran over to his prey, throwing his bow over his shoulder and drawing his Fang Dagger. The heart struggled to break free from the arrow, its dark blood streaming across the snow. Evan could see two rows of jagged yellow teeth, purple with the poison dribbling down them.

He carefully aimed and brought the knife down right into the thing's open maw. It screeched again, nearly causing Evan to double over in pain. Its fleshy body spasmed and collapsed, unmoving.

Evan breathed a deep sigh of relief and sat down, turning to look at the others. He frowned. The Silver Fangs still fought the enraged Garou. Three Wendigo were down and one Silver Fang was injured badly enough that another had to take his place while Hardtooth healed him.

The green mist still roiled beneath them at knee level.

Evan shook his head in denial. It didn't make sense. The heart was dead. The mist should be gone. He turned to look at the heart again, impaled on his arrow and knife. It didn't move. He grasped the knife handle and twisted, chopping the heart into pieces. Blood spilled out, released from the dead organ, but nothing else moved.

Evan spun around again, in near despair. Albrecht waded into the fray, swinging his klaive left and right, hacking the Fianna's arm off and disemboweling a Wendigo.

Evan cried out. "No! They can't help it!"

Albrecht gave him an angry look. "I got no choice!" he yelled. "I'm not losing any of mine to coddle them! This has gone far enough!"

In moments, the frenzied Garou were down. Evan couldn't tell if they were dead or if any still lived, unconscious from their wounds.

Albrecht ran his blade through the snow, wiping off the blood, and came over to Evan. He put his hand on his shoulder. "I hate to do that. You know I hate to do that. But I got two men badly wounded now. We've been through hell getting back to this side of the world. I couldn't let those guys take us down just because they're under Wyrm control."

Evan nodded, head hanging. "I don't understand this, Albrecht. The banetender—he said I had to strike its heart. Aurak agreed. I got it. But nothing's changed."

Albrecht frowned. "Look, kid. You did your best. I hate to say this, but are you sure it's not some sort of illusion? I mean, you're the only one who sees it."

Evan glared at Albrecht. "I'm sure, damn it! The ancestors showed it to me."

Albrecht nodded. "Okay. I accept that. If you're sure, I'm with you. But you have to decide: What are you going to do now?"

Evan hung his head again. "I don't know. If only Aurak were awake…."

Albrecht pulled Evan up from his sitting position. "*You've* got to decide this one. He's not getting up anytime soon. I've got reinforcements coming. We need a battle plan before they get here."

"Reinforcements?" Evan said. "From where?"

"All over," Albrecht smiled. "We got back to the North Country and heard about your war party up here. I gathered an advance group and hopped up to the Winter Wolf Sept; they told me where you guys had gone. I left orders for troops to gather from all over and follow me. They should be arriving sometime soon."

Evan looked at his packmate, eyes wide. "But I couldn't get the other tribes to budge. They all have their own problems."

"Still do. But I sent out a rousing call to arms that won some of them over. Not all of them, but enough. Look," Albrecht said, facing Evan. "I don't know what's happening in the material world now with your camp. These guys might just be the vanguard of more crazed warriors."

Evan shook his head. "Then why haven't others come over yet? No, it was my fault. Every time I shot an arrow at that thing, it hit a Garou in the material world. Don't ask me how; I've got no idea."

Albrecht frowned. "Maybe you're onto something here." He looked down at Evan's knife and arrow, both stuck in the ground. "Maybe you got the heart… or maybe you only got something that *looks* like the heart."

Evan's eyes widened again and his mouth dropped open. "A ruse? That means its heart could still be somewhere around here. Damn it! It used this *thing*," Evan kicked at the remains of the dead heart, "to fool me. It's so damn obvious! Why would its heart look like a real heart?"

Albrecht shrugged. "I don't know. I can't see what you see. But you've got to figure out where it *is* hiding."

Evan nodded, looking around, scanning the landscape.

Albrecht walked over to his soldiers. "I'll be right back, kid," he said. "I got to check on my unit."

Evan looked at the bodies of the fallen Garou. He wondered if it was hiding in them. Maybe that's why their rage lasted so long—they were possessed. But if that was the case, why couldn't he see the spirit here in the Umbra?

He reviewed what the banetender and the ancestors had said, supplemented by Aurak's discussion. The Heartsplinter had possessed the king-slayer Garou long ago. He remembered Crying Bird's words: *It has been free since the king-slaying. The Uktena only captured its heart. Its tendrils have always touched the descendants of those who participated in that slaying. You are the Healer of the Past. You must set things aright. You must atone for your ancestor's wrongs.*

Evan felt a lurch in his stomach and a chill up his spine as he realized what the ancestors had told him but which he had refused to see. The Heartsplinter touched the descendants of the slayer. Evan had to atone for her wrongs. *He was the descendant of the slayer.* He could see the Heartsplinter because it was in *his* blood. He wasn't its nemesis—he was its progeny.

He looked over at Albrecht and felt a terrible loneliness as he realized what he had to do. He watched his packmate slap his warriors on the shoulders, praising their battle skills and bolstering their morale. He smiled weakly. He would miss Albrecht.

He pulled his dagger from the ground and took a deep breath. Then he stabbed it into the Heartsplinter's heart, driving it into his own breast.

●　●　●

"My king!" Erik Honnunger cried, pointing to Evan Heals-the-Past, who had just driven a knife into his own heart and then collapsed into the snow.

Albrecht bolted over to his fallen packmate, a choking growl of worry escaping his throat. He bent down over Evan and looked at the wound. "Healer!" he cried.

Hardtooth ran up to Evan and placed his hands on his chest. The boy was already pale and growing cold, his breathing faint. He carefully extracted the knife, which had gone in deep, puncturing an aortal valve, and called upon his spirit power to heal the wound.

The flesh knitted itself but Evan came no closer to consciousness. His breathing grew more faint.

Albrecht howled in anger.

● ● ●

Evan opened his eyes. The mist was gone. The landscape revealed only snow, marked here and there with prints and the impressions left by combatants' bodies, but there was no one else near.

He stood up, surprised at the lack of pain in his chest. He looked down and saw that the wound was gone.

A bark of greeting startled him and he looked up to see a gray-furred wolf sitting nearby, watching him. He didn't recognize her.

She stepped forward, shifting into wolfman form, and Evan realized who she was.

"Thank you," she said, shifting into human form. Her skin was dark olive, her hair long and black. "For finally reversing my wrong."

Evan nodded slowly. "The king-slayer. What is your name?"

She shook her head. "It doesn't matter. My name should be forgotten. You have healed our family's wound." She turned and walked away, gesturing across the snow. "Come. It is time to return to the ancestors."

Evan nodded. "So it's all over then? The Heartsplinter is gone?"

"Yes," she nodded, beckoning Evan. "It died with your sacrifice."

He could see four wolves now, coming toward him from the direction she had indicated. Crying Bird, Swift Talker, Ironpaw and the Child of Gaia whose name he still did not know. They stopped, as if waiting for him.

Evan sighed and stepped forward, following his ancestor. He felt a tug at his shoulder, stopping him.

"It's not your time yet," a familiar voice said.

Evan turned to see Mephi Faster-Than-Death, leaning on his staff. Beside him stood a tall Silent Strider in full Egyptian regalia.

"Mephi?" Evan said. "You're dead, too? I thought you were supposed to be faster than that," he said with a smile.

Mephi smiled. "Very funny, Evan. No, I'm not dead. And you shouldn't be either."

Evan frowned. "I don't understand. I stabbed myself with a big knife. I definitely should be dead."

"Yeah," Mephi said. "Under any other circumstance, you'd be toast. But Shem-ha-Tau here says it's not meant to be." Mephi indicated the Silent Strider next to him. "Seems your favor for the ancestors gets you a 'get out of death free' card."

Evan looked back at the wolves waiting for him. They were gone.

He turned back to Mephi. "But if you're not dead, why are you here?"

Mephi smiled, winking at Shem-ha-Tau. "Silent Strider mojo. I finally got the answer to the big question."

Evan frowned. "What's that?"

Mephi shook his head. "Everyone will find out eventually. I can't say anything more than that. Death has to keep *some* secrets. Otherwise, it couldn't fulfill its role in renewal."

"That doesn't make any sense. Start over."

Mephi tugged Evan's elbow and took a step backwards. "Come on. Enough chatter. We've got to get back. I've got news for Albrecht." As said this, the smile left his face.

Evan nodded, confused. "Okay. But you will explain this eventually, won't you?"

Mephi didn't respond. He waved at Shem-ha-Tau, who raised his hand in farewell but said nothing.

Mephi drew a circle in the air with his staff. A moon bridge opened and he stepped in, pulling Evan in with him.

Evan coughed and spit up blood. He wearily opened his eyes, which seemed much more sluggish than a few moments ago. As they focused, he saw Albrecht staring at him with wide eyes and open jaw. The king howled with joy and shook Evan's shoulder.

"Thattaboy, kid!" Albrecht yelled. "You fought it!"

Evan sat up, feeling his chest his with hand. A scar ran down his left breast but was otherwise healed.

Hardtooth looked at Evan in amazement. "I thought for sure you had left us."

Evan smiled weakly. "So did I." He looked around, searching for Mephi. "Where'd he go?"

Albrecht looked around. "Who?"

"Mephi Faster-Than-Death," Evan said. "He was just with me."

Albrecht frowned and looked at Hardtooth, who shrugged. Albrecht looked back at Evan. "Look, Evan. You nearly died. You've been here the whole time. It must have been a dream or vision of some kind."

Evan shook his head and tried to stand. His legs were weak, so Albrecht stepped forward and let him lean on his shoulder. "I was dead. I went to the place the dead go on their way to the ancestor realms. Aurak called it the Path of the Milky Way, but I didn't see any stars. Mephi was there. He guided me back."

Albrecht looked disturbed. "I didn't know he was dead. That's too bad. He was a damn good Garou."

"No, you don't get it," Evan said. "He's not dead. He was alive. It was some sort of Silent Strider magic. There was another one there with him. He—" Evan stopped, a look of shock on his face. "I just realized. The other Strider was dead. He was a spirit. A Silent Strider ancestor spirit!"

Albrecht looked at Hardtooth again, a look of concern on his face. "The Striders don't have ancestor spirits, Evan. They're all lost."

Evan smiled, slapping Albrecht on the back as he leaned on him, stepping forward carefully, getting his balance. He was a bit dizzy. "Not anymore. I think Mephi's figured it out. That's the answer he talked about. The secret of his tribe's ancestors."

Albrecht smiled weakly. "Look, maybe you should lie down again. You're not making sense."

Evan laughed. "No. I get it now! Mephi's in the physical world. He stepped back through a moon bridge, while my spirit went back to my body here in the Umbra. We've got to step over."

Albrecht nodded. "Okay. We do need to see what's happening at the camp. Let's do it."

He growled a command to his soldiers and they all gathered around him. Hardtooth picked up Aurak's unconscious body and went to stand in the middle of the group. Everyone reached out to touch him and he nodded, parting the Gauntlet for them.

They stood in a field littered with bodies and blood. Snow and icy wind cut through the air, forcing them to squint.

Shapes moved toward them.

A figure stepped forward. Albrecht couldn't make out any features through the fast-falling snow, but he growled, a warning for it to keep its distance.

"Well, well," Mari Cabrah said, smiling wryly. She stepped closer, ignoring Albrecht's warning. "So King Albrecht finally makes an appearance."

Chapter Twenty:
The Last Valley

Albrecht chuckled, glad to see Mari alive and standing. "Yeah, I'm here, Mari. The traffic was a bitch. What happened here?"

"Mari!" Evan cried. He rushed forward and hugged her. She clasped him tight. Blood covered Mari's winter clothes, which were torn to shreds in various places. Only a few of the splatters seemed to be her own; a wound in her thigh looked bad, still glistening around a deep claw mark, but she didn't seem bothered by it.

A group of figures moved toward them through the falling snow, carefully stepping around the bodies. Mari nodded at them as they approached. Albrecht could now see the features of some members of the Silver River Pack, all of them but Carlita and Storm Eye. Among them were Garou he didn't know, some clearly Wendigo, others young Garou of various tribes.

"Everybody went bugfuck crazy," Mari said. "The Silver River Pack and I arrived back in time to see them freak out. Some of them got hit by arrows that came out of nowhere. Arrows I recognized." Mari patted Evan on the back and released him. "When they started disappearing into the Umbra, I knew that something more than a group rageout was up. I peered into the Umbra and saw Evan shooting wildly with his arrows, aiming at nothing."

"Not nothing," Evan said, flustered. "*The Heartsplinter.*"

Mari smiled. "I got the idea there was something going on I didn't understand. All I knew was that my packmate was in trouble. I started to step over but noticed a horde of wild-eyed Wendigo were about to do the same. I couldn't stop those guys, but I could stop the rest. The Silver River Pack and I did a hit and run—anytime somebody tried to step over, we hit him. They got so damn pissed, they soon forgot about anything but us."

Evan looked at the pack, growing tension in his voice. "Where's Big Sis and Storm-Eye?"

"They're alive," John North Wind's Son said. He had a large bite mark on his side and numerous claw marks up and down his arms. "But barely. We all took wounds while stopping them from stepping over."

"You guys did damn good," Albrecht said. "But why didn't the frenzy get you, too? Everybody else in camp succumbed."

Mari hung her head. The Silver River Pack did the same.

"We were *anointed* against it," Mari said, her voice cracking, as if she held back grief. "I'll… I'll tell you about it later. First, we've got to tend to the survivors. Most of these guys are only wounded."

Albrecht nodded, looking strangely at Mari. He'd never seen her so broken up before. He whistled to his group. Hardtooth and a group of warriors went out across the field, tending to the wounded.

"Is everybody back in control?" Albrecht said, looking at the strange Garou who stood near the Silver River Pack, each of whom appeared shell-shocked.

Mari nodded. "Everyone snapped out of it suddenly. I peered into the Umbra again and saw you leaning over Evan." She looked at Evan, punching him in the arm. "Gave me a scare there. But he popped up again as I watched."

Evan smiled and looked around. "Have you seen Mephi Faster-Than-Death?"

Mari looked surprised. "Here? No. Did he come with Albrecht?"

"No," Evan said, walking away, peering through the snow. "He came through the Paths of the Dead. He brought me back."

Mari shot a look at Albrecht. He shrugged and looked back at Evan.

"There he is!" Evan cried, pointing out across the tundra at a figure bent over one of the bodies. It looked to be giving the fallen Garou last rites.

Evan rushed over. Albrecht came right behind him, curious, joined by Mari.

Mephi Faster-Than-Death stood and watched them approach. He nodded at Evan, a silent greeting, and then bowed to Albrecht.

"So it's true," Albrecht said. "You really are here!"

Evan shot him a furious look.

Mari poked him in the arm. "I didn't believe you either," she said with a grin.

"It's really me," Mephi said. "I am glad to see you all. With you still standing, we have a chance."

Albrecht cocked his head curiously. "Something tells me you're the bearer of bad tidings. Okay, let's hear it."

Mephi cleared his throat and thought for a moment, deciding how to begin. "The army of the Margrave Konietzko and Queen Tamara Tvarivich is no more. They died fighting on the Plain of the Apocalypse."

Albrecht gritted his teeth and tightened his fists, shutting his eyes. He heard gasps from the gathered Garou, along with growls and whines from the younger ones. He opened his eyes again, staring steely eyed at Mephi. "You know this for sure?"

Mephi nodded. "I was there. I witnessed the Margrave's glorious death. He single-handedly slew a nexus crawler. Not just any crawler; this was the biggest one I'd ever heard of. Tvarivich… I didn't see her die. But she was outnumbered. It couldn't last long. I'm sure she killed the Wyrm army's general, though."

Albrecht's eyes narrowed. "Why are *you* still alive then?"

Mephi looked away, across the white tundra. "Believe me, it's not easy. So many people died and I just walked right out of there… Tvarivich demanded that I leave and find you, to tell you about what had happened. To make sure you prepared the last line of defense."

Albrecht looked away. He nodded. "You did right. I needed to know. It hurts like hell, though."

"That's not all," Mephi said, looking back at the king and meeting his eyes. "Tvarivich used her Ivory Priesthood secrets to open a portal into the Roads of the Dead. My ancestors were there. I walked with them. That's how I found Evan; they brought me to him."

Albrecht looked at Evan, a guilty look on his face. "Silent Strider ancestors?"

"They guide the dead to the lands of the ancestors. The roads are threatened by all sorts of creatures, but my ancestors know the short cuts and secret paths, ways to get newly departed spirits to their proper realms. I can't tell you everything—*I* don't even know everything. I just got a glimpse, really, but I learned some things on my journey." He paused, frowning, looking at each of them. "The gates of Malfeas have opened, spewing every last Wyrm minion. Something big and nasty is with them, destroying everything in its path. And I mean everything."

Mari frowned. "What sort of being is this? A new Maeljin?"

Albrecht growled. "Zhyzhak. This is Zhyzhak's doing." He slammed his fist into his palm in anger. "That bitch! She was dancing the Black Spiral. We fought briefly before she chickened out and jumped back into the Labyrinth. We got a note… from Antonine Teardrop."

"Antonine?" Evan said. "Where is he?"

"I don't know," Albrecht said. "But my guess is he's not in good shape. He was following Zhyzhak, hoping to prevent her from getting power. If Malfeas is emptying out… he must have failed."

"The Wyrm creatures are heading for the material world," Mephi said. "They're coming *here*."

Albrecht growled. "She said she'd be back, with the armies of Malfeas behind her. The bitch is looking for me. It's that goddamn prophecy. She probably actually believes it."

Evan looked uncomfortably at Albrecht. "What if it *is* true? What if she is destined to 'slay the last Gaian King?'"

"Oh for crying out loud! Not you, too? It's just a bunch of Black Spiral Dancer propaganda! I almost had her! Another few rounds and she would have been paste. She knew it, so she cut and ran. Had to go get allies to take me on. Well, we're going to be ready for her. Let her try!"

Mari smiled. "That's the spirit, Albrecht!"

Mephi looked around the field. "Not an ideal place for a last stand."

Albrecht nodded. "Yeah. We've got to move out, find a place to prepare for a fight. They can get us on all sides here. We need a cave or something."

"You said reinforcements were coming," Evan said. "How soon?"

Albrecht looked around. It was impossible to tell the time in the gloomy snowfall. "I don't know. I think we need to move on; they'll track us. We need one of the Wendigo who knows this area."

"We've got to tend to the wounded in the Umbra, too," Evan said. "Some of them might still be alive."

Albrecht sighed. "All right. Find some spirit-seers among the living and step over there and get them. With Mari in the lead."

Mari nodded. "Come on." She turned to the Silver River Pack. "Julia, we could use you." She looked at the group of other Garou who followed them. "Loper? Is that your name?"

The shaggy, unkempt Bone Gnawer nodded.

"You're a Theurge, right? Come with us." Mari walked away, gathering her group, Evan with her.

Albrecht looked at Mephi. "Any ideas?"

Mephi shrugged. "I'm not a full-moon warrior, but I know a lot of stories about last stands. I think this might well be the last of the last."

"Could be. Or not. That's not for us to decide. Our job is to fight until the last breath—and beyond if need be."

Mephi nodded. "You're the right one to lead this, you know. The Margrave and Queen Tvarivich... they were incredible. But me, I'm glad to add another chapter to the glorious saga of King Albrecht."

"Flattery will get you nowhere," Albrecht said, smiling. "You know, you could cut out back onto those Roads of the Dead. You don't have to fight this."

Mephi frowned, his jaw set. "Yes, I do. The roads offer no escape. I can't walk them again, not without permission. Not until I'm dead."

"That may be all too soon," Albrecht said with a sigh. He walked back to the center of the camp. Mephi bent down over another dead body and began mumbling.

Albrecht surveyed the situation. Nearly a quarter of the original war party was dead, most of them killed by other enraged Garou. Twice that number were wounded; about half of those were bad enough that they required spirit healing. The rest of the original army had made it out okay, relatively unharmed. They consisted mainly of the young kids who'd come with Evan and Mari from the Finger Lakes, along with a few Wendigo.

"King Albrecht," said a voice from nearby.

Albrecht turned to see a Native American man, tall and broadly built. He had a fresh, jagged scar across this throat but it had been healed.

"I am Painted Claw," he said. "War Chief of the Wendigo."

Albrecht offered his hand. "I'm glad you made it. We're going to need you."

Painted Claw looked back at the scattered Garou, most of whom—the living, at least—were now waking up. "And I am glad you are here." He stepped forward and took Albrecht's hand. "I was overcome by the Talon's power. I could not lead."

"Nothing to be ashamed of," Albrecht said. "If I'd been here as long as you had, I'd have succumbed too. I think it was so busy fending off Evan and enraging you guys, it didn't have enough power to spare for me."

Painted Claw nodded, staring at the Silver Crown on Albrecht's brow. "Perhaps. I am searching for Heals-the-Past, but I cannot find him."

"He's in the Umbra, tending to the wounded there."

Painted Claw gestured across the field, toward a group of Wendigo gathered around Aurak's body. "Aurak has awakened. He asks for Evan. I believe he wishes to see you also."

"That's some good news for once," Albrecht said, heading toward the old shaman. Painted Claw followed him.

Aurak sat up when he saw Albrecht coming. Two Wendigo bent down to let him lean on them. He was still very weak.

"King Albrecht," he said. "I am very pleased to see you."

"Feeling's mutual," Albrecht said, stooping on his knees so he was closer to eye level with the elder. "I was worried about you. It seems you're coming through, though."

"The poison is gone. The Heartsplinter's power is dead. I saw it all from my trance. I could do nothing, but I witnessed its form. It was as Evan had said, a mist. A mist that crept through us all."

"Well, at least it's gone now. One Wyrm threat down, a thousand more to go."

Aurak nodded. "I have been told about the Malfean army and the lost battle. But the Heartsplinter's defeat is a greater victory than you think. Our rage is our own now. The Wyrm cannot use it against us."

Albrecht shook his head. "I don't understand. What does that mean exactly?"

"Look into your heart, at your anger. When you heard the news of the Margrave and the Queen's fall, think of your reaction. Was it different than it would have been before the Heartsplinter's destruction?"

Albrecht thought for a minute. "Well, I was angry, but now that you mention it, I wasn't as outright pissed as I might have been before. I mean, not fighting pissed. More like cold, hard anger pissed."

Aurak nodded. "Already, our rage becomes more ours. Easier to control. No less powerful, no less stoked by news of calamity. But less wild, less out of control."

Albrecht nodded. "Yeah, I guess that seems right. Hard to tell. I'll wait for a real fight before I know for sure. That'll be the test."

Aurak shrugged. "When Heals-the-Past returns, will you tell him to see me?"

Albrecht smiled. "As soon as he hears you're awake, nobody will be able to keep him away." He stood up. "You get some rest. We're going to need your insight. The war party's hunt is not over yet."

Aurak nodded and relaxed. The Wendigo eased him back down.

Albrecht walked over to where Eric Honnunger stood with other Silver Fangs, watching over Hardtooth as he saw to the wounded.

"What's our status?" Albrecht asked.

"We have many wounded," Eric said, resting his hammer on his shoulder. "Hardtooth can't heal anymore and he's used most of his talens. Once the reinforcements arrive, we should be able to heal them all."

"Good. I need everyone we can get." He noticed a group appear out of nowhere near the center of the camp. "Mari and Evan are back, and they've got some wounded with them."

He walked over to meet them. Out of the eight Garou they had fought with, only four still lived, each standing weakly beside one of the shamans. The Fianna was among them, now missing his left arm, and the other three were Wendigo. Albrecht felt bad about having killed one of the Wendigo, but casualties were a fact of life for Garou.

A Native American woman stood next to Evan, tears streaming down her cheek. She walked away as Albrecht approached, trying to hide her tears behind her arm.

"That's Quiet Storm," Evan said. "She was good friends with Flint Knife. He didn't make it."

Albrecht nodded. "At least some of them are alive. By the way, Aurak is awake. He wants to—"

Evan was already running over to the elder. Albrecht shrugged his shoulders and looked at Mari. "You see the respect a king gets around here?"

Mari frowned sarcastically. "Smallest violin, Albrecht. I can't hear it over the wind. " She paused, looking out past the camp. "I thought of a place we should go."

"Yeah? Someplace defensible?"

"I don't know. I've never been there."

Albrecht cocked his head, waiting skeptically for details.

"Gather everybody around. I've got something to say."

• • •

Every member of the war party sat around the newly kindled fire. Many could only sit, for they were too wounded to stand. Mari stood by the fire, looking out at them all, making sure they were all present and paying attention.

She took a breath and began speaking. "The Silver River Pack and I chased the ferectoi leader of the Pentex commandoes back to an oil refinery. Just as we got there, the place blew up. Something hit it before us, and hit it hard. Everyone there was dead. I finished off the fomor and we scouted around, looking for whomever had taken out a whole base full of fomori and banes all by themselves."

She paused, looking into the fire. "We found her. She was wounded and dying. She'd used up the last of her reserves hurting the Talon." She looked back at the group. "She was called the Most Ancient of Bears, the oldest living shapechanger. She's dead."

The group broke into a collective gasp, punctuated by growls and whines. Aurak buried his face in his hands and his shoulders shook.

"Before she died," Mari continued, "she charged me with her dying wish." She pulled the tooth amulet from under her shirt. "This is her tooth. She said it would point the way to where we must go."

She let the tooth hang loose. It dangled in the air, twirling, and then began to float upwards until it hung perpendicular to the pull of gravity. The tooth's tip faced northwest.

"We must go northwest," Mari said.

Albrecht stood up. "We leave tomorrow morning. I've assigned guard duty already. Everybody else, get some rest. It could be a long march.

Evan looked at Painted Claw. The proud warrior gazed into the fire, his face expressionless. He had no reaction to Albrecht's taking charge of the party. Nobody else questioned it.

• • •

At dawn, they broke camp and departed, marching across the tundra. Snow had covered the tracks from yesterday's fight and mantled the bodies of the fallen. There was no time to dig graves in the hard, cold dirt or gather stones for a caern. The bodies would feed the ravens, something no wolf begrudged.

They walked for three days, leaving a trail marked by talens, short-lived fetishes created by the shamans. The talen spirits would alert and guide the reinforcements along their trail, which would soon be erased by snow.

They stopped every hour to check the tooth and make sure they still traveled in the proper direction. There were few landmarks on the open tundra and even the Wendigo were unfamiliar with the territory, farther north than their sept was used to roaming.

On the afternoon of the third day, they came to a pine forest, thick and untouched by human development. The Wendigo marveled at such an anomaly so far north, and many wondered why no tale had told of it and no hunter had discovered it before. The tooth pointed through the forest, so they arranged themselves in a loose line and wove through the trees. It slowed their pace but many were glad to see trees again.

That evening, as the full moon took to the sky, they came to a cliff face, a tall rock wall reaching at least a hundred yards high. The tooth pointed past it. They worked their way around to the right and came upon a tight passage between rock walls. Following its winding curves, they entered into a valley, barren of trees and covered with snow. Huge rocks lay in rough formations, resembling the mega-liths of Stonehenge or some other European sacred site.

Albrecht called a halt once everyone was in the val-ley. Mari stood in the center; the tooth pointed down.

"I think we're here," Mari said.

Albrecht sent scouts to all corners, looking for other passages. "This is a gem, Mari. Perfectly defensible. High walls and only one entryway—a tight one at that, about three men wide. We can hold off a lot of trouble from here."

Aurak walked around the rocks, rubbing snow away here and there. He called Evan over.

"Look," Aurak said, pointing at a large rock, taller than he was. "Pictograms."

Evan peered at the rock. He saw faint markings, slightly discolored. "I can't really read them," he said, his brow fur-rowing. "They're ancient."

"I do not think they are human or Garou. I think they are Gurahl."

Evan nodded. "Like the Most Ancient of Bears. This must be the remains of a Gurahl caern."

Aurak looked around. "I sense power. It may not be dormant."

He gathered a group of Theurges and began to scour the place for clues, seeking a pathstone or some other sign of a way they could use the caern. Aurak and a few sha-mans stepped sideways but didn't come back immediately. They reappeared a while later, walking in through the main passageway in the material world.

Aurak approached Albrecht and Mari. "This is a strange place. It is protected by great power. The Gauntlet leaving the valley is low; even an untrained cub would have no trouble stepping over. But not even I can pass back over. I had to leave the valley before I could pierce the Gauntlet again. No spirit or bane can penetrate this place without coming down the passage in this world."

"More and more this place seems designed for us," Albrecht said. "It's kind of eerie."

"There are spirits here," Aurak said. "In the rocks and in the snow-buried grass seed. They slumber deeply—too deeply to awaken without a long ceremony. It is possible that the power in this place makes them sleep."

Mephi Faster-Than-Death came up next to them, chewing his lip thoughtfully. "I've been checking this place out like the rest of you. I think I've heard of it before, though I don't know if I'm right or not. It's real obscure, more legend than fact. Garou have always claimed that the Silver Fang caern in the Urals was the first."

"I can attest to that," Albrecht said. "I just got back from there. It reeks of the primordial. There's a tree there older than God."

Mephi smiled. "Could be true. But. The Gurahl had caerns before the Garou. It's something Garou don't like to admit, 'cause it steals our thunder, but the evidence is out there." He opened his arms and gestured to the valley. "I think *this* is the first caern. This is the first place the Gurahl dedicated to the spirits."

Albrecht looked around. Aurak seemed to consider the idea and nodded, apparently accepting it.

Mephi continued. "This legendary first caern has a name among the Gurahl. It's called the Womb of Gaia. It's said that this is where Her first children gestated before they were born into the world. The Gurahl watched over them at the Dawn of the world."

Mari sighed and closed her eyes. "I wish we could ask the Ancient. But at least she led us here. We might find out its true nature soon enough, once the fight comes."

Albrecht called out and ordered scouts to leave the valley, searching for the reinforcements.

"Okay," he said. "Let's get ready to make our stand."

Chapter Twenty-One:
The Hidden Moon

The stars burned and fell from the sky, tearing flaming holes in the fabric of Creation.

Altair silently witnessed their screaming deaths while his septmates wept. The Stargazer stood on a moon path surrounded by his septmates, who watched in horror as the universe came apart.

"This can't be happening!" Canopus cried, raising his fists.

"The Apocalypse begins," Moon-Sister whispered. "So long foretold. 'All who are living today shall be the last.'"

Altair peered into space, into the vast distances. From the sept's vantage on the moon path, they could see the whole of the deepest reaches of the Aetherial Realm. Looming in the distance, growing ever larger, the Red Star approached, preceded by fiery destruction.

Meros' demesne—the planet Pluto—had already crumbled, knocked from its orbit and shattered into a thousand shards by the great red entity as it stormed past the outer barriers of the Near Umbra.

Altair looked at the falling star, a swirling, massive, molten shape wreathing the black hole in its center, sucking in all debris. The star crawled ever forward, aiming for the planets and devouring their Incarna spirits and servitors. He watched as Neptune shook and tumbled from its orbit, scattering water throughout the heavens.

A great being arose from the planet, half-human, half-octopus, trident in hand. She stabbed the black maw but could not withdraw her trident. She struggled with it for a moment, frozen in a tug of war, then stumbled and fell into the maw, disappearing from sight.

"Shantar!" Moon-Sister cried.

"The dragon ate her!" Canopus cried.

Altair frowned. Dragon? He looked at his septmates. "There is no dragon. Only an endlessly devouring mouth. A black hole."

Canopus and Moon-Sister looked at him as if he were crazy. The others also looked at him strangely.

"Can't you see it?" Canopus said. "It's a huge dragon, its tail stretching back into the farthest reaches, past our vision."

Altair nodded. He understood now. "You see with the eyes of hope. Your vision is clouded by reliance on forms. Forget what you know and see clearly. See the entity for what it truly is: a cosmic force of Uncreation."

They nodded slowly, barely comprehending. They were powerful Stargazers, but they had not yet learned to see past all the illusions their minds foisted upon them. When faced with the unimaginable, their minds sought to give it form, even if it was the very manifestation of formlessness.

"What does this mean?" Canopus said.

"The Wyrm is loose," Altair said. "It does what it does. It destroys."

"No," Moon-Sister said. "The Wyrm, once freed of its prison, is a force of balance. It is supposed to destroy only those things which are out of balance: the Weaver that chokes the universe."

Altair gave them a wry smile. "In a perfect universe, this would be true. But in a perfect universe, there would

The Last Battle

be no imbalance. The Wyrm is not truly free. It is loosed from its cage, but it is leashed to the will of its own corrupt children. Do you now see the dilemma of believing an illusion rather than the truth? The Wyrm has succumbed to its own lies, a story it told to those it hoped would set it free. Now, like so many beings, it is trapped by its own story."

"How can you be so damn cold?" Canopus yelled. "That thing is destroying all we know and love—the very planets themselves, damn it! And you sit here philosophizing about it!"

Altair raised an eyebrow. "What would you have me do? Fight it? To what end? It acts from ignorance. The cure is truth. How would you administer it?"

"I don't know! All I know is it's wrong to just sit back and… and *think* about it! We're Garou! It's our job to defend Gaia. To fight for her with our last breath."

"Fighting is not always about fists."

The black hole—the dragon—kept moving, approaching the orbit of Uranus. A huge shroud spread out from the world, like a cloak stretching across the sky. Ruatma went to war.

His form enveloped the dragon and held it. The universe seemed to freeze for a moment, each planet halting in its orbit as it waited, watching the outcome. Then the shroud burst and the dragon lunged forward, swallowing Uranus whole with one gulp. The remains of the shroud faded like wisps of smoke.

"It will soon defeat Lu-Bat and Zarok," Altair said. "Then it will reach the Pattern Web between the inner and outer solar system, between the Deep and Near Umbra. Can the Weaver ensnare it again?"

Two forms emerged from two planets, Saturn and Jupiter. One was a snowy owl, the other a massive human warrior with a king's crown and golden sword. Both engaged the dragon simultaneously. It responded by splitting itself, growing another head and two more arms. Two different jaws snapped at the Planetary Incarna, while six claws slashed at them.

The regal Incarna lasted longer than the others had, but soon faltered. They were devoured whole, each by different heads. The dragon flew a circle in the sky and continued on, heading toward the asteroid belt.

"Look!" Moon-Sister cried, pointing into the darkness below the dragon. "Rorg comes!"

A giant wolf stalked forth from amid the stones of the asteroid belt, a smoldering tail of fire trailing behind it. It charged the dragon, who veered from its course to meet it. Their collision flashed through the night, temporarily blinding the Sept of the Stars. When the Garou's vision cleared, they saw the wolf's jaws clamped onto one of the dragon's necks. The two entities thrashed about, struggling against one another.

Altair saw a fiery, quick stone pound its way into the black hole. Instead of being swallowed by it, it battered the pit's edges, managing to actually shrink its perimeter. Altair gasped. "Rorg's rage is greater than even I imagined."

Then the dragon spun, throwing the wolf from its throat. Its tail lashed out and split the wolf in two. A howl echoed throughout the immensity. With a last mustering of will, the wolf's front-quarters bolted forward and its jaws tore one of the dragon's heads from its neck.

The wolf faded, its form disintegrating, but the dragon roared in pain, writhing, its blood spewing from the wound.

Altair peered at the black hole, trying to see into its formless depths. He had seen a glimmer of something, a sparkling, like the light of a white star. Then it was gone. As the roiling hole in space moved forward, he thought he saw it again. This time, however, it seemed to have a form, a long sinuous snake within the heart of the Wyrm. A snake with the head and mane of a lion. Then it was gone, swallowed by blackness.

Altair looked at his companions. They watched the sky with looks of dismay. "Did you see something within the Wyrm?"

Canopus looked at him, eyebrows raised. "No. I saw it writhe in pain, but then it recovered and continued on."

"Curious," Altair said.

The dragon approached a vast spider web, spun across the bowl of the sky, separating the Near from the Deep Umbra. Tiny beings moved across the webs, Pattern Spiders preparing for the dragon's charge, strengthening the web against it.

The dragon hit the strands with its full force. The web bent inward but refused to break. The spiders furiously wove new strands, attempting to entrap the dragon before it could withdraw. It did not withdraw. Instead, it urged itself still forward, stretching the web ever more. The spiders altered their task and frantically tried to strengthen the web, but the strands began to fray, one by one. The dragon moved slowly, inexorably forward.

Then the web burst, scattered spiders in all directions. The dragon rocketed forward, into the Near Umbra. A great, shattering peal of thunder accompanied it.

Altair hung his head in sorrow.

• • •

In New York City, Kleon Winston, leader of the city's Glass Walker sept, frowned, staring at his computer screen. It had gone blank. He looked over at Diode.

"What the fuck?" he said. "I just lost all power."

Diode frowned, looking at her own laptop screen. "Me too. This is weird. I didn't think the Pattern Web could have a system crash...."

The windows of their fiftieth-floor office shattered, sending glass in all directions. Kleon and Diode hit the floor, grunting as shards dug into their skin. They both shifted to battle form and came up ready for action. Nothing moved.

Kleon crept to the window and looked out. Some sort of traffic pileup was taking place below, a number of cars crashed into one another.

Diode picked up a glass shard. "Holy shit. Something just killed every Pattern Spider we bound into the caern."

"That's not possible," Kleon said. "They're too many of them. Maybe they broke their fetish wards."

Diode shook her head. "No way. Something killed them. Look outside."

Kleon looked out the window again as the sound of honking horns grew louder. He looked down onto a traffic disaster. Every single light and sign had gone dead. Neon signs on buildings up and down the street had no juice.

"Something's fucking with the entire grid," he said. "First Black Spiral Dancers and sludge banes in the sewers—now this. What's going on?"

Diode shook her head. "I got a bad feeling about this, boss."

Kleon's cell phone rang. He answered it. "Yeah. Yeah? Shit. Okay, sound the alert. We're jumping ship." He hung up the phone and looked at Diode. "Everybody out. Looks like NYC's out of order."

Diode stared gap-jawed at him. "Out of order? Where we going?"

"We're taking King Albrecht up on his offer, like I knew we should've done already. We're joining the war party. Come on, we've got about fifty flights of stairs to get down."

"Shit! That's right—the elevators will be down. How we going to get to Central Park through that traffic?"

"The underground shortcut," Kleon said, opening the door and gesturing for Diode to go first.

"I hate the sewers," Diode said as she marched out the door.

• • •

"I said get your ass through that gate!" Mother Larissa said, waving her cane threateningly at Fengy.

Fengy whimpered and cringed back, holding up his paws. He stood by the edge of an open moon bridge. The last Bone Gnawer had already gone through, followed by Kleon Winston's Glass Walkers.

"Mother," Fengy said, "I'm not leaving you here by yourself."

"The hell you aren't!" Mother whacked him across the shoulders with the cane. "I can take care of myself. Been doing that since well before you were born! Now get out of here! The city's too dangerous even for our kind. Albrecht needs you."

Fengy whined again and hesitated. Larissa pulled back her cane and smacked him with all her strength. He shut his eyes and dove through the moon bridge. The gate closed behind him, leaving Larissa alone in the park. Even the humans had fled; everyone was trying to get home. City services were out all over, with no electricity or radio.

Larissa sighed and sat down. Folks these days didn't know how to live without those things. It was sad.

She heard a bird twitter and smiled, looking up into the foliage. "I'm glad someone's still here with me. I don't know how it's going to end, but it's definitely going to end. It'd be nice to see it through, but an old lady like me can't count on that sort of thing. At least I'll see it through here, from my own home!"

The bird twittered again.

"What's that? Then why'd I send everybody else away from home? Oh, they shouldn't be hanging out here. Everybody else is up north, with King Albrecht. If there's a chance of surviving this, it's with him. You and me, though, nobody's going to pay attention to small fry like us. We'll just wait here. See what happens."

Mother Larissa sat back, leaning against a tree. This was the quietest Central Park had ever been. Off in the distance, even the car horns had stopped. There was trouble out there, but in here, pure peace. She sighed and hummed an old tune from the 1930s.

• • •

At the Finger Lakes Caern, Alani Astarte watched the last full pack leave, disappearing into the moon bridge. When the silvery light went out, she shook her head and sighed.

Pearl River placed a hand on her shoulder. "Just us, Alani."

"Just us," Alani said. She looked out over the woods and the misty lake. "I just can't let it go. Too much beauty. Someone's got to see it till it's over. Beauty has to mean something in all this. Otherwise, what's it worth?"

Pearl River smiled. "I'm no warrior. I wouldn't be much good in the north. I sense that my heart belongs here."

"And I'm too old to fight," Alani said. "So here we are. We've got the lake all to ourselves."

The two women sat beside the lake and waited silently.

• • •

Altair watched as the black hole absorbed Nerigal and his planet, Mars. He knew that, with the spiritual reflections of the planets destroyed, cataclysms would soon appear in the material world. The eye of Jupiter would probably spew ejecta, throwing off the orbits of its satellites. It would all go downhill from there.

The Wyrm sped toward Earth, aiming for the Moon. Altair winced. With Luna devoured, all her powers would go with her, including the moon path he and his septmates stood upon.

He turned to face his fellows. "We have watched too long. I am afraid our own dooms will soon be upon us."

Moon-Sister wiped away a tear. "I have loved you all very much."

Canopus howled and the others joined in. A dirge of parting. Before it was complete, Canopus broke the howl, staring out into space, eyes wide and mouth gaping. The others followed his gaze.

The Moon was gone, but not devoured. The dragon circled in the sky, searching for its silver prey, roaring in anger. There was no sign of the white orb.

Altair smiled, pleased. "She has bought us some time. We must depart now."

The radiance beneath them dimmed. The moon path was failing.

Altair began walking, leading them back to the tower. "Come. There may just be time to open a final moon bridge before they all fail."

"I don't understand," Canopus said, following behind Altair but glancing back at the sky, looking for the Moon. "Where did Luna go?"

"She shed her skin," Altair said. "She metamorphosed into the invisible moon, the 'no moon.'"

Canopus blinked. "She can do that? Go from full to new without waning first?"

"Only at great cost to her power and servants," Altair said. "Already, many Lunes will have dissipated. We must hurry."

Moon-Sister smiled. "In the material world, a new moon means the sun's light is blocked by Gaia. But here, in the Umbra, she becomes intangible and invisible, the Keeper of Secrets. And not even the Wyrm can find her!" She laughed.

"Where are we going, Altair?" Canopus asked. "Where is there left to go?"

"To join King Albrecht's army," Altair said. "The last stand of Gaia's warriors. Now, Canopus, is the time when fighting means fists."

Chapter Twenty-Two:
Battle Plans

A howl echoed through the valley. Albrecht cocked his head and listened. "Scouts reporting," he said to Mari and Evan. They sat around a small campfire under a rock overhang in the chill, dim morning. "There are a lot of Garou coming."

More howls descended from the peaks of the valley wall, where the other scouts were positioned, watching in all directions.

"The reinforcements are here," Albrecht said with a smile. He stood up and strapped his grand klaive to his back. "Sounds like there's a lot more of them than I expected."

Mari and Evan stood up. Mari zipped up her winter coat. "They're coming from the Winter Wolf Sept?"

Albrecht nodded. "That's the closest moon bridge." He walked out across the valley. Garou were positioned around small campfires throughout the area. Mari and Evan followed close behind.

The king's guards assembled by the passage out of the valley. Eric Honnunger walked up to meet Albrecht.

"My king," he said. "I don't advise you to leave the valley. An enemy might use that moment to attack."

Albrecht frowned. "Have any scouts seen activity here or in the Umbra?"

Eric shook his head. "No, my lord. But that doesn't mean it's completely safe. I recommend sending out a small party to greet the reinforcements. They can ascertain if they're ours."

"You think this might be a trick?" Albrecht said skeptically. "The enemy disguised as an army of our own people? That's a bit far-fetched."

"So is this whole situation, Albrecht," Mari said. "I agree with your lieutenant. You shouldn't leave the valley. Once we determine if all is well, we'll bring the reinforcements in."

Albrecht looked at Mari, one eyebrow raised. "By 'we,' I assume you intend to go out there? It's okay for you but not me? I'm not an invalid, Mari."

"Grow up, Albrecht," Mari said. "You're the leader here. Delegate. You can't take on every task yourself."

Albrecht chewed his lip. "All right, all right. Go out there and make sure those guys are kosher. I left Thomas Abbot in charge; he should be leading the group. Eric, go with her and take ten warriors. Get some new moons, half-moons and crescents, too. If there's deception, they'll root it out."

Eric nodded and went to select his men. Mari smiled and followed him. Evan followed Mari, but Albrecht reached out and grabbed him by the collar.

"Oh, no," Albrecht said. "Not you. You're still recovering from that big hole you put in your chest. You're sticking with me today, kid."

Evan glowered but didn't resist. He shrugged and crossed his arms, waiting for Albrecht to tell him what to do. Albrecht smiled and walked back to the center of the valley, where a command center of sorts had been erected. It consisted of a cleared-out patch of ground where they could draw diagrams in the sand. An outline of the valley had been marked, along with various tactical points of reference.

Evan looked at it but didn't understand all the markings. "Hey, what does that mean?" He pointed to some pictograms drawn near the megaliths.

Albrecht glanced at the map. "Theurges. They're holed up behind the rocks. They can use powers and heal the wounded. I don't want them wading into the fray unless we fail to hold the line. If the enemy gets this deep into the valley, it's going to be a grand melee by that point."

"So what's the battle plan?"

Albrecht sat down on a rock that had been cleared and covered with a furred pelt. "I'll fill everyone in once Abbot gets here. No use repeating myself." He gestured at the space next to him. "This is your seat for the powwow."

Evan rolled his eyes. "That's not politically correct, Albrecht. A lot of my tribemates are justifiably sensitive about the misuse of their language and culture." He sat down anyway, smiling, glad to be beside the king during an important meeting.

Albrecht held out his hands as if to say, *O lord, why me.* "Okay. How about this: We'll call it an overview of our strategic-tactical procedures during the expected conflict."

Evan smiled and shook his head. "Too wonky."

Albrecht smiled. "War briefing?"

Evan nodded. "Succinct and descriptive."

"If we get through this thing alive, you're my new minister of propaganda."

Evan sighed, smiling, and looked down again at the dirt map, waiting for word from Mari.

• • •

The wind on the plain had died down. The day was cloudy and overcast but no snow fell. Mari and the Silver Fang guards stood at the edge of the forest, just within the tree line, watching the large army approach.

"You got an estimate on size?" Mari asked Eric.

"A hundred and fifty. Maybe two hundred," he said. "We expected fifty."

Mari nodded approvingly. "Something must have changed to bring them all out. Something more than just Albrecht."

Eric frowned, glowering at Mari. She gave him an indifferent stare. "Be realistic. They refused us before for good reasons. I can see them pitching in a few more warriors because Albrecht asked for it, but not this many. This looks more like an army of refugees than warriors."

As the army approached, it became clear that many of the marching Garou limped or leaned on others for help. About one-quarter of their number was already wounded.

Mari stepped forward. She spoke to Eric but still watched the army. "Leave half the guard here, hidden in the trees." She turned to look at Quiet Storm, the Wendigo new moon who had accompanied them from camp, and Loper, the Bone Gnawer Theurge. "You two are with us. I want a constant lookout. If you so much as get even a whiff of the Wyrm or something unusual, you let me and Eric know." The two young Garou nodded and came up close behind her.

She walked out of the forest with Eric, five Silver Fang warriors, Quiet Storm and Loper.

At the head of the army, a wolf halted and ran back into the formation. The formation opened up and a pack of men and woman marched forward, dressed in white winter furs. The leader held his hand over his eyes, squinting to block the glare of the snow, still bright even under the overcast sky. He threw back his head and howled a greeting to Mari.

She recognized the howl and returned one of her own, picking up her pace to meet him. "It sounds like Abbot and looks like him from here. You guys smell anything weird?"

"No," Loper said. "Only snow and Garou."

"Everything seems fine," Quiet Storm said. "Loper, how's the Umbra?"

The wolf squinted and stared off into the distance, as if daydreaming. "Empty. Nothing but wind spirits."

Quiet Storm nodded. She knew about the wind spirits. The Wendigo had already talked with them. The spirits promised to bring them news of any strange happening.

"Mari Cabrah!" Thomas Abbot called, waving his hand above his head.

"Abbot!" Mari yelled back, likewise waving.

"That's definitely, Abbot," Eric said. "If this is a trick, it's the best I've seen."

Mari ran the rest of the distance and clasped the old seneschal's hand. Abbot smiled, pleased to see her, and slapped Eric on the shoulder.

"It is good to finally meet friends again," Abbot said. "I'm not used to such a barren trek."

"It's damn good to see you," Mari said, looking out over the army. "Looks like you've been playing Noah."

Abbot smiled, but it was obviously forced. "We do have representatives from all the tribes. Many of them… had no choice. We've lost a lot of caerns, Mari. The northeast is a wasteland. Many of the survivors joined us because they have nowhere else to go."

Mari gestured towards the forest. "I suspected something bad was up. It's been no walk in the park here, either. Come on, let's get them into the valley."

"Valley?" Abbot said. He looked out over the woods. "I can't see it from here."

"It's well hidden," Mari said, leading him toward the trees. "These pines are larger than they appear from a distance. They hide the canyon. It's an ancient Gurahl caern."

Abbot raised his eyebrows. "Fascinating. And the king? How is he?"

"Albrecht's doing just fine," Mari said. "He arrived just in time to help us out of a jam. Even the Wendigo are relieved to have him in command. That's saying something."

Abbot nodded and gestured to the army. They followed behind him, looking eagerly at the trees like desert wanderers at an oasis.

• • •

As the sun set over the lip of the valley walls, the Garou elders gathered at the central command arena and sat in a circle around the dirt-drawn map.

Albrecht sat on the nearby rock, a long stick in his hand. He pointed it at the drawing of the valley passageway. "This is the only real way into the valley. Some creatures might be able to scale the walls, but they're steep and don't have many handholds. Just in case, we're positioning new moons and cubs along the clifftop perimeter with a stack of rocks to throw down at anything coming up.

"Flying creatures, of course, can just come straight in. That's why we've got archers here, here and here." Albrecht pointed to three spots in the valley, one to the rear, one in the middle and one along the clifftop lip of the passageway. "They'll have as many bane arrows and other talens as we can make between now and then."

Albrecht indicated Aurak, who sat nearby. "Aurak tells me that many spirits are fleeing the south, their homes destroyed. They're eager to help get revenge; it's proving no problem to pact them into service. Starting tonight, I need all the Theurges from the new army to get with Aurak on that. Also, anybody else who can handle fetish crafting, tell them to see Aurak. They've got to leave the valley to do it, so we've got a regimen of guards ready to escort them in and out."

Albrecht leaned forward and drew three lines blocking the place where the passage entered the valley. "As for our core defense—our muscle—there's five lines of our best right here, where the enemy has to go to get into the valley."

A Get of Fenris warrior stepped forward. Albrecht nodded at him, signaling that he could speak. "Shouldn't we try to stop them *before* they enter the passage?"

"Yes," Albrecht said. "We've got plans there, too. I'll get to those in a minute." He drew more lines at various places near the mouth of the valley. "The rest of our warriors—the backup—will be positioned here and here, ready to step in and fill the ranks for the wounded and fallen.

"Outside the valley, hidden throughout the woods, are a host of traps—mostly fetishes, but some clever trickster traps with trip wires and falling trees. They might take out a few of the enemy, but it's a delaying tactic at best. What it will do is slow them down while we drop some volleys of arrows into them. Once they're through, though, they'll hit the front lines I already described.

"Back here is the O/R. Packs of Garou runners will ferry the wounded here for healing. Once they're whole, they'll get in line with the backup, waiting their chance to rejoin the defense.

"The second line of backup is here to guard the shamans and half-moons who will be coordinating our spiritual defenses. We're lucky. There's no Umbral front to guard, thanks to the nature of the valley. But that also means we can't send out Umbral forces for hit-and-run; they wouldn't be able to get back in.

"The secondary backup is also ready in case the enemy does find a way to bypass the passage. They'll need to hold it off while the main defense falls back into our alternate plans. I'll discuss those later with the generals, who will explain them to their packs. Basically, there are a number of different formations to fall into in response to attacks from anywhere in the valley. For instance, if they break through the canyon wall here, we go to formation number five."

A Shadow Lord shaman stepped forward, waiting for Albrecht to acknowledge him. The king nodded at him. He pointed at the valley floor. "What if they have a thunderwyrm? It can come from anywhere below."

Albrecht looked at Painted Claw, who stood up to address the group. "My pack has experience against thunderwyrms. Pentex tried to hatch a brood near our forests a few years ago. The foundation under this valley is very strong, more so than most places. The thunderwyrms can break through it, but it will take them time. We will hear them and feel their vibrations long before they arrive. If so, Albrecht will call for formation number ten, where the secondary backup prepares to rush to the incursion point. All half-moon elders will join them and summon earth spirits to aid our defense." Painted Claw sat down again.

Albrecht put down his stick and stood up. "That's the basic overview. The details will be worked out with each pack, so they'll know their role and their alternate actions. Any questions?"

Nobody said anything. They all looked at the map, familiarizing themselves with it. Finally, True Silverheels, the elder of the Children of Gaia from the Finger Lakes Caern, stood up. Albrecht nodded at him.

"What sort of enemies are we expecting? New York was attacked by Black Spiral Dancers, banes and fomori. I have heard disturbing stories about the battle on the Plain of the Apocalypse, where it is said that the Margrave Konietzko and Queen Tvarivich fell. The sheer variety of foes there… if we are confronted with the same composition, we will be sorely tested."

Albrecht looked out at the faces watching him. "There's no reason to candy coat this. The battle on the plain was bad. But it was decisive, in our favor. A lot of creatures died there, thanks to the Margrave and Tvarivich's leadership. These things never made it to the material world.

What we've been fighting at our caerns up till now are the homegrown nasties. They've proved bad enough. Now, however, they're throwing everything they've got at us. This army's coming from Malfeas, which means it's full of the worst things imaginable. Things that can't even exist normally in the material world. I suspect they've found some power to get over that limitation.

"I don't know if we're the only ones targeted. There are surely other pockets of Garou resistance left around the world. The Wyrm forces will have to deal with them, too. If they split their forces, our chances improve. However… I think that Zhyzhak, the leader of a Black Spiral Dancer caern in New Mexico, did something unprecedented. She somehow unlocked the power of the Black Spiral Labyrinth and used it to lead the armies out of Malfeas. She swore she'd come kick my ass. I think this is her move."

The Get of Fenris snarled and spoke without waiting for permission. "Then we will gut her and choke the Wyrm with her intestines! Let her come! Hail Albrecht, true foe of the Wyrm!"

Others yelled out cries of affirmation and howls of glory. Albrecht didn't respond. He watched the faces of the elders, most of whom did not cheer, but they did nod sagely. None of them complained or seemed to disagree with what was said. That was a minor victory in itself, unprecedented in his previous history with them.

"Okay," Albrecht said, raising his hands for them to be silent. The cheering died down. "Like I said, that's the end of the briefing. Details to follow. Abbot here," he indicated Thomas Abbot, his steward who had led the reinforcements, "has been fully briefed. He'll help spread the information to the generals, who will in turn brief their packs. I want everybody fully prepared by dawn. All estimates from the spirits coming in seem to point to an attack sometime tomorrow night. We're done here. Now spread the word."

Albrecht walked away, joined by Evan and Mari. The gathered Garou rose and shuffled away, each heading for his assigned camp. The warriors stayed behind to get detailed orders from Thomas Abbot and Eric Honnunger.

Albrecht leaned against the cliff wall, beneath the overhang at his camp. He rubbed his forehead and slumped his shoulders.

"Something's bugging you," Evan said. "Spill it. You can hide it from the others, but not us."

Albrecht looked wearily at Evan and Mari. "I failed big time. It's all my fault we're in this mess."

Mari frowned. "What the hell are you talking about?"

Albrecht crossed his arms, still leaning against the cliff. "Tvarivich asked me to join her and the Margrave. He was gathering an army. She wanted me to lead it with them. I refused, too damn concerned about getting home."

"That doesn't sound selfish to me," Evan said. "You had no idea what was going on back here. Nobody could have predicted things would get this bad."

"The Plain of the Apocalypse," Albrecht said, staring out across the valley. "For Gaia's sake, if I only knew it would come to that... If I'd been there, maybe I could've turned the tide. You heard Mephi's report. If Tvarivich killed the Black Spiral Dancer general, the army would have been in disarray. I could have pressed that advantage. If we'd won there, this thing would be over."

"What makes you think that?" Mari said, incredulous.

"You've heard the legends about that place. The final battle was supposed to be fought there. What if that *was* the final battle? We lost. That means we're just part of the Wyrm's clean-up operation. If we'd won there, maybe Zhyzhak wouldn't have succeeded, or wouldn't be as powerful."

"You're wrong," Mari said with a growl. "This is the most egotistical bullshit I've ever heard. You would have died there with the rest of them. Your duty led you here, Albrecht. There's a reason for it. The Heartsplinter, the Ancient Bear, this valley—it's not coincidence. The last battle is meant to be here. It always has been—here on earth, not in some distant Umbral realm where no sane spirit actually lives."

Albrecht looked at her. "I don't deny there's some sort of providence in this place, Mari. But it feels a lot more like a final refuge than a battlefield."

"Quit this sulking," Mari said, pacing. "You've got a whole army of Garou who have fled their caerns to fight here with you. Get out there and show your face again."

"She's right," Evan said. "We're all feeling the weight of this, you most of all. But it's what you've been working toward since you were born. You're the king. You wear the Silver Crown. When they see that band on your head, they know they belong here, fighting for something greater than their own territory."

Albrecht stepped forward and smiled. "The tough love committee. Thanks." He stretched, standing at his full height. "You're right. No use living in the past, reliving bad decisions. I've got to get out there and review the troops."

"I'll come with you," Mari said. "I want to get sense of who we've got with us."

Evan yawned. "I'm going to bed."

They both looked at him, shaking their heads.

He shrugged his shoulders. "What? You said yourself that I'm still recovering. Come dawn, I need to help make fetishes. I don't have an endless supply of energy."

Albrecht nodded. "Okay, you're excused. See you in the morning." He turned and walked over to the nearest campfire, followed by Mari.

The Garou gathered there rose when they saw the king coming.

• • •

By the middle of the night, Albrecht and Mari had reached the mouth of the valley, where the hardiest of troops gathered.

"It's weird," Albrecht said. "I expected they'd be somber and grim. But most of them are excited."

"The moment long awaited has finally come," Mari said. "They've been told all their lives to prepare for the Apocalypse. Now that it's here, their waiting is finally over. It's time for action. Regardless of victory or defeat, they will die as Garou, howling as one to Gaia and the Moon."

Albrecht nodded. "I feel a bit of that myself. No matter what happens, we're at ground zero. The moment of truth. No more false victories and slow defeats. This will decide things."

"Even if we die, our lives will not have been wasted."

"No. We fought the good fight." Albrecht looked around, making sure no one else was in earshot. "I don't like the whispering I keep hearing, though. That 'last Gaian king' prophecy crap. Some of these guys are convinced my number's up."

"Who can blame them?" Mari shrugged. "Our lives are riddled with omens. So many of them are wrong, but enough of them are right."

"You don't believe this one, do you? I mean, it came from the mouth of an insane Garou. Not exactly the most reliable of oracles."

"Does it matter?" Mari met Albrecht's eyes. "If we die fighting, we will still have won."

"Yeah, but I refuse to buy into the idea that Zhyzhak—*Zhyzhak* of all creatures—can best me! It's just… demeaning. I mean, why can't I fight a nexus crawler like the Margrave? That's the way to go!"

Mari stared at him, exasperated. "You never fail to astonish me, Albrecht. You can turn a solemn discussion about our fate into a pissing contest with a Black Spiral Dancer."

"Hey," Albrecht said, frowning, "if it was you they were talking about, would you put up with it? Are you going to let Zhyzhak's legend beat you?"

Mari snorted, walking away. "Ha! That'll be the day. I could kick that bitch from here to Russia."

Albrecht growled in frustration. "Oh, I get it. My whining is only an issue because you think she can actually beat me! Think again, Cabrah. I nearly had her…"

Mari turned and gave him a smoldering glare. "Albrecht. Enough."

Albrecht grumbled under his breath, eyes rolling. He and Mari had arrived at the farthest campfire, the one that guarded the passage. It was manned mainly by Silver Fangs, but there were also Fenrir and Red Talons among them, those itching the most for a fight.

A Silver Fang warrior had just shifted to battle form, barking at another Garou, a young cub from the looks of it. The cub refused to back down.

"What's going on here?" Albrecht said. "I don't want any challenges going down. Do you hear me?"

The Silver Fang backed down, deferring to Albrecht. The cub stared at Albrecht in awe. He cautiously approached the king.

"King Albrecht?" he said, his voice low and nervous.

"Who are you?" Albrecht said, looking him over skeptically. The cub had no battle scars. "And what are you doing here on the front lines?"

The cub swallowed and looked away, too nervous to meet Albrecht's eyes. "My name is Martin, sir. I… I was raised by Aunt Loba."

Albrecht cocked an eyebrow. "Loba? Loba Carcassone?"

"Yeah," Martin said, frowning. "She… was killed. I came here. I want to fight with you!" He looked back at Albrecht, meeting his eyes.

"So you're the cub Abbot told me about," Albrecht said. "I'm sorry to hear about Loba. She was one of our best. I don't understand, though, why she didn't officially induct you into the tribe. You told Abbot she adopted you, saved you from the Seventh Generation. What was your parents' tribe?"

Martin looked down again, shuffling his feet. "I don't know. She wouldn't tell me. She said when I was old enough, after my Rite of Passage, she'd bring me to you."

Albrecht nodded. "She sure kept her secrets, a habit she developed under Morningkill's rule. I don't think anybody, even me, could win enough of her trust to learn them all."

"She had good reason," Mari said, watching the boy with a look of concern. "Everybody shunned her for years, refusing to believe what she knew about the Defiler Wyrm and its plots. She saved many children, although most of those she gave to the other tribes to raise. Martin, did she raise any other cubs besides you?"

Martin shook his head. He wouldn't meet Mari's gaze.

"You're welcome to join the army, Martin," Albrecht said. Martin smiled. "But you need to get your butt back where Abbot put you, with the shamans."

Martin's smile faded. He hung his head. "But I'm an Ahroun, born under the full moon. I can fight!"

"And you will. Believe me. Every damn one of us will get his claws bloody. But only the best, the most experienced belong here. Look at these guys," Albrecht said, pointing to various warriors. "You see those scars? You don't get those from shaving. Every one of these guys has been through hell and back and has the notches on his klaive to prove it. You'll get your chance, but these guys have earned the right to stand here. You haven't."

Martin nodded, his head hanging down. "Yes, sir." He shuffled away sulking, not looking back, heading for the megalithic rocks where the Theurges gathered.

• • •

Later that night, as the very first hints of dawn rose on the horizon, the howls of the sentries echoed through the valley. Eric Honnunger woke Albrecht.

"Our Umbral scouts are reporting something," he said. "They say it's important."

Albrecht nodded and stood. "Okay, take me to them." He looked down at Evan and Mari, sleeping soundly. He quietly picked up his klaive and followed Eric out of the passageway.

The scouts gathered just inside the main entrance. John North Wind's Son was with them.

"So what's up?" Albrecht said. "Good news or bad?"

John North Wind's Son looked sour. "My father came to me. I walked the perimeter in the Umbra, watching for signs of our enemy approaching. The sky was dark. The moon had not been seen all night, even though it should have been full. A great wind rushed through me and a voice spoke—the voice of my father, the wind spirit. He says that the stars have died."

Albrecht frowned. "What does that mean? I don't get it. I saw the moon just fine earlier."

"But none of us could see it from the Umbra. I searched the skies but I saw no lights, no stars. Only darkness."

Albrecht looked up at the sky, but the faint trace of the coming dawn blocked the light of the stars, had there been any.

A Garou broke through the ranks of defenders, rushing from outside the valley. "My lord! A pack approaches, numbering five!"

"Who are they?" Albrecht said.

"We cannot tell from this distance."

John North Wind's Son shivered and his hair seemed to move in a nonexistent breeze. "They are… the Sept of the Stars. From the Aetherial Realm."

"This can't be coincidence," Albrecht said. "These guys never leave their perch. Was that your father just now, whispering to you? How'd he get into the valley, past its wards?"

"He is outside, bellowing at me," John said. "Anyone in the Penumbra can surely hear him."

"But you're not in the Penumbra," Albrecht said, looking oddly yet approvingly at John North Wind's Son.

"I am his son," John said.

"All right," Albrecht said, turning to his warriors. "I want these guys checked for Wyrm taint, and I want a half-moon to make sure they're not lying. If they check out, let them in."

The scout ran back outside to convey the message. He returned a little while later. "There is no Wyrm taint on them and Dark Runner says they do not lie."

Eric Honnunger came down the passage, escorting the Sept of the Stars. Albrecht recognized Altair. The elder walked with a staff, more of an affectation or a fetish than a walking aid, for he was in perfect physical shape. The Stargazer elder could probably win out over a number of the warriors gathered here. He bowed before Albrecht, as did his followers.

"Greetings, King Albrecht," Altair said. "We have come to aid the last battle."

"We could sure use you," Albrecht said, offering the elder his hand. Altair took it gladly. "Last battle, huh? Is that written in the stars?"

"The stars have fallen," Altair said, releasing the king's hand. "The sky crumbles. Even the moon has gone into hiding. The Wyrm marches."

Albrecht frowned. "Fallen? As in gone for good? And what do you mean 'the Wyrm marches'? Not *the* Wyrm itself?"

Altair nodded. "The raw force of destruction, one of three primal forces, has been unleashed. Instead of restoring balance, it tears down everything in its path, leaving nothing to renew. It marches at the behest of its children. Their twisted worship warps its mission."

Albrecht said nothing for a while, staring at the sky. "You said the moon was in hiding. You mean Luna, right? If so, why'd I see her earlier?"

"Her material reflection still shines. Only her spiritual shadow is occulted. The Wyrm sought to devour her, but she sloughed her skin, leaving it nothing to grasp."

Albrecht smiled. "Good old Luna. As long as the moon shines in this world, we've got a chance."

● ● ●

On the following evening, as the sun sank low, the Garou took their places, waiting. The wind outside the valley wove through the trees, creating a low roar as branches swayed, but the interior of the valley was still; the walls blocked the worst of the wind's knives.

Two Wendigo shamans hid among the trees in the Umbra, watching for any sign of approaching spirits. The wind spirits flowed around them, John's father among them, bringing gossip from far realms, tales of torn and shattered places from which spirits fled.

Across the snowy tundra, a lone spirit came, flying on broken wings. The crow fluttered to the ground beneath a tree, cawing a desperate message. The shamans looked at one another and then stepped through the Gauntlet, into the material world. They ran for the passageway, howling.

As their howls reached the scouts on the peaks, different throats repeated them, yelling them into the valley. The camp below stirred. Every Garou listened to the howls and looked at one another, their jaws set and weapons ready.

The enemy approached.

The Last Battle

Chapter Twenty-Three:
The Last Gaian King

The dragon thundered through the pitch black Umbral sky. The broken paths and realms below lay in darkness; the Moon hid her silver light. The dragon thudded to the ground, its claws gripping into the ephemeral dirt of the Penumbra, the spiritual reflection of the material world. It opened its jaw and bit into the air, tearing a chunk of invisible threads from the fabric of the Gauntlet.

It poked its snout through the hole and sucked in its breath, drawing the Gauntlet into its maw. Like a sheet crumpled into a ball, the Gauntlet peeled away, sliding into the dragon's endless stomach.

A terrible rending sound echoed through the Penumbra and the material world as the wall between the two realities collapsed. The ground began to shake as the two worlds merged, matter and spirit colliding like tectonic plates.

Spirits materialized all over the planet, their ephemera transforming into flesh and blood, their subtle forms drawn into dense matter by the physical world's immense gravity. The realms of the Spirit Wilds manifested in forests, fields, streams and in cities. Ancient spirit oaks thrust up from concrete, towering past skyscrapers. Rivers rerouted themselves as their sentient spirits gained sway. The cities, bereft of Pattern Spider spirit protectors, crumbled. People ran riot throughout the streets, chased by mythological beasts made real.

The forces of the Wyld ran amok, freed from the limits of the Weaver's webs and the wall of the Gauntlet. They began to enact ancient vendettas against humans, hunting and killing them. Chaos reigned.

Then the dragon finished its meal and stepped forward, stamping its foot onto the earth. It slid forward, fully entering the material world onto the vast plain outside King Albrecht's valley holdout. The tundra shook. The snow exploded into steam.

Drawn there by an urge even it didn't understand, it raised its head and vomited a black, oily ball of muck. The thing unraveled as it rolled, spooling off banes and monsters. The creatures rose, dripping with the Wyrm's slime, casting about for prey.

The last being to rise from the muck roared in exultant victory. Her massive battle form was taller and broader than before, her fur matted with the Wyrm's slick digestive juices. She raised her hand and unraveled a barbed whip, bringing it down with a terrible crack that split the air like thunder.

Zhyzhak's minions, the army of Malfeas, turned to watch her, waiting for orders.

Zhyzhak sauntered past the Maeljin Incarna, horrendously malformed beings whose eyes watched her, tinged with hate and fear. They once ruled in Malfeas; now they begged at her feet.

She walked past them, staring at the forest ahead, growling. "What's going on?" she cried. "Why did we stop here? Where's Albrecht?"

A mewling, whining Maeljin, crouching by her leg, spoke. "The Wyrm cannot penetrate the Gauntlet around the valley."

Zhyzhak backhanded him, sending him tumbling through the blasted rocks, now bare of snow. "DuBois, you bastard! Don't lie to *me*!"

Another Maeljin approached, although she kept out of arm's reach. "For once, DuBois speaks truth, Zhyzhak."

Zhyzhak's eyes narrowed. "Aliara! If this is a trick!"

A new Maeljin—the short and pudgy Doge Klypse—stepped forward. "No trick! The Wyrm has been halted in its tracks."

Zhyzhak glared at Klypse. She stared up at the dragon, which sat unmoving, its eyes closed. She could sense a boiling, frantic energy in it, but it felt trapped, confined by some unknown force.

Zhyzhak screamed and snapped her whip. The barbed tail instantly severed the heads of three banes. Zhyzhak smiled at the comical look on their faces as they died. She turned to face the valley, snarling. "Albrecht! This won't stop me!"

She marched forward, cracking her whip in the air. "Come on! We'll charge in ourselves!"

A tall, thin Maeljin refused to move. He yelled at her. "We cannot enter! The Gauntlet is torn everywhere but there—that is why the Wyrm cannot move forward. We have no power to traverse it. Only those spirits and creatures who already possess material bodies can pass through."

Zhyzhak screamed and spun around, bolting at the Maeljin. She landed on his chest, knocking him to the hard ground. Her jaw slavered inches from his nose. "Thurifuge! You lazy bastard! You will do as I say!"

Thurifuge, his eyes half-lidded, seemed unconcerned about the proximity of her snout. "I have no choice, thanks to your usurpation. You are the teacher's pet for now, Zhyzhak. But even you can't undo the power of that valley from outside."

Zhyzhak growled, drawing back her claws. "We undid the Weaver's web! There should be no more Gauntlet!"

Doge Klypse stepped forward again. "Clearly, something else is powering this wall! Perhaps it is…" he shuddered in disgust, "…the Earth Mother herself."

Zhyzhak stood still, thinking. She looked at the valley. Her snarl slowly became a grin. She barked a series of terrifying laughs and crawled off Lord Thurifuge. "Then I will tear it down from within! Once it's down, you follow!"

She roared to the assembled creatures and marched off toward the valley. A number of banes, monsters and Black Spiral Dancers fell in behind her, but more of them stayed behind, watching her go. They turned to watch the Maeljin.

The former Lords of Malfeas gathered together, watching Zhyzhak storm her way toward the forest.

"I almost wish she would fail," Thurifuge said, sneering at her rapidly departing figure.

"Then you're a fool," Aliara said. "Victory is almost in our hands, but it depends on her."

"I don't believe your theory," DuBois said, still rubbing his injured jaw. "If she falls, *we* will rule again."

Aliara looked at her co-conspirators. "Your raw desire blinds you." She looked back at Zhyzhak and her army. Even reduced in size, it still consisted of nearly five hundred creatures. She didn't know how many Garou huddled in the quaint valley, but she doubted they had near that many defenders. She smiled. The object of her own desire would soon be within reach: the entire universe reduced to rotting feces shat forth from the Wyrm's filthy anus.

● ● ●

"Hold positions, goddamn it!" Albrecht yelled. He pointed his klaive up at the Garou archers who tried to scramble down the valley walls, abandoning their posts. They froze at the sound of his growls, afraid to continue down but also afraid to return.

"I don't care what you see!" Albrecht said, sheathing his klaive and grasping a handhold on the cliff face. He pulled himself up, reaching for more handholds, scaling the sheer wall. The deserters scrambled back up the wall as he climbed higher.

Albrecht gritted his teeth and kept pulling himself up. It wasn't an easy climb, although it was better from inside the valley than outside, where the wall was even steeper and more sheer. He finally reached the lip and tugged himself over. Garou archers—those who had not attempted to desert their posts—grabbed his arms and helped lift him up.

He stood on the rocky path that followed the topmost lip and stared out across the tundra, at the sight that had spread fear among the ranks. He felt a lurch in his stomach.

A vast serpent sat on the plain, coiled around itself like a mountain. Just looking upon it wrenched his guts and sent an instinctual signal to his brain, screaming for him to run. He growled to hide the chill, turning the growing frenzy into resolve. Aurak was right; it was easier to control his rage now than it had been before. He still had to fight against the panicked urge to run, but he didn't feel the same uncontrollable anger that he often used to counteract fear.

Tiny figures approached en masse, a horde of creatures running for the valley, screaming and yelling. Leading them was a large Garou. Zhyzhak.

He turned away from the dragon and looked into the eyes of the archers. They met his gaze, searching for some sign of assurance, some excuse not to throw down their weapons and flee.

He growled and stepped forward, placing his hand on one archer's bow, then raising it and pointing it toward the onrushing army. He spoke in a steely voice. "See those bastards out there? Shoot them."

The archer blinked and nodded, shaking off his unreasoning fear. He snarled and pointed his bow at Zhyzhak. He raised it higher to adjust for the distance and released the string. The arrow shot into the sky, arcing high and descending again, hurtling toward the distant Garou. It *thunked* into the ground inches from her feet, causing her to veer from her course.

Zhyzhak looked up at the cliff and howled, snapping her whip wildly before rushing onward again.

"See?" Albrecht said. "It's that easy. Next time, hit her."

The archers roared and raised their bows, hurling arrows into the massed army. The barbs struck a number of the enemy forces, knocking them down. Those behind the fallen did not bother to veer aside; they rushed on, trampling and killing those the arrows had already wounded.

The archers cheered and nocked new arrows, drawing them back and releasing them simultaneously. The swarm of bane arrows dug into more flesh, wounding and killing scores of creatures.

Zhyzhak entered the trees, protected from the arrows.

"Keep firing at the army," Albrecht said. "Take out as many as you can." He stepped to the edge and looked down into the passage. "You," he said, grabbing the arm of an archer. "Get ten guys to watch the passage. As soon as you can see them, fire away. I don't want a single creature to reach the front lines without at least one arrow in it."

Albrecht ran back to the place he had climbed and began to lower himself down, hurriedly grabbing handholds and feeling for footholds.

A voice at his shoulder startled him. "Let me take you down," Painted Claw said. He floated in the air, riding a vortex of icy wind, using a rare Wendigo power.

Albrecht smiled and let the Ahroun wrap his arms around his shoulders, lifting him off the wall. He descended rapidly and Painted Claw released him just above the ground. He landed on both feet and waved at the Wendigo.

Painted Claw rose up again, heading up to join the archers. Albrecht knew he would be back to aid the front lines as soon as the enemy arrived.

Albrecht headed for the command center, the place where the Theurges positioned themselves. Mari and Evan waited there for him.

"Mari!" he yelled. "They're coming. We need to be up front."

Mari nodded and put her hand on Evan's shoulder, squeezing it tight.

Evan had a frustrated, pained expression on his face. "Let me go up there with you, Albrecht."

Albrecht shook his head. "You stay here, with Aurak. The shamans need a line of defense."

"He's right," Mari said, releasing his shoulder. "You can do more from here."

Evan gritted his teeth. "But I won't be with you."

Albrecht gripped Evan's arm and released it. "You will. Just not physically."

"It's not the same," Evan said.

"Hey, somebody's got to protect our backs. That's what your bow is for."

Evan nodded and punched Albrecht's arm. "If you say so." He looked at Mari and smiled, but his eyes were clearly sad.

"This isn't the end, Evan," Mari said. "We'll make it through this."

Albrecht stepped away, signaling Mari with a nod that they had to go. She met Evan's eyes one last time and turned away, jogging with Albrecht toward the front lines.

As they ran, a slender, lean Crinos form joined them.

"Mephi," Albrecht said, "you ready to play herald again?"

"Absolutely," Mephi said. "Just tell me a message and point out who needs to get it and I'm there."

"Your speed's going to come in handy," Albrecht said. "Glad you're with us."

They approached the rear line of warriors amassed by the passage. The warriors moved aside to admit the king and his entourage. Albrecht's place was in the fourth line, where he could bark out orders and coordinate the fighting, but also close enough where he could jump into the fray himself as needed. Mari took up a fighting position beside him, while Mephi stayed behind, ready to convey orders to any place in camp at Albrecht's command.

A snarling growl broke out in the front line, followed by howl of challenge. A screeching roar responded within the passage and the first line of Wyrm creatures hit the first line of Gaian defenders.

Albrecht howled a call to battle and the Garou tore into the malformed creatures. The first wave fell within moments, torn apart by the expert claws of the frontline Garou, each a high-ranking warrior. A howl of triumph went up, followed by a cheer from those within the valley.

The second wave pounded down the passage, their bodies riddled with arrows from above, snarling and screaming for blood.

• • •

Evan watched the battle from a distance, his bow ready with an arrow nocked in case he needed to use it. Aurak stood by his side, lightly pounding a drum. The fetish held a great war spirit from the Battleground realm, ready to manifest as soon as Aurak pounded the proper series of beats.

Behind them, Martin paced, his claws opening and closing, itching to fight. Most of the shamans intently watched the battle or prepared to release spirits bound into fetishes or talens. Some watched the tops of the walls or the rear of the valley, scanning for trouble from other directions.

Martin shifted to dire wolf form and bolted forward, faster than the Theurges could react. He shot past Evan and ran toward the front lines.

"No!" Evan yelled. "Get back here! You're not ready!"

Martin either didn't hear or refused to listen. He ran into the crowded fifth line and was lost to sight in the fray.

• • •

Zhyzhak rushed down the passage, arrows bouncing off her fur. The oily residue from the Wyrm's stomach provided a near-frictionless surface. The arrows couldn't find purchase.

She burst into the rear ranks of her army, shoving aside scrags and skull pigs, pushing to reach the front. As soon as the army realized she was there, they let out an exultant cheer and moved aside for her.

She lunged forward and into the line of Garou. Her jaws snapped down on a Fenrir's neck. She clamped down hard and shook her head, thrashing the trapped Garou to her right and left, knocking aside his compatriots. She released him and drove her claws into his belly, yanking out a handful of guts. The Fenrir collapsed, wheezing as air escaped from the ragged holes in this throat.

Zhyzhak stepped over him and slashed at more Garou, looking past them, searching for signs of Albrecht.

The Garou pressed forward, a small charge instigated by something behind them. Their ranks opened enough to admit a white-furred Garou. King Albrecht immediately fell upon Zhyzhak, knocking her over.

She snarled and scraped her claws against his metallic silver fur, screaming in pain at the burning contact. She spat a foaming green fire at him, pissed that he'd use the same trick as last time they clashed. She hooked her whip around his neck and squeezed.

Albrecht's claws tore off chunks of the slimy ichor that protected Zhyzhak's flesh. Before he could penetrate her skin, his throat closed up, squeezed by her whip. He leaped back with a burst of strength, almost pulling the whip from Zhyzhak's hands, and slashed down with his klaive. The blade, supernaturally sharpened by an earth spirit Aurak had bound into it, sliced cleanly through the whip, tearing it in two. Albrecht fell back as the tension suddenly released. He yanked the whip from his throat and threw it on the ground.

Zhyzhak howled in rage, clutching the other end of the broken whip, staring at the remains of her beloved fetish. Her eyes squinted and her jaw opened wide, a deafening growl exploding from her throat.

She launched herself up and forward, barreling into Albrecht. She drove the king against the canyon wall, knocking the breath out of him. Her claws drilled into his chest, tearing away the silver armor as if it were paper, drawing gouts of blood.

Suddenly she stumbled, weak in the knees, her blows glancing off the king. She limped backwards, confused, and looked down at her stomach. Albrecht's klaive jutted from her guts, exiting out her backside. She felt a sudden wave of fear and clutched at the klaive's handle, tugging it with her fading strength. It slid out, nicking her spine. She spasmed as the nerves ignited in pain, dropping the klaive to the ground with a clatter.

Albrecht slowly rose, obviously in pain, his veins inflamed with Zhyzhak's poison. He grunted and swayed unsteadily. Zhyzhak stumbled backward, clutching her gut. Albrecht's klaive lay on the ground. Almost instinctively, ignoring the screaming in his veins, he snatched the weapon up.

A horde of Garou warriors leaped between him and Zhyzhak. Creatures fell upon them, inserting themselves between the Garou and their queen. Hands lifted Albrecht up and carried him away, back down the passage. A mob of creatures tugged Zhyzhak back, dragging her down the path.

Mephi Faster-Than-Death ran over to Evan and Aurak. "The king needs healing!"

Aurak shifted to wolf form and ran after Mephi. Evan snarled and chased after them. If his job was to protect Aurak, he could do that by Albrecht's side.

The elder pushed the warriors away and bent over the king. Albrecht shivered in a fever, fighting a toxin in his bloodstream. Aurak shifted into human form and drew a handful of leaves from his pouch, placing them on Albrecht's torn and bloody chest. He spoke a few words and the leaves shriveled, drying instantly.

Albrecht's eyes opened. Aurak and Evan leaned over him, faces taught with concern. His fever was gone and the pain in his limbs dissipated.

Aurak nodded, relieved. "The Crawling Poison was strong, but the spirits of Pangaia are stronger."

Albrecht sat up, looking at the pass. Warriors bunched around the entry, still fighting the incursion. The enemy had not broken through. Garou in dire wolf form ran back and forth, dragging wounded warriors away from the front lines, back to the healers in the valley.

"Where's Zhyzhak?" Albrecht said, standing up.

"She was pulled into the forest," Mephi said. "Presumably for healing."

"Have they sprung any of the traps?"

"Most of them," Mephi said. "As far as we can tell, falling trees took out a few of the enemy. But that didn't slow them down much."

Albrecht nodded, examining his klaive. Blood caked the fine silver-steel alloy. "At least I got a piece of her."

• • •

Zhyzhak grunted as the maggots crawled through her guts, secreting a mushy substance that scarred over her torn flesh. She rubbed the bumpy scar on her stomach where the klaive had entered. It itched annoyingly.

She spat onto the ground and kicked the solicitous healers away. She looked around and gestured to four packs of Black Spiral Dancers. "You! Who has patagia?"

Nine of them nodded, grunting and hooting, opening their arms to reveal flaps of skin connecting their underarms to their torsos.

"Follow me!" Zhyzhak led them to a large stand of trees near the cliff face. The trees towered upwards, almost reaching the cliff's peak. She reached up and grasped a limb, pulling her body up. "Climb!"

The Dancers spread out among the trees and began to climb them, cackling and barking as they moved higher and higher.

A loud cracking sound reverberated through the air. One of the tree trunks swayed, then snapped and tumbled to the ground. The Dancer climbing it leaped away, spreading his skin flaps. They caught the wind and he glided down in circles, cursing and gnashing his teeth as the others laughed at him.

"Climb!" Zhyzhak yelled and the laughing stopped. The Dancers hurried their pace, rushing to the tree tops.

Once everyone was positioned, Zhyzhak pointed across the empty space to the cliff top, where archers aimed arrows at them. She snarled and launched herself into the air, her own patagia skin catching the wind and carrying her upwards. The other Dancers lurched into the sky with her, veering in different directions to catch the wind gusts.

Arrows rained down on them. Two Dancers gurgled loudly and fell, arrows buried deep in their chests. Three more Dancers howled as arrows pierced their limbs, but they kept climbing, catching new winds.

Two arrows bounced off Zhyzhak's hide. She huffed and huffed, drawing deep breaths, and belched a gout of green flame at the row of archers. They leaped back, screaming in pain, dropping their bows as they frantically tried to extinguish their burning fur.

Zhyzhak landed on the ledge and waded into them, knocking three of them over the side with one blow. The Dancers landed at other places on the ledge and slashed into the defenders, who dropped their bows to deal with the assault claw-to-claw.

Zhyzhak didn't bother with them. She screeched in what sounded like a bat language and leaped forward, shoving aside more defenders, until she reached the far ledge. She looked down into the valley and saw her prey.

Arms spread wide, she vaulted over the edge, falling fast toward the valley floor, followed by four other Black Spiral Dancers.

She rocketed at King Albrecht's head. The king turned to see her coming and tried to dodge out of the way, but she changed her flight path to intercept him. A sudden wind cut under her, picking her up and throwing her back, out of control. The icy air pounded into her, freezing her lungs, and bashed her against the rock wall.

She slid to the ground, hitting hard, stunned. She saw a young Wendigo standing next to Albrecht, directing the wind that tore at her fur. The king's accursed packmate.

Six howling Gaian warriors landed on her, slashing at her wrists and legs, pinning her down. She closed her eyes and spat a curse in a language harmful to human ears. Her skin burst, revealing new, warty gray hide. Her body warped and spasmed as she grew to huge proportions, three times her normal size.

The combined strength and weight of the warriors were no match for her Wyrmish power. She flung them away with ease, cackling through a disfigured throat. Her body vibrated, muscles growing and shrinking, contracting and expanding. Her claws grew into miniature scythes, dripping with venom. She roared in laughter, thinking of the irony. She had been taught this power by Duchess Aliara when she had attained the fifth rank. Now, she ruled over that Maeljin Lord.

She paced forward, glaring at the warriors. Their courage faltered and they hesitated to engage her.

King Albrecht strode forward, heading straight for her, swinging his accursed klaive. She wouldn't be so stupid as to let him land a blow this time.

A weight landed on her shoulders and something tore at her ears. Before she could react, her left ear was ripped from her body while a claw dug into her gums, wrenching her head back with incredible strength. She lunged backwards into the wall with massive force. The attacker on her back grunted, letting go.

She spun around and sliced at the attacking Garou. He howled in agony as her claw flayed his bicep from his left arm. She hesitated, surprised. Her assailant was a mere cub. How had he delivered such pain?

The cub stared at her, his eyes pits of rage. He leaped up and clamped his jaws around her throat with such speed she could only stumble backwards in shock. She snatched at him with her claws but couldn't tug him from his grip. She felt his teeth penetrate her muscles and saw her own blood spray across the Garou's fur.

She poked her thumb into the boy's eye, her sharp claw popping the gelatinous flesh like a bubble. His jaws opened, screaming, as his hands went up to protect his eye. She swatted him away, relishing the crunch of his bones as he tumbled into the wall.

She spun around to look for Albrecht and saw his other packmate, the Black Fury sow, hands open wide, pointing at her. Ten wasps shot from her hands, diving through the air in curving arcs. They drove straight into Zhyzhak's eyes. She howled and reeled, plucking the flying claws from her face. Her eyes were mangled orbs hanging from their sockets. She was completely blind.

She smelled Albrecht's scent and snarled. She bunched her legs up under her and leaped into the air, spreading her wings. She vaulted away from him, flying erratically across the valley. She thudded into another wall and sniffed, smelling for her enemies. Their scent was distant. She had crossed the whole valley in one leap.

She dropped to the ground and moaned, clutching her skull.

• • •

Albrecht cursed as Zhyzhak leaped away from his klaive strike. She shot across the valley and slammed into the far wall. He looked down at Martin, Loba's adopted cub. The boy thrashed in pain, clutching his lost eye. Albrecht had never seen a Garou move so fast—and he'd seen the best of the best. The boy clearly had abilities well beyond what even elders could do.

He bent down, offering the boy his arm. "It's all right, kid. Losing an eye is nothing. Come on, get up!"

Martin opened his good eye and stared at Albrecht, frowning. He relaxed, as if the pain had gone. His jaw opened into a crooked grin and he began to laugh.

Albrecht stared in shock at the cub as a cracked, hoarse female voice rumbled from his throat. With the same speed he had shown earlier, he snatched at Albrecht's hand, pulling him close. Before Albrecht could react, Martin's other hand yanked the Silver Crown off his head.

Martin rolled away, clutching the crown with both hands, laughing in that eerie voice. Albrecht stared at him, aghast. Nobody had ever touched the crown before without screaming in pain as the silver burnt their flesh. Even those who had dared to touch it couldn't budge it from his head. Only he could take it on and off.

Martin halted, staring at Albrecht with wide eyes, and dropped the crown onto his own head.

His forehead bubbled and extruded outwards. The skin split in a horizontal line across his brow, revealing a red orb with a catlike pupil. The eye began to glow, radiating a sickly red light in a swath before it.

Martin laughed again in that strange female voice and then screamed in the spirit tongue. The words rang out, echoing louder than his normal voice could have sounded. It sought out the ears of every Garou and insinuated a message: *Flee!*

The warriors holding the entry to the valley howled in fear and fell back, scattering across the valley. The Wyrm forces cheered and broke through, chasing after them, falling on their backs, hacking and slashing with claws and teeth.

Albrecht roared a command for his Garou to stop and fight but they didn't seem to hear. He recognized the power that compelled them, for he was immune to it. The Silver Crown.

He rushed at Martin, raising his klaive.

Martin leaped back, yelling again: *Defend me!*

Mari Cabrah barreled into Albrecht, knocking him over. Her rear claws slashed at his legs, tearing open wounds. He snarled and hit her in the chin with his klaive's pommel. She reeled aside, clutching her jaw.

Then Evan leaped on him, punching him with fists. Albrecht grasped his waist and lifted him up, throwing him aside. He rolled in time to avoid three Wendigo who rushed his position.

Albrecht snarled, backing away from his own army.

• • •

Altair stumbled aside from the passage entrance. He clutched his left arm; he could no longer move it. He had fought in the second line, using his advanced fighting skills to keep the Wyrm forces at bay. Then his companions broke and ran, listening to a voice that carried across the valley.

He looked over at Martin and groaned when he saw the cub's third, red glowing eye, just below the silver band on his brow. The prophecy had come true. The omen Loba had most feared about the boy. *And the armies of destruction marched forth, led by the child that should not be and bearing the sign of the eye of the devourer upon its brow.*

Martin had clearly used the Silver Crown's powers of command, bolstered by the hypnotic red eye, to orchestrate a terrible rout of Garou forces.

Then he heard the voice, the strange, warbling female voice issuing from Martin's throat. It was not Martin's voice. He frowned. He knew that voice. He had heard it before. Ruatma, the Incarna of Uranus, had spoken a prophecy about Martin, but he called him 'the Shadow Queen.' Altair had always wondered about the gender discrepancy; he now understood. Martin was possessed by a spirit, one so subtle and powerful it had gone undetected even by the greatest seers. He silently cursed himself for letting Loba keep the boy away from other Garou for so long. They might have sensed it before this disastrous moment.

He saw King Albrecht, backed against a wall by his own warriors. They slashed at him, keeping him from approaching Martin. *Why doesn't Martin's voice affect me?* he wondered. *Have I progressed that far beyond illusion?*

He shook his head and bolted forward, charging at the boy. Martin, who watched King Albrecht, failed to see the large Garou coming straight at him. Altair grasped the boy's head in both his hands, holding tight, keeping Martin from turning his eye upon him. His palms burned where they touched the Silver Crown and he grunted in pain. He leaned his jaw against the boy's ear and whispered two single words, backed by all his power: "Break free."

He released Martin and leaped back, but the boy was insanely fast. He spun and hurled himself at Altair, driving his claws into his chest. Bones cracked and the Stargazer fell, shocked at Martin's speed. His vision faded as his heart's blood spilled onto the ground, but he saw Martin shake his head, clenching his eyes shut. The third eye's lid lowered, shutting off the crimson light.

• • •

Martin opened his eyes and moaned in his own voice. He watched Altair's eyes close and looked down at his own hands, streaked with the Stargazer's blood.

"No," he said, shaking his head. "No. Not again." He howled, clutching at the third eye on his forehead, clawing at it.

Some force worked against his muscles, drawing his hands away from the eye. An old woman's voice inside his head said: *Succumb.*

Martin wailed in anger and clutched the Silver Crown. He screamed with all his might, in his own voice: "Get out!"

A wrenching pain shot through his skull, as if someone had driven a knife into his forehead. A shape shot out of his third eye, slapping onto the ground.

The manifest spirit looked like a shard of glistening wet shadow that had somehow crawled from a dark, moist cave. It writhed up and glowered at Martin. It had no eyes but he still knew it watched him. He realized that his command, bolstered by the Silver Crown, had forced the thing from his soul.

He growled, crouching low, moving toward it. It backed away. He could sense its fear now. He leaped forward and slashed at it, catching its bottom edge as it shot to the side. He tore a piece of inky blackness from it and the rest of it unraveled. Wisps of dark smoke dissipated with a faint, distant scream. An old woman's scream.

Martin looked over the battlefield and cried out. Garou fought creatures throughout the valley, stumbling and slashing at one another. King Albrecht fought his own warriors. He buckled under the assault, beginning to falter, his fur red with his own blood.

• • •

Albrecht stumbled to the ground, bleeding from a dozen wounds. Five Garou lay dead before him. Two of them were some of his best warriors. He'd had to kill them with his own hands. More warriors moved in, hot for his blood.

A black-furred dire wolf bolted into them, dropping them like dominos. A gray Garou kicked another warrior away and shook an open flask of water at Albrecht. The water hit his wounds and immediately closed them, sealing the cuts.

"Evan?" Albrecht said, choking out the words from a parched throat.

"Yeah," Evan said, growling at a Garou who crouched nearby, threatening to approach Albrecht. "It's me and Mari." The black dire wolf shifted to battle form and slashed at the Garou on the ground, forcing them back. "We're okay now. Back to our senses."

Albrecht blinked, catching his breath. "Why you and not them?"

"The red light," Evan said. "It was controlling us. I don't know what it did to us, but as soon as it went out, I was in control again. I think these guys are still under the influence of the crown."

Albrecht growled. "I don't know how that kid got it, but I've got to get it back!"

• • •

Martin felt his forehead. The eye was still there. He cautiously willed it to open. The red light spread outwards. He took a deep breath and yelled, calling on both the power of the eye and the Silver Crown. *Wyrm forces: retreat!*

Every Wyrm creature in the valley reacted as if shocked by an electrical jolt. They then ran for the passageway, retreating as commanded. Many moaned and wailed as their limbs acted against their own wishes, carrying them away from the fight.

• • •

Zhyzhak ran, her sense of smell and hearing her only clue as to the beings scrambling around her. She had an insane urge to flee, to retreat from the valley. From the sounds, it seemed her army was doing that very thing. She howled in anger and ran into a wall.

As she stumbled down, her hand brushed against the lens fetish that still hung from her neck, the lens she had used to track the Red Star through the Labyrinth. She growled and yanked it out, placing the lens like a monocle in her eye.

She looked around and chortled. She couldn't see people or things, but their supernatural powers glowed like little lights. Their fetishes shone through the pitch black of her blindness, allowing her some semblance of sight.

The urge to depart the valley was gone. She lunged forward, searching for the one fetish that mattered. There, across the way, it shone, floating in the air, buoyed by the head that wore it.

She growled and dropped to all fours, charging forward. She would not be denied this time.

Zhyzhak collided with the Garou body attached to the glowing fetish. She snarled and dug her jaws into him, clamping them down into what felt like his shoulder. Her claws latched onto the arms, pinning them to the side, while her rear claws dug away, tearing into his legs and guts.

A gargled cry of pain and shock greeted her and she clamped down deeper, exultant. The body collapsed and stopped moving. She felt blood still pumping in the veins by her mouth and slashed with her claws again, tearing away at the flesh until she was sure he was dead.

She released the body and howled with joy, placing a paw over her prey's chest.

Then she stopped, sniffing, confused. She looked down. The cursed Silver Crown still glowed, wrapped around the now lifeless head. But the scent was all wrong. It wasn't Albrecht. It was that cub who had attacked her earlier.

She screamed in rage and vaulted away, searching with her single lens for any sign of Albrecht. All she could see were shining fetishes and active spirits. She dove to her left, toward a cluster of them, and howled as her jaws bit into flesh.

• • •

Albrecht stepped forward and stumbled. He was weaker than he'd thought. Too much blood loss. He had to move.

He watched Martin's body as Zhyzhak leaped away from it. She had finished him off in mere seconds. The kid never had a chance.

Mari howled in pain as one of the Garou sank its teeth into her flanks. She spun and threw him off, wheeling around again to bury her own teeth in his throat. The Garou thrashed and stopped moving. All the immediate threats were gone. No Garou moved nearby. The valley was filled with wounded and dead Garou. Across the way, a single group of shamans and straggling warriors fought to defend themselves against Zhyzhak.

Mari limped forward and collapsed, unconscious. Evan ran to her side, hugging her neck. Tears streamed down his cheek. He had taken wounds himself; Albrecht was surprised at how long he had stayed up. Evan had used his last healing fetish on him. Albrecht wasn't sure it would be enough.

He crawled forward, unable to stand. He used his hands to pull himself forward, moving slowly toward Martin's body.

He gritted his teeth, trying to shut out the screams of his warriors as they fell beneath Zhyzhak's blind assault. The Black Spiral Dancer was more powerful than he had ever seen her before.

He reached Martin's body and grasped the crown. He thrust it onto his head and shut his eyes, calling out to the power within it. *Falcon! By the power of the Sun and Moon that forged this crown, give me the strength to destroy that bitch! If it's the last goddamn thing I do!*

The crown exploded with light, a bright smoldering gold and silver. Albrecht felt new strength enter his limbs. He saw an ephemeral haze of wings and feathers all around him. He stood up, lifting his klaive, stalking toward Zhyzhak.

He reached her side but she didn't react. She was too busy chewing at a Silver Fang shaman to hear or smell him. Her eyes were red pits of raw flesh. As his klaive swung back, she caught its movement in her monocle. She rolled to the side, avoiding the brunt of the blow. It split her stomach open, spilling her guts across the ground.

She howled and leaped at him but he easily sidestepped her, the crown's strength increasing his speed. As she shot past him, he swung his klaive again and sliced her torso in half.

She sucked in a shocked breath and fell, her front claws scrabbling at the air as her rear quarters tumbled away from her front half. A dying growl croaked out of her, rattling away into silence.

Albrecht stepped back, his strength ebbing. The Silver Crown shattered, its metal pieces flying in all directions. The gold and silver aura went out and Albrecht collapsed.

• • •

The dragon buckled, thrashing its tail across the plain, knocking banes into the air and across the ground.

The Maeljin Incarna stared at it, worry furrowing their brows.

"First a retreat, then this," Doge Klypse said. "Has Zhyzhak failed?"

Aliara cursed and drew her slender sword. "Do you see? The Wyrm prepares for its final meal. I was right."

The dragon opened its maw and began to suck in mammoth gusts of air. Banes hurtled through the sky and into its gullet. The retreating army, milling around outside the forest, waiting for new orders, scattered and ran. Their strength was useless against that inexorable force. They fell and flew backwards, sucked into the Wyrm's mouth.

"No!" DuBois yelled, losing his footing as the force of the Great Devourer began to draw him in. "I don't understand!"

Aliara stabbed her sword into her own gut, collapsing to the ground. "It… eats…the corrupt." Her body, no longer resisting the pull, shot into the air and down the dragon's throat.

The remaining Maeljin screamed and tried to resist, but their powers were nothing against the being they had worshipped for millennia. One by one, they flew down its throat and into its furnace of utter destruction.

Once the armies were devoured and the last bane eaten, the dragon snapped its tail forward and bit its tip. It slurped and sucked at the scaled appendage, drawing it into its throat like a snake eating a mouse.

Eating its own tail, it shrank, becoming ever smaller, until there was only a tiny, infinitesimal point left. The point exploded outwards into a white star, brilliant against the empty night, and then went out.

● ● ●

Altair, his breathing slow and labored, tried to smile. He had dropped in and out of consciousness, trying to muster the strength to live. He had witnessed Martin's victory over the bane within him and knew that both prophecies had come true. The Perfect Metis was both the world's doom and its savior. Too bad Zhyzhak had killed him before he could further assert his powers against the Wyrm.

He watched as the black hole beyond the valley's passage slowly ate itself. As the singularity burst into a pinprick of pure light, he marveled at the star. His tribe's symbol was a star. He had suspected when he witnessed the Wyrm's battle with Rorg that more was afoot than mere appearances suggested. He had seen his tribe's totem, Chimera, deep within the black hole.

Perhaps it had eaten something that disagreed with it, something that had fought from within to reverse its course and return it to its natural cycle.

He pondered this for a moment and then stopped breathing.

• • •

Albrecht stumbled and collapsed, landing beside Evan and Mari. Both his packmates lay still, unmoving.

He rolled onto his back and let out a deep breath. Nothing in the valley moved. Everybody was dead or dying. There were no healers left to restore them.

Albrecht sighed, watching a bright white star appear briefly in the sky before winking out, leaving only black emptiness.

He scanned the bodies, looking for Mephi Faster-Than-Death, hoping the galliard had survived. Somebody had to tell the tale. But there was no sign of his body anywhere.

He closed his eyes, tired beyond tired. He wanted nothing more than to rest. After a while, he stopped moving.

The battlefield was silent. Garou bodies lay scattered across the valley floor. Snow slowly began to fall, descending from the blackness.

• • •

A figure stirred near Albrecht. Mari Cabrah opened her eyes, feeling a terrible pain in her ribs and chest. She looked over at Evan and Albrecht and choked back a sob. She watched the snow fall slowly over them.

She looked out over the valley and watched the snow pile up around the megaliths, pregnant with the slumbering spirits none of them could awaken. She wondered: Was there even a world left for them to awaken into?

She closed her eyes, feeling her body grow numb, but then snapped them open again with a growl. She remembered. Her duty was not yet done.

Her hand fumbled in her pocket and withdrew the nut she had taken from the Most Ancient's tangled hair. *Nothing else matters*, the Ancient had said. Mari looked at it, examining its seamless, hard surface. With her other hand, she used her claws to dig into the hard dirt, wincing in pain with the strength it required to open a hole big enough for the small object.

She placed the nut in the hole and scraped the loose dirt on top of it, covering the hole. She waited, watching. Time passed, moments impossible to count. Nothing happened.

She closed her eyes, tired and numb, and forgot what she was waiting for.

The snow fell, covering her with its mantle, wrapping her and her packmates beneath a single white sheet. A cold wind whistled through the valley, blowing the snow in small circles as it fell.

From the ground by Mari's hand, a single green shoot rose from the earth.

About the Author

Bill Bridges is the author of four previous Werewolf novels (**The Silver Crown, Tribe Novel: Bone Gnawers, Tribe Novel: Stargazers** and **Tribe Novel: Wendigo**) and is the line developer for White Wolf's **Mage: The Ascension**. He is also the co-creator and developer of the *Fading Suns* space fantasy universe for Holistic Design, and has numerous writing credits throughout the roleplaying and computer game industry. He currently lives in Tucker, Georgia with his wife and three cats.

Acknowledgments

The author would like to thank the many authors who have contributed to the world of **Werewolf** over the years. Their many threads began the tapestry of this story.